The Warrior Worlds

Also by Stephen Renneberg

THE MAPPED SPACE UNIVERSE

The Mothership
The Mothersea

The Antaran Codex
In Earth's Service
The Riven Stars
The Spawn War
The Warrior Worlds

SF/TECHNOLOGICAL THRILLERS

The Siren Project
The Kremlin Phoenix

The Warrior Worlds

Stephen Renneberg

This novel is a work of fiction. Names and characters are the product of the author's imagination, and any resemblance to actual persons, living or dead, is coincidental.

Copyright © Stephen Renneberg 2022

Stephen Renneberg asserts the moral right
to be identified as the author of this work

Author website
www.stephenrenneberg.com

ISBN: 978-0-9941840-8-5

All rights reserved. No part of this publication may be reproduced, stored in a retrieval system, or transmitted, in any form, or by any means, electronic, mechanical, photocopying, recording, or otherwise, without the prior written permission of the copyright owner.

Illustration © Tom Edwards
TomEdwardsDesign.com

For Elenor
For All Time

Mapped Space Chronology

3.4 Million Years Ago to 6000 BC
Earth's Stone Age (GCC 0).

6000 BC to 1750 AD
Pre-Industrial Civilization (GCC 1).

1750 - 2130
The rise of Planetary Industrial Civilization (GCC 2).
The First Intruder War – unknown to mankind.
The Mothership (MS-First Contact 1)
Start of the Blockade.
The Mothersea (MS-First Contact 2)

2130 - 2643
The spread of Interplanetary Civilization (GCC 3) throughout the Solar System.

2629
Marineris Institute of Mars (MIM) perfects the first stable Spacetime Distortion Field (the superluminal bubble).
The MIM discovery leads to the dawn of Inceptive Interstellar Civilization (GCC 4).

2615
The Solar Constitution ratified, establishing Earth Council (15 June 2615).

2644
First human ship reaches Proxima Centauri and is met by a Tau Cetin Observer.

2645
Earth Council signs the Access Treaty with the Galactic Forum.
First Probationary Period begins.

Tau Cetins provide astrographic data out to 1,200 light years from Earth (*Mapped Space*) and 100 kilograms of novarium (Nv, Element 147) to power human starships.

2646 - 3020

Human Civilization expands rapidly throughout Mapped Space.

Continual Access Treaty infringements delay mankind's acceptance into the Galactic Forum.

3021

Dr. Anton Krenholtz discovers Spacetime Field Modulation.

Krenholtz Breakthrough enables transition to Incipient Interstellar Civilization (GCC 5).

3021 - 3154

Mass migration dramatically increases human colonial populations.

3154

Human religious fanatics, opposed to interstellar expansion, attack the Mataron Homeworld.

Tau Cetin Observers prevent the Mataron Fleet from destroying Earth.

3155

Galactic Forum suspends human interstellar access rights for 1,000 years (the Embargo).

3155 - 3158

Tau Cetin ships convert human supplies of novarium held in Earth stockpiles and within ship energy plants to inert matter (as human ships landed at habitable planets).

3155 - 4155

Human contact with other interstellar civilizations ends.

Many human outposts beyond the Solar System collapse.

4126

Earth Navy established by the Democratic Union to police mankind when Embargo is lifted.

Earth Council assumes control of Earth Navy.

4138

Earth Intelligence Service (EIS) established by the Earth Council.

4155

The Embargo ends.

The Access Treaty is reactivated, permitting human interstellar travel to resume.

The second 500 year Probationary Period begins.

4155 - 4267

Earth re-establishes contact with its surviving colonies.

4281

Earth Council issues Sanctioned Worlds Decree, protecting collapsed human societies.

4310

The Beneficial Society of Traders established to manage interstellar trade.

4498

Quantum Instability Neutralization discovered (much earlier than galactic powers expected).

Mankind becomes Emergent Civilization (GCC 6).

The golden age of human interstellar trade begins.

4605
The Vintari Incident.
The Antaran Codex (MS1)

4606
The Battle of Tresik Prime.
End of the Blockade.
In Earth's Service (MS2)

4607
The Nan Chen Disaster.
The Xil Asseveration.
The Riven Stars (MS3)
The Siege of Serris Orn.
The Spawn War (MS4)

4608
The Fall of Earth
The Warrior Worlds (MS5)

Notes:
MS: Mapped Space
GCC: Galactic Civ. Classification system.
Asseveration: A solemn or emphatic declaration.

Chapter One: Earth

Human Homeworld
Sol System
1.0 Earth Normal Gravity
498.7 light seconds from Sol
20 Billion Humans
10 Million Terrestrial Amphibians

"Race you to the top," Marie yelled, leaping out of the snowskimmer before the skids had settled.

I pushed the gullwing door up, caught my bulky boots on the door frame and fell head first into a snowdrift. Marie looked back, saw me disappear beneath a cloud of powder and laughed, then ran to the summit. Breathing heavily and grinning in triumph, she watched me plod up the slope toward her covered in snowflakes. It wasn't the romantic moment I'd had in mind for the big question, but nothing ever worked as intended with her.

When I reached the top, she dusted snowflakes off my face and shoulders. "For an ultra-reflexed super spy, you're kind of clumsy. You know that?"

"It's these damn snow boots."

"I think your fancy bio circuitry gizmos don't like the cold."

"Bionetics, not circuits," I said, taking her in my arms.

She smiled, cheeks flushed in the cold alpine air. "You'll always be a stumbling bio-bot to me."

We'd been together for a solid month, mostly at her family's estate near Bordeaux where I'd come clean about everything: the gene resequencing, the bionetic system threading my body, my years of deep cover for Earth Intelligence Service, even my sordid family connections. For the first time in our lives, there were no secrets between us, no more lies, and it felt good.

Lena Voss, my EIS controller, would be furious. She'd always known this day was coming, but would never get used to having a former Separatist sympathizer knowing my secrets. Not the missions I'd run or how cozy we were with the Tau Cetins, just the personal stuff: who I was, what I did, and how. Marie didn't like it, but she accepted it was part of the package and the lying, while not forgotten, was the past.

We looked into each other's eyes, surrounded by snow covered mountain peaks beneath a cold blue sky. She gave me an expectant look, dusted a snowflake off my cheek and waited me out. Realizing the time had come, I reached into my pocket for the Witari diamond ring I'd been carrying for far too long.

"Marie," I said, surprised how awkward I sounded, "there's something I've been wanting to ask you, for a long time."

"I'm a size four," she said mischievously, enjoying my discomfort.

"Since when?"

She made a fist and lightly punched my shoulder.

"I was wondering...if you would do me–"

A solitary boom thundered above us, shattering the alpine silence. We looked up as a circle of super-heated air expanded high in the sky and a tiny speck punched into the upper atmosphere. It quickly became a flaming meteor, trailing fire and black smoke as it dived toward us, much too fast for a controlled entry.

"It's small," Marie said, gauging its size with an expert eye.

It was silvery-white with a tapered nose and aft mounted delta wings. Long before we could read its hull markings, my bionetics matched its profile.

"It's a D-forty gunship. Six-man crew."

The orbital defender was at least Mach five over safe descent, radiating atmospheric shock waves from her glowing hull as her skin peeled away in the thickening air. The gunship streaked over our heads, slammed into a high rock wall and exploded, raining fiery debris into a nearby valley.

"Oh my god," Marie whispered, horrified.

I slid the engagement ring back into my pocket as my eyes followed the smoky contrail into an empty blue sky, wondering what had caused such a disaster. Those gunship jockeys were the hottest young pilots in the navy. There was nothing they couldn't handle, yet she'd dropped like a stone as if her entire crew were dead before she hit the atmosphere.

"Let's go," I said uneasily as quiet settled over the European Alps once more.

"Go?" Marie said surprised. "Where?"

"Off this mountain." I felt very exposed, just the two of us standing alone in bright colored ski suits on stark white snow. I took her hand and we slipped and slid our way down to the snowskimmer.

"Destination Chalet," I said as we climbed inside.

The gullwing doors lowered and the engine came to life, then the skimmer kicked up swirling eddies of powder as we glided over the snow toward our mountaintop resort. A thin pillar of smoke was rising from the gunship's wreckage, but no emergency craft had yet appeared.

"Should we try to help them?" Marie asked.

"Help who?" I said, certain there were no survivors. "Comms On. Set channel: high mountain rescue." The comm system activated, unexpectedly crackling with static. "Hello, ski patrol?"

We waited for a reply, then Marie said, "The mountains must be blocking the signal."

"From all three ski-sats?"

We watched the sky through the snowskimmer's transparent bubble as our skimmerbot followed the tourist trail back to the resort. It was a row of high alpine chalets atop Aiguille du Midi with panoramic views of Vallée Blanche. A broad walkway linked the luxury guest suites to a central restaurant and bar with a pressure field equipped viewing deck.

No one came out to secure our skimmer as it settled, and the glass-walled restaurant, bar, ski shop and famed Vallée Café were all empty. The tourist shuttle was missing from the landing pad atop the guest center and the rescue jumper and the other snowskimmers were gone. When we'd left three hours ago, the bustling little resort had been full of staff, guests and day trippers. Now it was deserted, except for a handful of cleanerbots vacuuming floors and replacing towels and sheets.

"Where is everyone?" Marie asked as we climbed out of the skimmer.

"They left in a hurry," I said, eyeing abandoned luggage waiting beside open chalet doors. "Traded weight for people."

We hurried along the walkway to our room. The front door was open and the floor to ceiling windows overlooking the valley were clear, not opaque as we'd left them. The mood screens on the interior walls were blank, and a rustling sound came from the bathroom.

Marie and I exchanged uncertain looks, then I cautiously approached the doorway. Inside was a chrome plated, gold and silver egg on metal legs with triple jointed arms and a flex mounted rotating eye. The cleanerbot was polishing already spotless taps as if its next recharge depended on it.

"Bonjour Madame et Monsieur," it said with a silky smooth voice, sensing our presence and turning toward us.

"Why'd everyone leave?" I asked.

"Do you require extra towels or toiletries today, sir?" its diminutive interactive intelligence asked, switching to my preferred language.

"No." I turned to the nearest mood screen and spoke to the room AI. "Display news, headlines only."

A room sensor followed my eyeline, activated the gray wall I was looking at, and filled it with white static and a black rectangle containing white text.

No Signal.

"There are thirty five thousand channels in fifty languages on that thing," Marie said.

"Not today." I turned to the windowed wall, looked out at tranquil alpine beauty as far as the eye could see, and knew it was too quiet. "Pack your bags. We're leaving."

We hurried into the bedroom and emptied our wardrobes.

"I don't suppose you're hiding a gun in there?" Marie asked as I stuffed clothes into my suitcase.

"Sorry, the Spawn ate my last one. Haven't had time to replace it."

"All I have is this." She held up a small needler just big enough for the palm of her hand.

"You brought a gun on holidays?"

"Someone had to," she said with a wry smile.

"Hmm." I glanced at the elegant, utterly useless lady's weapon. "Nothing bigger?"

"Hand cannons are your department."

Cursing my carelessness, I tapped my suitcase's close panel, waited for the hiss of the vacuum seal to end and set it to auto-follow. Marie did the same, then we went back into the lounge room followed by our suitcases.

"Have a nice day, sir," the cleanerbot called from the bathroom.

"It's too late for that," I snapped. "You got any hunting weapons up here?"

"No sir. Weapons are prohibited in the high alpine zone. Would you like new soap?"

I gave Marie an exasperated look and headed for the front door. A high pitched scream sounded as a shiny, metallic object streaked down out of the sky and slammed into the snow close to the ski shop.

"Uh-ho," I said, watching steam waft from the small impact crater.

"What is that?" Marie asked, rushing forward for a better look.

I caught her arm and dragged her back before she could show herself. "Suitcases, wait," I ordered as I hustled her into the marble bathroom.

"You don't think it's them, do you?" Marie whispered with rising horror. "Not here. Not on Earth."

"It was a drop pod." I turned to the fastidious cleanerbot. "I want extra towels. Double what we have."

"Certainly, sir. It is my pleasure to provide you with more towels."

The obliging, gold plated tap scrubber hurried through the front door to a housekeeping trolleybot outside. When it reached the trolley, an energy blast struck it horizontally, shattering its torso and hurling dismembered arms clutching white towels onto the walkway.

Marie gasped. I pulled her into the bathroom where we pressed our backs against the wall, out of sight of the front window, straining to hear. Soon, the metallic clang of heavy robotic feet landing on the walkway rang out. There was another weapon flash and the clatter of cleanerbot parts, then clanking footsteps marched along the walkway, pausing to look into each room. The footsteps grew louder until they reached our door and the distorted reflection of a silver bipedal form appeared on the mirror-like bathroom taps.

Attracted by our bags near the door, it came into the room and studied the mood screen hissing with static. It took a few more steps and looked down the hall at the freshly made bed while its distorted reflection, shimmering with the glow of a contour shield, slid across the polished taps.

It looked into the bathroom as we pressed our backs against the wall, scarcely daring to breathe. It was a step away from seeing us, then the whine of a vacuum cleaner caught its attention. It charged outside and blasted another defenseless cleanerbot while Marie and I exchanged relieved looks.

She opened her mouth to speak, but I cut her off with a sharp look and a finger to my lips. She nodded and we listened in silence to its footsteps clank to the end of the walkway. It leapt onto the shuttle pad, paced across to the far side and jumped out onto the snow. We waited a long time, hearing no more of it, then a cleanerbot started vacuuming a few rooms away.

When no energy blast signaled the cleaner's destruction, I stole a peak through the bathroom door, finding no sign of the intruder, a Spawn autac. I'd seen their kind before. Autacs, AUTomated Aware Combat units, came in many shapes and sizes, although bipeds were the most common.

"It's gone," I whispered, relaxing.

"What's an autac doing on Earth?"

"Nothing good," I said apprehensively.

"It was big."

"Yeah, it was an elite."

Flanker-elites were heavy assault units with a form hugging contour shield that made them almost invulnerable to weapons not firing static force penetrators.

"They'll think the chalet is abandoned now. Maybe we should wait for dark."

"I don't fancy getting down off this mountain at night," I said, certain if the Spawn were attacking, it would only get worse the longer we waited.

"Sirius," Marie said somberly, "do you think it was sent to kill you?"

"Not this time." The Spawn had reason to want me dead, but an assassination would best be done covertly. A Spawn hit squad wouldn't shoot a D-forty out of orbit. I wasn't that important, and it would attract too much attention–Tau Cetin attention. "I need to contact Lena."

"The maglev to Grenoble might still be running," Marie suggested.

"Maybe."

We hurried down toward the snowskimmer with our suitcases trundling behind, stealing a peek into the snow crater on the way. The drop pod was at the bottom in a pool of steaming snow-melt water. The top had cracked open into four triangular pieces revealing a chamber lined with field generator rings and no controls. The flanker-elite had squeezed inside by folding its legs behind its back and had pulled itself out by its fingertips.

"How does it steer?" Marie asked.

"It doesn't. They drop it onto an entry vector and gravity does the rest. It aerobrakes all the way and soaks up the impact with an inertial field."

"Looks uncomfortable."

"Not for an autac. The Tau Cetins gave us the schematics in case the Spawn ever used them against us."

"How many do they need for an invasion?"

"More than one. Come on. Let's get off this mountain."

Marie told the bags to mount the rear luggage rack while I searched the skimmer garage for something with more kick than her toy needler. All I found was an emergency kit with a signal gun inside.

When I joined Marie in the skimmer, she pointed at Point Sella on the edge of the Giant's Tooth where the nearest resort was perched. "It might have gone over there."

"Whoever warned us, warned them too," I assured her, then addressed the skimmerbot console. "Destination: Chamonix. Full throttle."

We lifted off the snow and headed down the track into the valley. The skimmerbot expertly handled the path while we watched the sky, searching for more drop pods, but all we saw was the thin white contrail of a commercial high liner cruising the mesosphere.

"The commercials are still flying," Marie said. "That's a good sign."

"Unless they don't know the Spawn have landed." She gave me an anxious look making me immediately regret my words. "Or maybe the Tau Cetins have already chased them off."

It took human ships the best part of four days to reach Tau Ceti from Earth, but our galactic superpower neighbors could be here in the blink of an eye, if they knew we needed them and had the ships to spare.

The snowskimmer lurched back, kicking up a bow wave as it tried to contain its speed down the steepening slope, then Marie pointed across Geant Glacier to four tiny forms racing over the snow.

"Look! Speed riders!"

The power skiers had their knees bent and their impeller poles tucked under their arms for flat out, straight line speed. Long fanning snow wakes rose behind them, while their eyes were locked on the exit off the glacier.

"They're sure in a hurry," I said, and rapped my knuckles on the skimmerbot console. "Hey! Go faster."

"For your safety, Monsieur," the skimmerbot replied, "speed restrictions apply in high mountain areas."

The skimmer tilted further back on its heels, sending more snow jetting from beneath its hull as it fought the steep slope.

"Sirius," Marie said slowly, peering into the distance.

"Is that an autac?"

She pointed across the glacier toward a conical dark rock called Aiguille du Toule, where a metallic quadruped stood watching the power skiers. It had short legs with metal grappling hook feet and an angular body coated in thick armor. A short barreled weapon extended from its front above a black sensor strip that ran back along its sides to a rear mounted field accelerator. Even in the bright sunlight, the glowing aura of its contour field was clearly visible.

"It's a rhino."

They were a mainstay of the Spawn's Clan Imperial Battle Corps, a cross between a battle tank, heavy artillery and a bull in a china shop.

Its thick body shifted slightly to aim its cannon, then a brilliant orange energy burst pulsed from the weapon. The power riders peeled apart in pairs as the blast vaporized the snow between them, then they continued racing to get out of range.

"That's a nasty horn," Marie said.

"It's a heavy assault unit, definitely not here for me." I studied the skimmer console with growing frustration. "How do I switch to manual?"

"Manual piloting is prohibited in high mountain areas," the skimmerbot replied.

"That's what you think," Marie said, drawing her lady's pistol and firing a needle-like projectile into the sealed control module in front of my knee.

"Hey! Careful with that thing!" I said as the skimmer veered off course, then the panel in front of me opened and an emergency steering column slid out.

"You wanted manual control," she said lightly.

I grabbed the wheel, turned to get us back on course, overcorrected and sent the skimmer lurching the other way.

"Warning! Stability alert," the skimmerbot announced as we tilted sharply.

"Twist the side-grips to power the effectors and push for power," Marie explained.

I steered against our tilt, throttling back on the high side effectors and the skimmer leveled off, then I leaned into the wheel for more speed. "I got it."

"You're a quick study."

"I should be, ma'am, I fly starships for a living."

The extra power sent us racing down the hill toward the snow covered glacier. The slope eased as we slid onto the long winding run to Chamonix while off to the right, the power skiers were about to overtake us.

The rhino leapt off its conical peak, then its rear-mounted field accelerator glowed, propelling it through the air like a buffalo-sized cannon ball. It cut the distance by a third before plunging onto the snow and disappearing in a white cloud. A moment later, it charged into view, its grappling claw toes splayed for traction. After a few steps, it leapt into the air, propelled by a burst from its rear-end accelerator, gobbling up the distance to the power skiers.

"It's fast," Marie said as the power skiers glanced back fearfully at the bounding autac.

"They're not going to make it."

The rhino landed, charged and jumped again, only this time its field accelerator didn't glow. Instead, at the apex of its leap, its horn flashed, hurling another orange energy burst at the power skiers. It struck a girl in the back, vaporizing her torso and scattering her limbs and red blood across the starkly white snow. Her three companions crouched for more speed and veered to the left, away from the rough ground ahead of them. The rhino landed in a cloud of white powder, slewing sideways as it turned to follow them while I swerved the skimmer toward the skiers.

"Not that way," Marie said, eyeing the rough snow and ice ahead.

"Get the strobe gun. Load it."

She gave me a puzzled look, then retrieved the bulky

signaler from the emergency kit and slid a cylindrical round into the chamber.

The rhino leapt and fired again, melting a channel through the snow and throwing up a wall of steam between the power riders. They began slaloming left and right, making themselves harder to hit as they passed in front of us. We crossed their tracks ahead of the charging rhino, heading for lumpy, snow covered mounds while they continued on toward the easy, northern route down the mountain.

"You steer," I said, taking the strobe gun and pushing my gullwing door up.

She grabbed the wheel with both hands, keeping us straight, while I leaned out over the snow and fired. The flashing red strober passed above the rhino's armored body, then it lurched sideways evasively, kicking up snow and veering toward us, misreading the brilliant light as a weapon. The strober slowed to a hover behind the rhino, flashing bright red pulses designed to summon rescuers in the dead of night.

I pulled myself back in, slammed the door down and took the wheel. "I got its attention," I said, watching it race after us on the rear viewscreen.

"Now what?" Marie asked anxiously, glancing back through the skimmer's canopy at the metal beast on our tail.

"Now it tries to catch us," I replied as we entered the rough. Fractured ice began hammering the skimmer's underside, bouncing us into the air.

"Danger! Entering Seracs du Geant is strictly prohibited," the skimmerbot declared.

"Yeah, yeah, we know," I muttered as the skimmer plowed through snow drifts covering ridges of cracked ice, compressed into a concertina by the glacier. The broken ice shook the skimmer violently as I fought to keep control and the rhino rapidly closed the distance.

"Return to the freerun trail immediately or you will be

fined for safety infractions," the skimmerbot ordered.

The rhino reached the rough and vaulted into the air, propelled by its field accelerator.

"Watch out!" Marie yelled, looking up through the bubble as it came racing through the air toward us.

The rhino dropped into the snow with a thunderous crack of shattering ice and vanished beneath a plume of white powder. As the snow cloud cleared, Marie fixed her eyes upon a deep, dark hole behind us.

"It fell in!" she exclaimed.

"It took the scenic route," I said, fighting the controls as we bounced across the fractured ice, crashed through another snow drift and slid out onto the narrow run south of the Seracs du Geant rough. A sickening grinding sound came from the skimmer's battered effectors while the steering pulled to the left, forcing me to counter steer to stay on the track.

"How'd you know?" Marie asked.

"You told me; people fall down there all the time." I grinned. "Rhinos too."

We followed the ski run away from the fractured glacier which shuddered behind us as if struck by an earthquake. The roar of shattering, falling ice filled the air as the big autac tried to batter its way free then an orange energy blast exploded from the snow and hurtled skyward.

"It's trying to shoot its way out," Marie said alarmed, looking back through the skimmer's transparent canopy.

"By the time it gets out of there, we'll be long gone."

Far down the mountain, the three surviving speed riders crossed the Tacul Glacier. They waved to us and headed for the Mer de Glace, the final stage of the descent.

"It'll send a signal," Marie said apprehensively.

I nodded. "They could be waiting for us at the bottom," I conceded and turned toward Glacier du Tacul. "We'll get rid of the skimmer in Chamonix."

* * * *

At the bottom of the Mer de Glace, we turned onto a track through snow covered trees leading to the town center. The skimmer's damaged effectors were sputtering, scraping the ground and dragging us offline. Two thirds of the way down, the left side died completely and we careened into the forest, hit a tree and rolled down the hill. Emergency pressure fields pinned us to our seats as the canopy cracked, then we slammed into a tree and came to a bone jarring halt.

The pressure fields deactivated and Marie fell sideways onto me as the locking bolts on the gullwing door above us detonated, hurling it into the trees. Cold air and snow flurries wafted into the cabin as Marie gave me a dizzy look.

"Next time Earth's invaded, I'm driving," she said.

I grunted at her ingratitude, then we climbed out into knee deep snow. Running back up through the trees was a path of destruction littered with broken skimmer panels, torn branches and all our clothes.

"Oh no," Marie cried, picking up several torn items. "They're ruined."

"We'll buy new clothes in Paris-Elbe."

She sighed and tossed them away, then we waded through snow down the hill. At the edge of the forest, we studied a row of three and four story buildings with high angled roofs across the road.

"They've still got power," Marie observed, watching snowflakes dart from pressure field enclosed balconies.

There were people on balconies watching the sky and a few uncertain faces peering out through windows. Others were hastily packing bags and children into ground vehicles as fully loaded ground cars sped past. Thin columns of smoke rose into an empty sky above the town center although there were no autacs in sight.

Rising in the distance above the rooftops was the

maglev's gleaming white conductive rail, held aloft on white stanchions. The track lights were on and the station's holo boards were all active.

"It's still intact," Marie said with relief.

"Let's go." I said, then we ran across the road and headed for the nearest cross street. After we'd passed a dozen houses, a sleek, dark blue train glided into the station.

"We'll get the next one," she said as it slid out of the station, heading west.

At a picturesque house, a graying couple came out in such a hurry that they carried their bags in their hands and didn't bother to close the front door. They ran to their car and threw their bags roughly inside.

"What's happening?" I asked.

"Am-East was attacked," the man replied as he climbed into his car.

America-East was home to more than a billion people, a mega-urban running along North America's Atlantic coast from Nova Scotia to Florida.

"What kind of attack? How big?" I demanded, fearing a repeat of Niedarim, the Spawn bombardment that had reduced the Lhekan homeworld's cities to boiling lava plains in a matter of hours.

"It was dark," he mumbled, trying to close his door.

I planted my snow boot on the door frame, jamming it open, and grabbed him by the collar. "Was Am-East bombed?"

"I...I don't know."

"What did you see?"

"Lights...Lights in the sky, then...the holo-comm went down. Everything's down."

I hesitated. "Why are you running?"

"I...I saw falling stars." He looked at the sky. "Up there!"

"How many lights?"

He stared at me, confused and afraid. "Thousands." He

grabbed my wrist and tried to break free. "Let me go!"

I saw the fear in his eyes and stepped back from his car. "Sorry."

He grunted indignantly as the door slid shut, then reversed out, spinning his wheels on the icy road before speeding off.

"Aerobraking drop pods look like falling stars," I said.

"If there were thousands…"

"They'll be all across Europe by now. And America." The few autacs we'd seen were on the fringes of the drop zones. The main battles would be down on the plains among the big cities. "Let's go."

We hurried along the road, passed by cars heading west toward the Mount Blanc Tunnel to Italia or the White Road Superway to France, the fastest routes out of the mountains. A few houses further on, an old man stood on a roof peering through a large biscope.

"Hey!" I yelled, "What do you see?"

"Fires. Traffic," he replied and wandered off to another part of his roof.

At the end of the street, we spotted a dark blue gendarmerie patrol craft flying low over the rooftops. Its lights were flashing and armed officers with light assault weapons hung from open side doors watching the ground. It flew toward the fires burning around the city center and passed out of sight, then we hurried along a broad avenue toward the maglev station. Green lights on the elevated conductive rail began flashing as another train came racing in from Geneva.

"We can make it," Marie declared, wanting to run, but I caught her arm.

"It's an intercity. It's not going to stop."

The maglev express hurtled through the station at a thousand kilometers an hour, then an orange energy blast from the city center struck the conductive rail, tearing a huge gap in it between two stanchions. Debris showered the buildings as the train shot off the track and crashed into the far side stanchion, obliterating it instantly. The massive train dropped onto the ground, smashing through the town like a supersonic wrecking ball, destroying everything in its path.

"Oh no!" Marie cried in horror as a river of fire tore through Chamonix. The lead carriages slammed into the far hills and disintegrated while those following skidded over the ridge into the next valley.

"We need another way out," I said.

We ran toward a cluster of shops on the outskirts of the town center, then the high pitched whine of magnetic accelerators sounded as gendarmes opened fire with kinetic rounds, useless against Spawn contour shields. The boom of a rhino's horn and the shriek of flanker energy weapons replied, silencing the human rail guns, as a burning gendarmerie patrol craft flew overhead trailing black smoke. It lurched out of control as a dead gendarme hung limply in his door harness, blood and energy burns staining his chest. The aircraft crashed into nearby houses and exploded as the screams of shocked onlookers filled the air.

I pulled Marie into a doorway as the sound of weapons fire approached, then she drew her needler.

"What do you plan on doing with that?" I asked.

"We have to help," she said, flushed with anger.

I put my hand on her toy gun. "You'll only get yourself killed."

"We've got to do something!"

"We will, but not here. Not now."

"Sirius," she whispered, "if they're in Am-East and here..."

"I know. They're everywhere." I put my arm around her shoulders. "There's an EIS station in Paris-Elbe. I'll contact Lena there."

"We don't even know if Paris still exists."

"Only one way to find out." I summoned a map of Chamonix from my bionetic memory, looking for a way out of the Alps.

Marie watched me staring into space, guessing what I was doing. "Anything?"

"The airport's too far and the gendarme base will be guarded, if it hasn't already been destroyed. I'm looking for something of no military value." I scanned the map, searching for a place where we could beg, borrow or steal transport. "There's a mountain rescue station not far from here. That way." I pointed north of the fires burning beneath the maglev line.

I cleared the map from my mind's eye, then we ran along the avenue, staying close to the buildings. Even though it was late afternoon and peak shopping time, the streets were almost deserted. We crossed under the maglev rail east of the train wreck fires and entered a plaza lined with cafés and restaurants. Shots rang out from a side street ahead, then we slipped into the doorway of an abandoned café and listened as the shooting got closer.

Two gendarmes ran into view, firing handguns back the way they'd come, barely aiming. A white flash hit one in the back, killing her instantly while her companion kept running. A small, inverted pyramid with sensor spines extending from each corner flew into view, silently following him. The gendarme fired at it, but the tracker evaded the shot, then a large metallic biped came leaping through the air and landed beside him. The gendarme emptied his pistol into it, but the autac's contour shield deflected every shot.

The autac was a flanker-elite, taller and faster than a man, more heavily armored than a recon-flanker, with an angular black, rotating sensor for a head. Its downward sloping shoulders were abnormally wide and ended in ball-mounted energy weapons that could rotate in any direction. A pair of meter long, articulated arms equipped with four-digit 'hands' extended from its waist, giving it a non-human, misshapen appearance.

The elite snatched the pistol out of the gendarme's

hand, severing the man's fingers, then threw the weapon and fingers away. The gendarme stared at his bloodied hand in shock as the autac grabbed his throat with a grip sizzling with electrical flashes where the contour shield pressed against skin. The heavy flanker lifted the gendarme off the ground, holding him steady while the inverted pyramid scanned him with a thin blue beam. The gendarme clawed at the elite's hand through the sparking contour shield to no effect. When the tracker completed its scan, the elite snapped the man's neck and tossed his body into a nearby map kiosk, shattering its illuminated data pane.

The floating pyramid scanned the other dead gendarme while the flanker-elite raked the buildings and several parked cars with energy blasts from its shoulder cannons. The cars burst into flames and the buildings collapsed, then three people emerged from a hiding place down the street and tried to run. The flanker killed one and let the other two escape while one of its articulated arms made a minute adjustment to its left side shoulder cannon. It randomly destroyed several more buildings before starting down the street we were hiding in.

"Down," I whispered and we both dropped to the floor.

A burst of energy pulses smashed the restaurant to our right, swept above our hiding position, blowing out the rear wall, and continued on through several more buildings to our left. The elite followed the inverted pyramid down the street, firing randomly before leaping over a row of apartment buildings and passing out of sight.

"It let two escape," Marie whispered.

"To spread fear."

We waited until we were sure the autac had gone, then hurried to the mountain rescue station. It was surrounded by a high stone wall and inactive perimeter sensors. The metal gate across the driveway had been holed by an energy blast and hung at an odd angle.

Taking cover behind the wall, we peered past the

wrecked gate to a row of landing pads. Two of four rescue jumpers were burning with the charred remains of their pilots still at the controls, killed as they tried to take off. Beyond the jumper pads were wrecked cars, more bodies and a two story office building with a rooftop aerial and walls riddled with blast holes.

"They left two jumpers," Marie said puzzled.

"No pilots. They weren't taking off."

"I'll fly," she said, avoiding looking too closely at the blackened corpses.

"I've got bionetics, ultra-reflexes and maps in my head."

She scowled. "That'll only win you so many arguments."

We ran inside, past the two burning wrecks to the third jumper. It had a capsule shaped fuselage, vectoring thrusters at each quarter and a transparent sphere up front with a single pilot seat and good all round visibility. I climbed into the pilot's seat and started the engines while Marie took the medic's jump seat behind me.

"The power cells are at sixty percent," she warned, peering over my shoulder, then the stone wall beside the landing pads exploded.

"Too late now," I said, feeding power to the engines.

The rescue jumper lurched into the air. With our skids almost touching the ground, I banked sharply, staying low to avoid line of sight with the autac outside. A rhino charged through the break in the wall as we flew behind the rescue headquarters. It fired after us, demolishing a corner of the building, then we cleared the back wall and skimmed low over the road. The rhino leapt onto the building's roof, ran to the edge and fired again, but I pitched up and the blast passed beneath us.

We flew on over the rooftops and dropped into a street, using the houses for cover. Orange energy blasts blew the buildings apart, then we slewed into another street, almost collided with a car going the other way, and raced toward the towering rock wall of Le Brevent. It was too high to climb with a rhino blowing its horn behind us, so I followed the road along the northern side of the town toward the White Road Superway.

On the south side of Chamonix, the Mount Blanc Tunnel was choked with burning cars, blocking the Trans Alpine Expressway. Many people were sheltering behind the vehicles as a rhino stood on top of a heavy loader firing at the traffic. It shifted position and turned toward us.

"It's seen us!" Marie called.

I dived as an energy burst flashed across the town, passed close above us and demolished a four story apartment building. I rolled the jumper down to the River Arve, a mountain stream with high banks crammed with buildings. Rhino blasts flashed blindly after us, shattering ancient houses on both sides of the narrow waterway.

"Sirius!" Marie yelled as a covered pedestrian bridge appeared ahead.

"I see it."

I waited until the last moment to vector the thrusters. We hurdled the bridge, shaving tiles off the roof with our landing struts, then dropped back into the gully as another blast flashed above us.

We followed the river as it turned to the north and passed out of range of the Chamonix autacs, then the valley angled down toward the town of Servoz and the fertile lowlands to the north west.

"Once we reach the plains, we'll head for Paris-Elbe."

"If it's still there," Marie said pessimistically.

If the Spawn had destroyed Am-East, the other mega-urbans would be gone too, and it would only be a matter of time before they ruled all of Earth and its few survivors.

* * * *

The rescue jumper's thrusters began to sputter an hour from Paris-Elbe.

"The power cells are flat lining," I said as we began losing altitude.

"There's a village over there," Marie said, pointing over my shoulder.

The nav screen had been giving me 'No Signal' all the way from Chamonix, leaving me to navigate by dead reckoning and bionetic mind maps alone. There were no shuttle ports nearby, so I aimed for the nearest cow paddock and used what juice we had left to break our fall. Close to the ground, I lost all four thrusters, missed the paddock and nosed into a stand of trees. The landing skids took the impact and tore off, then we belly-slid into an oak tree and came to a jarring halt.

Marie looked through the cracked piloting sphere at the thick foliage above and said, "At least they won't see the jumper from the air."

"If they're looking for us, they'll find us," I said, reminding her we couldn't hide from Spawn tech even if we had years to prepare.

"Good thing they have more important things to worry about than us."

We abandoned the rescue jumper and made our way to the edge of the trees. To the east was a group of flat roofed structures sheltering a variety of aging farmbots while to the north was a small village surrounding an intersection of narrow country roads. Between us and the village, somewhat isolated from the other houses, was a small chateau showing no vehicles or people.

"It's quiet enough," I said uncertainly, then we crossed a green field to the chateau.

No one answered the front intercom, so we walked around to the rear looking for an easy way in. Behind the house was a garage with two empty car spaces and a gray dust cover over a long slender shape. I pulled the cover back to discover a red two-wheeler with a raked wind capsule enclosing the driver and adaptive pressure fields for the passenger.

I whistled appreciatively. "Someone likes to go fast." I checked the console and smiled. "The cells are fully charged."

"It's kind of big for a bike," Marie said, unimpressed.

"This is no mere bike." Its sleek lines, adaptive aerodynamics and large trailing wheel were unmistakable. "It's a gyrodragster. Fastest thing on two wheels."

She gave me a dubious look. "You know how to drive this thing?"

"They pretty much drive themselves."

"I'll take that as a no."

I smiled. "We'll start first thing in the morning."

We headed back to the house, looking up at the sky in search of shooting stars. Very high up was a long dark shadow gliding toward the north west.

Marie gasped. "There they are!"

My bionetics profile matched its outline to my Tau Cetin catalogue of all things Spawn. "It's a spawncarrier, an invasion ship."

They were operated by Clan Imperial Battle Corps; less well armed than spawnships, but with double the mass and built to carry millions of spawnwarriors and autacs for the sole purpose of planetary conquest. A few had been seen during the attack on Serris-Orn, the Tau Cetin homeworld, but they'd never got close enough to launch an assault.

The Spawn's main invasion force was supposed to be out in the Cygnus Rim, consolidating recent conquests while the Tau Cetin Fleet was tied down at home. After the Ornithians had defeated the Spawn at Tau Ceti, they'd assumed any surviving spawncarriers in the Orion Arm had withdrawn, but they'd been wrong before and the behemoth floating above us confirmed our great and powerful protectors had got it wrong again.

"Where are the Tau Cetins?" Marie wondered with

growing despair.

"They're here," I assured her.

Our nearest neighbors were less than twelve light years away, and the only civilization this side of the galactic core powerful enough to stop the Spawn. They had to know by now that Earth was being invaded. The Ornithian Consociation had guarded the Orion Arm for millions of years, had emerged victorious from The First Intruder War long before mankind had even set foot on Mars and had stopped the Matarons from exterminating us centuries ago. They were supposed to protect us from enemies far more advanced than us, so where were they?

It was a question every human being on Earth was asking.

High in the upper atmosphere, tiny points of light streamed from both sides of the spawncarrier. They fanned out across the sky, tens of thousands of them, dropping like falling stars across Europe, just as they had done across the Americas hours before. Suddenly, the spawncarrier's black silhouette raced across the sky and vanished, then a trio of mirrored slivers of light streaked above us so fast they came and went in an instant, painting three lines of light across the heavens.

"Thank God!" Marie exclaimed with relief, beaming a smile at me; freezing when she saw my stony face. "What is it? We're saved."

"Are we?" I asked uncertainly, watching twinkling stars fill the sky and fall to Earth unmolested.

"But...the Tau Cetins..."

"...have a great fleet, but a weak army."

The Spawn also had a mighty fleet, almost as powerful as the Ornithians, but the Spawn were a land power with near limitless resources and a capacity to replace losses at a phenomenal rate. The Tau Cetins did not, and that was our greatest problem.

"Are we still going to Paris-Elbe?" Marie asked.

"There's nowhere else, not on this continent."

There were EIS stations in Am-West and Tokohama, but we couldn't reach either, and even if we could, if Paris-Elbe was gone, they would be too. And this landing was hours after the first, making it the second wave, or perhaps the third, confirming it was no mere raid. Was that why the Tau Cetins hadn't attacked the drop pods, because it was already too late?

I kept my thoughts to myself as we crossed the manicured lawn, then Marie blasted open the back door with her needler and we went inside. The chateau was lavishly appointed, decorated in third generation cyber-humanism, all blue velvet upholstery, concealed interactives and psycho-soothing mood lighting.

"Not what I expected," Marie said, sinking into a deeply padded chair that sensed her high stress levels and began massaging her neck with pressure fields. She exhaled slowly, put her head back and closed her eyes.

"The house must have back up cells," I said, suspecting the countryside's power grid had already been cut. "I bet they've got a fancy foodbot here."

She opened her eyes. "Non!" she said dramatically. "I will cook."

"You? Really?" I was so used to machines preparing our food, it never occurred to me that Marie had culinary talents.

"It's in my blood," she said with a flourish, emphasizing her French accent. "You check the wine cellar. It'll be a good one."

"Anything in particular?"

"Red and dry, and bring its friends. Lots of friends."

* * * *

"I'm impressed." I said with a satiated sigh after a delicious meal.

"It's called agneau de pauillac."

"Delicious. The best lamb and garlic I've ever had."

"It was my mother's recipe, from thirteenth century Aquitaine."

"I'll have Izin program the recipe into the galleybot."

"Sacrilege!" Marie declared, feigning indignation. "It's a family secret."

"Handed down from generation to generation, I suppose."

"Of course."

She held out her glass, which I refilled from our second bottle. Hoping the Spawn wouldn't attack tonight, I topped up my glass, celebrating what might be our last meal in style.

We sat at one end of a beautifully polished dining table that could seat twelve, drank from synth-crystal goblets and ate off the finest carbonized porcelain plates I'd ever seen, all beneath a gently glowing diffusion chandelier floating above us. Whoever owned the house had spared no expense replicating chateau style living, even if on a small scale, and they'd left it all without a second thought.

A muted boom thundered from far away, snapping us out of our reverie. We exchanged anxious looks, rushed to a large window and peered out through sheer curtains. The fields outside were deserted, lit only by soft moonlight. Beyond them, the village windows flickered with candles and log fires and the rooftops were silhouetted by the glow of a distant, burning city.

"How close are they?" Marie asked.

"Not close. Not yet." I put my arm around her shoulders, found she was shivering slightly, although it wasn't cold.

"How long can we hold out?"

I considered lying, but said, "They're using contour shields."

"We have the Tau Cetin ammunition."

The Ornithians had designed static force penetrators for us to manufacture, but each round cost a small fortune to produce and there wasn't anywhere near enough of them. Only our most elite forces had penetrator ammo, intended for guerilla war, not set piece battles.

"There are stockpiles, but only for I-F units," I said, dashing her hopes.

Our Intuitive Fighters were zygote constructs, super soldiers genetically engineered with a sixth sense for survival. We always knew if it came to this, Earth's conventional military forces would be annihilated, leaving I-F as our last soldiers standing. Their mission was to make Earth a poisoned chalice, although the Spawn would never willingly withdraw. That was simply not their way.

If the attack had come in ten or twenty years, we might have been able to equip our regular forces for the fight, but the Spawn were too smart for that. Mankind was the most technologically primitive interstellar civilization in the galaxy, the absolute bottom of the ladder, but a handful of I-F super soldiers had given the Spawn a nasty surprise, and they weren't about to let that happen again.

We'd shown our hand too soon, and it was my fault. My mission.

Most civilizations used handheld energy weapons, but building novarium reactors the size of walnuts was still beyond us. Even so, our magnetically accelerated, hypersonic rail guns were effective against unshielded targets, and thanks to Tau Cetin genius, penetrators made them shield busting death dealers. Teched-up alien blasters might be the holy grail, but our humble rapid-fire kinetic weapons got you just as dead, especially down in the weeds of ground combat.

"Why don't the Tau Cetins come back?" she wondered.

"They will. I bet they're up there right now, destroying spawnships by the dozen."

"I think...I think they've abandoned us," she said fatalistically.

"No. They'll come back." They had to.

* * * *

We climbed onto the gyrodragster early next morning. When the twin engines began to purr, our visorless helmets came to life, displaying speed, power level and compass heading in a strip below our eyes. A 'location unknown' warning appeared in my head-up display when the global guidance system failed to respond, so I summoned a bionetic map into my mind.

"Two wheels," Marie said warily, slipping her hands around my chest. "It's not stable."

"That's what the gyros are for." I retracted the support struts and the monster bike remained rock steady. "See?"

"Wait 'till we're moving," she said doubtfully, then the air around us wavered as aerodynamic pressure fields formed between the long windshield and the rear wheel.

I selected automatic gearing and let the bike roll out of the garage. She was four meters long, over two thousand kilograms in mass, and deceptively light to the touch. Dynamic traction axles, variable geometry pressure fields and gyro-stabilization made her forgiving of mistakes, although they wouldn't save us from a six hundred kilometer an hour collision.

"See? Easy, like riding a bike," I said with a grin as we cruised past the house, onto the little country road out front.

I twisted the throttle, felt an intimidating surge of power and hoped the bike's AI would compensate for my inexperience. Hiding my surprise from Marie, we motored past a sign naming the village ahead as Sainte Vertu. Little houses and quaint shops lined both sides of the street leading to an intersection of narrow roads. Old men sitting on tiny round tables outside a café recognized the bike, but not us, and called out a challenge. I ignored them, drove on to the intersection and followed a sign indicating Paris-Elbe was a hundred and sixty kilometers away.

"This isn't north," Marie said as we left the village behind.

I found Sainte Vertu on my mind map and saw where we were headed. "The main road's up ahead."

We drove west through green fields, patches of forest and rustic farmhouses, keeping the speed down on the narrow road. If not for smoke on the horizon, the tranquil rural setting would have lulled us into thinking all was right with the world. We passed blacked out villages and dead transmission towers which should have been pulsing the cross country feeder beam. Among the fields, machine sheds were filled with farmbots waiting for a recharge while farmers checked their crops, unable to tend them without machines.

"You think they know what's happening?" Marie asked.

"They know."

We drove on through quiet countryside, then came upon an eight lane, divided freeway. I stopped at the edge of the road to study the scene. The northbound lanes were deserted while the southbound side was crammed with skimmers, light wheelers, heavy transports, high speed commuter buses and short range auto-taxis, all at a standstill. In frustration, many people had abandoned their vehicles and were streaming south on foot while others, unwilling to abandon their possessions, honked horns and yelled angrily at each other. Some tried to get off the road, but crash barriers locked them in and the nearest off-ramps were jammed. There were no gendarmes to direct traffic, and with the number of abandoned vehicles mounting, no possibility the congestion would clear for days.

A group of bedraggled refugees, weighed down by bags and children, approached us with desperation in their eyes.

"De l'eau, s'il vous plait," a woman with a child begged

in a husky voice. *Water please.*

I lowered the pressure field and nodded to Marie who retrieved a water bottle from the storage compartment and handed it to the woman who let her child drink first.

"Merci, Madame," the woman said with relief, then took a sip herself.

"Did they bomb the city?" I asked.

"No Monsieur," she said wearily, "but there is…a lot of fighting." She went to hand the bottle back, but Marie refused to accept it.

"You keep it," she said, glancing meaningfully at the children.

"Thank you, Madame."

A group of men behind her were eyeing our ride, whispering to each other, so I raised the pressure field and started toward the northbound on-ramp before they could do more than talk. Several of them tried to cut us off, but I accelerated past them onto the freeway and headed for Paris-Elbe. Apart from a few stragglers on foot, we had the road to ourselves, letting me crank up the speed.

We raced past many small towns untouched by fighting and the regional cities of Auxerre and Nemours where sporadic fires were burning. When we crossed the Loing River, waves of off-white strikebots with Democratic Union markings flew low and fast over our heads heading north. There was at least a thousand of them, bombers and fighters, skimming the trees at hypersonic velocity, followed by a thin line of manned control craft directing the airstrike. Behind the four engineered command craft were hundreds of dark green troop transports with armor clad soldiers manning door guns and more troops visible inside.

We stopped to watch as sonic booms thundered from the sky and cheers and honking horns rang out from the traffic chaos of the southbound lanes. People waved and cheered as if victory was within their grasp.

"Finally!" Marie said excitedly, waving and smiling,

then she sobered when she saw I wasn't rejoicing. "You don't think they have a chance."

"No, they don't." I knew they'd be slaughtered, but I couldn't bring myself to say it, not that I needed to. My face said it all.

"So why are they attacking?"

"What else can they do?"

We started north again, soon reaching the outskirts of Paris-Elbe. We entered an old arrondissement filled with four story buildings and stopped on a hill with a view of the europolises of central Paris. They were great rectangular structures many kilometers long and over a thousand meters high. The flat roofs were crowded with shuttle pads and the sloping walls were lined with balconies and planter boxes overflowing with flowers and vines that gave the walls an overgrown, green appearance.

The europolises were inhabited by the wealthy urban elite who rarely ever set foot in the grubby, crime ridden alleys below, and they stretched from Versailles in the west, across northern Europe to the Elbe River in the east. The vast mega-urban was mainland Europe's greatest cultural, economic and industrial center, although the pillars of black smoke rising all across the horizon signaled it was now the site of vicious street fighting.

White and orange energy blasts flashed from autacs in the streets, up into the europolises, while human tracer arced from the balconies in reply. Fiery explosions erupted from the sides of the europolises while human artillery maintained a constant bombardment of Spawn held territory.

Democratic Union attack craft swarmed like protective insects around the gigantic structures, strafing Spawn positions on the ground while energy blasts flashed up at them from a thousand places, destroying our fighters with frightening efficiency. Circling at the periphery of the battle were dozens of manned control craft, working with soldiers on the ground to vector airstrikes and coordinate tactics. Whenever the controllers ventured too close to the battle, energy bursts flashed up from the ground, turning them into fireballs, degrading human command and control.

Streaking through the frenzied swarms of white and silver Union fighters were a handful of black hulled, Spawn strike craft. They were many times faster than their human adversaries and enormously outnumbered, yet their armored hulls and glowing contour shields rendered them almost immune to human air-to-air weapons. They swept through the Union squadrons with strafing energy weapons, making pass after pass, shooting our fighters down with ruthless efficiency.

"Where's I-F? Why don't they help?" Marie said.

"Orders."

"They could make a difference."

"The Union Army's going to be destroyed. I-F can't stop it."

"So they're hiding!"

"They're doing what they were created to do. They're surviving."

I-F had been trained not to be drawn into unwinnable battles like these, but to bide their time and hit the Spawn later, when they least expected it.

We skirted the battle and headed east toward the EIS station. I followed the side streets along the river searching for a way across, but all the bridges over the Seine had been destroyed. We passed Parisians wielding primitive weapons and forming barricades in alleyways and on street corners while gendarmes directed traffic and shot looters, all seemingly unaware their opportunity to escape the dying city was rapidly slipping away.

A little further on, we found an ancient stone bridge that was damaged, but still standing. We drove across it thankful for the gyros and continued east through increasingly deserted streets. Several kilometers beyond the river, we came upon a smoldering gendarmerie vehicle in the middle of an intersection. I circled it slowly, spotting two charred corpses in the front seat and the body of a third officer lying face down on the road nearby. I stopped beside the body, which had a blackened, fist-sized wound through its torso.

"Why are we stopping?" Marie asked.

"Weapons," I replied and retrieved the officer's stun pistol and a small automatic gun. I stripped the charred corpse of reloads, climbed back onto the drag bike and handed the gun to Marie.

"You're riding shotgun," I said, then a glint of sunlight caught my eye.

It was a recon-flanker, walking along the road scanning buildings a block away. The bipedal autac was smaller than a man, more lightly armed than an elite, with a short barreled energy weapon instead of a right forearm, and a disk-shaped, planar shield emitter on its left forearm instead of a full body contour shield. It turned toward us, detected the gun in Marie's hands and immediately aimed its cannon arm at us.

"Watch out!" Marie cried.

I twisted the throttles, hurling the bike forward as it fired. An energy pulse flashed behind us as our twin engines roared and we raced away through the narrow streets. The buildings obscured its aim, then it raced out of the side street at a full sprint and fired again. I swerved to the right as an energy blast flashed by, shattering a building, forcing me to veer back across the road to avoid being crushed by falling debris. The autac sent another energy blast flashing past as I lay the bike hard over and went into a cross street without braking. The bike's traction controllers, variable axles and gyros glued us to the road, then we straightened and I piled on the speed.

"Freeway," Marie said, pointing at a ramp ahead.

The autac appeared on the rear viewscreen, chasing us at a full sprint. It raised its cannon arm as I turned onto the ramp and fired. The blast shaved the bike's pressure field as we reached the top and became airborne, then the gyros howled, ensuring a perfect two point landing. Now on an empty freeway, I went full throttle. The twin engines screamed like wild cats as my HUD's speed indicator numbers blurred and the aerofield pressed us onto the road.

The recon-flanker leapt into the air, hurdling the on-ramp to reach the freeway, but we were already too fast. Calculating it couldn't catch us, it stopped suddenly and tried to snipe us with a precision shot. Its weapon flashed and I swerved, losing control. The energy pulse swept past as the bike wobbled, then the AI reshaped the aerofield, adjusted the axles and steered us out of trouble.

"Good recovery," Marie said, relieved.

"It wasn't me."

The recon autac lowered its weapon arm as we topped six hundred kilometers an hour while the aerofield pinned us to the road. When the autac was no longer in sight, I eased off the throttles and let our speed bleed away.

"Sirius Kade, drag racer," Marie joked. "Who knew?"

"First and last time I'm ever getting on one of these things."

"First time?"

I checked my bionetic mind map, looking for the shortest route to the EIS station. It was on the south bank of the Marne close to the freeway and well away from the battle now ranging through Paris-Elbe's europolises.

"Not far now," I said, looking for a way off the freeway.

I'd never been to the Paris-Elbe Station, didn't know anyone there, but that didn't matter. It would be a relief to be among friends again and find out what was happening to the rest of the world.

* * * *

The EIS Station was in Chalifert Arrondissemont thirty

clicks east of the old city. My bionetic mind map led us through largely deserted streets to a six story, light industrial building surrounded by a three meter high wall capped by flickering sensor beams.

"They've still got power," Marie observed.

"Emergency cells, almost depleted," I said, slowing as we approached the entrance.

The heavy metal gate was open and the armored autoturret covering it failed to track us as we drove in. Beyond the checkpoint was visitor parking and a dirty, windowless building bristling with commlinks. I ignored the ramp down to the underground vehicle stacking facility and parked close to the entrance, facing the road in case we had to get out fast. Well dressed, chisel-faced men should have been shoving automatic weapons in our faces by now, demanding identification.

"Nobody's home," Marie said suspiciously.

"They've been hit," I said, noting the building's lights were out, the exterior wall panel was blinking and the automatic front doors were slightly apart.

"Are we going inside?"

"Yes."

I turned the bike off and climbed the stairs to the door. It was wedged open by the bloodied hand of one of those chisel-faced guards I'd been expecting. I forced the door open and found a charred hole as big as my fist in his back and an automatic weapon clutched in his other hand. From the smell, I knew he'd been dead a while, and his gun's ammo display was on zero.

"He didn't die wondering," I said, certain he'd emptied his magazine into whatever had killed him.

A second guard lay in the darkened foyer with only a blackened hole for a face. I ejected his weapon's magazine and confirmed none of the remaining rounds had the telltale purple ring of static force penetrators. I set his useless weapon down and pushed my bionetic listener to maximum. Hearing only the distant hiss of static, we crept through a security checkpoint into a dark corridor where a woman lay face down in a pool of blood. At the end of the corridor was an open door with a malfunctioning DNA scanner and a large dark room crammed with wall screens hissing white noise.

Wrecked consoles, overturned chairs and corpses wearing virtual reality headsets filled the room. Most had been killed while seated, some while running for the exits, and everywhere I looked, VR headsets blinked ghostly light onto the faces of the dead.

Marie was ashen faced. She kept her burp gun level, forgetting how useless it was against Spawn contour shields. In the center of the room was a hole reaching up through the floors above to the sky and down to the lowest sublevel. Lying in a shallow crater six levels below was a drop pod, peeled open and empty.

"How'd the Spawn know the EIS were here?"

"The snakeheads told them," I replied. Our ancient enemy, the reptilian Matarons, had been spying on Earth for millennia. They knew every high priority target on the planet, and even if they hadn't blabbed to the Spawn, there was simply no way to hide an EIS station's signal traffic. "Would have taken them out in the first wave, before they even knew what was happening."

I removed a headset from a dead operator and pulled it on. My bionetics fed in my security clearance, then I whispered, "Search comms log for recipient, Sirius Kade, Oh-Zero-Sixty Command." The headset showed there was a message waiting for me, now more than thirty hours old. "Play message, Lena Voss."

VR data link damaged. Routed to screen three, appeared in front of my eyes.

I discarded the headset as Lena's face replaced white static on the nearest wall screen. The Oh-Zero-Sixty regional commander wore a gray, Earth Navy pressure suit with no rank and the visor fully up. She was in a dimly lit room lined with screens and full of Earth Navy officers in p-suits on high-gee couches. They spoke in controlled, efficient voices, watching the screens rapidly updating with contact markers, range circles, course vectors and gravity zones.

"Sirius," Lena said in a hushed voice, "If you receive this message, your orders are to get off Earth any way you can. I'll send instructions to our surviving stations on unoccupied worlds. I can't say more, the Spawn are intercepting all our comms. The–"

"BRACE FOR LATERAL-GEE!" blared behind her, drowning out her words.

Lena lay back on her couch, wincing as the ship went to military power. The acceleration overwhelmed the inertial field, flattening her face against bone as the ship shuddered from a blast wave. It performed another high-gee evasion and she blacked out while loose equipment flew across the screen. Her lifeless body lay pressed against her couch for several seconds before she regained consciousness and her face returned to normal.

She coughed, trying not to vomit, then an officer offscreen yelled, "Damn it! My leg's broken."

Lena leaned toward the comm unit again. "The Spawn hit the Council Meeting in Kinshasa. Killed them all, including Kaneko."

Marie gasped at the news the Democratic Union's president was dead.

"Giannelli wasn't there," Lena added. "He was evacuated from Earth and sworn in as Union President two hours ago. The PFA, the Indian Republic and the Calies are all trying to figure out who they've got left. Giannelli's issued the Survival Protocol on behalf of the Council. A PFA secretary I've never heard of seconded it from Sino City while the Spawn were beating down the doors of the Great Hall behind him." She shook her head grimly. "We're abandoning the Solar System, Sirius, saving the fleet. The Tau Cetins haven't told us where we're going, and even if they did, I couldn't tell you. Just get off the planet. Earth is lost."

On a system projection behind her, a cluster of spherical lights bloomed above Neptune, then a calm, synthetic voice announced:

"ENS KANSAS...DESTROYED."

"ENS CAIRO...DESTROYED."

"ENS YUNNAN...DESTROYED."

"ENS BRISBANE...DESTROYED."

"PREPARE FOR EMERGENCY BUBBLE."

"*WARNING!* MINIMUM SAFE DISTANCE NOT ACHIEVED."

Lena glanced over her shoulder, then leaned toward the comm set. "The Spawn changed tactics, Sirius, they're–"

The screen went black, displaying a simple message in white letters: *Transmission Terminated.*

"They can't just leave us," Marie said shocked.

"They already have. They don't have a choice."

"But...what are we going to do?"

"What she said. Get off the planet."

"How?"

"Find a ship. Steal one if we have to."

"We could stay here, and help."

"With what?" I asked, holding up the gendarme's stun pistol. "This?" I shook my head. "If the Tau Cetins can't stop them, what hope do we have?"

She studied the bodies in the room, and nodded. "Roissy is the largest spaceport in Europe."

"It'll be crawling with Spawn."

"Orly is smaller. It'll be less of a target."

They were about the same distance away. Roissy was north, Orly west, but Orly was an intra-system hub, not a true starport. Any ships there would be interplanetary slow haulers and micro-jumpers.

"We need a starship," I said, my mind made up. "It has to be Roissy."

Metallic footsteps rang out above us, heavy and fast.

Our eyes followed the clatter of metal feet across the ceiling, then I grabbed Marie's arm and we ran back through the building, and out to the dragster. Before she was even settled, I had both wheels spinning on the gravel, throwing the big bike forward.

Two stories up, a wall exploded. An elite stepped to the edge, targeting us with its twin shoulder cannons as we went through the gate. I lay the bike hard over, pushing the gyros and axles through a sharp turn as two energy blasts flashed after us. They cratered the road behind us, then I straightened the bike and piled on the speed as the elite leapt from the EIS station.

It landed on the road and fired after us again as I swerved into a narrow side street and sped away between parked cars with barely enough room to pass. We raced through narrow streets and lanes at high speed, periodically glimpsing the elite giving chase, but we were faster through the maze and soon left it behind.

"It's not following," Marie said at last, watching over her shoulder.

"We just went to the top of the kill list." The recon-flanker back on the freeway would have reported us to its big brothers, but we were nobodies then. Now we were EIS fugitives on a fancy set of wheels. "We've got to ditch the bike."

We raced west through narrow roads toward Montevrain, a small commercial center now a ghost town. Deciding to dump the bike, I drove through a shop front window, showering shelves of holographic product displays with crystalline shards. We left the gyro bike there, out of sight of the road, and slipped out into a laneway.

"Roissy's too far to walk," Marie said.

"I'll hot-jack a car," I said, waggling my bionetic fingers at her meaningfully.

She gave me a bemused look, then I began checking every car we passed. I skipped those with sophisticated security systems and picked a small three wheeler with an egg shaped nose and sloping rear window. It was a Fiotti, old and gray, barely fast enough for the freeway, and the polar opposite of the flashy, over powered gyrodragster. Hoping the Spawn would pay it no attention, I put my index finger on the touch pad, linked with the car's crude control system and unlocked the doors.

Marie looked impressed. "Interstellar spy, hunted enemy of the Spawn, and car thief." She gave the car a disparaging look. "It's kind of ugly."

"It's perfect," I said and climbed inside.

We followed my Paris-Elbe mind map north west, crossing the Marne at Thorigny and passing under a double maglev line that was no longer working before entering a maze of streets south of Roissy Spaceport. It was dark by the time we reached Mitry-Mory, an old industrial part of the city abandoned long before the Spawn had arrived. There was graffiti on every wall and the destitute and dangerous prowled the shadows. Burnt out, rusting derelict cars lined the streets, stripped of parts and tagged with gang signs. Our little Fiotti looked almost at home, too poor to rob, which is why in spite of furtive glances from the lurkers, no one approached us.

Soon we turned into a narrow street and headed toward buildings silhouetted by the orange glow of fires burning at the spaceport. We passed abandoned warehouses, then a slender bipedal form faster than any human darted through our single beam headlight. It came around for a closer look, then I jammed on the power, sending the little car buzzing between abandoned vehicles and rubbish piles as street idlers watched from dark doorways and darker alleys. The recon-flanker chased after us, easily closing the distance.

"Faster!" Marie urged, glancing back.

"This is faster."

Marie emptied her burp gun through the rear window, but the flanker deflected the attack with its arm-mounted planer shield, then a man stepped out in front of us. He stood in the midst of our single headlight, looked me straight in the eye, and made a sharp, sweeping motion with one hand toward a side street. I swerved, narrowly avoiding running him down, lifting one wheel off the road as we took the corner. The Fiotti scraped a rusting freight loader, tore off a fender as it bounced clear and was lit up by a bank of eight brilliant floodlights, blinking on ahead of us. I shielded my eyes with one hand as I realized the eight lights were hurtling toward us.

"Sirius!" Marie yelled, tensing for a collision.

I swerved the Fiotti into a wall as a massive twenty two wheeler thundered past, struck the back corner of our little car, tearing it off, then slammed into the recon-flanker as it came around the corner. The prime mover carried the autac across the road and crashed into the rusting cargo loader, crushing it.

The truck's cab door opened and the driver jumped down while the man who'd waved us into the side street ran up. Both men produced small automatic weapons and raked the pinned flanker mercilessly until their ammo ran out, administering vigilante vengeance, street style.

"You alright?" I asked.

Marie nodded, shaken but unharmed, then I kicked my crumpled door open and we climbed out. Across the road, the two gunmen inspected their handiwork, grinning to each other. The pointing man lit up a fumer to celebrate while the driver lifted a short range communicator to his lips.

"Nous avons trouvé un maigre," he said, *We got a skinny one*.

"Bon travail, Equipe Deux," replied from the communicator, *Good work, Team Two*.

The two men grinned maliciously, looked and fought like common street thugs, but whoever they were talking to spoke with military crispness.

"Nice work," I said, looking over the shredded autac,

its planer shield disk still glowing.

They exchanged curious looks, studied us both, then the driver's eyes narrowed. "Are you Kade, Monsieur?"

I hid my surprise, but considering they'd just butchered an autac, I decided on the truth. "I am."

He lifted his communicator to his lips. "Je l'ai trouvé," he said, *Found him.*

"We need to get to the Spaceport," Marie said.

"Ha! You and ten million others," the pointing man declared.

"Come with us," the driver said, lighting up a fumer even more pungent than his companions. I hesitated, then he added, "Or stay here and die."

"We'll come," I said, wondering how he could possibly know my name.

Exhaling smoke laced with something that made my eyes water, the two street hoodlums led us into a labyrinth of filthy back alleys and derelict buildings so lawless even the Spawn feared to enter.

* * * *

The two Parisian autac muggers led us into a disused engineering works filled with dusty, rusting machines. Moonlight streamed through holes in the roof and five vagrants with a scrawny dog sat around a campfire sucking stimhalers. The pointing man nodded to the vagrants, who recognized him and removed their hands from hidden weapons, then we went down stairs to a basement, through a hidden door into a grimy corridor lit by a solitary glow tube. They showed us through another door into a clean, well-lit waiting room with an optical sensor and an armored door.

"Wait here," the truck driver said, then he and his companion went back the way we'd come.

"Now what?" Marie asked.

I sat on the couch and looked at the sensor mounted

high in one corner. "We wait, while they confirm our identities." I patted the seat beside me. "Smile."

"I don't feel like smiling, and I'm not EIS," she said, sitting down.

"Guilt by association."

Soon, a slender woman in her mid-thirties with heavy eye makeup and a tight fitting dress opened the armored door. "Monsieur Kade?"

"Everyone knows my name, and I didn't even make a reservation."

"I am Caliste Faucheux, head of the Collectif du Côté Est."

"Right," I said like it meant something to me.

"It's a Paris crime syndicate," Marie explained with a sideways look.

"Criminal one day, freedom fighter the next," Caliste said, confirming Marie's assessment. "Follow me, s'il vous plaît."

She led us through a large room filled with military personnel in battle fatigues and local criminals in skin tight shirts and dark jackets. They spoke softly into an odd assortment of communication devices hard wired to wall connections, studied maps and cleaned weapons.

"We use cables to remote comm stations so the Spawn cannot track our transmissions," Caliste said. "Before the invasion, we used this system to avoid the Gendarmerie. Now it serves another purpose." She led us to a door guarded by a pair of Union Army troopers and turned to Marie. "You will wait here." She motioned to a small, uncomfortable looking chair beside the door.

"She comes with me," I said.

"She will be quite safe here, unless the Spawn attack."

"I'll be fine," Marie said and sat down, then Caliste showed me into an office with table and chairs on one side and a flat screen map of western Paris-Elbe on the other. A group of civilians chatted with several high ranking officers and a young lieutenant who looked completely at ease in spite of being in the company of his seniors. One of the civilians, a well-dressed, silver haired gentleman who looked as if he'd just come from a board meeting, detached himself from the group and came to meet me.

"Sirius Kade. Welcome," he said with a smooth, Anglo accent, then nodded to Caliste to give us a moment. "Geoffrey Northcott. Delighted to meet you at last. Lena has told me so much about you and your exploits."

When we shook hands, I felt my palm tingle as our bionetics linked, but no data came through. "She didn't know I was coming this way."

"She told you to leave and to do that, you need a ship."

"You spoke to her?"

"Spoke? Hmm...Not exactly." He looked into my eyes the way Lena did when she was waiting for me to figure something out. The way Lena did! He smiled conspiratorially and his voice sounded in my mind. *Yes, my boy. Now you've got it.*

He was mega-psi, like her, part genetic accident, part bio-engineered miracle. There were four of them, only four, in all of humankind. They were a forced evolutionary advance whose existence was a closely guarded secret, not just from our enemies but our friends as well.

"She was on a ship orbiting Neptune," I said. "That's a long way out."

"Yes, but close enough," Geoffrey replied meaningfully, close enough for their minds to meet.

"You're a lot older than she is."

I was the first, that survived, he replied telepathically, leaving me in no doubt that he was the ranking Earth Intelligence Service officer on Earth. "And not that old. I'll have you know I'm a sprightly one hundred and thirty six, which is why I agreed to a rear area posting. Unfortunately, Earth is now the front line."

"Were you at Chalifert, when the pod dropped?"

"No, Geneva. I tried to get back to London-Mid, but

the Channel crossings have all been destroyed, so...here I am." He slid a hand under my arm and guided me to the others. "Let me introduce you to our little resistance cell. Our lovely host, you know."

Caliste nodded graciously. "You are too kind, Lord Geoffrey."

"*Lord* Geoffrey?" I said surprised.

He gave me an embarrassed look. "A minor affectation. I am a Viscount by birth, not that such things count for much these days." He motioned to the Union Army officer. "General Anton Delatte, Union Army, FranCorps commander, Paris-Elbe West."

The general gave me a curt nod. He wore a purple beret above a black moustache and was clearly impatient to begin. "Monsieur Kade."

Lord Geoffrey indicated the Earth Navy officer. "Commodore Amara Geurrant, flag officer commanding Earth Naval Base Roissy."

She was swarthy skinned, late forties, with dark eyes and a uniform soiled with ash and dirt, having barely escaped Roissy Spaceport with her life.

"Bienvenu, EIS," she said wearily.

Lord Geoffrey introduced the Chief of Police, the Mayor of Paris, a local Union boss, the City Engineer, a liaison from the German side of Paris-Elbe, then last of all, the young lieutenant. "And this is Lieutenant Dickson."

He wore light armor and had a red, triangular shoulder patch with a clenched chainmail fist inside; an Iron Fist. Dickson was young, but not fresh faced, with an athletic physique and the cold, humorless eyes typical of his kind. The zygote super soldier was as far from a standard human as Lord Geoffrey himself, although in a completely different way, and if rank had been the determinant, he wouldn't have made it through the door. From the way the others ignored him, they didn't realize what he was, or that he'd be fighting the enemy long after they were all dead.

"Kade," the young officer drawled with a North American accent, shaking my hand with a grip that almost broke bones.

"Lieutenant Dickson is the ranking I-F officer in Paris-Elbe," Lord Geoffrey said.

"How many men do you have?" I asked.

"Not enough," Dickson replied evasively, unwilling to share specifics with any of us, even his military superiors.

"Can we begin now?" General Delatte demanded impatiently.

"Of course," Lord Geoffrey replied amicably, turning to me, "I asked them to wait for you, so you can report our situation to Lena."

The FranCorps commander turned to the flat screen depicting a hundred kilometer wide plan of metropolitan Paris-Elbe from Rambouillet in the west to Reuil-en-Brie in the east. The central area around the old city was colored red, as were the industrial areas to the north and two pockets to the east.

"The red areas are under attack or controlled by the Spawn," the general began. "They're jamming our communications, however, optical drones confirm heavy fighting north of the old city in the europolis zones from Satrouville to Saint-Denis. They have also isolated our forces at Montrouge, south east of the Seine, and in the Creteil area." He pointed to the two red rings south of the main battle. "These positions are held by the ninth and seventieth brigades respectively." He grimaced. "We have no way to relieve them. It is only a matter of time before they are wiped out."

He let that sink in before continuing. "A courier from Fifth Army HQ in Toureine informs me that Marshal Rousseau has abandoned all hope of relieving Paris-Elbe. The entire army is now withdrawing toward the Massif Central, where they intend to dig in."

"Non! Non! They must do something," the Mayor of

Paris exploded.

"What can they do?" General Delatte snapped. "We have no orbital support. Our infantry weapons are useless. Our heavy weapons cannot sustain contact long enough to overload their shields. And our air units are no match for theirs. If the army does not withdraw, they will be annihilated. The Spawn have refused all attempts to negotiate a ceasefire. Their intention is clearly the complete destruction of our forces."

"They won't negotiate," I said. "They want Earth as a base to use against the Tau Cetins. We're just in their way."

"In their way!" Caliste exclaimed indignantly.

"Earth's the closest habitable planet," I explained. Our proximity to Tau Ceti gave us a special relationship with our great and powerful neighbor, and painted a massive target on our homeworld.

"Thank you, General," Lord Geoffrey said and motioned to Amara Geurrant. "Commodore."

She stepped forward, bleary eyed, looking like she hadn't slept in days. "My news is no better. Roissy naval base has been utterly destroyed, along with nine ships caught on the ground, including the battleship Temeraire."

"What about the rest of the fleet?" the Chief of Police asked.

"I've had no contact with them since global comms went down," she replied.

"They're gone," I said. "Most of them."

"Gone? Where?" the City Engineer asked.

"They jumped out yesterday, with the Tau Cetins."

Caliste's eyes bulged incredulously. "They left us to the Spawn?"

"The Council activated the Survival Protocol," Lord Geoffrey explained. "And rightly so."

"What is this Survival Protocol?" she demanded.

"It means we're on our own," I said. "Our ships are no

match for the Spawn. Any that stayed would have been destroyed. So, they saved what they could."

"Cowards!" she spat.

"A fleet-in-being is better than no fleet at all," Lord Geoffrey said gently.

The people of Earth had never really understood what it meant to have an enemy millions of years more advanced than us. Now they were learning the hard way.

"Any word on the rest of the planet?" I asked.

"I've had no contact with other commands in over forty hours," General Delatte said. "There were reports of landings on every continent before comms went down. Nothing since."

"I can confirm through EIS channels that our ground forces are being driven back on all fronts," Lord Geoffrey added.

"How many cities have been destroyed?" I asked, fearing a Lhekan-style genocide.

"None. Not one," Lord Geoffrey replied. "The Spawn are occupying the mega-urbans, not destroying them. They know the Tau Cetins won't bombard our population centers from orbit."

"They're using us as meat shields," I said.

Lord Geoffrey nodded. "So it appears."

"The Tau Cetins should have stopped them from landing," Caliste declared angrily.

"They tried," Commodore Geurrant assured her. "We've seen Tau Cetin ships attack four times since it began, but each time they appear, the Spawn retreat. When the Tau Cetins leave, the Spawn return."

"Why do they leave?" Caliste asked.

"They have more to defend than Earth," Lord Geoffrey explained. "The Spawn are attacking weaker worlds all across the Orion Arm, avoiding a direct engagement. If the Tau Cetins stationed a large fleet here, many other worlds would be defenseless. If they left a small force, the Spawn would return in strength and destroy it in detail."

It's what Lena meant when she'd said the Spawn had changed tactics. Weakened by their defeat at Serris-Orn, they'd switched to drop and run tactics, hitting the Tau Cetins where they were weakest, their allies.

"They're leaving us to die," Caliste said bitterly.

"They're trying to destroy the invasion ships, to stop attacks on all worlds," Lord Geoffrey stated.

"The Spawn have them chasing ghosts," I said, recalling the spawncarrier's sudden retreat yesterday when three Tau Cetin arbiters had appeared overhead. A somber silence settled over the group as they digested the severity of the situation.

"The Survival Protocol means I-F now have responsibility for defending Earth," Lord Geoffrey said. He turned to Lieutenant Dickson, who stood unobtrusively at the back of the group. "Isn't that so, Lieutenant?"

All eyes turned to Dickson, who shifted uneasily. "Yeah...that's right."

"*Lieutenant* Dickson," Major General Delatte said scornfully, "is only here because you insisted he be present."

"He's here," Lord Geoffrey said, "because his forces will soon be all that's left of Earth's military. That's why all I-F units are now free to operate independent of the chain of command."

"What!" the general exploded.

"I-F will lead the resistance. Any military or civilian personnel who wish to fight may place themselves under their command, if I-F will have them."

The general looked Dickson over dismissively. "He is a junior officer. What does he know of grand strategy?"

"The strategy's decided, General," I said. "It was decided years ago, by Earth Council, by our weakness, by our enemy's strength. We knew this day might come and there was only ever going to be one strategy."

"What strategy is that, Monsieur Kade?" the general

demanded icily.

"To make Earth the bitterest pill the Spawn ever swallowed. To make them regret ever setting foot on this planet. We can't beat them in a stand up fight, but I-F will make them bleed." I turned to Lieutenant Dickson. "Right?"

"Yes sir," he said with steely resolve.

"How are they going to do that?" General Delatte asked.

"That's for them to decide," I replied. "Right now, the best thing you can do is scatter your forces before the Spawn destroy them."

General Delatte bristled. "No! We have to regroup. We must counter attack."

I shook my head. "With what? Weapons that can't penetrate their shields? Aircraft they shoot out of the sky at will. General, the Spawn have the most powerful army in the galaxy. You're never going to beat them in set piece battles. Even the Tau Cetins won't try that."

"I'd listen to him if I were you, Anton," Lord Geoffrey said diplomatically. "Save as many lives as you can. We're going to need those men one day. Don't let them die for nothing."

Delatte hesitated, torn by an order he knew he had to give.

"The Spawn are growing stronger, General, as we grow weaker," Commodore Guerrant said. "They already have air-to-orbit supremacy. Soon our forces won't be able to move in the open, perhaps at all. You cannot stop them."

Delatte weighed up her words in silence, stared at Lord Geoffrey who nodded, then his shoulders slumped ever so slightly. "Very well. I will order a general dispersal, every man for himself." He looked Dickson over uncertainly. "I'm glad I'm not you, Lieutenant. God help you." He gave us all a defeated look and went off to save what he could of his disintegrating army.

I turned to Dickson, who now had the weight of the world on his shoulders. "Have you got a weapon I could use," I asked, hoping he'd let me join him.

"You won't need it, Sirius," Lord Geoffrey cut in. "You're not staying."

"I'm sure as hell not leaving, not now. Besides, you heard her," I said, nodding to Commodore Guerrant, "Roissy's destroyed. There's no way off the planet."

Lord Geoffrey turned to the others. "I'd like a moment alone with Captain Kade," he said, then waited as they filed out. When they were gone, he produced a small EIS jamming device that would scramble any unwelcome snooping.

"Is that necessary?" I asked after he activated it.

"Miss Caliste is a most enterprising host. Right now, she's discovering her listening devices are no longer functioning. She won't return, because we like to pretend we trust each other." He pocketed the device. "There's a ship waiting for you at Roissy."

"But the Spawn–"

"Destroyed the naval base. They're allowing civilian vessels to leave unmolested."

"Why?"

"Refugees spread fear and defeatism to other worlds." He glanced at the door, knowing Marie waited beyond it. "You brought your girlfriend."

"Fiancé...almost."

"You realize you're putting her in danger?"

"We're all in danger."

"You're wanted. She isn't."

"I know, the Consortium have a price on my head, but I can–"

"No. I meant the Spawn. They have two lists, one for high ranking Earth officials–I have the honor of being fourteenth on that list–and another for people our Mataron friends want for their own reasons. You, my dear boy, are number one on that list.

"Hazrik a'Gitor?"

"Yes, Hazrik," Lord Geoffrey said, confirming the snakehead spymaster hadn't given up hope of overseeing my public execution. "I have many associates listening at keyholes, even on Kif-atah."

"That's no reason for me to leave Earth."

"Perhaps not, but this is," he said, extending his hand as if to shake, although this time he clearly had something else in mind.

"Hmph." I took his hand, letting our bionetics mate, then a massive system upgrade streamed into my bionetic memory, rewriting how my sensory inputs were processed.

"Someone's been busy," I said wryly.

"We analyzed how the Spawn disabled your bionetics at Serris-Orn. This won't entirely stop them, but it will slow them down."

"They didn't penetrate my bunker,"

"Only because they were in a hurry. If they catch you again, this will ensure your nerve endings are destroyed, isolating your entire system before they can penetrate it. We call it autonomic bunkering."

"It's not going to make me deaf and blind, is it?"

"No, but you won't be able to utilize your bionetics until we put you though a rather painful cell regeneration process."

"If you can do it, so can the Spawn."

"They can try, but they'll need a bionetic key to connect your system, which I'm told has over a hundred octillion combinations."

"Sounds like a lot."

"You'll die of old age before they figure it out."

"I feel safer already," I said, attempting to release his hand, but he kept his grip, continuing our interface.

"Lena wants you off world. So do I. I'm giving you everything we have on Earth's current situation."

"Can't you just..." I waved my fingers at the side of

my head, "send it to her."

"She's too far away now. And make sure the Tau Cetins get a copy, so they know how bad it is down here."

Thousands of reports from EIS, Earth Navy, UniPol, Union Army, PFA Army, Republic Armed Forces and the Caliphate flowed through our palm link into my bionetic memory, along with news bulletins and battle imagery from every continent. Last of all was a think tank analysis of Spawn capabilities and tactics.

"I thought you had no comms," I said.

"EIS has underground data links. The Spawn will find them eventually."

"The military don't know?"

"No, they'd want access. The increased signal traffic would make them vulnerable to detection."

I skimmed the data gathered from around the world. There was a tremendous amount of it, gathered in an extremely short time under the most difficult circumstances and it told an appalling story.

In Asia, the PFA's Northern Army had been defeated west of Jinan and was falling back toward the Taihang Mountains, while the Mumbai Supermetro had surrendered and its defenders were withdrawing into the Himalayas. The Delhi Supermetro was still ours, the only one of Earth's four collective government capitals still in our hands, but it was cut off and would soon be taken.

In Africa, the Cali Corps had been wiped out defending Cairo-Delta, and on the west coast, Kinshasa and Lagokuta had both fallen.

In North America, Democratic Union armies had suffered heavy casualties and civilian street fighting had erupted in both Am-East and Am-West. The Continental Commander had reported he'd lost both coasts and his armies were retreating inland.

The Russians were faring no better. Their ground forces were surrounded on both sides of the Urals and an e-plant had been hit, vaporizing the northern third of the

Moscow-Nov mega-urban with catastrophic loss of life.

In the southern hemisphere, South American forces had disintegrated and all attempts to withdraw into the Andes had failed. In Australia, the southern half of Aus-East was occupied, the northern half encircled, and many survivors were scattering into the interior to fight a guerilla war. Most desperate of all was the Antarctic Garrison, which had been driven onto the Larson Ice Shelf and was slowly freezing to death with no hope of rescue.

Of all the mega-urbans only Tokohama and London-Mid were still in our hands, largely because geographical factors were hampering the Spawn attack.

Lord Geoffrey remained silent as I ran the reports through my mind's eye, growing increasingly disheartened, then when the data transfer finished, he released my hand.

"Is there any good news?" I asked.

"Most of the fleet escaped, as far as I can tell, and all our I-F units survived the initial assault."

"I didn't see any I-F reports."

"They don't send reports. They'll avoid contact, wait for the initial momentum to fade, then make a jolly nuisance of themselves."

"Jolly?" I said, marveling at his optimism.

It wasn't that I-F were so much stronger than regular soldiers, it was that their psionic ability gave them a tremendous tactical advantage. They were Intuitive Fighters–the true meaning of I-F–with a sixth sense that told them what the enemy was going to do before he did it. It was that anticipation that made them faster than the Spawn's technological terrors, although they were painfully few in number.

"Any off world news?" I asked.

"Nothing from the Core Systems. We received a lot of maydays from inside the Solar System and our observatories report big explosions across the Marineris Supermetro and among the trans-Jovian cities. No word on the others."

It was grim tidings all round.

"So how do I get out of here?"

"My people are holding a ship called the Niobe for you. Pad eight seventy-one."

"For me and Marie," I said, correcting his error.

"Of course. Ask for Hannes Mertens. Tell him I sent you and he has my permission to launch. One of Caliste's men will guide you. Good luck, Sirius. Give my regards to Lena."

"Same to you. And…don't get caught. You won't like Spawn interrogation methods."

"I have no fear of drowning," he assured me, revealing he'd read my report detailing how the Spawn had played upon my greatest fear. "And my terminal safeguard is active," he added, confirming they'd never take him alive.

"I hope it won't come to that," I said, and went outside to Marie. Before she could ask a question, I whispered, "We've got a ship."

She looked relieved, then one of Caliste's heavies in a dark coat with a meticulously manicured Van Dyke and a smoldering fumer wedged between his lips said, "Ready, Monsieur?"

"Yes."

He led us through a tunnel to an old warehouse now filled with injured Parisians and wounded soldiers, many with horrific wounds. A handful of nurses and a single doctor treated them, but the medical staff lacked for everything and could do little more than watch their patients die. Beyond the makeshift aid station was another poorly lit passageway, this one lined with long pipes that hadn't carried water in centuries.

"This passes under the spaceport. It will take us close to your ship," Van Dyke said and turned to Marie. "Watch out for the rats, Madame. They bite."

"Rats?" Marie said alarmed, then Van Dyke hurried into the shadows with us following close behind.

* * * *

Van Dyke used a physical key to open an ancient mechanical lock, shouldered a corroded metal door open and led us into a dark storeroom stacked high with dust covered containers.

"The freight elevator doesn't work," he said. "Use the stairs. When you get to the top, go right."

While we eyed the stairs, he pulled the door shut behind us.

"Thanks," I said as the key rattled in the lock, then we climbed the stairs to a collapsed warehouse that had fallen in on top of an eight wheel freight handler.

We clambered over debris to the outer wall where we got our first look at the terminal. It was large and circular and there were still some lights on. Most of the windows had been blown out by shockwaves and the aerobridges fanning out from it were all blacked out. Off to the north was a cluster of pads littered with the smoldering wrecks of navy ships destroyed on the ground, still glowing hot. Elsewhere, work crews with flickering fusion welders patched holes in civilian ships, hurriedly preparing them for space, some with civilians milling around their landing gear trying to buy passage.

The direction of the pad numbers indicated eight seventy-one was off to the east. There was only one ship out that way, a skeletal container hauler with a boxy crew section in the bow, four engines astern and five horizontal rings mounting the star drive's spatial distorters between them.

"That must be the Niobe," I said.

"The Society's office is still open." Marie nodded toward a small, well-lit building with the letters BST glowing over the entrance. "We might have messages."

There was no telling where the *Niobe* would take us or when we'd have a chance to get in touch with our crews again, and the spaceport did look deserted.

I nodded. "OK."

We ran across several empty landing pads to the Beneficial Society of Traders' main European office. The normally locked security doors were wide open and the contract terminals on the floor and the private booths at the back were still active. Normally, captains would be scanning cargo contracts and whispering with associates, even at this late hour, but for once, the place was empty except for a cleanerbot diligently scrubbing the floors.

When we approached the private booths, a flickering service hologram appeared, smiled as if she knew us both and asked, "Comment puis-je vous aider?" *How may I help you?*

"We want to access member comms," I said.

"Yes sir. Please be advised, we have forty minutes of emergency power remaining."

We hurried to adjoining signal suppressed booths guaranteed to resist any human eavesdropping, ensuring Society members could conduct the most delicate commercial discussions without fear of arrest. The Society's policy of 'don't tell, don't get caught' famously annoyed UniPol while allowing members to maximize profits as creatively as they liked.

The booth scanned my DNA then the screen revealed I had a message waiting for me from Triton Central. It was from Jase, my co-pilot, sent two hours before Lena's message. He'd called me almost daily since Marie and I had arrived on Earth, pretending to update me on the *Silver Lining's* repairs, but really so he and Emma could pester me about whether or not I'd popped the question. By contrast, Izin, my engineer, hadn't called once, not surprising considering tamphs had no interest in small talk and even less in human relationships.

I activated the message and an image of the *Silver Lining's* bridge appeared. Jase was on my couch with Izin on one side and Emma on the other. Sitting at one of the disused science stations was a fresh faced navy ensign trying to look all-military and not fooling anyone. She was stiff and jittery, and clearly afraid.

"Hi Skipper," Jase said, "the navy's ordered us out of the system. I wish I could tell you how to find us, but they won't say where we're going. The ensign over there's going to plug in the coordinates just before we bubble, like they don't trust us to keep a secret."

The ensign turned to Jase. "Ninety seconds, Captain."

"See how polite she is." He grinned. "Me, a Captain!"

"You're wasting time," Izin snapped, glaring at Jase with bulging blue-green amphibian eyes.

"He's just jealous she doesn't call him Captain," Jase confided.

"Fleet command confirm jump approval, all ships," the ensign announced.

Emma Hadley leaned forward and spoke fast. "Hi Sirius. I hope you're both OK down there. Stay safe."

"The TCs are covering our retreat," Jase said. "Don't worry, Skipper, we'll take good care of the Lining for you. And keep your head down. Earth looks like crap from out here."

"Inputting superluminal transit coordinates, Captain," the ensign declared. "Compiling course simulation. Vector profile, complete. Mass intersection probability, zero. Initiate superluminal field activation sequence."

Jase winced and whispered, "She says stuff like that all the time. It's very confusing."

Izin tapped instructions into his console and replied to the ensign. "Sequence commenced. Superluminal field formation in ten seconds."

"She's got him talking like her now," Jase said, shaking his head. "Got to go, Skipper. We'll be waiting for you...somewhere."

The screen went blank then I stepped out of the booth. Marie was already waiting for me.

"They're OK," she said of her own crew. "They

hitched a ride with a Cali junk dealer."

"At least they're alive," I said, then we hurried outside and up into the aerobridge.

The long windowed corridor was dark, except for moonlight, and none of the security checkpoints were manned. The normally glowing arrivals and departure screens were all dead, and while a few shops along the promenade still had lights, there was no one in them.

"Eight seventy-one's a long walk," Marie said, noting the powered walkways had all stopped.

"They'll wait," I assured her, then flashes from the ground lit up the aerobridge. We stole a look outside as flanker-elites stormed the Society offices and blasted the helpful hologram when she appeared to greet them. "Uh-ho. We shouldn't have gone there."

"But…the Society's got the best–"

"Nowhere's secure," I said, cursing myself for being a fool, noticing a large, dark shape was now floating above the Society building. "They were watching my account."

A crash of tearing metal sounded as flankers broke through the ceiling and began searching the promenade.

"They're in the terminal," she whispered anxiously.

"Come on." I grabbed Marie's hand and pushed open an emergency exit.

We ran down fire stairs to the ground floor door and stole a look outside. Elites were tearing the Society offices apart while other autacs in the terminal engaged in an equally destructive search. On the other side of the aerobridge, an emergency services building stood in darkness with its garage doors open and its fire engines gone.

"Over there," I said.

We sprinted to it through the darkness and hid in the shadows inside, watching the Society building collapse and autacs fan out searching the area. Several came toward us as a spherical, snake-armed reaper and a spawnwarrior in full battle armor descended from the craft inside repeller fields.

"It's me they want, not you," I said, certain we had only moments before the Spawn came charging into the building. She wasn't on any list, but that wouldn't stop them shooting her to get to me.

"What are you saying?" she asked with mounting fear.

"They won't kill me. They'll give me to the Matarons."

Her eyes widened in horror. "No. Sirius, No!"

"I'll escape. I'll find a way."

She looked around, desperately. "We'll hide."

I shook my head. "They'll find us," I whispered, certain it was hopeless. "Remember, pad eight seventy-one. The Niobe. Ask for Hannes Mertens. Tell him Geoffrey Northcott sent you."

"I won't," she said as tears welled in her eyes.

"You will." I put my arm around her for the last time. "It's the only way,"

"I won't leave you."

"You won't have to." I pressed the gendarme stunner into her side.

"Sirius! Don't!"

"I'll always love you," I whispered and fired.

She convulsed. Her eyes closed and her body went limp, then I carried her back into a storeroom and lay her down in the dark. I retrieved the small box I'd been carrying for almost two years, briefly admired the Witari Diamond ring inside, wishing I'd given it to her sooner, and slipped it into her pocket.

"Hold this for me," I whispered, kissed her forehead and covered her with fire retardant sheets from the shelves.

I left the stunner beside her and hurried back through the empty garage. A beam light winked on from the Spawn transport above, illuminating the building, then I walked out into the bright light with my hands on my head, making it clear I was surrendering without a fight.

The spherical reaper glided away to the right, giving the spawnwarrior a clear line of sight. His shoulder mounted cannon locked onto me, then the flanker-elites leapt forward, landing in a wide circle around me.

"So many of you guys, for just one of me," I said.

The spawnwarrior raised an arm fitted with a spherical attachment and fired, sending a man-sized burst of ball lightning toward me. It enveloped my body, sending pain exploding through my nervous system. I fell to my knees and slumped face first onto the ground, numb all over, but still conscious.

The snake-armed reaper scooped me up like a rag doll hanging face down, then a bright, vertical beam floated us up toward the dark triangular craft hovering above. As the ground dropped away, the flanker-elites moved off across the spaceport toward the naval base, leaving Marie safely asleep under the sheet.

I was carried up through a circular opening into the craft's belly, then the hatch irised shut with a metallic clang, blanketing me in darkness, cutting off my last sight of Marie's hiding place, of freedom and of Earth.

Chapter Two: Kif-atah

Mataron Homeworld
Matar System (G2 Binary)
Inner Pegasus
1.18 Earth Normal Gravity
214 light years from Sol
4.1 Billion Reptilians

A wave of heat flooded the cold of stasis sleep as harsh violet light pressed against my eyelids, forcing me awake. My coffin-like sleep chamber was open and filling with stiflingly dry air as needles that had trickled life sustaining nutrients into my body now throbbed with stimulant. The resistance field pinning me down faded and I convulsed, drawing air into my lungs for the first time in weeks.

Strangely familiar, yet incomprehensible whispers broke into my thoughts. They flowed around me like a river, then the needles withdrew and my bunkered bionetics, sensing the alien implements were gone, reached out for sensory input. Life signs data flashed through my mind's eye, confirming I was suffering from chemical paralysis, but was otherwise unharmed.

Terminal safeguard deactivated, flashed before my eyes as my bionetics decided to let me live. The safeguard had activated automatically thanks to Lord Geoffrey's update, but the stasis chamber's intrusions hadn't been quite enough to trigger self-termination.

I opened my eyes, squinting against the harsh glare of a bright purple sky. Triangular reptilian faces looked down at me from both sides of my stasis coffin, studying me through vertical-slit eyes evolved for Matar's brilliant sunlight. Their beta-keratin soaked skin was hard and segmented, perfectly adapted to Kif-atah's arid environment, although it made their faces almost as incapable of expressing emotion as Izin's. The red and brown variations in color and pattern made them all uniquely distinctive while their clothes identified their status. The military snakeheads wore reddish-brown uniforms with bronze-colored insignia while the civilian security types were dressed in sleeveless blue jackets.

My bionetic listener activated and suddenly began translating their familiar hissing directly into my mind.

"–he strong enough for sentencing?" a military officer demanded.

"He will be," a blue jacket replied.

"What are his injuries?" an officer with a silver insignia asked.

"None, sir. He surrendered without a fight."

"I will inform the Blademaster. Send him to the cells for now."

"And the others?" the first blue jacket asked.

"Will any survive?"

"No, their injuries are too severe. They would be dead now if not for stasis."

"Hsssht!" the officer hissed irritably. "Stake them on the Scalded Plain. The scorids can have their flesh."

The military officers departed, then two blue coats lifted me out of the stasis chamber. I was on the back of a ground transport, along with seven other coffins laid out side by side. Each one contained a human prisoner, some wearing Earth military uniforms, some civilian. All had energy burns and open wounds. Some were missing limbs, although none had received medical treatment. The Spawn had simply de-animated them upon capture and shipped them off to the Mataron homeworld with no thought for their survival.

The transport was parked in the courtyard of an ancient, gray stone fortress stained with red dust and crowned by guard towers. Above an arched entryway was a faded Mataron sign my bionetics translated to:

Trel'sitar Prison
Directorate of Discipline

Trel'sitar was infamous, once the stronghold of a Landed Lord killed in a brutal blood feud long ago, the great fortification had fallen into disrepair only to be resurrected centuries later as a maximum security prison. The Mataron Triumvirate sent enemies of the Supremacy there for execution in accordance with snakehead warrior-cult traditions and for the amusement of the general population.

Still too numb to walk, the blue jackets dragged me across the dusty courtyard toward an arched entrance. At three meters tall, the snakeheads carried me with ease. In their inhospitable gravity, I struggled to lift my head, gaining mere glimpses of the forbidding walls towering above me. The weathered stonework contained slit windows for ventilation and had shiny metal sensors attached to it for all round surveillance.

More forbidding than the walls was the oppressive heat. Kif-atah's dry atmosphere gave Matar's yellow sunlight a purple tint that threw a strange cast over everything, especially the red dust. Before we reached the arched entry, my mouth was dry and the sweat beading on my skin was evaporating as fast as it formed, warning this was no world for soft skinned humans.

We passed under the arch, through double metal doors, into a labyrinth of dark, musty passages. The blue jackets handed me off to a pair of prison guards in gray uniforms carrying two meter long stun staffs. They dragged me through corridors lined with corroded metal doors, feeble lights and sensor nodes. The other guards showed little interest in me, confirming many humans had seen these passages before me.

My escort stopped in front of a large metal door, rolled it sideways and threw me in onto a worn stone floor. My senses were immediately assaulted by the reek of feces and strange body odors, then one of the guards drove his staff into my back for no reason and slammed the door shut with a clang.

I lay face down on dry stones, heard shuffling movements from the shadows and the tinkle of water in a tiny basin nearby. Three vertical slit windows high on one wall cast slender violet sunbeams onto the floor, providing the dungeon's only light and air. I lifted my head as lanky, snake-eyed denizens emerged from the darkness, their eyes fixed malevolently upon me as they prepared to give me a proper reptilian welcome.

Two Gienans and a Minkaran watched apprehensively from one corner, but dared make no move to help me. I forced myself to my knees, trying to hide how weak I was after my long stasis sleep, but only succeeded in showing I lacked the strength to stand.

"Hey," I said to my reptilian cellmates. "Nice dungeon."

No one returned the greeting, then three snakeheads sauntered toward me maliciously clenching and unclenching their long bony fingers. They carried no weapons, giving me hope they'd do no more than beat me senseless.

The biggest one stopped and sniffed the air.

"Human...stink...like tarkul," he hissed.

I didn't know what a tarkul was, or how it could possibly smell worse than this putrid dungeon, not that it mattered. They were here to stomp on my face, not give me a bath.

I struggled to my feet, made fists and tried to look like a fighter. They weren't fooled and hissed with amusement, raising their whip-like tails in readiness.

"Not the tails," I said wearily.

The reptilian who'd objected to my tarkulian odor came toward me, signaling he was the alpha snakehead. He lifted his tail into the air as if to whip me, then punched me squarely in the face, sending me reeling back onto the floor. Stunned, I stared up at the arched stone ceiling, blinking stars from my eyes as blood oozed from my nose and hissing laughter filled the air. Slowly, I pushed myself to a sitting position, knowing worse was to come.

"Good one," I said, feigning a smile and stumbling to my feet. I was so groggy, I was seeing double, and neither image would stand still. "My turn." I threw a drunken hay maker that missed both of him and almost sent me back to the floor.

"Humans...are weak," the alpha sneered as hisses of encouragement sounded from the reptilian audience.

He launched himself into the air, executing a classic Mataron spinning tail strike. His tail flicked back as he spun through the air, then whipped forward toward my face. Halfway through his turn, a huge dark hand caught his tail and jerked it back, snatching the snakehead out of the air. His tail straightened as he was swung violently through a half a circle and plowed head first into a stone wall.

Shocked, hissing gasps came from the reptilian onlookers as a large humanoid stepped out of the darkness. He was shorter than a Mataron, not as broad shouldered as a Syrman, but stronger and faster than both and twice as mean.

I sighed with relief, wiped blood from my mouth and surrendered the floor to the big Kesarn. "OK. Your turn."

In a fury, the alpha got to his feet, shook his head to clear it and signaled his two companions to attack together. The hulking humanoid stepped forward as one of the betas charged. With a lightning fast punch, the Kesarn drove his fist into the taller reptilian's chest, hurling him back the way he'd come, then the alpha leapt forward, spearing his tail toward the Kesarn's face. The muscular humanoid caught the tail's tip in front of his large brown eyes and snapped the alpha to him with one hand, punching the snakehead's face with the other. The blow was so hard, the reptilian's head recoiled back, shattering his neck.

Shocked gasps sounded from the shadows as the watching snakeheads recoiled in horror. Even I winced, never have seen a Mataron killed that way before.

The Kesarn tossed the alpha's corpse at their feet and hissed at them in their own language, "This human is mine!"

The snakehead cheer squad glowered in silence and backed away as the Kesarn motioned for me to follow him. Every hateful reptilian eye was fixed upon me, so I waved a finger back and forth between me and my protector, making sure they understood we were a team, even if I did the bleeding and he did the killing. From the resentful way they slinked off into the darkness, I knew they got the message.

Having made one friend and many enemies, I followed the Kesarn to a stone bench running along the far wall. There was empty space all around us, leaving me in no doubt whose dungeon this was. I sat and rested my pounding head against the wall, pinching my nose, trying to stem the blood.

"Sirius Kade," I said with a nasally twang. Courtesy of the Tau Cetins, both the snakehead and Kesarn languages were in my bionetic memory, although Kesarn was a little guttural for the human tongue.

He stared into space as if already bored by my presence. I'd only met one Kesarn before and he looked much like this one and was just as friendly. Both were a head taller than me, had dark brown leathery skin, large sunken brown eyes beneath a massive bone slab of a brow and a flat nose with a single horizontal slit nostril. They were from a high gravity world, accounting for their thick bones and rippling muscle, and while they were famous for their heal suits, this one was dressed only in a dark jacket and trousers.

"Thanks for not letting them beat me to death," I said.

"Didn't do it for you."

"Oh…well, thanks anyway."

The Kesarn watched the snakeheads whispering among themselves. "He was planning to kill me. They still are." He kept his eyes on them as if eavesdropping.

"You can hear them?"

He tapped his ear with one finger. "Sonic implant."

"Right," I said slowly, looking him over. "What are you in for?"

"Murder."

"You killed a snakehead, on Kif-atah?…Gutsy move." Or stupid.

"Seven." He looked at the corpse of the alpha lying on the stone floor and revised the count. "Eight."

"Eight?" I said impressed. "I'm sure you had a good reason, for every one of them."

"Yeah." He gave me a meaningful look. "They talked too much."

I suspected he was making a joke, but didn't dare ask in case he wasn't.

A circular metal hatch in the ceiling slid open and flexible packets dropped through the hole. The prisoners raced toward them, elbowing and punching each other aside to get theirs.

"Wait here," the Kesarn said and walked to the center

of the room. He fixed his gaze on one snakehead clutching a handful of packets to his chest and held out his hand. The Mataron hesitated before sullenly giving him one packet.

"All of them."

The snakehead hissed resentfully, handed over his entire stash and dashed off to steal a packet from another snakehead before retreating into the darkness. The Kesarn tossed three packets into the corner where the Gienans and their Minkaran ally were standing. They scooped them up with grateful looks, then the Kesarn returned to our corner. He dropped one in my lap, tore the end off another and poured its contents into his mouth.

I opened my food packet, saw fleshy meat in a pungent liquid that made my nose wrinkle and cautiously sampled it. The bitter concoction made me gag, and I spat it out like poison.

"It's protein," the Kesarn said, finishing his first packet and opening a second.

I looked into the ration pack doubtfully. "I don't think my stomach can handle Mataron microbes."

"It's irradiated."

"Irradiated sewerage," I said, baulking at putting more of the foul tasting mix in my mouth. "So, how are we getting out of here?"

"No one escapes Trel'sitar," he said chewing mechanically.

"We'll be the first," I assured him. When he said nothing, I added, "There's got to be a way out."

"Escape, no. Out, yes."

When he didn't explain, I pulled another tooth. "How?"

"Get sent to a penal colony."

"Ah, and escape from there. How do I get transferred?"

"Survive the trials."

"You're not talking about a court hearing, are you?"

"No." He glanced at my slop satchel. "Eat."

That's why he forced snakehead slop into his stomach, for fuel. Irradiated sewerage or not, if I was going to escape, I'd need my strength so I took a breath and poured the vile tasting concoction into my mouth. Fighting the urge to vomit, I ate it all and reached for another of his unopened food packets. He gave me a sideways look, realized I would do whatever it took to escape, and made no move to stop me.

He watched me eat it all with silent approval and said, "Tahl Rete."

I gave him a puzzled look.

"That's my name. Tahl Rete."

* * * *

Next day, four lanky guards with stun staffs entered the dungeon and fixed their eyes upon me.

"Remember what I told you," Rete whispered.

"I will."

They led me out through a maze of dark corridors to a gravity lift that carried us up to a circular meeting place atop the fortress. There were no walls, only a ring of large columns supporting the ceiling with brightly colored silk-like curtains strung between them. The setting was reminiscent of the ancient caravans that had plied Kif-atah's deserts over seven hundred thousand years ago and were now Mataron folklore.

Hot dry air wafted through the gently swaying silks, giving glimpses of a sprawling city of weathered stone and dark metal to the south. It was Vaset'al, Kif-atah's capital city, stained red by desert dust, simmering under a relentless baking sun, and home to a quarter of the Mataron homeworld's population.

The buildings were mostly four and five levels high with shaded, central courtyards and shutters on every level that could be sealed against the dust storms. The courtyards were ornately tiled and decorated with spiny white plants although there were no fountains, no exposed water anywhere which would have rapidly evaporated in the parched atmosphere.

Narrow lanes separated the tightly packed buildings which filled the plain to the southern horizon and beyond. Above the urban sprawl, passenger and freight capsules moved at tremendous speed, suspended between pairs of transit rails by an ingenious distortion of the positron binding nuclear force, not magnetism. We'd been trying to figure that one out for centuries, but still hadn't cracked it. It was one of the more mundane reminders of just how far ahead of us the snakeheads were.

Industry was indistinguishably blended with housing and mostly below ground where it was cooler. Small passenger craft flew above the positron rail network, followed no marked flight lanes and landed on elevated lily pads that shaded the narrow streets below. Pedestrians and small vehicles crowded the alleys which were shielded from the sun by dusty triangular sails. There were no shops or street stalls, as they were all underground and highly stratified by class.

In spite of the sun shades and shutters, snakeheads preferred the dry baking heat of the central latitudes to the moderate polar regions. Water was scarce on Kif-atah, which was why it was pumped via underground tunnels into gigantic cisterns below the cities. The cisterns had been created from natural aquifers in ancient times, and had determined the locations of Kif-atah's major cities. The reptilians had the technology to bring water to the planet, but not to restrain Matar's heat from turning it to vapor, transforming Kif-atah into a super-hothouse nightmare, so they'd long ago abandoned any thought of terraforming.

North of the fortress was an arid plain of red soil tinted by the purple sky, and covered by billowing shade sheets shielding moisture-injected succulent plants from the harsh sun. The shaded succulent plantations reached off to a crystalline plain radiating with heat, creating a shimmering mirage that kept Mataron hatred for mankind burning as fiercely as their sun. The fused plain had stood that way for fifteen hundred years, and as far as the snakeheads were concerned, it would stand that way forever more.

Or at least until human civilization had been exterminated.

The black crystal wasteland had once been home to an ancient city that had survived wars, blood feuds, dust storms and centuries long droughts, but not an encounter with human isolationist fanatics. They'd detonated their ship's e-plant upon landing, vaporizing the ancient center of Mataron civilization and turning our xenophobic neighbors into a remorseless enemy. Every offer of compensation from Earth had been refused, while reptilian unwillingness to forgive the past and embrace the future had imprisoned them more than us, isolating the Mataron Supremacy from much of the galaxy.

Trel'sitar Fortress had seen the blinding white flash on the horizon that had killed so many and turned desert to glass. Its ancient walls had been scalded by the blast, although its distance from the epicenter had saved it from destruction. Surviving the attack had made the fortress a symbol of Mataron strength, which was why they'd turned it into snakehead supermax, the most feared place on Kif-atah and one of the hellholes of the galaxy. Gathered now in this ancient monument to retribution were my accusers, a triumvirate of judges on high backed, throne-like chairs representing snakehead society's three factions.

In the center, representing the Military Order, was a reptilian in a brown uniform decorated with gold insignia. To his left, was a female representing the Priesthood. She was draped in flowing yellow silks and had a thin golden circlet set with nine bright red stones on her head. On the third throne was an old male in a long sleeved, crimson tunic with dark blue trousers. He wore an ornate, jeweled dagger strapped to his left arm above the elbow and a large five pointed star on his chest. He represented the wealthy Landed Lords, medieval style barons who fought blood feuds with each other and whose private armies served as a counter to the power of the rigid Military Order.

Functionaries sat at long tables in front of the judges, sorted by faction. Many wore data-monocles over one eye and whispered into small communicator disks attached to their palms. One snakehead close to me was hissing into his hand, yet not a sound reached me through the palm-comm's suppression field.

At a small table on the far side of the functionaries were four black uniformed officers with ornately decorated quantum blades strapped diagonally across their chests. They were Black Sauria, the shadowy fourth arm of the Mataron power structure. They had no seat on the Triumvirate, no power of decree, yet they were more feared than any who sat upon the Three Thrones. Their leader was Hazrik a'Gitor, Blademaster of the Black Sauria, the one snakehead who wanted me dead more than any other and who most certainly had elevated me to first place on their hit list.

Hazrik fixed his eyes upon me as soon as I entered. I nodded to him like we were old friends, knowing we were mortal enemies. He made no response, tilted his head to listen to one of his aides whisper something to him, never taking his vertical slit eyes off me. He had a haughty, triumphant look, as if he'd just won a personal duel and was about to mount his enemy's head on the wall.

The Lord Justice-General of the Military Order motioned to the court herald, a young reptilian in a rust-red formal jacket and kilt. The herald carried a maroon staff which he pounded on the floor for silence while my two guards shoved me into the center of the chamber. My ultra-reflexes saved me from an embarrassing fall, then the two guards saluted the Three Thrones and withdrew.

It seemed careless to leave an enemy alien alone, so close to the judges, then I realized the stone circle I stood in was anything but decorative. I extended my hand, activating a translucent green shimmer that numbed my fingertips. With my faith in snakehead paranoia restored, I bowed gracefully to the judges, one hand across my waist.

"Sirius Kade, at your service," I said with a flourish.

"The prisoner will not speak unless addressed by the Court," the herald hissed.

"As a duly accredited representative of Earth, I demand diplomatic immunity and request any charges against me be heard by an impartial arbiter, as is my right under Article Six of the Access Treaty."

Article Six handled dispute resolution, and if they bought it, any request they made to what was left of Earth's government would confirm my credentials and give the Tau Cetins a chance to free me.

"The Triumvirate does not recognize Access Treaty provisions in relation to capital crimes against the Supremacy or its citizens," the Lord Justice-General declared. "Petition denied."

"Your honor, I was captured on the human homeworld by the Spawn and brought here as a prisoner of war, not a common criminal."

"The details of your arrest are inconsequential," he said, not about to free me on a technicality.

"If the prisoner speaks again without permission," the court herald announced, "he will be fitted with an auditory restraint."

I opened my mouth to protest, realized speaking would get me gagged, and shut up, then the herald pounded his staff on the stone floor. "The charges shall now be read."

The Lord Justice-General flipped his data-monocle down over his left eye. The lens-like device glowed and snakehead scrawl scrolled across its surface. "The prisoner Kade has been found guilty of extra territorial killings of Mataron citizens and acts of subversion against the Mataron Supremacy as listed in the procedurals."

I waved to get his attention. He glanced at me, ignored my gesticulations and continued without pausing.

"With the convicted now present, the Triumvirate will determine sentencing."

I raised both hands, waved like I was flagging down a ship in orbit while carefully remaining silent.

"In compliance with–" The Lord Justice-General stopped, irritated by my silent shenanigans. "What is it?"

"Every one of those Matarons was killed in self-defense."

"All relevant evidence has already been presented. This is sentencing."

"By who? Him?" I asked, indicating Hazrik.

"The prisoner will be silent!" the court herald shouted.

I pointed at the Lord Justice-General. "But he said I could speak."

The representative of the Priesthood, the Lord Justice-Spiritual, leaned forward. "In your absence an impartial advocate stated your case, addressed all of the evidence, and confessed to all of your crimes."

"Confessed!" I exclaimed.

"The facts and evidence were conclusive, the confession comprehensive and the verdict unanimous," Lord Justice-Temporal, representative of the Landed Lords added.

Hazrik a'Gitor stood up and waited in respectful silence.

"The court recognizes the Black Sauria representative," the Lord Justice-General said.

"Prisoner Kade is an avowed enemy of the Supremacy," Hazrik declared. "He is attempting to make a mockery of the Triumvirate. We request his date of execution be set for this day and he be cut and hung from Traitor's Wall by sun fall."

"We will decide how the Triumvirate views the

prisoner's behavior," the Lord Justice-General stated sternly.

"And whose spine is cut on Traitor's Wall," the Lord Justice-Temporal added, revealing there was no love lost between his Landed Lord faction and the Black Sauria.

"I meant no disrespect," Hazrik said stiffly.

"Your honor," I said, trying to find a way to use Tahl Rete's advice, "the Matarons I killed died in the service of your world, and I took their lives in the service of mine."

"Your point being?" the Lord Justice-General asked.

"The Matarons I killed died with honor. In tribute to their courage, and my own, I request a sanctified death."

The court room exploded with outraged voices, then Hazrik bellowed, "He's a human! Our sworn enemy! He cares nothing for our ways."

The herald pounded the stone floor with his staff. "Silence! Silence," he yelled until calm was restored.

"Do you realize what you are asking, human?" the Lord Justice-Spiritual demanded.

"I do. The Totemic Trials are known and respected, even on Earth," I lied, having never heard of them before Tahl Rete told me about them the night before. Still, it was better than being left to bleed to death, hanging by my ankles on Traitor's Wall.

On the other side of the room, a female Mataron in violet robes, the color of the sky, the Mataron color of mourning, stood.

"The court recognizes Karna i'Talso," the Lord Justice-General said as a respectful hush fell over the chamber.

"A traitor's death does no honor to my husband," she said, "or speed his journey."

"So it is written in the Hallowed Shirah," the Lord Justice-Spiritual intoned.

"This is a trick!" Hazrik shouted.

"Do the Black Sauria believe in nothing but the

blade?" the Lord Justice-Spiritual asked.

"Are your dead not revered, as are ours?" the Lord Justice-Temporal added.

I suspected Hazrik cared as much for their ancient superstitions as I did, yet faced by such questions, he faltered.

"They are revered," he replied icily, "but this human does not deserve a sanctified death,"

"The bereaved of our fallen heroes do not agree, Hazrik a'Gitor," the Lord Justice-Spiritual declared, glancing at Karna i'Talso. Two other females in violet morning robes stood, indicating they also gave their consent.

The three judges exchanged looks of agreement, perhaps more to annoy the Black Sauria than appease their gods, then the Lord Justice-General proclaimed, "It is decided!" He nodded toward the Lord Justice-Spiritual, handing authority to her in her capacity as High Priestess.

"The prisoner Kade," she announced, "a noble Warrior of Earth, has agreed freely and without fear, to sanctify his life for those he has slain. By widow's assent and in full knowledge, he shall face the Totemic Trials as ordained by the Father Seer Asud a'Tugul. The Great Spirits of the burning land, of the furious sea and of the eternal fire shall be his judges and may their verdict honor our fallen heroes."

In a fury, Hazrik got to his feet and strode out, followed by his three Black Sauria companions. He'd plotted and schemed for years to bring me here, to give me a traitor's death, to watch me bleed on Trel'sitar's infamous wall of death, and at the moment of his triumph, three widows, a snakehead priestess and Tahl Rete's coaching had snatched it all away.

If they hadn't been watching me, I'd have grinned, then I remembered what lay ahead. A sanctified death was still death, but at least it would be quick.

* * * *

When the guards returned me to the dungeon, Tahl Rete was gone. He'd used the widow's ploy himself to have his sentence commuted from certain execution to probable death by Totemic Trial. It was a clever ploy, too clever for someone from the remote Cygnus Rim. He knew far more of Mataron traditions than he should have, and I wondered why.

No Kesarn had ever faced the challenge of the Mataron Totems. If he survived the ordeal, he'd be famous, at least on Kif-atah where the trials were broadcast in all their gory detail to the planet's population. They were as much blood sport as spiritual test, and unfortunately for us, the snakehead spirit world was not known for its mercy.

With Tahl Rete gone, I was acutely aware of furtive reptilian eyes watching my every move. If they wanted to kill me, now was the time. Their hand was stayed only by the prospect of facing the big Kesarn's revenge when he returned to find me dead.

When the food satchels dropped a few hours later, I grabbed what I could, certain I was going to need all my strength for the Totemic Trials. Evading lunges from belligerent snakeheads, I retreated to my bench and gulped down the food before it could be taken from me.

With a bulging stomach, I dozed as purple sunlight beaming through the slit windows crawled across the floor. Sometime after sunset, the metal door slid open and guards came in guiding a floating stretcher carrying Tahl Rete's battered body. His clothes were torn and singed, his body covered in burns, welts and scratches, patched with white skin seals, and a gray rigid bulb covered the stump of his right forearm.

The stretcher rolled to the vertical in front of me, dumping him on the floor with no regard for his injuries. He grunted and lay where he fell while the guards withdrew. I moved to help him up, but he waved me away, warning me with a look that he could not show weakness in front of the snakehead prisoners. He got to his knees, stood stiffly through gritted teeth and walked to the bench, showing our cellmates he was no cripple, then he sat down beside me, suppressing a groan. He might have looked dangerous to the reptilians on the other side of the dungeon, but it was obvious to me it had taken all his strength just to walk a few steps.

"You don't look so good," I whispered.

"Alive...is good," he wheezed and closed his eyes.

A group of Matarons cautiously approached, eyeing the Kesarn, wondering if they could finish what their Totemic Spirits had started.

"Can you fight?" I whispered.

"I am fighting...to breathe," he rasped.

"That's what I figured."

I stood to meet the Matarons challenge, certain any sign of fear would end badly for both of us. They looked down at me with amusement, then over my head at Rete.

One of the betas from my welcoming committee waved me aside and said, "We want him, not you."

"We're a set," I said, guessing I could kill one of them before the others impaled me with their tails.

The beta, intent on becoming the dungeon's next alpha, launched a predictable spinning kick at my face. I rolled under his foot with ultra-reflexed speed, came up behind him and drove my fist into his spine below his twenty fifth vertebrae, just as my EIS hand-to-hand instructors had taught me to do years ago. His major spinal nerve center exploded with pain and he dropped to his knees, paralyzed. I could have snapped his neck, but that would have only made more enemies, so I let his face smack the stone floor.

I let his companions watch the alpha-wannabe writhe in agony at my feet and said, "I'm feeling better today…much better."

They exchanged furtive looks, getting my meaning,

then I pointed to the shadows they'd come from.

"Your side." I stuck my thumb over my shoulder at Tahl Rete's bench. "Our side." I pointed at their humiliated, former leader. "Wrong side."

I stepped back, never taking my eyes off them, giving them room to retrieve their paralyzed companion while snakeheads watching from the far side of the dungeon began yelling.

"Kill him!"

"He's just a human!"

With the audience baying for blood and their snakehood in question, they counted the odds and liked the answer.

"I can't beat all of you," I admitted in a low voice, "but I will kill the first one who makes a move." I smiled. "Maybe the second."

Snakeheads were tall, fast and agile, with muscles like wire and plated skin tougher than leather, but they had pain points and I knew them all, not that that would save me if they rushed me all at once.

Tahl Rete fixed a withering stare upon them and forced himself to sit up as if preparing to join in, although it was a bluff. He could barely stand, let alone fight, but the snakeheads didn't know it. They glanced at him apprehensively, then one grabbed the foot of their paralyzed companion and dragged him away. The others, seeing the odds turn against them, hesitated.

"Go!" Tahl Rete bellowed.

The remaining snakeheads backed away sullenly. When they rejoined their gang in the shadows, I sat beside Tahl Rete.

"Now we're even," I said.

"They'll be back," he whispered, supporting his broken ribs with an arm across his chest.

"Good thing Kesarns heal fast."

"No heal suit," he said, easing his back against the wall. Heal suits gave the Kesarn tremendous recuperative powers, a necessary tech for a self-reliant race that travelled great distances alone.

"When are they taking you out of here?" I asked, hoping for his sake it would be before it was my turn to face the Totemic Trials. I didn't fancy his chances if he had to deal with our cellmates alone.

"Soon, once the transport to Zjal-kor arrives." It was the labor camp he'd won the right to call home, until they worked him to death.

"We'll bust out of there together," I promised.

"Yeah," he grunted, doubting I'd survive the trials, then the ceiling opened and food packets poured in.

"Don't you go running off now," I said and joined the scramble for tonight's special.

* * * *

Tahl Rete told me what he could of the trials over the next few days. They were modeled on three phantasms of snakehead superstition that gave meaning to their brutal culture's class system. Magrod the Purifier was the symbol of the Landed Lords; Varidon the Dispeller represented the Military Order; and Felrum the Silent embodied the Priesthood. There was a pantheon of others, notably Golat the Dispenser, the Black Sauria's overlord of death who, fortunately for the condemned, played no part in this particular ritual. The trials were a test of endurance, vision and ingenuity; attributes the snakeheads believed essential for surviving Kif-atah's harsh environment and feudal political system.

"Move fast," Rete whispered, "and never go back."

"Is that what you did?"

"You won't survive…what I did."

"What was that?"

"Killed everything."

"At least you thinned them out for me."

"No," he whispered and fell asleep sitting propped

against the wall.

Next day, while we were feasting on snakehead food satchels, I asked, "How'd they capture you?"

"They didn't."

"You let them capture you?" He looked away and again I wondered how someone from the galactic rim knew so much about snakehead culture. "You killed seven snakeheads just to get arrested?"

"One wouldn't have been enough." He put his head back and emptied a ration pack into his mouth.

"Enough? To get sent here? To Trel'sitar."

He tossed the empty packet into the corner and looked at my last, unopened ration pack. "You going to eat that?"

"You've had four." He stared at me in silence, confirming food was the price of his scintillating conversation, so I shrugged and gave him my third pack.

He ripped it open and started eating. "They're hiding something here."

"Matarons are xenophobes. They hide everything. They'd lie about the sky being purple if they could get away with it."

"From the Spawn," he added.

I blinked. "But they're allies."

"Supposed to be."

The Spawn had almost wiped the Kesarn out in the First Intruder War over two thousand years ago. By a cruel twist of fate, their homeworld lay on the Spawn's main access route into the Milky Way, which was why Kesat had been one of the first worlds to fall, although the Kesarn never ceased fighting and paid a terrible price for their stubbornness.

After Kesat had been liberated in the first war, the fiercely independent Kesarn had withdrawn from the Galactic Forum and the Access Treaty, a move accepted because of what they'd suffered. It made them unique in all the galaxy, free to go where they pleased with no formal Treaty obligations and an open invitation to rejoin the galactic community at a time of their choosing. That gave Tahl Rete reason enough to hate the Spawn, but his people had nothing to do with the Matarons.

"You're a long way from the Cygnus Rim," I said.

"I was looking for something." He fixed his eyes on the reptilian gang whispering in the corner, listening to their conversation. "Didn't find it."

"A 'thing' or a prisoner?"

"Either."

"You don't know?" I asked, and he clearly didn't. "Did the Tau Cetins send you?"

The Kesarn had long been the eyes and the ears of the Tau Cetins in the Cygnus Rim. It was why the Spawn had crushed them, why they had their unique arrangement with the Forum, and if a Kesarn was here looking for anything, it didn't take a genius to suspect Ornithian scheming was behind it.

"What do you know of Tau Cetins?" he asked suspiciously.

"Oh, we go way back."

He gave me a long, studied look. "Who are you?"

"A friend of Gern Vrate," I said, naming the one Kesarn I knew.

"Hmph...Vrate has no friends."

"Yeah, he's not the most personable Kesarn I've ever met, not like you." Vrate was a tracer; part bounty hunter, part mercenary, part freedom fighter. His kind worked alone, were well paid for their services and had a shadowy relationship with the Tau Cetins. Considering very few Kesarn ever ventured into the Orion Arm, I wasn't surprised my new best friend knew Vrate, or at least of him. "So you're a tracer?"

"No."

I nodded to the Minkaran and the two Gienans huddled together in the corner. "Could it be one of them?"

"It's not them."

"How do you know?"

"Too weak. They couldn't hurt the Spawn."

"Hurt the Spawn, how?" I asked. He didn't answer, I suspected because he really didn't know. "The Tau Cetins gave you no clues?"

He gave me a sideways look, but didn't deny the Ornithian connection. "I was told I'd know if I found it."

"Hmm...and have no tales to tell if the Spawn interrogated you."

Considering how big Trel'sitar was, how many passages and subterranean chambers it had, the snakeheads could be hiding anything or anyone in the bowels of the fortress. Being a civilian prison of no military value, it was just the kind of place the Spawn wouldn't pay close attention to.

"May we join you?" a softly spoken voice with a lisping accent asked.

I turned to see the Minkaran and his two Gienan friends standing before us. The Minky was slightly taller than a human with dark purplish skin, slender arms and legs and delicate facial features. The two Gienans by contrast were about my height with muscular physiques covered by thick orange and black striped hair. They had vaguely feline facial features with light green eyes framed by long eyelashes, a small flat, black nose above a slightly protruding jaw and a mouth filled with a double row of small sharp teeth. The Minkys were herbivores and the Gienans were not, which was why the peace loving Minkarans had saved themselves from the Spawn by signing the Xil Neutrality Pact and the Gienans had bravely thrown their lot in with the Tau Cetins.

"Help yourself," I said, motioning to an empty space on the bench.

They sat down then the Minkaran said, "I am Lorilso. This is Torataya and Nesaroiya." He introduced the two Gienans who inclined their heads in greeting. "Neither speak your language." He turned to Tahl Rete. "We do not recognize your species, friend, but we thank you for the food you gave us. We are sorry to see you are hurt."

"I'll live," Rete growled through the pain of broken ribs.

"He's Kesarn," I explained. "So, who'd you kill to get thrown in here?"

"No one. We are..." he paused, trying to remember the word, "...students of...old buildings."

"Archeologists?"

"We were excavating ruins on the fifth planet of a yellow star not far from here when the war began. The Matarons declared us spies and sent us here."

Matar was a binary with a faint F-type companion and a couple of G-types close by. The yellow stars were all well outside Matar's heliosphere, making them neutral territory, not that that made any difference to the xenophobic reptilians.

"Matarons don't like snoopers near their homeworld," I said.

"We were not snooping."

"You're welcome to camp on this side of the dungeon," I said, glancing at the snakehead gang eyeing us. "Safety in numbers."

"I am no match for even one Mataron," Lorilso admitted, "but my companions are quite formidable, as several other prisoners have discovered."

I glanced at the two muscular Gienans sitting beside him, watching with alert, predatory eyes. Lorilso translated what he'd said to me and they grinned with razor sharp teeth. One of them absently picked his teeth with a short claw that extended from his furry fingertip. They might have been eggheads on their own planet, but in here with no weapons, messing with them was a bad idea.

"Well, since you put it like that," I said, "you're doubly welcome."

More so for Tahl Rete than me. I'd be gone soon, but at least he'd have protection while I was away, and in case

I didn't make it back.

* * * *

In the days following our alliance with Lorilso and the Gienans, Tahl Rete's wounds festered in the putrid dungeon. I tried to get him treatment, but the guards ignored my demands, then one morning after the food drop, the dungeon's metal door rumbled open and four guards marched in. I thought they were here to take Tahl Rete to hospital, but two priests in maroon robes and skull caps appeared carrying ornately carved spears with barbed blades. The guards motioned for me to stand, avoiding using their stun staffs in case they hindered the spirits' power to decide my fate.

"Remember, run, don't fight," Tahl Rete whispered.

They put me in the center of a procession of reptilian priests waiting in two lines in the corridor. A drummer began a slow beat and the priests started chanting, eyes forward and solemn, pounding their barbed spears on the stone floor with each step. We slow marched through dark passages, down ancient stone stairs, to a rectangular hall lined with robed acolytes standing at attention. Waiting at the end of the hall was the high priestess from the sentencing hearing, flanked by a high ranking prison officer. Hazrik and two of his flunkies stood off to one side, dressed in Black Sauria armor with ritual blades sheathed. Behind them all were three floating telebots transmitting proceedings to a planetary audience and an accelerator portal in the shape of a stone arch filled with soft blue light.

The procession came to a halt and the priests pounded their staffs on the floor twice more, then the drumming stopped. The two robed snakeheads who'd escorted me from the dungeon walked me up to the high priestess and stood silently at attention.

"I am warden of Trel'sitar," the prison officer beside

the priestess said. "Are you fitted with a suicide device?"

"I'm here to live, not die," I replied evasively.

"He's an Earth Intelligence Service operative," Hazrik said. "He has one."

The high priestess accepted Hazrik's contribution with a hint of irritation, then fixed her eyes upon me. "You have freely chosen to submit yourself to the Totemic Trials, human. Do you swear not to use technology to subvert the will of the spirits?"

"I do," I replied solemnly, faithfully pledging not to use my terminal safeguard, unless I changed my mind.

"The human warrior known as Kade," she said, "convicted of crimes against the Supremacy, in honor and penitence of those slain by his hand, offers restitution to the bereaved of the fallen. Through the Cleansing of Magrod, the Control of Varidon and the Discipline of Felrum, he consigns his Life to the Kif-oyene. His destiny now lies in their hands."

The Kif-oyene were the Mataron Pantheon, worshiped by a planet full of superstitious snakeheads and represented in the trials by three paramount spirits. With ritualistic solemnity, a hundred spears began pounding the stones in unison as dirge-like chanting filled the air once more. In spite of their civilization being technologically far superior to ours, there was a brutishly primal aspect to their culture that mankind had left behind long ago, proof that technology alone was an insufficient measure of achievement.

With the beat resonating through the chamber, the high priestess stepped aside and motioned me toward the accelerator portal. Having no choice, I climbed the stairs, shadowed by the small telebots, and stepped into the accelerator field. It swept me away through a subterranean passage at tremendous speed. Tiny tunnel lights flashed past as a point of violet light appeared ahead, then I felt a sudden deceleration and was thrown out onto a semicircular stone platform at the edge of a scorching desert.

I tumbled onto searing stones that burnt my hands, forcing me to my feet as a wave of heat hit me. Shielding my eyes from the glare with one arm, I looked out over a blistering, barren plain beneath a cloudless, purple sky. It was dotted with iron-rock pillars weathered by dust storms and radiated more heat than Earth's harshest desert. In the distance, heat shimmers boiled off the horizon, blurring what lay beyond.

The three telebots flew out of the accelerator behind me and began circling, showing their world audience how feeble the soft skinned human was beneath Kif-atah's unrelenting sun. Their live feed made Mataron Totemism a blood sport and it was my blood the watching audience wanted.

I searched for the dark red banner Tahl Rete had told me marked the way out. All I could see was a sliver of red swimming in the heat shimmers, and below it, a tiny blob of blue light where the accelerator portal waited. My heart sank as I realized how far it was, how quickly the heat would sap my strength in Kif-atah's heavy gravity, and how vulnerable I'd be among starving and thirsty magrods desperately fighting to survive.

A serpentine rack displaying ancient Mataron implements of war stood to my left, filled with long swords, short spears, spiked maces, razor whips, war hammers, shields and various body armors unsuited to the human form. I approached the rack, then one of the telebots flew in low and projected an image of the high priestess before me, resplendent in flowing yellow silks and a jeweled circlet.

"Condemned of Kif-oyene," the iridescent hologram said, "before you lies the Burning Plain of Magrod, a holy ground where the weak are slain and heroes rise. Endurance and courage you must have, but only the pure of heart shall triumph. To consecrate your way, select one sacred implement, but once chosen, it shall appear no more."

The hologram vanished although the telebot remained floating above me. Tahl Rete had chosen a large two handed sword, a fearsome weapon that could cleave a man in half with a single stroke, and it had nearly cost him his life. I walked along the rack studying every item, certain there was one right choice.

Search: Mataron Totemism, Magrod, I thought. My bionetic memory knew every criminal within a thousand light years, but almost nothing of Mataron spiritualism, so its response was not particularly helpful.

> MAGROD (1): EQUATORIAL WASTELANDS, KIF-ATAH.
>
> MAGROD (2): THE PURIFIER, MATARON TOTEMIC.
>
> ALSO: THE CLEANSING ONE, THE BURNER OF DESERTS, THE PIERCING DEATH, THE FORGE MASTER.
>
> MAGROD (3): SYMBOL OF THE MATARON LANDED LORD CLASS.
>
> MAGROD (4): CARNIVOROUS XENO-STYRACOSAUR, KIF-ATAH.

Tahl Rete had encountered a large quadruped with a hide so tough, his great sword couldn't penetrate it. I guessed that was the carnivorous xeno-styracosaur, although there were no images of it. He'd killed it by driving his blade through one of its eyes, striking bone, but failing to penetrate its brain. Enraged, the creature had crushed his hand, almost trampled him to death, and hunted him for a long time before finally dying of blood loss. Rete's experience convinced me swords were not the answer. And from the look of them, most were too heavy for me anyway.

I wandered alongside the shields and body armors, glanced at the merciless sun and decided I needed something light enough to carry across the desert. My eyes settled on a black lance a meter and a half long, topped by a long blade whose edges curved to a sharp point.

"The Piercing Death," I muttered, wondering if the lance might penetrate a magrod's thick hide.

I lifted it off the rack, tested its weight with both hands and thought it resembled the barbed spears the priests carried. It was heavier than I wanted, but could be balanced on my shoulder or used as a walking staff. While I was still testing the spear, a time limit expired and clamps locked around the other weapons, then the high priestess appeared again.

"A wise choice, Condemned One. The Blessings of Kif-oyene shine upon you this day."

"You never said that to Tahl Rete," I replied, satisfied with my selection.

The holographic priestess vanished while the telebot stayed close as I practiced with my new spear, sweeping it from side to side, blocking and lunging. Once I had a feel for my new weapon, I followed weathered stone steps down to the desert and started across. There was no path indicating the way and no footprints on the hard packed ground, so I headed for an iron-rock pillar out in the desert hoping to find shade where I could rest.

The dry, gritty ground quickly became an oven, evaporating my sweat as soon as it formed. I marched toward the rocky pillar at a steady pace, using my lance as a walking stick, while Matar climbed into the sky and my skin began to burn. It took several hours to reach the pillar, then I slumped in its shade to regain my strength.

"Burner of deserts," I panted, setting my back against the spire and recalling the cryptic phrase my bionetics had reported. "They ain't kidding."

A distant roar rolled across the desert, reminding me it wasn't the heat I had to fear. I searched the barren plain for any sign of the beast, but saw only sun bleached boulders and small thorny plants. Tahl Rete had warned me the emptiness was an illusion, and that I wouldn't see the magrod until it was on top of me.

I tried to gauge the distance to the red blur in the heat shimmers, but it seemed no closer. Kif-atah was larger than Earth and the horizon deceptively far, throwing off my sense of distance. Tahl Rete had made a straight dash for the way out, gambling on keeping his time in the sun to a minimum. It was a good plan, but I didn't have his staying power. I needed to rest periodically and I needed shade for that, which only the pillars could provide.

The three telebots that had followed me from the portal floated in the air nearby, teasing their audience with vision of how quickly I tired. They'd be reveling in the prospect of seeing a human shredded before their eyes, confirming how weak we were.

"What are you looking at?" I muttered, closing my eyes to the harsh glare, preparing to head back out into the sunlight, then I heard a faint drumbeat.

It came from above, from the rock pillar. I heard it again, one note, coming from a rock ledge four meters above me. It looked like a natural feature, but when I stood, I saw it had been carved from the rock centuries ago and weathered by time. A snakehead could have reached it with one leap, but it was a tricky climb for a human.

I wondered if it was worth the energy, then it sounded again and I knew I had to try. I left my lance on the ground and pulled myself up the rough rock face. When I reached the ledge, I found a tiny grotto had been cut deep into the rock, leading back to a shallow basin filled with water. Above the pool was a small stone spout from which a droplet fell into the water, making the drumming sound.

I pulled myself up and crawled eagerly into the grotto. The entrance was barely wide enough for human shoulders, then it opened into a small circular chamber high enough to kneel in. Close to the basin, my skin prickled from a weak pressure field shielding the water from the harsh desert heat. I pushed my hands through with only a little effort and cupped warm water into my mouth, drinking until I could swallow no more. My thirst quenched, I splashed water on my face, head and clothes to cool off.

Refreshed, I climbed back down, hoisted my spear onto my shoulder and struck out for the next rock pillar, convinced they were the key to crossing the desert. Tahl Rete, in his dash across the burning ground, had missed them completely, although Kesarn required less water than humans.

One telebot took up position behind me while the other two raced ahead. One went directly toward the distant banner and passed out of sight while the other veered off to the left and hovered several clicks away.

"There's one over there," I said, realizing the telebot was tantalizing its audience with images of the nearest magrod.

When I was halfway to the next pillar, I noticed the hovering telebot was drifting toward my path. There was no breeze to carry my scent, so either the magrod could see me, or the telebot was herding it toward me.

I picked up the pace to get ahead of the cheating telebot. When I neared the pillar, I came upon a skeleton bleached white by the sun. Its bones were partly buried in the sandy soil and broken in several places. I knelt and blew dust off the triangular reptilian skull, revealing it had been crushed by a great weight. Beside the skeleton was a forked spear. I picked it up, finding its shaft was broken, although its two metal prongs were still intact. While I examined the weapon, the tailing telebot came in close and projected the holographic priestess beside me.

"Condemned of Kif-oyene, one sacred symbol only may you wield. Choose again if you wish, but any symbol chosen appears no more."

I remembered her earlier praise of my choice, dropped the damaged weapon and grabbed my lance. "I'll keep this."

"Such is your right," she said and vanished.

The telebot returned to its shadowing position while the second bot fell in behind me, following my footsteps, moving faster than before. The beast had my scent and liked what it smelled. It wasn't charging, but it was closing the distance.

I broke into a loping run, burning energy and fluids at a prodigious rate while the thump of my boots pounded across the plain. A throaty roar sounded behind me and the thunder of heavy footfalls exploded though the hot, still air. I glanced back, saw a rounded, rust colored shape twice my height racing after me as I sprinted into the shade of the spire. I dropped my lance, launched myself at the pillar and scrambled up into the safety of the tiny grotto.

Breathing hard and feeling like I was on fire, I reached though the thermal field and splashed water onto my face and into my mouth, then the grotto shuddered as the magrod reared up and slammed its feet against the pillar's side. Tiny rock fragments from the ceiling showered me as a booming roar blasted into the tiny cave.

A dragon's head, surrounded by a horned frill peered in at me with flaming red eyes. It bellowed again, revealing thick yellow teeth, blasting me with its stinking breath as its rough, purple tongue shot into the grotto toward me. I rolled sideways behind the cave wall as the giant tongue swept past my face into the pool.

Capillaries in the tongue soaked up the precious water before my eyes. When the basin was dry, its bloated tongue probed from side to side, searching for me, but I pressed myself against the cave wall just out of reach.

Realizing I'd escaped, its tongue flowed past my eyes, back out through the tunnel into its mouth. The angry magrod swallowed the water, snorted and growled, and let its forelegs thud down onto the ground.

I stared in dismay at the empty basin as a single drop fell from the spout and splashed onto the damp stone. I'd swallowed a little water before the magrod had sucked the water trap dry, but not nearly enough to quench my thirst.

With a drying mouth, I crawled out to the ledge and watched the four legged dragon sniff my lance uncertainly. It lowered its head, revealing a narrow fold of pink skin behind its armored frill, and sniffed my footsteps on the ground. It had a scaly hide, short legs and broad feet with four toes, but no claws. As it quartered back and forth, its nostrils flared in confusion, then with a snort, it wandered off into the desert.

I settled on the ledge to watch it meander away, knowing I couldn't risk climbing down until it was far away. With a telebot observing me closely, I rested in the shade while Matar climbed higher into the purple sky. When I hadn't seen the magrod in a long time, I dropped down, grabbed my lance and headed for the next pillar.

The desert now radiated heat like a fusion furnace, scalding my skin and draining moisture from my body. After a brutal march across hard packed ground, the second telebot appeared, signaling the dragon had lost all interest in me. The third telebot, however, did not return, warning at least one beast blocked my path.

Matar was over three hundred times brighter than Earth's sun, and even though Kif-atah was a long way out, it was no place for soft-skinned, water dense humans. With every step, my lance grew heavier and increasingly hot to the touch, but I didn't dare leave it behind.

When Matar neared its zenith, flying creatures began circling in the distance, no bigger than dots in the sky. They were scavengers, living off the desert dragon's leavings and the remains of condemned prisoners found wanting by Kif-oyene's pantheon.

After two hours in the unforgiving sun, with lips cracked and dry, I fell to my knees exhausted in the shade of the rock spire desperate for water. The ledge was just above me, no higher than the others, yet it seemed an impossible climb. A telebot came in close, floating just out of reach, watching my face, waiting for me to collapse.

"You'd like that wouldn't you," I croaked hoarsely, then dragged myself up the rock face to the ledge where I found a basin full of water.

"Thank Kif-oyene!" I muttered and crawled forward, pushed my head through the thermal field and submerged my face in the water. I gulped down as much as I could, drenched my hair and clothes to cool off and rolled onto my back, intending to complete the crossing at night.

"Condemned of Kif-oyene," the high priestess' voice sounded from the ledge, "you must cross the Burning Plain by Matar's slumber, else Magrod's Might will have prevailed and a coward's death will be yours."

"Now you tell me," I mumbled. The holy snakehead had read my mind, confirming this was as much a test of speed as endurance.

She disappeared, then with no way to carry water, I forced myself to drink as much as my stomach could hold.

Metabolize stomach fluids, I thought, commanding my body to digest the water now rather than over the next day. It was a bionetic function designed to counter excessive blood loss, which I hoped would stave off dehydration.

With a stomach full of water, I clambered down and gauged the distance to the next rock pillar. It was far to the right, increasing the distance to the exit by a quarter. I was close enough now that the heat shimmers no longer blurred the horizon. In their place was a flat mesa with a long red banner fluttering high above it and an accelerator portal on a stone landing at its base. I gave the distant pillar one last look, knew I couldn't stay in the sun that long, and decided to follow Tahl Rete's advice to move fast.

I grabbed my lance and headed straight for the red banner with the two telebots in tow, one low and close, the other high and circling. I forced myself to move fast, ignoring the sweat bubbling off my skin, hoping my bionetics could keep my fluids up. The price of turning water into plasma at an unnatural rate was increasingly severe stomach cramps, while the bloated feeling of a belly used as a water tank faded away.

Three hours later, the mesa towered before me. Sunlight reflected off polished metal where the third telebot was hovering ahead, watching my approach. It looked to be alone, but the frill-necked dragon was so well adapted to the terrain, I might be staring straight at it and not see it.

When I neared the hovering telebot, a bionetic message flashed before my eyes:

METABOLIZATION COMPLETE.

My stomach cramps eased, then as I drew level with the telebot ahead, a rust red boulder uncoiled before me. A massive dragon head lifted up and turned toward me, red eyes flaring. The giant reptile climbed to its feet, never taking its eyes off me, and let loose a blasting roar that turned my blood cold in the boiling desert.

Suddenly it charged, opening its massive jaws as it galloped toward me. When it was almost on top of me, I hurled my lance at its mouth, aiming for its exposed throat. The magrod turned its head away and the lance glanced harmlessly off the thick scales plating its head. I threw myself sideways with super-reflexed speed as it thundered past and rolled to my feet with a desperate look toward the accelerator portal. Its ancient stone stairs were close, but the dragon would easily chase me down if I ran toward them.

The magrod turned sharply in a cloud of dust, furious

at my escape. It snorted and charged again while the three telebots circled in close, enthralling their audience. I feigned to the left, luring its weight that way, then leapt to the right as it careered past. It came to a stop, roaring in frustration and paced toward me, determined not to let me use its weight against it again.

"Not as dumb as you look, are you," I said, spotting my lance on the ground nearby.

My first attack had proven the lance could no more punch through the magrod's scale armor than Tahl Rete's two hander, yet the high priestess had said it was a good choice. The failure wasn't the weapon's fault, it was mine, how I was using it.

The beast stalked me as I edged toward the lance. It snarled, baring its yellow teeth, as I recalled every Mataron trick EIS instructors had ever thrown at me, searching for a clue. The training simulations had used a vast array of weapons, from quantum blades to shoulder cannons, fighting with speed and agility. Matarons were tall and lean, faster and more acrobatic than humans with harder skin, but extremely vulnerable to cold and virtually night blind due to the glare filters on their eyes. Agility was their strength, which was why the water traps were an easy leap for them, a difficult climb for me.

An easy leap? That's what the training sims all had in common; jumping snakeheads.

I reached down for the lance, never taking my eyes off the desert dragon, and slid my hands along the shaft to just below the curved blade. Holding the neck of the lance with both hands, I waited. When the magrod charged, I darted forward, slammed the base of the lance into the hard ground and pole vaulted into the air.

The beast roared and snapped up at me in frustration as I caught a horn jutting from its armored frill and swung onto its back. I slid my hand along the lance and drove the blade into the soft pink flesh beneath its frill. The lance went in deep, severed muscles and nerves and struck bone.

Blood gushed from the wound as the creature bellowed in pain and its head dropped sharply. The dragon's full weight drove its head into the ground, hurling me clear and snapping its neck with a sickening crack.

I landed hard, momentarily stunned as the magrod lay on its side wheezing for air, its neck drenched in blood. It was suffocating to death as a severed artery spilled its blood onto the plain.

A shadow passed over me, then a thin, bony creature with broad leathery wings landed near the dying dragon. Other desert scavengers circled above, some settling nearby, all ravenously eyeing the stricken monster.

Not wanting to be mistaken for an appetizer, I got to my feet, gave the magrod a wide berth and ran across the desert toward the mesa. Nothing followed me as I stumbled up the stone stairs toward the glowing accelerator portal and looked back to see a winged scavenger land on the magrod and peck its side with a sharp triangular beak. After several strikes, it tore a scaly plate off, screeched in delight and plunged its beak into the bleeding flesh from the still living carcass.

The magrod could do no more than blink and wheeze as other scavengers joined in, watched by two telebots relaying the dragon's end to millions of snakeheads across Kif-atah. The third telebot followed me toward the accelerator, the second alien in a week to slay their feared dragon totem and a puny human at that.

Eager to escape Matar's vicious gaze, I stepped into the accelerator and was carried away at great speed. Tunnel lights flashed past me, then I was deposited in a small cavern with a walled pool. Standing in the center of the pool was the statue of a Landed Lord holding my lance triumphantly above his head. On one side of the pool was a table set with an assortment of foods and on the other, a multi-armed bot floated above the stone floor. Beyond the fountain was another equipment rack identical to the first, now with one empty place where my lance had been.

The multi-armed bot scanned me from head to foot and sprayed my burnt and blistered skin with a cooling mist as three telebots flew out of the accelerator behind me.

"You are fit to continue," the medbot said and returned to its standby position, then a telebot projected an image of the high priestess in front of me.

"Condemned of Kif-oyene, the Burning Plain of physical life have you crossed. Cleansed by the journey, purified by the heat of the desert, tested by the beasts of Magrod, you stand triumphant, the mighty Door The First stands behind you. Two more beckon." She motioned to the fountain and the table. "Drink now of the healing waters, eat the foods of renewal, and proceed through Door The Second to be judged anew."

"Thanks," I croaked and looked into the clear, cold waters of the fountain.

Tahl Rete had told me they were laced with a broad spectrum regenerative and to drink as much as I could, so I cautiously spooned a little into my mouth. It had a subtle sweetness that started my body tingling immediately. I shrugged uncertainly, drank my fill and went to the table which was set with a selection of unappetizing vegetables, animal remains and bowls of black and red insects.

"No wonder they're so skinny."

I avoided the intestines and insects, ate as much sliced cactus as I could stomach and returned to the fountain to wash it down, feeling much better. With the effects of dehydration fading, I approached the serpentine rack where a telebot projected the holy snakehead once more.

"Condemned of Kif-oyene," she said, "before you lies the Seething Sea of Varidon. Endurance and purity, you have proven, but true courage rises not from the storm of battle, but from the tranquil waters of resolve. Select one sacred implement to consecrate your way. Once chosen, it shall appear no more."

Tahl Rete had selected a battle axe, anticipating another beast fight, but it had proven useless against the ethereal Varidons.

Search: Mataron Totemism, Varidon, I thought, hoping my bionetics would help me avoid repeating his mistake.

> VARIDON (1): PTEROSAUR, EXTINCT 150 MYA, LATER SAUROSALIC PERIOD, KIF-ATAH.
>
> VARIDON (2): THE DISPELLER, MATARON TOTEMIC.
>
> ALSO: THE NIGHT TERROR, THE REVEALER OF COWARDS, THE GREAT DECEIVER.
>
> VARIDON (3): SYMBOL OF THE MATARON MILITARY CLASS.
>
> VARIDON (4): MYSTICAL PSYCHO-KINETIC WRAITH.

Facing the Varidon was a test of courage, not combat. The Landed Lords trained armies to control land, to master the physical world, but the Military Order trained warriors to overcome their fears, to master the emotional world. That's why Tahl Rete's axe had been the wrong choice and why I ignored the weapons.

"I need a talisman against fear," I said, focusing on the small statues and carved jewelry.

My eyes settled on a faceted jewel hanging from a silver chain. I lifted it off the rack, wondering if it had more than a symbolic purpose and held it up to the light of a burning torch on the cavern wall. It didn't sparkle or refract the light indicating it wasn't translucent.

"It's no diamond."

I held it in my palm as I looked at the other trinkets, intending to put it back when light poured between my fingers. I opened my hand and the light slowly faded, then closed it again and the jewel glowed once more.

"Huh...Thermal powered."

My bionetics called Varidon the Terror of the Night and Tahl Rete had said it was dark on the other side, too dark to see clearly.

"Are snakeheads afraid of the dark?" I wondered, recalling they were night blind. I shrugged uncertainly and pulled the talisman's chain over my head. "I'll take this."

The clamps locked in place and the holy hologram said, "A brave choice, Condemned One, but not unwise. The Kif-oyene exalt courage, even among the damned."

I wrapped my hand around the talisman and let my palm's heat charge it up as I walked toward the accelerator portal. Soft light flooded between my fingers, growing steadily brighter until it became a radiant star.

"Impressive thermocouple."

I took a series of deep breaths, oxygenating my blood and wishing I'd paid more attention to Izin's attempts at teaching me how to swim, then stepped into the accelerator field and was carried away at high speed to face the Mataron Lord of Fear.

* * * *

The accelerator hurled me from the heights of a sheer cliff into a star filled night. I flailed and fell blindly toward infinite darkness, my heart pounding. A wind appeared from nowhere, became a screaming gale, and thunder and lightning shattered the darkness as torrential rain poured from the heavens.

I crashed head first into a choppy sea, whipped to a frenzy by the wind, and sank in a swirl of bubbles. The three telebots dived into the water around me, emitting no light, watching me sink into the oily blackness as my fear exploded.

I released the talisman, letting it hang by the chain

around my neck, and thrashed frantically to the surface where a big wave pushed me under again. On the brink of drowning, I bobbed up, coughing and spluttering, gasping for air. In the feeble starlight, through towering waves, I glimpsed far away rock walls rising on all sides. I wasn't in a sea, but an immense cavern filled with water, one of Kif-atah's subterranean cisterns.

The icy water cooled my talisman, extinguishing its light as two telebots moved through the water, oblivious to the rise and fall of the waves. A massive swell, bigger than the first, rolled over me, submerging me in blanketing darkness. On the edge of panic, I fumbled for the talisman with one hand and swam with the other the way Izin had taught me.

When I reached the surface, I saw through sheets of rain that the stars were still twinkling, silhouetting the white capped waves. A piercing shriek rang out behind me. I spun toward it as a ghostly form swept out of the darkness. Its face was demonically reptilian with curved flaming eyes, razor-like teeth, thin bony arms and skeletal hands with stiletto-claws for fingers. Arms wide, it shrieked again and slashed at my face. I pulled back through the water, shielding my face as claws ripped through my skin, sending pain exploding along my arm.

More shrieks erupted from the shadows as a wall of water hit me. With one hand on the talisman and my blood clouding the water, I pulled myself back to the surface. A varidon wraith came screeching out of the darkness and slashed my face, then another shrieked behind me. I spun around, raised the talisman and opened my hand, spraying it with light, intending to fight it off, but the apparition screamed in fury and dissolved before my eyes.

I stared at empty air, realized its weakness was light, and wrapped my hand around the jewel to recharge it. The darkness rang with blood curdling screeches as the reptilian specters circled. They were everywhere, more unseen than seen, shrieking above the howl of the wind and crash of the sea. They were trying to get behind me, forcing me to spin in energy sapping circles as I held the talisman above the water, opening my hand each time they dived, driving them back with the light.

The waves were so high, I could no longer see over them. I was trapped in an endless sea, shrouded in darkness, surrounded by phantoms, yet a nagging thought kept fighting to be heard: I was in a cistern not a sea.

I remembered it was a test, a puzzle, and it had a solution, then a mountainous swell lifted me above the other waves and I glimpsed impossibly far rock walls, further away now than before. I turned in circles, looking for the accelerator out of there, but there was no sign of it, nothing to cling to, no hope of escape.

I slid into a deep trough, filled with confusion, surrounded by great waves, plagued by nagging doubts. How could the walls be further away, the waves so high? How could such a storm exist in a subterranean lake?

Encircled by the screams of demons, I looked up at thousands of twinkling stars filling the night sky and realized there was no sky, no stars. There couldn't be, not in a cistern. If there was no sky, none of it was real.

The telebots circled at the edge of my light, unaffected by the howling wind and the rolling sea. A demonic wraith came screeching out of the darkness and lunged at me, but this time I didn't evade. I opened my hand, flooding it with the jewel's light, and it vanished, dissipating some of my fear.

I tried to understand the illusion, to think clearly, and the wind and rain eased. I realized it was a fantasy of my own making, powered by my innermost fears. My mind destroyed the deception, calmed my emotions, and stilled the waves, dissolving the shrieking wraiths into nothingness. I breathed deeply and the sea flattened, revealing the cistern's stone brick walls were astonishingly close.

"It's an illusion," I whispered as my fears disappeared,

although the bloody gashes remained. The harm had been real. It was my blood in the water, but only because I'd allowed my emotions to deceive me.

The lake became tranquil and a red banner appeared hanging from a wall a short distance away. There was no sign of the accelerator portal, then the cistern began to drain. My feet touched solid ground and the water vanished, leaving me standing on a dusty, stone floor in an ancient cavern. A short distance away, well-worn stairs led up to the accelerator portal, now glowing with life.

It all been a trick of holograms and pressure fields, stimulating the emotions and confusing the mind, sensing and reacting to the intensity of my feelings. And all it had taken to sweep away the delusion was a few clear thoughts.

One of the telebots approached and the high priestess appeared in a glow of golden light. "Condemned of Kif-oyene, the seething sea of the emotional world have you mastered through the power of a clear mind. No longer the slave of fear, you have earned the right to proceed to the final test."

The priestess disappeared and the starry lights above deactivated, leaving the cistern in a darkness broken only by the light of the accelerator. Tahl Rete had never realized it was an illusion, but had overcome moderate seas and prowling wraiths with brute force and courage, never surrendering to fear.

I walked to the accelerator in bone dry clothes, dripping blood from slashed skin. I'd always feared drowning, never having learnt to swim until Izin had come along. I gave the ancient cistern one last look, wondered if I really had overcome my worst nightmare, and stepped into the portal.

* * * *

The accelerator deposited me and the three telebots in a

rectangular chamber with stone block floors, thread bare Military Order wall tapestries and a healing fountain with an ancient tribal warrior at its center. The fountain was flanked by a medbot and food table and at the end of the chamber was an equipment rack beside a square doorway. A pressure field filled the doorway, blurring a black and gray landscape flowing with movement.

The medbot sprayed my wounds with white, numbing skin seals and declared, "You are fit to continue."

I drank from the fountain, visited the table for a protein boost and went to the rack, now with two vacant places.

"Condemned of Kif-oyene," the holy hologram said, "purified of form and ruler of emotion you are, yet the fires of mind, the basis of consciousness, remain untamed. Select a sacred symbol to aid your struggle, Condemned One, pass through Door the Third and face your final judgment amid the Fires of Felrum."

Search: Felrum, I thought, then my bionetics gave me what little it knew of this final piece of snakehead superstition.

FELRUM (1): VOLCANO, RUKHESA POLAR FAULT ZONE, KIF-ATAH.

FELRUM (2): THE SILENT, MATARAN TOTEMIC.

ALSO: THE SLAYER OF MIND, THE SHIELD OF THE SEEKER, THE DISCIPLINARIAN, THE TRUTHBEARER.

FELRUM (3): SPIRITUAL GUIDE OF THE MATARON PRIESTLY CLASS.

FELURM (4): PYRO-SAUROPSID, KIF-ATAH.

The holy hologram said this was a test of the untamed

mind and one of the totem's names was 'The Disciplinarian', suggesting it was a test of mental discipline, although Tahl Rete had not seen it that way. To him, it was simply a test of survival where one weapon was as good as another. He'd gotten through this trial like he had all the others, with speed, brute force and a little luck, although he'd never solved the puzzle.

"Felrum The Silent?" I said thoughtfully, walking alongside the equipment rack, searching for a key to this puzzle. "The disciplined mind doesn't chatter. It has to be tamed, that's why he's silent." I glanced at the blurred pressure field and recalled Tahl Rete's warning. "Fires were everywhere…but she said the fires of mind were the basis of consciousness...which evolves. It's a…mental battlefield." I winced in frustration, wondering what weapon would suit such a battleground.

"Condemned of Kif-oyene," the snakehead priestess said. "Choose now or forfeit the trial."

"Don't rush me."

Tahl Rete had picked a long bladed cleaver, which he'd put to good use, but it had cost him many burns. All his choices had been poor because Kesarns were fighters. They liked big weapons and Tahl Rete had never figured out the clues. Considering my skin wasn't as tough as his, I couldn't afford to make his mistakes, and didn't fancy fighting pyro-sauropsids with a sword. There had to be a better way.

"Felrum The Truthbearer," I muttered, wracking my mind. "He knows truth…How does a priest know truth?...He rejects untruth…How does a priest reject untruth?" My eyes flittered desperately from one weapon to another, settling on four shields placed side by side. "He shields himself from evil. He's silent, disciplined and…wise."

One shield was long and narrow, surrounded by barbed points, just wide enough to protect a lanky reptilian body, but too thin for me. Another was rectangular, made of a bronze-like material and emblazoned with a snakehead skull, but it wouldn't provide much protection against fire. The third was a large round shield made of thick gray wood, with an outer rim of metal and covered with a cracked, leathery hide. It was a conscript's shield, giving good all round protection, but the dry wood and leathery skin looked flammable and would leave my head and legs dangerously exposed. The last was a large golden shield, oval in shape with spikes protruding from its top, bottom and center. It was the kind of shield a medieval snakehead would have marched into battle with, and being all metal, it would not catch fire.

"The shield of the seeker," I said triumphantly and lifted it off the rack.

It was heavy and lugging it up the side of a volcano would be hard work, but this was the last trial and I could afford to expend my remaining reserves of energy. I slid my arm through the leather back straps and swung it from side to side, then rested it on the ground by its bottom spike finding it made a good one-man shield wall.

I stepped back from the rack and turned to the High Priestess. "I'll take this," I said and the clamps locked over the other items on the rack.

"A foolish choice, Condemned One," she said. "The Kif-oyene revile the yoke of greed, for it consigns the faithless to eternal torment."

"I meant that one," I said, pointing at the long thin shield, then changed my mind and pointed at the round shield. "No, that one."

The high priestess ignored my pleas and disappeared.

"Oh Kif-oyene," I muttered miserably and walked to the doorway. Two telebots floated through the pressure field to watch my arrival while the third hovered behind me.

Beside the doorway was a stone pedestal and basin filled with a dark, oily liquid. Its pungent smell wrinkled my nose and sent my bionetic sniffer into a frenzy.

WARNING: POISONOUS SUBSTANCE.

AMMONIUM HYDROXIDE, ZINC BORITE, SEVEN UNKNOWN MOLECULES DETECTED.

"And smells like toxic waste."

There was a metal ladle resting on the lip of the basin, but I dipped a finger into the oil uncertainly. My skin began to sting, so I quickly pulled it out and wiped it on my shirt, finding it had turned my finger an inflamed pink color.

"Can't drink it, can't wash in it, but it's here for a reason," I said with a sinking feeling.

With no faith in my magnificent golden shield, I stepped through the door's pressure field to face my untamed mind in the fiery hell of Felrum.

* * * *

Beyond the third door was a narrow ledge overlooking a volcanic precipice. A waterfall of orange lava cascaded into the gorge at one end, feeding a molten river that flowed far below me, while towering behind me was the blackened stone wall of an ancient keep. It was midmorning, yet the Mataron sun was low on the horizon, confirming this was one of Kif-atah's polar regions. The planet's atmosphere was far too dry for snow and ice and the heat radiating off the lava made the air hot, albeit noticeably cooler than the baking plains of Magrod.

Mount Felrum rose on the far side of the gorge toward a summit belching black smoke. Acrid gasses hissed from its ashen slopes as glowing hot rivers of magma snaked down its sides and cascaded into the lava flow in many places. The volcano appeared to be on the brink of an eruption, yet it was another illusion. The Matarons had the tech to control the lava flow, the magma chamber levels and the pressure of venting gases. They were keeping the volcano on a knife's edge simply for the spectacle of it.

Barely visible in the belching smoke, fluttering high above the caldera, was a long red banner indicating the way out.

I peered over the edge at the boiling river meandering through the chasm below. "Izin would love this," I said, certain my acrophobic engineer would be pressed against the keep wall in terror, then my sniffer flashed a message into my mind.

WARNING: CONTAMINATED ATMOSPHERE.

SULPHUR DIOXIDE,HYDROGEN SULPHIDE DETECTED.

Not life threatening, but it explained the rotten stink in the air.

Spanning the gorge was a flimsy suspension bridge reaching across to blackened cliffs honeycombed with dark caves. Pairs of eyes peered from the shadows, already aware of my presence.

With the telebots watching my every move, I worked my way along the ledge to the suspension bridge and started across with my golden shield in hand. More beady eyes appeared as Tahl Rete's warning rang in my mind.

"Stay away from the caves. That's where the felrum live."

The giant boulders lining the sides of the lava river were strewn with Mataron bones, thousands of them, turning the black rocks white. They weren't whole skeletons, just single bones thrown from the warrens after they'd been picked clean.

When I was halfway across the rickety bridge, a dark red lizard emerged from a shadowy cave and fixed its bronzed eyes upon me. Its snout was long and narrow and its skin reflected the light as if it was rusted metal. It watched me briefly, then scuttled up a vertical rock wall with powerful, clawed feet.

I reached the far cliff and climbed steep stairs carved into the rock, polished smooth by time. They led to a winding path through rough-hewn rock, past caves and lava flows. The scratch of claws and hissed breathing filled the air as the felrum awakened, emerged from their caves and came after me.

My path opened onto a small plateau with an ancient snakehead shrine set below a high cliff. Crumbling stone columns surrounded the statue of a headless priestess with one arm pointing toward the summit and the other holding an engraved tablet. Below her was a small walled pool filled with the same noxious oil that had filled the basin at the doorway. The pillars, the stone floor and the statue were all sooty black, yet the pool was spotlessly clean. I reached for the lip of the low wall surrounding the pool and felt a weak pressure field push against my hand. It kept the ash away, preventing it mixing with the oily substance in the pool.

"Hmm…Must be useful," I said, eyeing the ladle on the pool wall.

I hurried from the temple, saw dozens of lizards ambling toward me, and loped up stairs cut into the cliff with all three telebots in tow. The stairs emptied onto a narrow path running alongside a bubbling lava stream. A felrum on the other side fixed its eyes upon me. It was over a meter long with short, powerful legs and a thick tail. It moved along the opposing rock face, gripping cracks with its claws and hissing angrily as it stayed with me, then the path angled away and I left it behind.

The fumes burned my lungs and I began coughing up phlegm. I came upon a Mataron boot with a half-eaten reptilian foot inside, and a little further on, the path branched. I chose the steepest way, hoping it was the fastest route to the summit.

I soon heard hissing and a large felrum scuttled into

view, gripping the rock at eye height. Its mouth opened, revealing a jaw rimmed by a ridge of razor sharp bone, not teeth. It inhaled the foul air, wheezing constantly as it inflated its lungs, then a stream of fire spurted from its mouth, coating my shield in flames. The felrum spit burned away, turning my glittering metal shield sizzling hot.

"Argh!" I moaned as my arm was seared purple, forcing me to drop the shield.

The felrum started inhaling again, inflating its bellows-like lungs with a long wheezing in-breathe. When its lungs were full, it spat another stream of fire at me. I leapt sideways, dodging the fiery spurt that splashed over the rocks behind me. When it began its next rasping inhale, I grabbed my shield.

Tahl Rete had warned me against puncturing the felrum's incendiary sack, so I slammed the shield's bottom spike into the creature's head. There was a crack of bone as the spike punctured its tiny brain, then the fire-lizard fell onto the ground. Air exhaled from its lungs as green, oily spittle drained from its mouth and trickled toward the burning rocks.

"Uh-ho," I muttered and ran up the path.

When the green spit reached the flames, it ignited. Fire raced back along the green fluid into the felrum's mouth, causing it to explode like an incendiary grenade and scattering burning flesh in all directions.

With my left arm stinging from shield burns, I switched the golden hotplate to my other arm and followed the path to a small stone bridge. The far end had collapsed into a narrow lava stream, although the gap was small. The scraping of clawed feet sounded, then a long snout and bronze eyes appeared behind me. It began a wheezing in-breath and ambled toward me. I ran onto the bridge and leapt over the lava to the far shore, landing hard and jarring my knee. The felrum stepped onto the bridge, its bellows now full as I hurriedly limped away.

When it reached the collapsed end of the bridge, it spat fire at me, but the flames fell short. Other fire-lizards rushed onto the bridge, crowding together while I stumbled up more stone stairs and left them behind.

The path forked again and I came upon a round wooden shield with a severed Mataron arm still in the straps. It was the conscript's shield, and its leathery covering was stained black, but not from fire. I touched the shield, felt my fingertip burn from oil soaking the leather.

"Ah, that's what it's for," I said and pulled the severed arm from the straps. It had been gnawed off, not burnt.

The wooden shield showed no signs of fire damage, so I dropped my glorious golden fry pan and slid the wooden shield onto my good arm, surprised by how light it was.

A telebot swooped down and the high priestess appeared beside me. "Condemned of Kif-oyene, one sacred symbol only may you wield. Choose again if you wish, but once made, that symbol may you wield no more."

"I'm switching."

"Such is your right, Condemned One, for better is it to discover wisdom late, than not at all."

"So I traded up?" I asked hopefully, but she disappeared without answering.

I shrugged and continued up the path, finding it easier going in the heavy gravity with the lighter wooden shield. The path emerged beside a large lava flow so hot I had to keep the shield between me and it. The path was steeper now, reaching toward the thick smoke billowing from the volcano's mouth, turning the sky black.

Just before the path turned away from the lava flow, a felrum dropped off a ledge and landed before me with lungs fully inflated. It spat immediately, barely leaving my time to angle my shield. When the flames struck, a circular energy field radiated off the face of my shield driving the fire and heat back toward the lizard.

It was a planar shield that lasted until the flames dissipated.

The felrum started sucking in air for another attack, so I charged forward and kicked it into the lava river. It squealed as it landed on the boiling magma, hissed furiously as lava ate through its plated hide, then its incendiary sack exploded, tearing the creature apart.

I stepped back from the lava flow and inspected my wooden shield. The leathery material on the front was now dry, but it still showed no signs of scalding.

"It's a liquid thermocouple," I said, realizing the oil turned heat into energy to power the planar shield. My problem now was that the oil was gone and my shield was useless.

With new found respect for my conscript's shield, I hurried up steep stairs, through a narrow crevice onto a gently sloping rock shelf with a crumbling shrine at its center. Felrums were scrambling up onto the ledge and waddling toward me, trying to cut off my escape. With my leg still aching from the fall at the bridge, I hobbled along the cliff wall to the shrine and ladled oil onto my shield from a pool beneath a priestly statue.

With my planar shield recharged, I emerged from the shrine to find felrums between me and the path to the summit, many with fully inflated lungs. There was no other way, so I raised my shield and charged. When I reached them, they spat fire at me while I angled the shield at each attack. The planar shield blinked on and off multiple times as I ran through a gauntlet of fire, then I reached the stairs and raced up through a narrow passage toward the summit.

With felrum stalking me from all sides, I emerged onto a flat shelf surrounded by rock walls. The red banner fluttered on the far side amid belching black cloud, and between me and it was a huge bull felrum, five times larger than any I'd seen, tearing at the scorched remains of a Mataron corpse. The telebots began circling, revealing this was an amphitheater for the pleasure of the audience, with only one way through.

The bull felrum let out a blood curdling roar and started toward me, wheezing as it inflated its gigantic bellows. The huge male blocked my path as the scraping of clawed feet from females coming up behind grew louder.

I stepped into the arena, keeping my shield up, angled toward the beast, and edged around it toward the volcano. When its chest had doubled in size, its eyes flared, its head lunged forward and its giant mouth opened unleashing a torrent of fire. The planar shield blinked on, protecting me from the inferno while the bull's lungs emptied, then when the firestorm faded and the shield deactivated, I raced past the wheezing, inhaling monster's legs toward the red banner and the smoke below it.

The enraged bull felrum paced after me, sucking air, inflating its chest, but I was too quick. I plunged into the smoke, but my shield slammed into an invisible barrier which hurled me back. I fell hard, cracked my skull on the volcanic rock and almost passed out as the giant fire breathing lizard marched toward me, lungs fully inflated. Its head lunged forward and I rolled sideways onto my knees, bringing my shield up as fire slammed into it. The planar field blinked on, holding back the flames until the inferno died away.

I got to my feet and retreated toward the invisible wall, keeping my round shield facing the bull felrum as smaller females emerged from the stairs to join him. I reached blindly into the smoke with my scalded arm, felt a powerful force blocking my way, holding back Mount Felrum's roiling breath.

I pushed hard at first, unable to penetrate it, then as I tired, my hand sank slowly into the field. It was an inertial barrier, not a force shield, and it would let me through if I made no sudden movements. Fighting the urge to run, I eased myself into the field, felt it press against my body.

When my shield touched the barrier, it was pushed away, dragging me back toward the bull felrum. The giant pyrosauropsid was at the edge of the smoke, inflating its massive bellows, as if it knew I could not pass. I tried to pull the shield after me, more slowly, but the barrier pushed it firmly away, forcing me to choose between safety and freedom; the final test.

I dropped the shield as the bull felrum's eyes flared and eased myself into the inertial barrier. The beast's head lunged forward, jaws opening wide, and a great jet of flame came roiling at my face. I resisted the urge to run, knowing any sudden movement and the inertial field would hurl me back into the flames. Fire blasted the energy barrier and fanned out before my eyes, almost touching my face, but I kept my nerve and slipped deeper into the field. When the conflagration died, the giant lizard roared with rage and black smoke closed in around me.

I was lifted off my feet and swept away through the smoke, over the glowing orange caldera of Mount Felrum, to clean, cool air on the summit of a mountaintop. I stood on a stone dais overlooking stairs down to a circular terrace flanked by three ornate statues, one for each of the Totems. A medbot and a glowing accelerator portal waited beyond the statues while the volcano was now visible far off on the horizon. Beyond the terrace was a panoramic view of snowless, polar mountains and deep valleys as far as the eye could see. I took in the view briefly, then followed the stairs down to the terrace where a telebot brought the high priestess to life in her flowing yellow robes.

"Reprieved of Kif-oyene, the flaming torments of mind hold you no more. Through purity, tranquility and discipline, you stand free in the three worlds, found worthy by the Great Spirits. Your life is spared so you may labor in penance for your crimes. May your years be long and many, and your payment made in full."

She gave me a long look, clearly surprised I'd

survived, and disappeared.

"What, no parole?" I asked wearily.

The three telebots flew off between the snakehead statues into the accelerator while I coughed soot from my lungs. The medbot approached, scanned me head to foot and cut away my clothes until I was wearing nothing by my boots. It sprayed misty white seals over my burns, paying particular attention to my mutilated shield-arm.

"Your injuries will heal," it said, and presented me with a dull gray, one piece prison suit with Mataron scrawl on the back.

"Any other colors?" I asked.

The medbot made no reply, so I pulled on the prison garb and stepped into the accelerator, too tired to care where it took me next.

* * * *

The accelerator returned me to Trel'sitar Prison where a group of Black Saurians in full body armor were waiting for me. Two of them took up positions either side of me, then Hazrik a'Gitor emerged from the shadows and looked me up and down.

"You are harder to kill than a Turian sand-leech, Kade," he said, eyeing the milky white patches covering my skin. "You're the first human ever to survive the trials."

"Ah, that was nothing. You should try going ten rounds in the Grotto, bare knuckles."

Hazrik grunted. "It would have been better for you to have died out there."

"I survived your trials. I'll survive your prison planet too."

"You will never see Zjal-kor." He motioned to the two Saurian guards who grabbed my arms and lifted me off the floor.

"Hey!" I shouted angrily, trying to break free. "Your

whole planet saw me beat those trials. You can't touch me, not now!"

"I never challenge the will of the Spirits," Hazrik said with false piety. "You will die Kade, but not by my hand. I have something far worse in store for you."

He gestured to the two apprentice assassins, who seemed intent on separating my arms from shoulders. They carried me past him, while I yelled, trying to break free.

"Put me down! I want to talk to the priestess."

They carried me out of the chamber, twisting and kicking. I drove my boot into the leg of one, then the other fired a stunner into my back. I went limp and spots flashed before my eyes as they dragged me through dark passages, down into the bowels of Trel'sitar Prison. They weren't taking me back to the dungeon where Tahl Rete was waiting, but somewhere far below ground.

I was completely lost by the time we entered a circular chamber. They dropped me onto a large round trapdoor, then a white beam winked on above me and the door irised open beneath me. The suspension beam lowered me into darkness, deposited me on cold stones and winked out as the door closed.

The pungent stench of rotting flesh assaulted my nostrils as my eyes adjusted to the gloom. I was startled by a half-eaten Mataron head infested with black worms an arm's length away. Its neck was in stringy tatters from having been torn from its torso.

I covered my nose and mouth and crawled away from the rotting head, taking in my surroundings. It was a dark chamber with a glimmer of light coming from a ventilation shaft high on one wall and the drip of water echoing off stones. Bones were scattered all across the floor, stripped of flesh. Some were long and slender Mataron bones. Others were alien to Kif-atah, although none were human.

A clicking sound came from the darkness, sending a

chill down my spine. I froze, straining to hear, peering into the shadows, then it came again, very slowly.

Click...click.

I got to my feet and backed toward the feeble light coming from the vent as the clicking continued, followed by a louder, sharper snapping of jaws.

Activate infrared, I thought and retrieved a Mataron thigh bone from the floor, holding it like a two handed club.

The bionetic filaments in my eyes ramped up my thermal vision, revealing a skimmer-truck sized red ghost lurking in the shadows. It was so big, my snakehead thigh bone would be no defense, and I was too weak to run, not that there was anywhere to go.

The infrared mass lumbered toward me, its footfalls reverberating heavily through the subterranean vault like a measured drum beat. It seemed to be studying me, determining what kind of creature had fallen into its lair, then my DNA sniffer began to read it.

NON HUMAN LIFE FORM DETECTED.

The clicking became louder as it drew nearer.
Identify species.

COLEOPTERAN INDICATORS.

Closest match.

I needed my bionetics to find a weakness and fast, but before it replied, the air exploded with thundering footsteps. The infrared blur charged, growing rapidly in size until it towered above me. I glimpsed a massive curved body, bright yellow in color with dead black eyes, black legs and antennas. I swung my puny club, shattering it against the creature's armored carapace to no effect.

Its enormous mandible came close to my face as an antenna-manipulator closed around my chest and lifted me off the ground. I squirmed and pushed against it with both hands, but it was far too strong. It could have cut my chest in half with a simple snap, but instead it lifted me up close to its two large spherical eyes. The mighty insect studied the fragile, helpless ape, then my bionetics flashed its conclusion into my mind.

NISK.

The giant beetle held me eye-to-eye, observing me like a specimen. I'd seen its kind before, but never one that big or that color. Precisely drilled holes were visible on its mandible, shiny yellow carapace and antenna-manipulators where its technology had been surgically removed.

Humans, like most species in the galaxy, implanted their tech and genetically re-engineered their bodies to interface it, but not the Nisk. They bolted it onto their exo-shells, preferring technology to serve their bodies rather than the other way around. Without its attachments, the giant coleopteran could have been mistaken for a monster rather than a highly intelligent being from an advanced, if reclusive society.

The Nisk used vocalizers to make themselves understood, as no species I knew could speak, or even understand their language without translators. I'd mostly dealt with the slow witted drones and a few highly intelligent attendants, although my linguistics base knew basic Nisk. Strangely, my bionetics hadn't recognized the Nisk clicking, making me wonder if it had been speaking at all, or just clicking hungrily.

"Don't eat me," I said, raising my hands in surrender.

The Nisk stopped its unintelligible clicking, more curious than hungry. The insectoid cave dwellers always made my skin crawl, even though they had a reputation for keeping to themselves and a general disinterest in other lifeforms.

Dreaming-seeker-voice...you? appeared in my mind, clear and loud.

I recoiled in surprise. "You're telepathic?"

My bionetic base had no record of the Nisk possessing tele-psi abilities, but we only saw what they wanted us to see, met who they let us meet. We didn't even know how intelligent they were, although it took serious brain power to transmit thought.

No...not him...not him...no. Its head rocked from side to side as it babbled to itself, then the giant coleopteran fixed its dead eyes on me again. *Who?...Who speaks?*

"I...don't understand."

Dreaming-seeker-voice...searching...Why?

"I don't know what you're talking about."

There was an unsteadiness and a desperation in its thoughts, warning me this telepathic beetle was dangerously unstable. The Nisk were vegetarian, ate blue fungus and sugar, not Mataron flesh which must have been affecting its body chemistry. Being imprisoned in a Mataron dungeon for who knew how long, all alone and forced to eat condemned prisoners to survive had driven it to the brink of madness.

Dreaming-seeker-voice calls...calls...Make it stop! STOP!

"You've been here way too long," I whispered, then spoke loud and slow. "I have traded with one of your worlds, with Krailo-Nis."

Its huge head lifted slightly. "Krailo-Nis? Krailo?... Krailo!"

"Yes! Krailo-Nis. It's a beautiful planet. Lots of fungus and clouds and...swamp." It was a horrible, boggy world, consumed by the blue cyanobacteria they called food and honeycombed with tunnels and caverns filled with tens of billions of creepy crawly coleopterans.

"Krailo-Nis...System Ikatir," it clicked out loud, trying to remember, saying something my bionetics was finally able to translate.

"Right!" We called the system Nisk-Draconis, but at least I was getting through to it. "It's nine hundred light years from Earth. That's where I'm from, Earth. I'm human, a prisoner, like you."

"Human?...Human," it clicked slowly, fighting confusion. "You understand Nisk."

"Only if you speak slow. Use little clicks."

Iskeratul Strain, appeared in my mind.

"Iskeratul?" I said uncertainly, having never heard that word before. The Nisk classified the various offshoots of their civilization as 'strains', or at least, that was our best translation of whatever they had in mind.

Twenty one thousand nine hundred forty kirats, Litchik-Nis distance.

Krailo-Nis was the only Nisk world in Human Mapped Space, but we knew there were other Nisk worlds scattered throughout the galaxy. And Krailo-Nis, with all its tens of billions of inhabitants, was just a remote outpost far from their origin world.

"Is Litchik-Nis your homeworld?" I didn't know how far a kirat was, but I guessed it meant Litchik-Nis was very far from Earth.

Nisk strains, origin all, Litchik-Nis.

"Ah huh," I said, relaxing, hoping we'd soon be friends and I'd be off the menu.

"My name is Sirius Kade," I said, tapping my chest.

"Human-Kode-Soris?" it repeated, mutilating my name in a few clicks.

"Close enough...What's your name?"

"Name?" it clicked absently, trying to remember.

"You do have a name, don't you?"

Iskeratul-consort-Girutonak.

"OK, glad to meet you...Girutonak."

Girutonak! Girutonak! Girutonak! it sang as if the mere mention of its name–his name–triggered a frenzy of thought.

"Now that we know each other's names, and we're

friends, could you put me down?" I waited, but he was staring off into space as if he forgot I was there. "Hello? Girutonak?" I whistled to get the coleopteran's attention. "Are you in there?"

Girutonak dropped me on the ground and scuttled off into the darkness. I landed hard on my back, feeling my wounds tear under the snakehead skin seals, then I sat up slowly and watched the Nisk's massive infrared blur chattering to himself in a dark corner of the dungeon. Whatever he was saying, it was too fast and incoherent for my bionetic translator to make sense of.

"That's one crazy bug," I muttered, thankful he hadn't eaten me and wondering how long it would be before hunger and madness changed his mind.

* * * *

We know where you are, a voice whispered in my dreams. I listened, straining to hear more, but nothing else was said. I decided it was a trick of my mind, then became aware of disturbing, physical sensations.

I snapped awake to find the giant yellow coleopteran standing over me, his giant insectoid foot on my chest pinning me to the floor. With surgical precision, he ripped the sleeves and trouser legs of my prison fatigues into strips and peeled off the skin seals exposing my festering wounds to the air.

"What are you doing?" I yelled, trying vainly to break free.

Human-Kode-Soris, move NOT.

I stopped struggling, then Girutonak's huge head dropped toward me. His mouth opened, and for a moment I thought he was going to eat me, but his mandible stopped short of touching my skin. He coughed, as if choking, and a droplet of bile the size of my fist fell from his mouth and splashed over my wounds. It stung for a moment, then my skin went numb. Girutonak convulsed, drenching my body in a thick translucent gel that numbed my cuts and burns. When my front was fully coated, the giant coleopteran rolled me over and vomited onto my back. I dry retched in disgust, recognizing the sickly sweet smell.

"You're a Nisk royal!" I wheezed, face down on the stone floor.

No human had ever seen a royal, let alone been slimed by one. They alone produced niskgel, the liquid gold, the elixir of life it was now coating me with. Niskgel was one of the rarest, most precious substances in the galaxy, an exotic substance so bizarre, its composition could not be synthesized. Many had tried, human and alien, and all had failed.

"Royal?...Yes...Consort...Iskeratul Strain," he clicked.

Royals were the high caste rulers of the Nisk, hidden from all except their attendants and revered by trillions of Nisk throughout the galaxy. They were so revered, no aliens of any race were ever allowed in their presence.

"What are you doing here?" I asked, flinching as a drop of niskgel splashed onto a horribly blistered burn.

"Biped-reptilian-creatures...study-probe-hurt...study-probe-hurt," he clicked absently as he coated my body in niskgel, turning my skin numb and soaking the ragged remains of my clothes. Just breathing its cloyingly sweet odor eased the volcanic burning in my lungs.

"Are all royal-consorts healers?" I asked, still unsure if he understood my language or was reading my mind.

"Nisk-consort-protector...not healer." He shuddered and a telepathic wave of grief washed through my mind. "Girutonak failed...Failed!...FAILED!"

His niskgel massaging became forceful, squashing the air from my lungs.

"Argh! Easy!" I yelled.

Girutonak stopped rubbing as he realized his fractured mind had almost fractured my rib cage.

"Apologies...Human-Kode-Soris," he clicked, easing the pressure on my back.

"What did you fail?" I asked, looking over my shoulder as a drop of priceless niskgel splashed onto my leg.

"Not what...no," he clicked softly, tiptoeing around memories too painful to bear, then he rolled me over. "Why does Dreaming-seeker-voice...call...you?"

"Me?" I said surprised, and remembered my dream. "You heard the voice?"

"Dreaming-seeker-voice not weak, not like... Human-Kode-Soris. Powerful...like..." He shuddered as if crying, overwhelmed by emotion. "Like...Irukoochati."

"Iru-what? Is that another Nisk? Are they here too?"

"No...Irukoochati is...not here...She is..." he clicked slowly.

"Were you her consort?"

"Yes...Nisk-consort-protector," he replied with great sadness.

Something had happened to his mate, and perhaps that, more than the Mataron probing, was what had driven him mad.

"I'm sorry."

"Rest...Human-Kode-Soris...Dreaming-seeker-voice...comes."

"No one's coming," I said gently.

This giant yellow insectoid might once have possessed a refined intellect more advanced than any human mind, but it had been torn apart by Mataron probing, by half-forgotten memories and by impenetrable grief. I wondered if it was his voice I'd dreamt of, if in his madness, he was creating fantasies of escape where none existed. Not for him, or me.

He rolled me onto my back, then an irresistible thought flashed into my mind, *Open Human-Kode-Soris.*

Like a puppet, I opened my mouth and kept it open, completely in his power while he coughed a drop of niskgel into my mouth.

Swallow!

Unable to resist, I gulped down the niskgel, then he released me. I coughed and gagged, but it was too late, the niskgel was down and my mouth and throat were turning numb. I dry wretched and coiled into a fetal position, fighting dizziness.

Human-Kode-Soris sleep now. Grow strong. Survive.

My vision blurred as I was paralyzed by Girutonak's precious stomach bile. My face flushed with heat and I fell into a deep, niskgel induced delirium from which I could not escape.

* * * *

Days passed in a confused nightmare of charging beasts, violent seas haunted by screeching wraiths and flaming rivers of lava burning me alive. Staring at me through the visions were huge black coleopteran eyes, unblinking and cold. Occasionally, a barely audible voice called maddeningly to me through the niskgel delirium. I couldn't discern the words, only sense hopelessness and futility in them, then after a long tormented sleep, the hallucinations cleared momentarily.

We can't reach you, the dreamer whispered from afar before fading into oblivion.

I strained to hear more, but the haunting visions returned, drowning out the dreamer. After a long delirium, I awoke with a shudder. Girutonak was shaking me, trapped in his own torment.

What does it want? Make it stop! His thoughts bellowed into my mind.

"Make what stop?" I asked confused, finding it hard to speak through the bitter stickiness in my mouth.

The dreaming-seeker-voice. Make it stop.

"You hear it too?"

It dreams!...Why does it dream?

"I don't know," I croaked, desperate for water.

Girutonak released me, folded his legs and slumped

onto the stone floor beside me. He convulsed and chattered madly to himself, too fast for my bionetics to translate. It was coleopteran sobbing, although there were no tears–Nisk had no tear ducts.

I got to my feet unsteadily, still giddy from the niskgel. My skin was sticky from Girutonak sliming me while I slept, healing my wounds, but I felt younger and stronger than I had in years. Niskgel was rumored to be an alien fountain of youth, and considering it had healed me faster than a medbot with a cell regenerator, I could see why.

I patted his trembling head, trying to comfort him, not that he felt my hand through his thick shell. After a while, he noticed me standing beside him, my hand on his shell.

"You healed me," I said. "Why?"

I die here...Human-Kode-Soris must live.

I hated to disappoint him, but once Hazrik discovered his pet Nisk wasn't going to eat me, he'd find another way to ensure I never got off Kif-atah alive.

"You're strong, Girutonak. You'll survive."

No!...Reptilian-biped-Matarons...must kill...Iskeratul-consort-Girutonak.

"Don't talk–...think like that."

I know...what they did.

"Who? The snakeheads?"

Matarons study. Others kill! All dead. ALL DEAD!

"What others? Who did they kill?"

Human-Kode-Soris...must...live. LIVE! he screamed it into my mind.

I pressed my hands to my ears, doubling over in pain. "Stop!" I yelled, almost blacking out as his anger exploded inside my head. I dropped to my knees.

ALL DEAD...DEAD...DEAD!

"Girutonak! Stop!" I begged as spots flashed before my mind.

The telepathic cries ceased as Girutonak came to his senses. He stood and lifted me off the stone floor, pulling me in close to his dead black eyes. I exhaled with relief, thinking it was over, then a thousand hot spikes speared into my mind, overwhelmed my bionetic bunker and filled it with terrifying images and sounds. I saw millions of giant beetles clicking together, an immense circular ship filled with the population of an entire world, and a catastrophic explosion that vaporized them all in an instant. I struggled to take in the horror and magnitude of the disaster as a strange alien word was seared in my mind. It had been Girutonak's sole reason for living, and it was now mine.

Irukoochati. Irukoochati! IRUKOOCHATI!

Over and again, the deranged Nisk drummed the thought into my little mind, then a bright light beamed down into the dungeon. Girutonak dropped me on the stone floor as snakeheads in battle armor and carrying two handed energy weapons descended from the circular ceiling hatch.

Girutonak stared down at me, paying them no attention.

Human-Kode-Soris... survive...in my place...You are me...Protector.

It was a plea for help, and a demand that speared with crushing force into my mind. I staggered back, unable to speak, holding my head, close to passing out.

You are me... Human-Kode-Soris...Remember... Irukoochati.

"No!" I whispered through gritted teeth, realizing what he was about to do.

Girutonak, swept by vengeance, charged the guards. He scooped one up and tore his body in half, turned to another and crushed his head. A third guard raised his gun, but Girutonak struck him with an antenna-manipular and hurled him into a wall. The other guards, terrified by the rampaging Nisk, opened fire together, raking Girutonak's massive carapace with energy pulses, shattering his shell and splattering blood and mangled flesh across the floor. The royal-consort's legs collapsed and his massive shell thudded onto the floor. Close to death, his head turned to me, whispering one last thought.

Save...Irukoochati.

Girutonak's enormous head dropped onto the floor as panicked reptilian guards continued blasting his body long after he was dead. When they finally stopped shooting, two snakeheads grabbed me by the arms and hauled me into the suspensor beam.

"Where are you taking me?" I demanded, still groggy from Girutonak's telepathic assault.

The snakeheads kept a crushing grip on my arms as the suspensor lifted us out of the dungeon, then dragged me into an accelerator that carried us to the top of one of Trel'sitar's towers. We were deposited in a chamber flanked by three archways, each opening onto a hexagonal landing pad with sweeping views of the desert and Vaset'al far below. The guards marched me through one of the arches to a prison transport, threw me inside and locked the hatch behind me.

The prisoner compartment was lined with small windows and bench seats, and a snakehead guard sat with a blast rifle on one side. Tahl Rete was slumped opposite him, barely conscious. The Mataron directed me to sit beside Rete, who took a few moments to recognize me.

"I thought...you were dead," he said weakly. His wounds were purple and festering and the stink of rotting flesh wafted from the stump of his right arm.

"I'm in better shape than you," I replied, thinking he'd be dead before we reached our new home, then I scraped niskgel from my skin and wiped it on his wounds, watched suspiciously by the guard. I put some on his stump seal, but didn't dare remove the fetid bandage.

"What are you doing?" Rete demanded, tensing as I touched his rotting flesh.

"Saving your life." When I finished with his front, I pushed him forward and coated the welts and broken skin across his back. "These aren't all from the trials."

"No," he replied, confirming our cellmates had taken their revenge on him after all. "The Gienans…tried to stop them, but… there were too many."

"Broken bones?"

"Some," he replied, not bothering to give me a count.

The engines whined and we lifted off. I got a glimpse of Trel'sitar's dry, rust colored walls, then we flew away over the shade plantations while I finished coating his wounds. When I was done, I eased him into a sitting position.

"That's all I can do."

"Less pain," he mumbled as the niskgel tranquilized his wounds.

"Better than a heal suit."

"What is it?"

I opened my mouth intending to tell him, but found I could say nothing of the niskgel or Girutonak. "Something I got…after the trials."

"Hmph…I guess they like humans more than Kesarn," he said, thinking it came from the Matarons.

The shade plantations gave way to the barren wasteland human terrorists had created fifteen centuries ago. Red dust covered its unusually flat, crystalized surface, flattened and melted by the blast wave.

"They'll never forgive you for that," Tahl Rete said, following my gaze through the small window.

"Never," I agreed.

The transport shuddered, rolled to port and began to drop out of the sky. I caught Tahl Rete as he slid onto the floor, hanging onto him as the ground raced toward us.

Our guard pulled himself to the intercom and yelled, "Pilot! Why are we descending?"

The pilot's unconscious face appeared on a small screen, blood trickling from the flattened auditory bulges that passed for his ears. An emergency pressure field pinned him to his seat while his vertical slit eyes pointed away from each other, no longer under his control.

"Uh-ho," I muttered, pulling Tahl Rete to me and bracing for impact.

A surge from the transport's emergency repulsors hit us with high-gee, breaking our fall and almost tearing the Kesarn from my hands. He groaned from grinding broken bones as I stopped him sliding across the deck. I glimpsed the desert outside, then we pancaked hard onto the ground, kicking up a thick red dust cloud that blanketed the windows.

I released the Kesarn, tensed to launch myself at the guard, and froze when I saw he already had his weapon aimed at us. I raised my hands, signaling I wasn't about to do anything stupid, and switched my gaze to the comm screen. The pilot lay slumped over the controls in front of cockpit windows shrouded in roiling red dust.

I suspected the Black Sauria had brought us down, trying to make my death look like an accident, but not sabotaging the emergency crash system was uncharacteristically sloppy for the murderously efficient Saurians. The guard glanced at the screen, saw he was alone with us and slid his weapon's power level to maximum, following Mataron security protocols: if in doubt, kill the prisoners.

The guard raised his blast rifle and took aim, but shuddered involuntarily, unable to fire. With crazed, fearful eyes, he slapped the wall panel with one hand. A boom filled the compartment as the hatch was jettisoned, then a reptilian appeared out of the dust cloud and climbed up into the compartment. He was dressed like a Mataron military officer although there was something wrong about him, about the way he moved. He was short for a snakehead and his eyes were strangely rigid, as if he didn't see us. He stepped over Tahl Rete, approached the guard without a word, and held out his hand. The guard hissed in distress and gave the officer his weapon, who immediately used it to splatter the guard's brains across the cabin wall.

The officer turned to me, but still seemed not to see me. "Hello Sirius, I've been waiting for you."

I knew that voice. It didn't match what I was seeing, then the illusion vanished. The Mataron officer became a tall, ebony skinned woman wearing a dark hood and long cloak.

"Lena!" I blinked in surprise.

"What trickery is this?" Tahl Rete wheezed.

"Hurry," Lena said, helping me to my feet. "They'll have a rescue squad here in no time."

"You brought us down?" I knew she was mega-psi, had insidious psionic powers, but nothing like this, then it hit me. "You're the dreamer!" The voice in my dreams.

She aimed the blast rifle at Tahl Rete lying helpless on the floor. "Who's this?"

I stepped between them, thinking she was going to kill him too, ensuring there were no witnesses. "Tahl Rete. He saved my life."

"Did he..." she said thoughtfully.

"He's coming with us." Not giving her a chance to refuse, I dragged him to his feet.

"If you insist," she said and dropped the blast rifle on the deck.

I helped the Kesarn hobble to the hatch, but he was too weak to climb down. "Sorry about this," I said and shoved him out.

He fell onto the crystalized ground with a grunt, then Lena and I jumped down and took him by the arms. A diminutive figure appeared from behind the transport in a thermal suit with the glare visor down. He was carrying a long barreled shredder in one hand and an omnitool in the other.

"It's good to see you, Captain," Izin's muffled voice sounded from the helmet as he holstered his weapon and turned to Lena. "The pilot's dead and the crash beacon has activated. I've disabled the energy cell dampeners. They'll detonate in a few minutes. It'll look like an accident, at least initially."

"That'll give us a head start," she said.

"They won't find our remains," I said as we helped Tahl Rete through the thinning red dust.

"They'll be looking for escaped prisoners on foot," she replied as an off-world skimmer truck approached, stirring up more dust.

It had a narrow strip window across the cab, no identifiable markings and hatches too small for humans and Matarons. When it stopped, we dragged Tahl Rete into a windowless cargo compartment crammed with cube-shaped containers labelled in a characters my bionetics identified as Risuleon.

"Go!" Lena yelled through a door barely high enough for a tamph, then the effectors floated us off the ground and the truck glided away over the dead plain.

I turned to Tahl Rete, who lay on the floor, eyes closed. His normally dark skin was now pale, and a putrefying green in places. "You going to make it?"

"I'm not dying on this dust ball. I'll just rest here," he growled and passed out.

"We can give him medical treatment on the ship," Lena said.

"A Risuleon ship?"

"Good guess," she replied and led me into the cab where a diminutive humanoid, smaller than Izin, sat at the controls.

He had a furry face with luminous green eyes flecked with gold, a dark nose with widely separated round nostrils and a small mouth. His arms were muscular and disproportionately long, at least to my eyes, and he wore a shiny brown, skin-tight jumpsuit that covered all but his face. I'd never met a Risuleon before, scarcely even knew of their existence. They were friends of the Tau Cetins, which was why I had their essentials stored in my bionetic base.

"They come, they come," the little Risuleon said in a

sing-song, high pitched voice. "Haven't seen us yet."

A muted thunderclap sounded behind us as the transport's fuel cells exploded, scattering wreckage across the glassy desert and blowing away the truck's dust tracks.

"They won't like that," the little arborean chuckled gleefully.

"This is Shilu," Lena said. "He brought us here."

"Hello Kade. You are hated by reptilians." He glanced at me with sharp, darting eyes, immediately detecting my curiosity. "We like you already."

I smiled. "Thanks for rescuing me. You came a long way."

My bionetics told me the Risuleons were an Orion Arm civilization, albeit a distant one. They were a medium power with three densely populated worlds and hundreds of tiny orbital outposts scattered across half the galaxy.

"Yes, yes, Piralea is far. Too far for humans," he sang.

His homeworld was over five thousand light years from Earth, a near neighbor by galactic standards, but far outside Human Mapped Space. And it was small, with gravity almost half of Kif-atah's.

"I didn't think low-gee races came to Kif-atah," I said, surprised he wasn't in braces.

"Yes! Awful planet. Why would we come? Awful gravity, awful reptilians. Nothing to like here. Nothing, nothing at all."

"You can say that again," I said, giving Lena a bemused look.

"Should I? Say it again? Why would I? Oh yes, for emphasis! Terrible place. Too dry. Too many reptilians."

The little Risuleon clearly had no love of Matarons, and while he appeared harmless, his people had refused to sign the Xil Neutrality Pact, making them either brave or stupid.

"I asked the Tau Cetins to help get you out," Lena explained. "And they asked the Risuleons who have special landing rights here."

"We help our friends," Shilu added. "Our friends help us. Ornithians are our friends. Good friends." He gave me a knowing look. "Now humans, friends too."

"Unfortunately," Lena said, "they kept you in Trel'sitar much longer than we expected."

"That was Hazrik's doing." I wanted to say he'd tried to feed me to a giant beetle, but again, I was prevented from uttering any word of the Nisk. Strangely, mega-psi Lena missed it completely.

"We've overstayed our clearance," she added. "If we don't get out of here soon, they'll board us. They're already suspicious."

"Maybe they will, maybe they won't," Shilu said mischievously. "Maybe we won't let them!"

"We watched your trial, Captain," Izin said. "That's how we knew you were still alive, and where you were."

"You are quick, and have good balance, for a human," Shilu said.

"You know us?" I asked.

"We saw your world, when it was cold. And white!"

"During the last ice age?" I asked.

"Yes, yes," Shilu said. "Too cold for us. We don't go back."

"It's getting cold again," I said.

"We know. A pity. Celestial mechanics. Changing orbit. Very difficult."

Earth had been holding off the next ice age by boosting greenhouse gases, but the planet's increasingly elliptical orbit was bringing the planetary summer to a close after nearly fifteen thousand years. Now the polar ice was spreading once more, forcing more and more people to migrate to warmer worlds.

"We've got a launch window in two hours," Lena said. "They've ordered us not to miss it."

"Lucky they decided to move me today," I said.

"Not luck," Lena said meaningfully. "The warden just

had a...change of mind." Her look told me she'd changed it for him.

"Does Hazrik know?"

"Not yet."

"I wouldn't want to be the warden when he finds out," I said.

Shilu turned the skimmer truck onto a divided road running across the crystallized plain from new Vaset'al to the spaceport. We blended in to a long procession of multi-carriage haulers shuttling goods between the new capital and the spaceport, although our vehicle was clearly not Mataron. Stretching away from the road on both sides was a dusty plain containing a hatched pattern, which was all that remained of the old capital's street grid.

"This is where it happened," Lena said, fascinated.

"The hypocenter was over there, about seven clicks," I said, pointing to the north.

It was a gross violation of the Access Treaty that had driven the Galactic Forum to impose a thousand year Embargo on mankind's interstellar access rights and forced the Tau Cetins to prevent the Matarons exterminating us. A millennium without interstellar travel had played havoc with our colonies. Many had survived, but some had descended into barbarism or simply vanished without a trace. The Matarons now used the plain to fan fear and hatred, rather than learn from history, forgive the past and move on to a brighter future.

The blackened skeletons of melted buildings stood where the e-plant had detonated, now stark reminders of what had happened all those centuries ago.

"I'm surprised anything survived," Lena said.

"Nothing did," Izin declared. "The Matarons deceive themselves. They created those ruins after the explosion."

"Anything to keep the hate burning," I muttered, studying the charade with dismay.

"Humans are not so bad," Shilu said, "for a predator species. You learn. You grow. You look ahead. Awful reptilians do not. They look back. Always back. Never forward."

I checked my bionetic base, finding the little arboreans were omnivores like us. "Risuleons eat meat. Doesn't that make you a predator species too?"

"Not like you, as you are not like them," His eyelids fluttered in an alien blinking response I didn't yet understand. "Awful reptilians are hated. Humans are not."

"Humans did obliterate their capital city," Izin said dryly.

"Yes, yes, when very young," Shilu agreed. "And embargoed for it, only once. Three times for awful reptilians. They never learn."

"Wait. The Matarons have been embargoed three times?" I said incredulously.

"Oh yes. Should be still, but the Forum took pity. Let them out early. Now they betray us all. Evil, awful reptilians."

Our first offence had cost us a thousand years, but repeat offenses incurred increasingly heavy penalties to give the offending civilization time to evolve. We'd studied our history openly and honestly, and learned from it, but Shilu was convinced the Matarons had not. Their fixation on the hatreds of the past, their inability to forgive, had embittered them, making them one of the most despised civilizations in the galaxy.

"Embargoed three times," Lena said thoughtfully. "Hmm, I never knew."

"No reason you should. It was long ago. Before humans," Shilu replied. "They attacked us once. Awful reptilians. We built a colony. Too close to them. In our space. Not theirs. No warning! Just kill."

"What happened?" I asked.

"The Ornithians destroyed them. Their fleet. Their base. No more!" His eyes blinked again. "Ornithians are good. Awful reptilians are bad."

"Considering your history with the Matarons," Lena

said, "how come you have landing rights here?"

"Forum says so. Access to land for us, access to space for them. For parole."

"Ah, I see. The Matarons had no choice," I said, "not if they wanted their interstellar access rights back."

"Yes! Now we land. Often!" His eyes fluttered with amusement. "We don't even like coming here!"

"So why'd you agree to parole them?" Lena asked.

"Awful reptilians hate visitors."

I grinned, beginning to appreciate the Risuleon's wicked sense of humor. "I think we're going to be real good friends."

Shilu's eyes blinked. "We think so too."

"So what's with the suit?" I asked, looking at his shiny brown body suit.

"Kif-atah very heavy. Suit keeps me light."

"It's an antigravity suit?"

"A filter. A shield. Same thing. Piralea is small, beautiful, very rare."

"There are many small worlds," Izin said.

"Yes, yes. But, magnetospheres are weak. Not on Piralea. Ours is very strong. We travel far. To find suitable worlds. Very few like Piralea. Even rarer than Earth."

The fake ruins passed out of sight as a high wall appeared on the horizon. The bows of ships docked there rose beyond it, almost all Mataron. It was a sign of how few alien ships they allowed to land on Kif-atah, and of snakehead unpopularity.

"I thought it'd be bigger," I said, guessing the Mataron homeworld's only spaceport was barely the size of a secondary landing ground on Earth, which had immense starports on every continent.

"They do not trade," Shilu said. "Not like humans. Or us!"

"You're a trader?" I asked.

"I serve the Watch."

I gave Lena a questioning look.

"That's their civilian intelligence organization," she explained. "They help the Tau Cetins."

"Yes, yes, we do," Shilu said seriously. "Awful reptilians be very angry. If they knew. Now hide please."

We went back into the cargo compartment and closed the cab door while Shilu drove through the starport's security checkpoint. Once inside the walls, Lena opened the cab door and we watched through the front window while staying out of sight. The spaceport was a maze of narrow, one way streets flanked by high, landing pad walls. Each pad was fully enclosed, monitored by automated sensors and locked away behind armored doors.

Shilu drove slowly through the spaceport, along one-lane roads filled with pedestrians clinging to wall shadows and hiding under shade cloths from Matar's brutal heat. Enclosed bridges spanned the roads while the upperworks of Mataron ships peeked above the landing pad walls. It was archetypally Mataron; cramped, crowded, hot and secretive.

Eventually, Shilu turned into a covered drive blocked by heavy doors. He transmitted his key and the doors slid aside, then we drove into a circular docking bay surrounded by high walls. In the center was a small, golden ship so shiny it was hard to look at in the harsh Mataron sunlight. It stood on three spindly legs, comprised two opposed cones joined at the base, and had a rounded bulge ringed by dark, oval windows amidships. A large rectangular door was open in the lower, downward pointing cone revealing a hangar deck crammed with small craft.

I'd never seen a Risuleon ship before, yet there was something vaguely familiar about it, although it wasn't the color or the skinny legs. While I tried to recall what it was, four tiny craft flew out of the hangar deck. Each had a bubble cockpit and was flown by a single pilot.

The craft rolled acrobatically for no reason, passed

dangerously close to each other for fun, never touching, and finished their antics perfectly positioned above us. Each craft locked a tow beam onto one corner of the skimmer truck, and together they lifted us off the ground and carried us into the hangar deck.

"Impressive flying," I said.

"Risuleons have highly developed spatial awareness," Izin said as the skimmer truck was lowered onto the flight deck.

"And no fear," Lena added.

Ship's gravity took over, giving welcome relief from Kif-atah's heavy grip. It took me a moment to find my low-gee legs, then Shilu showed us out. An assortment of small craft were crowded into the hangar deck, so close they almost touched. Tiny toy bots began unloading the truck as the four tugs squeezed into their allotted parking spaces with only millimeters to spare. A group of spindly medbots arrived and began fussing around Tahl Rete who lapsed in and out of consciousness.

"He will be cared for," Shilu assured me, then a familiar voice called out from behind me.

"You don't look half bad for a dead man," Jase said with a broad grin. He gave me a bear hug, crushing my almost healed skin.

I flinched. "Ugh."

He released me quickly. "Sorry Skipper."

"It's good to be back. Are you alone?"

"Emma's with her old man, helping Navy get a handle on Hardfall's defenses. And I didn't want to risk bringing her along, just in case. Don't tell her that."

Marie was standing behind him impatiently, hands on hips. I smiled with relief, went to wrap my arms around her, but she slapped my face. Hard!

"Ow!" I felt my jaw, searching for broken bones. "What was that for?"

"For shooting me at the spaceport!"

"It was only a stunner!"

"I was numb for a week."

"They would have killed you."

"I know." She grabbed me and kissed me passionately. When she let me up for air, she added softly, "And that's for not dying!"

"I told you I'd make it," I whispered.

"Hmm," she said, almost forgiving me.

A Risuleon voice made a ship wide announcement my bionetics could only partially translate: "Ship lift in– *untranslatable time units*."

"You are welcome to watch us lift, Captain Kade," Shilu said. "Kif-atah is as ugly from space, as it is on the ground. You will see."

Chapter Three : RS Busho

Risuleon Starship
Interstellar Transit
Matar System to Outer Lynx
706.8 light years
11.4 light years per hour arbitrary velocity
62 hours duration

The *Busho's* bridge was a dome-shaped compartment in the ship's central bulge. A continuous screen filled the curved overhead above the deck, concealing how low the ceiling actually was. The screen gave an uninterrupted view of the high walls surrounding the landing pad and a clear view into the cloudless violet sky as if we were standing on an open air platform. The illusion was only broken by Risuleon symbols on the screen marking gravity zones, orbitals, celestial objects and stellar nav points.

We shuffled to one side of the bridge to stay out of the way of the crew during launch. Jase banged his head on the invisible sky-dome, grunted and rubbed his forehead.

"Fourth time I've done that," he whispered. "It's a ship for midgets."

"I find it quite roomy," Izin said, reaching up and touching the sky.

In the center of the bridge was a five-sided command station with four officers at the controls, all wearing one piece Risuleon gravity suits. They sat in elevated positions looking down onto the central console containing an intricately detailed, isomorphic projection of Kif-atah's surface, from the spaceport at the center to the new city on one side and distant red-brown ridges on the other.

A vertical white line indicating our ascent vector reached from the spaceport to the spatial projection on the dome-screen. Floating before each officer was a translucent plane of soft light filled with Risuleon characters and at the end of their arm rests were circular touchpads over which their slender fingers rapidly moved.

Shilu climbed the metal ladder to his high backed couch, placed his hands on the interface pads and a light pane illuminated before him.

"Ship ready for lift-unlock, Captain," the officer to his left said in Risuleon. Bionetics translated his words for me and Lena while the others watched on without understanding.

Shilu entered a long and complex security code with both hands simultaneously, then a synthetic voice announced, "Lift-unlock accepted. Sealing ship."

"Field hover active…Landing legs retracted…Ready to lift," the engineer said.

"Compact, isn't it?" Marie whispered, appreciating the elegance of Risuleon design.

"Yeah, like a shoebox," I replied.

She touched the sky projection deceptively close to our heads. "We should get one of these."

"We'll get one on the Risuleon black market," I said, knowing that was the only way we'd get past Forum prohibitions against technology transfers, then navigation, tactical, sensors and engineering officers all spoke in turn.

"Kif-atah Control has approved our ascent vector."

"Mataron Security has disabled their weapons locks."

"System Tracking confirms no routing conflicts to translight activation coordinates."

"Engine charge optimized."

"Lifting," Shilu announced and in the blink of an eye we were in space and moving away from Kif-atah's violet atmosphere at tremendous speed.

I blinked in surprise. "Wow! That was fast!"

Jase grinned. "Yeah, they have crazy sublight."

The command station isogram changed to a line through shrinking gravity circles in space leading away from the planet.

"Risuleon ship Busho," a Mataron voice sounded in the Risuleon language. "Return to spaceport immediately."

"Return?" Shilu said indignantly. "You told us to leave."

"Return immediately or you will be fired upon."

"Spatial geometry normalizing," the engineer reported as our little ship raced through Kif-atah's large gravity well toward flat space. "Approaching translight threshold."

"Three Mataron ships have increased energy output ten to the fifth power," the sensor officer announced.

"Mataron Control, do not fire. We will return when launch guidance terminates," Shilu said.

"The Mataron ships have left orbit," the sensor officer announced. "They are charging weapons."

"It didn't take them long to figure out where you went," Lena whispered to me.

"We are the only alien ship launching," I replied.

Isomorphic images of three Mataron warships appeared above the command console, engaged in a stern chase. Mataron ships were significantly more advanced than the *Busho*, yet the snakehead cruisers were still falling behind.

"Risuleon ship, this is your final warning," a voice bellowed into the bridge.

"Final? Yes! Goodbye," Shilu said and tapped his console. The dome spatial projection and the Mataron cruisers vanished as the *Busho's* sensors retracted and were replaced by our course simulation, plotting our trajectory through the Matar System into interstellar space. "Very slow reptilians."

"Translight field stable," the engineer announced. "Elongating."

The bridge officers tensed, eyes locked on their translucent light panes, more afraid of what they were now doing than of the snakehead cruisers. For several seconds, they held their breaths, frozen in place.

"Elongation, nine degrees and stable," the engineer said at last and they all relaxed.

"They mess with their bubble geometry," Jase whispered to me.

"It makes their superluminal drive unstable," Izin said.

"Field shaping is experimental, even after four thousand years," Shilu said to us, in our language.

"Why do it?" I asked.

"We must go fast."

I clicked my fingers, recalling what was familiar about the *Busho*. It was how she tapered at both ends.

"It's your hull geometry," I said. "It reminds me of Tau Cetin and Kesarn ships." They were long and slender because both used Ornithian star drive technology. "You stretch your bubble for speed." It was the key to transgalactic travel.

"Stretch, a little," Shilu conceded. "Nine percent. No more. Enough to go fast."

"Your approach is reckless," Izin said and turned to me. "Their bubble could collapse at any time, Captain."

"We shape, because we must," Shilu replied, irritated

by Izin's presence. "We need eight point zero."

"GCC?" I said.

The Forum's Galactic Civilization Classification system identified how advanced a civilization was based on its star drive technology. The system was logarithmic, with each level requiring ten times the arbitrary velocity of the level below. Under the all-powerful Access Treaty, civilizations were freely given the astrographics necessary for safe navigation according to their GCC, providing they respected Galactic Law and each other. And there was no practical alternative to the Access Treaty.

Superluminal fields caused curvatures of spacetime so extreme that no signal could pass through them, rendering starships blind to the infinite navigational hazards of interstellar space, not least of which was undetectable-at-a-distance dark matter. Transiting gravitationally curved space at superluminal velocities caused catastrophic field collapses while collisions spelt instant death. The solution was Galactic Forum astrographics, which identified the hazards and simulated their movements with infallible accuracy. Without them, every journey was a dice roll and the odds got worse with distance.

Mapping the invisible across cosmic distances required the most advanced technology, possessed only by the galactic superpowers, the Level Ten's: the Tau Cetins, the Ovani, the D'kol, the Yhinsar and the Girria. There were other greater civilizations known to myth and legend, but they had long lost interest in galactic affairs and played no part. It took millions of years to climb the greasy pole of galactic power, yet the enterprising Risuleons had found a shortcut.

"Our worlds are rare," Shilu explained. "To find them, we must go far."

"Ah, you stretch your bubble to raise your GCC," I said. "You're pumping your rating."

"Yes, yes! Eight is better than seven."

"Any chance of teaching us that trick?"

"We say yes. Access Treaty says no."

The Access Treaty gave young civilizations a chance to grow at their own pace, before they made too many mistakes. Sometimes it felt like a straightjacket, but it had saved mankind from Mataron vengeance, so we couldn't complain. It was a rules based system that had stood for millions of years and it worked, or it did until the Spawn showed up.

"What does eight point zero buy you?" Jase asked.

"Buy me?" Shilu asked confused, then his eyes fluttered as understood. "Ah, buy! Yes. Half the galaxy."

"And it costs you what, a few ships blowing up?" Lena asked.

"More than a few," Shilu admitted. "But we have three homeworlds now, and many friends."

"I'd take that deal," Marie said.

"Is your sublight propulsion as unstable?" Izin asked.

"No, no," Shilu replied. "Very stable."

"So your fighters are fast," Lena concluded.

Shilu eyed Lena suspiciously, wary of betraying Risuleon state secrets. "Fast, yes," he replied guardedly.

I recalled the acrobatics of the four tow craft that had loaded the skimmer truck into the *Busho* at the spaceport and imagined those piloting skills controlling agile fighters. I gave my little Risuleon rescuer an appreciative look and turned to Lena, certain she hadn't busted me out of Kif-atah to take me joy riding in Risuleon speed boats. "What now?"

"We're rendezvousing with the Tau Cetins. I'm going with them and…you're going to find your brother."

"My brother?"

"Oh man," Jase groaned. "Not him."

Canopus Rix was a criminal, a murderer, the head of the Drake Chapter of the Pirate Brotherhood and one of the most wanted men in all of Mapped Space. I'd seen him once in twenty years and we hadn't exactly parted on good terms. "What for?"

"You're going to offer him a deal, one he won't refuse if he knows what's good for him."

* * * *

The *Busho's* cramped medical compartment had four rectangular bunk-plates beneath ceiling mounted strip sensors. Tahl Rete lay unconscious on one, floating inside a pressure field with his legs hanging over one end, bent at the knees. The strip sensor above him glowed white while two fist-sized ellipsoid-medbots swept soft yellow light over his body, regenerating his damaged skin. The Mataron stump seal was gone, replaced by a white cylinder that sealed his forearm all the way to the elbow.

A medbot led me to a metal bunk-plate and said, "Stand here. Remove your clothes."

I stripped off my tattered prison garb, which it carried away in a green beam and dropped down a chute, leaving me standing naked and filthy on the pristine deck. I'd lost weight and the niskgel had healed my cuts and burns, now hidden beneath layers of grime.

"Lie down," the medbot said when it returned.

The metal bunk-plate looked cold, but when I sat, a pressure field stopped my naked skin touching it. I lay down and the overheard sensor illuminated above me, turning my body translucent. I rolled left and right, watching my bones and organs move inside me.

"Do not move," the ellipsoid ordered.

"Sorry."

I became motionless while the sensor looked me over. When the scan finished, the overhead light went out and the medbot told me what I already knew. "You have high levels of dehydration and malnutrition."

"Hmph. I hope you're not charging by the hour."

"There are also indicators of ectodermal acceleration syndrome, cause unknown," the medbot added, then overhead panels either side of the sensor strip opened and a pair of slender nozzles lowered toward me like snakes. "Close your eyes and hold your breath."

I did as instructed, then the nozzles sprayed a warm blue liquid over me. The bunk's pressure field caught the liquid as it drained from my body and funneled it into deck receptacles. When my skin was spotlessly clean, the nozzles retracted into the ceiling, revealing freshly formed pink skin where my wounds had healed with surprising speed. I went to touch a line on my arm where a varidon had slashed me, but the medbot blocked my hand.

"No touching!" it snapped sternly.

I relaxed, feeling the pressure field close around me and warm air blow over my naked body, drying my skin.

"What about my clothes?" I asked.

"They were contaminated and have been recycled. Sustainment is preparing replacements."

"Copies? No thanks. They were snakehead prison clothes. I want something human."

"Specify cultural and professional requirements."

"Earth starship captain. Civilian. Utilitarian. Not too fancy. Jacket, shirt, pants, boots and ah...an energy blaster with a personal force shield."

"Suitable clothes will be prepared. Armaments will not be provided."

I shrugged. "It was worth a try."

The ellipsoid floated away, then I climbed off the bunk-plate and approached Tahl Rete. He too was naked, revealing a thickly muscled physique substantially heavier than a man's, except in one regard.

"Hmm, a bit lacking down there big fella," I said, glad the Kesarn were no match for humans in at least one department.

One of his medbots floated to my side and asked, "What is the gelatinous substance on the Kesarn's wounds?"

Girutonak's memory sent a shock of fear through my mind as I realized it was referring to niskgel.

"What substance?"

"Traces were detected on your body and in your clothes prior to recycling."

I felt a tremendous compulsion to lie, to conceal any hint of the Nisk. "Are you sure?"

"Was it a Mataron substance?"

"I...I don't know."

"It is disrupting our tissue regenerators."

"Get rid of it. Wash it off."

"Organisms disrupting ship systems must be analyzed to ensure they pose no biological threat to the crew."

Incomprehensible Nisk clicking sounded in the back of my mind, gripping me with fear, fear the Risuleons would identify the niskgel, that they would discover Girutonak's secret. My secret.

"But you destroyed my clothes."

"We did not realize the contaminant was bioactive."

The medbot hovered over Tahl Rete's body collecting niskgel from his skin with a beam, then it placed the sample in the circular opening of a wall mounted machine. The niskgel formed a liquid sphere, like water in zero gravity, and the shiny cylindrical housing surrounding it began to glow softly. Four sensors extended and beamed different colored lights into the watery sphere.

"What are you doing?" I asked apprehensively.

"The sample contains multiple genomes. Our genetic spectrometer will separate them and identify the bioactive substance."

"How many sequences?"

"There are four elementary chains with multiple mutations."

Four genomes? Human, Kesarn, Nisk and microbes native to Kif-atah, all tangled together in a vastly complex puzzle.

"Why are they mutating?" I asked, suspecting I knew the answer.

"The bioactive substance is highly mutagenic, causing

chain entanglement."

"How long until you split them?"

"Three days."

The Nisk clicking suddenly grew louder, then like an automaton I reached for the spherical sample, intending to destroy it. The Risuleon ellipsoid flew in front of my hand, stopping me reaching into the analyzer.

"No further contamination is permitted," it declared.

"Of course," I said, pulling my hand back as my ears rang with terrified Nisk chatter.

It didn't matter I was among friends, only that I fulfilled the deranged coleopteran's dying wish. It was more than a compulsion, it was an obsession, one I didn't understand and couldn't resist. I had to destroy the floating globule of Girutonak's stomach bile before the Risuleons realized what it was, and ruined everything.

A display illuminated above the analyzer with dozens of double helixes, slowly rotating as one. They were of different lengths with many missing sections, wound together like a Gordian knot. As the tangled, genetic mass revolved, a tiny part of one helix formed in an empty space, the first piece of an immensely complex puzzle. There were billions of pieces missing, but the Risuleons would find them all, including the Nisk, in just three days.

"Your clothes are ready," a medbot announced.

They were laid out on a deactivated bunk-plate. The jacket was longer, the boots shorter and the colors darker than I liked, more in keeping with a Core Systems fleet trader than a freelancer on the fringe. But they were a vast improvement on the Mataron prison garb I'd been wearing and they were a perfect fit.

"You do good work," I said, looking for a mirror.

"The other humans are waiting for you in compartment nine, deck four."

I glanced apprehensively at the genetic spectrometer which was slowly filling gaps in the chains, then turned to Tahl Rete. He was sleeping soundly and still had a thin sheen of niskgel on the worst of his wounds.

"You should wash him. If that substance is a biohazard, you're endangering the crew by leaving it on him."

"The Kesarn is in a biocontainment field and poses no danger to the ship. However, now that we have a viable sample for analysis, fully decontaminating him will aid his recovery."

Two nozzles lowered from the overhead and gave the Kesarn a cleansing blue shower. When it was complete, they reapplied their healing mist.

"All gone?" I asked as the nozzles retracted.

"The mutagenic agent has been sterilized. It no longer poses a threat to the crew."

That left only the dirty brown, watery sphere in the analyzer as the last trace of Nisk DNA aboard. On the display above it, another link appeared in a chain as the next piece of the puzzle was solved. Girutonak's mind block shivered with fear, filling me with a determination not to allow the Risuleons to finish the job.

I gave Tahl Rete a farewell look, said, "Hang in there, big guy," and went in search of the others.

* * * *

"We saw three big troop carriers and a spawnship before we jumped out," Jase said, recounting the invasion of Earth as we sat squeezed around a small table in the *Busho's* miniature mess deck.

Food preparation machines against one bulkhead dispensed meals from an extensive menu while screens on another displayed various ship status reports. For my first Risuleon meal, I selected a boiled, flightless bird and vegetables, supposedly palatable for humans. It was soft to the touch and bland to the taste, but a marked improvement over snakehead slop satchels.

"The Tau Cetins only had two of their big ships to

cover our retreat," Jase continued. "Not enough to take on four spawnships, even if three of them were transports."

"Spawncarriers are not transports," Lena said. "They're powerful, capital ships."

"They're a modern version of the ship that brought my ancestors to Earth," Izin said.

The ancient Spawn mothership that had crashed on Earth thousands of years ago had been crippled in the First Intruder War and forgotten when the war moved on to other battle spaces.

"Where was the rest of the TC fleet?" I asked.

"At Syrma, disrupting an invasion of Sarlo," Lena replied, "and protecting Gienah and a dozen other systems." She gave me a grim look. "Sarlo fell, but the Spawn only managed to hold the smallest continent on Xanseb. The Gienans destroyed the other bridgeheads with Tau Cetin help, before the Spawn could take the big cities."

"Those furballs are tough fighters," I said.

"Their technology is superior to the Syrmans," Izin added.

"The Gienans learned from our experience on Earth," Lena said. "They kept the Spawn out of most of their major cities, although they couldn't stop them taking their smallest continent. The Tau Cetins now have ships over Xanseb, preventing the Spawn from dropping more troops, but it's too late to bombard the bridgehead."

With Tau Cetin help, the Gienans were a formidable proposition. Their weapons were effective, their military efficient, and if the Ornithians could keep the Spawn out of the orbital drop zones, they had a fighting chance.

"The Tau Cetins gave them priority over us," Marie declared bitterly.

Lena shook her head. "No, they didn't. The Spawn feigned attacks in the Outer Bridge to draw the TCs toward the Perseus Arm. That's when they hit us. By the time the Tau Cetins realized what was happening, the

Spawn were in our mega-urbans, and it was too late."

The Outer Bridge was where the Orion and Perseus Arms intersected, at the end of the Orion Arm furthest from the galactic core. It was beyond Human Mapped Space and at the outer limit of the Tau Cetin's central sphere of influence. That's why they'd taken the bait.

"The Tau Cetins helped us save what we could," Lena said. "It was risky, considering Serris-Orn's defenses are still down. Most of Earth Navy got away, thanks to them."

"Us too," Jase added.

"After the Tau Cetin victory at Serris-Orn," Lena continued, "we expected the Spawn to withdraw, or at least wait for reinforcements. No one thought they'd switch to drop and run landings against the minor allies. No one knew there was a Spawn Invasion Fleet hiding in interstellar space, waiting for Serris-Orn to fall. When the Spawn realized the Ornithians had concentrated their fleet to defend their homeworld, they dispersed theirs and hit as many targets as possible. Now the Ornithians are spread thin, guarding everyone, chasing shadows."

"How thin?" I asked.

"The Spawn are hitting non-Pact worlds within twenty thousand light years of Tau Ceti, usually with three or four assault carriers escorted by one spawnship."

"If the Spawn concentrate their forces," I said, "they could destroy the Tau Cetins in detail."

"They won't," Izin said. "The Spawn are a land power. Their army is their real strength, not their navy, and ground combat is the Tau Cetin's weakness. If the Spawn concentrate their fleet again, they'll risk giving the Tau Cetins the chance of a decisive victory. The Spawn made that mistake once. They won't do it again."

Ornithian ground forces were well equipped and well trained, but small in number, and they could not replace losses the way their populous enemy could. The Spawn had only built a large fleet to challenge the Tau Cetins, and after it failed, they reverted to type. They could afford to lose many surface battles and still win the war, while one catastrophic mistake could cost the Tau Cetins everything. And one day, reinforcements for the Spawn Battle Fleet would arrive from the Minacious Cluster, to use the bases created on many conquered worlds against the Ornithians.

"The Tau Cetins are soft," Izin continued. "They should destroy the Spawn from orbit while they can. Allowing them to hold densely populated worlds is a foolish strategy."

Lena gave Izin a withering look. "The Tau Cetins won't murder billions of innocents to liberate conquered worlds."

"That is why we will lose," Izin said. "If the Tau Cetins were the invader, the Spawn would not hesitate to obliterate their own cities to destroy them."

"And everybody dies," Jase said sourly.

"There would be survivors," Izin insisted.

"We're not the Spawn," Lena snapped, irritated by Izin's lack of concern for civilian lives, and because she knew he was right.

A tense silence settled over the group, then I asked, "When are we going back, to liberate Earth?"

Lena frowned. "There are over a hundred thousand autacs and at least ten thousand spawnwarriors on Earth and in the Sol System colonies. They're there to stay."

"Because Earth is the closest habitable planet to Tau Ceti," I said.

She nodded. "The Spawn won't give it up. The TC home fleet is pinned down covering Earth, while their Grand Fleet is scattered, protecting everyone else."

"Making them weak everywhere," I said, realizing much had changed since my holiday on Kif-atah. "So how'd you find me?"

"Marie told me you were captured in Paris-Elbe, and I knew from Lord Geoffrey the Matarons wanted you. The rest was easy."

"When I came to in Paris and saw you were gone," Marie said, "I knew you'd surrendered to the Spawn. I made it to the Niobe just in time. Got as far as Procyon Station before her people arrested me." She nodded disdainfully at Lena.

I smiled, doubting Marie would have gone quietly. "You were lucky to escape."

"She didn't escape," Lena said. "The Spawn are letting civilian ships leave the occupied worlds, flooding Orion with refugees."

"They are masters of psychological warfare," Izin added, "spreading fear and defeatism among their enemies."

"Earth Navy kept me locked up for weeks," Marie continued. "No one would tell me what was happening."

"You were in protective custody while I procured transport to Kif-atah," Lena explained.

"You could have told me."

"I needed complete secrecy, and considering your past sympathies, I don't trust you."

"You didn't tell us anything and we've never been Separatists," Jase said. "You don't trust any of us."

"I trust Sirius, to handle all of you, but he wasn't around."

Marie scowled. "The first I knew we were going to Kif-atah was when we landed there."

"She kidnapped us right off the Silver Lining," Jase added.

"Extraordinary times require extraordinary measures," Lena said, dismissing their concerns. "Now that Earth has fallen, the Separatists are becoming increasingly emboldened."

"Earth hasn't fallen!" Jase snapped.

Lena sighed wearily. "It's in open revolt, but we don't control it."

"Neither do they!"

"It's only a matter of time," she declared. "That's why

we need to cripple the Separatists, before they can exploit the situation. They actually believe the Spawn are on their side, helping them."

"The Spawn will destroy them, when it suits them to do so," Izin said.

"We can't wait for that," Lena said, turning to me. "You must convince your brother to break his deal with Separatists. The Sep Fleet won't survive without access to Brotherhood bases."

"He'll never go for it."

"He might, if you're the one making the offer."

"Are the Risuleons going to blast his fleet if he says no?"

"They won't be there. You're going in the Silver Lining. The Tau Cetins are bringing her to the rendezvous."

I smiled sourly. "We'll be dead before we get anywhere near him."

"Why don't the Tau Cetins take us to Rix?" Marie asked. "Just seeing one of their ships would make an impression."

Lena shook her head. "The Drake fleet would scatter, not talk."

"What am I offering?" I asked.

"Anything they want."

"Suppose he wants his own planet?"

"Give it to him. Give him two. We don't care. Lie if you have to. With the Spawn on Earth and some of the big Core System colonies on the Sep side, we're struggling to keep our fleet going. We need those Brotherhood bases for our ships, and any of their ships that'll fight alongside ours. This is right from the top."

"What if he refuses?"

"If the human race is going to survive, Sirius, we have to stop fighting each other. The civil war must end. Mankind must unite, otherwise we're finished. Earth Council will back you all the way. Any deal is better than no deal."

"The Consortium will keep fighting," Marie said. "They have the money and the ships to do it."

"We'll deal with them in good time," Lena assured her.

The Consortium had started the Human Civil War. They'd funded it, secretly controlled it and intended to reshape human civilization into their own criminal enterprise. If they got their way, the rest of humanity would be nothing more than serfs in their economic empire. But powerful as they were, they needed secret bases to break the Earth Navy blockade, otherwise Separatist holdouts would soon be on their knees.

"So we're working for you now?" Jase asked.

"No. Sirius works for me. You work for him."

"Me too?" Marie asked.

"All of you. Or I'll drop you at the first habitable world we pass, human controlled or not."

They exchanged dubious looks, not realizing who they were dealing with.

"She means it," I said.

"Same pay?" Jase asked opportunistically.

"Bonuses and splits, as before," Lena promised.

"No. We want…double bonuses on trades and triple merc rates for missions," Jase bargained.

"Done," she said simply.

"Damn!" Jase winced, realizing he could have asked for ten times as much and she'd have agreed.

Lena gave Izin a long look, waiting for his answer.

"I've suspected for some time this was the arrangement," he said indifferently.

"You didn't say anything," Jase said.

"I shouldn't have had to."

I turned to Marie who nodded, grudgingly.

Lena gave me a satisfied look. "Once you've finished with your brother, go to the Earth Navy base on Uralo IV. The Tau Cetin courier ship stops there now. Send me a report and wait for further orders."

I turned to Marie, having second thoughts about risking her life on this unlikely mission. "Maybe you should go with Lena. We can handle this," I said, nodding to Jase and Izin.

She scowled and placed the jewelry box I'd slipped into her pocket in Paris-Elbe on the table in front of me. "You think you're going to leave me behind again? And you haven't even given me this yet."

Jase smirked as I picked up the ring box, but didn't open it.

"You're not going to forgive me for Paris, are you?"

"Not until I've made you pay, and you've asked properly. And I want to meet this infamous brother of yours. If Canopus Rix of the Pirate Brotherhood is half as bad as they say, I might not even want to be part of your family."

* * * *

That night, asleep on my tiny cabin's pressure plate, I dreamt of coleopteran clicking. It began as a faint whisper in the dark, grew slowly louder, becoming frenetic and fearful, then alien shrieks filled my mind as a great circular ship was consumed by plasmatic fire. The chattering staccato of hideous, skin crawling multitudes was snuffed out in an instant as millions died, never knowing why.

I awoke suddenly, expecting to see melted forms all around me, but the cabin's soft light showed I was alone. I'd lived the nightmare for hours, unable to break free, only it wasn't a dream. They were Girutonak's memories, as real to me as they had been to him, as personal as if I'd been there myself.

"Intercom on. Lena Voss," I whispered hoarsely.

Lena's disembodied face appeared, floating before me, lacking the shimmer of a hologram. "Sirius?" She squinted, wiping her eyes. "Do you know what time it is?"

"Yeah. Late. I mean...early."

She leaned toward me, studying my face intently. "What is it?" she asked, her mega-psi abilities failing her the one time I needed them most.

I wanted to tell her about Girutonak, of the millions of coleopteran ghosts haunting my dreams, of the fiery cataclysm in space. Most of all, I wanted to warn her I was unfit for duty, but when I tried to speak, no words came out. The Nisk mind block was growing stronger by the day and my capacity to resist ever weaker. Girutonak's memories were taking over my mind and there was nothing I could do to prevent it. If Lena could only see it, she'd know how to stop it, but I couldn't speak the words and she remained uncharacteristically blind to my thoughts.

"Sorry," I said, realizing calling her had been a mistake. "It was...just a nightmare."

She nodded sympathetically. "It's understandable, considering what you've been through. Do you want me to have the Risuleons give you something to help you sleep?"

"No. I'll do it."

"OK. Relax Sirius. You're safe now. Intercom off."

I lay back on the pressure field, but rather than return to sleep, I wondered how close the nosy Risuleon medbots were to identifying Nisk DNA in the sample they'd taken from Tahl Rete. The thought of them discovering the Nisk filled me with dread and an inexplicable sense of betrayal. Filled with an urgent desire to ensure the Risuleons failed, I went down to medical. Tahl Rete was still unconscious, although his color had improved and his wounds were no longer festering.

"How is he?" I asked as a medbot came to meet me.

"We have repaired his broken bones. His right arm was decaying. We had to amputate to the elbow."

"I hope you're going to grow him a new arm," I said, studying the white cylinder now sealed all the way up his bicep.

"We are not equipped for alien reconstructive cloning."

I turned to the DNA analyzer. Its four arms were circling the liquid sphere, slowly untangling the extremely complex genetic puzzle. The number of entwined chains had decreased as simpler Mataron microbials had been identified and removed. Many broken chains remained, and hidden among them were the disjointed segments of three complex life forms.

"You're making progress," I said.

"The genetic analysis will be complete in twenty two hours."

"What's taking so long?"

"The mutagenic compound is constantly modifying all structures, inhibiting sequence assembly." The little medbot floated between me and the analyzer, unintentionally stopping me reaching the watery sphere. "Is there something you require, Captain Kade?"

"Yes, I'm…having trouble sleeping. What have you got?"

"Approach the dispenser." The medbot waited while I walked across to a small shelf. A panel opened and a small, circular blue patch floated out. "Place that on your forehead when you require sleep."

"What is it?"

"A hypnagogic suppressor."

"Is it quick?"

"It will induce deep sleep within three to five seconds."

"Hmm…No stimhalers?"

"Chemical remediation is not required or available."

"OK, I'll give it a try. Thanks."

I pocketed the patch and returned to my quarters, but didn't use the Risuleon sleep inducer. Instead, I floated in my cocoon field staring at the overhead, wondering what that giant beetle back on Kif-atah had done to me.

* * * *

"Our fighters use spatial grapples," Shilu explained while giving us the five credit tour of the *Busho*.

He indicated six small spacecraft parked on one side of the hangar deck, each barely four meters long. They were shaped like three-pointed stars with inward curving sides on the horizontal plane and a trailing stern point twice as long on the vertical. Their non-reflective hulls were blue-gray in color and in the center of the three-pointed stars were shallow dome-shaped cockpits, too small for a human. The tiny fighters were the ship's only armament, although Shilu wouldn't give us details. "Grapples compress spacetime. On three axes. Ahead of the craft."

"Like a bubble?" Jase said.

"No, no. Different. Bubbles surround. Grapples extend."

"You pull the fighter through spacetime?" I asked.

"Yes, and no. Slide forward, through steep curvature. Falling and pulling, in three directions."

Marie paced around one of the fighters, paying particular attention to the points of the star. "It looks very maneuverable."

"Yes, yes," Shilu replied. "The grapples steer."

"It's the opposite of interstellar travel," Izin said.

Jase gave Izin a puzzled look. "Opposite how?"

"A ship is stationary, or moves slowly inside its superluminal field. That ensures no momentum, no kinetic energy, no build-up of relativistic mass. Spacetime moves elastically around the bubble, not the ship, but these fighters have high velocity through spacetime. There is no bubble. Their velocity produces inertia and kinetic energy, which is why they can never reach the speed of light."

"Correct," Shilu said, uncomfortable at the ease with which Izin had grasped their propulsion concepts.

"No getting past Albert," I said. The Risuleons had a brilliant innovation, but it was strictly sublight.

"What is Al-bert?"

I smiled. "A funny little guy with curly hair, bushy eyebrows. Been dead a couple of thousand years. He figured out space for us."

"Ah! Like Bajii. Our greatest genius."

"What's its top speed? Half-light?" Jase asked, sizing up the Risuleon fighter like it was a souped-up skim-racer.

"Fast," Shilu replied evasively.

Jase studied the cramped cockpit and the unfamiliar controls inside. "Hard to fly?"

"For you, yes. For us, no. Our ancestors were tree dwellers. They leapt from tree to tree."

"That's why you have a heightened spatial ability," Izin said.

"We understand geometry."

Jase's eyes narrowed hopefully. "Any chance of taking one for a spin?"

"No, none. You would not fit." Shilu motioned toward a hatch. "This way."

We crouched through the hatch into a recycling compartment. Like everything else on the Risuleon ship, it was a fraction the size of our reprocessing systems. A single waste tank dominated the center of the compartment, surrounded by five cylinders containing extraction and processing machines.

"Do not cross that line," Shilu said, indicating a white circle around the machines.

"Your miniaturization is impressive," Izin observed appreciatively.

"You chemically deconstruct waste. We atomize it. And assemble molecules as required. Our way is more efficient."

Strategically placed Risuleon symbols warned to stay outside the safety line. Inside the circle, a soft hum came from the central machine while heat radiated off one of the cylinders and a thin layer of ice covered another.

Coleopteran clicking began whispering to me, growing louder as we moved around the recycling system, urging me to protect Girutonak's secret no matter what the cost. With a shudder, I realized what it wanted, then in a dream, I feigned a stumble and fell toward the hot cylinder. I stuck my hand out to break my fall, pressing it against hot metal. My palm sizzled, filling the cramped compartment with the stink of burning flesh, and fell onto the deck holding my wrist in agony.

"Argh!" I groaned, staring at my blackened hand, refusing to activate my bionetic pain blockers so the others saw the pain was real.

Marie grabbed my wrist, horrified. "Sirius!...It's bad!"

"It's no plasma burn," I said through gritted teeth.

"We have to get you to sickbay," she said, pulling me to my feet.

"Medical emergency," Shilu announced to the ship. "Prepare for burn treatment."

I pulled free of Marie's grip and gave her a reassuring look. "I'm OK. You finish the tour. I'll go to sick bay."

"I'll take you," she insisted.

"No, I'm fine," I assured her, taking a deep breath. "Really."

Before she could argue, I hurried back through the hatch and headed to medical where three Risuleon medbots were waiting for me. One scanned my hand while the other two hovered close by.

"This will sterilize the burn and eliminate the pain," another medbot said, spraying a fine mist over my hand's blackened flesh, instantly numbing it.

"We will regenerate the damaged organic material," the third medbot said.

I glanced at Tahl Rete. "How is he?"

"The Kesarn will be conscious soon," one medbot replied, then floated toward an empty bunk-plate. "Use this medical station, Captain Kade."

I ignored the instruction and stepped toward Tahl Rete, while the other two medbots fussed over my burnt hand. With my good hand, I took the sleeping patch they'd given me hours before and pretended to rub my forehead, holding the patch firmly in place.

"He looks a lot better," I said, feigning interest in the Kesarn. I became irresistibly drowsy and discretely pocketed the hypnagogic inducer. "I don't feel so good."

My knees buckled and I fell sideways, flailing with my damaged hand, plunging it into the genome analyzer. I snatched at the watery sphere, forcing it between my fingers and splashing it onto the surrounding metal. The globule disintegrated, poisoned by the sterilizing agent on my hand, then I collapsed onto the deck, fast asleep and beyond the reach of coleopteran clicking.

* * * *

Marie was sitting beside my pressure-plate when I awoke hours later. My hand was numb to the wrist, immobilized inside a white paddle.

"How are you feeling?" she asked.

I yawned, surprisingly rested from the effects of the hypnogic inducer. "Better."

A Risuleon medbot floating beside me said, "You will be able to remove your hand from the dermal regenerator shortly. You will wear a cytokinesis glove until cell restoration is complete."

"I hope I didn't break anything," I said, hoping I did. There was no watery sphere floating in the genome analyzer and the multi-helix jigsaw image was gone from the display.

"No equipment was damaged, although the bioactive sample was destroyed."

"I'm sorry to hear that," I lied.

"It was our fault, Captain Kade, not yours. Your human physiology reacted adversely to our hypnagogic suppressor. We failed to correctly calibrate it for your species."

"No harm done."

The medbot floated away, then I glanced at Tahl Rete who still dozed beside me. His pressure field was now opaque below his chest, hiding his nakedness, and folded neatly on a shelf behind his bed were freshly synthesized Kesarn clothes.

Marie followed my gaze. "He's really from the Cygnus Rim? I've never met anyone from that far out before."

"The Spawn almost wiped his people out."

"What's he doing here?"

"He didn't say. Kesarn don't talk much."

"We talk," Tahl Rete murmured and opened his eyes. "This is no human ship."

"It's Risuleon." I glanced at the low ceiling. "Watch your head."

He felt his bandaged chest and the pad over the side of his face with his good hand.

"They had to take more of your arm," I added.

"Hmph," he grunted indifferently, knowing he'd get a replacement eventually, then eyed Marie suspiciously.

"That's Marie," I said.

She smiled. "Welcome to the Orion Arm."

He acknowledged her with a look but made no attempt at small talk.

"Was it worth it?" I asked. "Going to Kif-atah?"

"No."

"You sure it wasn't one of the Gienans? I never liked the way their eyes always followed you."

He turned his head toward me. "I thought it might have been you."

"Oh yeah? What changed your mind?"

"You talk too much."

Marie smiled. "I have that problem with him too."

"The Tau Cetins must have paid you well, to take such a risk," I said.

"No money," he replied, no longer hiding his connection with the Tau Cetins. They had a close but strained relationship with the Kesarn, built on a common desire to defeat a mutual enemy.

"They should have told you what you were looking for."

"Wouldn't have made any difference."

"I figure they didn't want you telling the Spawn what they were interested in, if you were interrogated. You can't give the game away, if you don't know what the game is."

"Hmm," Tahl Rete agreed.

"Makes you kind of expendable, doesn't it?"

He replied with stony silence, telling me he'd already come to the same conclusion.

"So how'd they expect you to know when you found what they were looking for?" A faint clicking sounded in my mind, warning I was treading on dangerous ground.

"I'd know."

I wanted to ask him if he could have been searching for a Nisk prisoner. I tried to form the words, opened my mouth to speak, but the clicking grew louder and the mind block stronger.

"You must have your suspicions," was all I could get out.

Instead of voicing them, Tahl Rete glanced suspiciously at Marie.

Sensing she was not welcome, she kissed me on the forehead. "I'll see you later, Sirius," she said and headed for the door.

"My homeworld's occupied by the Spawn," I said, once we were alone. "Anything that hurts them, interests me."

Tahl Rete gave me a long look, recognizing we had that in common. "Who do you work for?"

"Earth Intelligence Service," I replied, abandoning all pretense. "You?"

"The Kesarn Teraal." When he saw I'd never heard of it, he added, "Similar to your EIS."

I wasn't surprised the Tau Cetins had neglected to mention the Kesarn secret intelligence service, but keeping us in the dark was to no one's advantage, except the Spawn's; something we'd have to raise with them, and soon.

"The Spawn are doing to us what they did to you."

"I know." His stony exterior slipped a little, then he finally decided to share. "The Sibylline of Uvo told the Tau Cetins there was something on Kif-atah."

"The Uvo?" I said surprised. They were spiritual aesthetics, one of the oldest communicating races in the galaxy, teachers to many of its great and powerful, yet lacking any real power themselves. "What does Kif-atah have to do with them?"

"I don't know, but those Uvo witches have their ways, and the Tau Cetins listen to them."

"Why didn't the Tau Cetins come themselves?" One TC arbiter would have been enough.

"They feared the Matarons would have destroyed whoever, or whatever they had."

"How were you supposed to get him out?" I asked, then the clicking exploded in my mind, deafeningly loud, strangling my ability to speak.

"They said I'd find a way," he closed his eyes wearily. "Those Uvo witches got it wrong. There was nothing there. Never was."

Silenced by the mind block, I watched Tahl Rete slip off to sleep, certain the Uvo had been right all along. There had been a prisoner, a Nisk Royal whom Tahl Rete would have recognized if he'd met him, but he never did. Now Girutonak was gone, driven mad by memories he couldn't bear and all trace of him removed by his captors.

Now, only I knew the truth, and I could tell no one.

The Nisk prisoner of Trel'sitar was dead, slaughtered by the Matarons, and though I didn't know why, I feared the hope of freedom for half the galaxy had died with him, lost forever.

* * * *

That night I stayed late in Marie's room, receiving her tender care after weeks apart and experimenting with the more sensual effects of the Risuleon pressure bed. With my stunt at the Paris Spaceport forgiven and only a single bunk-plate in her room, I retired to my own quarters to sleep. When I entered, I found Lena sitting on my cabin's tiny couch.

"You obviously weren't that badly injured," she said wryly, well aware of where I'd been and what I'd been doing.

"I'm a highly trained EIS agent, with genetically engineered powers of recovery, and phenomenal physical endurance," I replied dramatically.

She smiled and motioned to two DNA encoded boxes on my side table. "They're for you."

I ignored the ammo box and unlocked the pistol case. Inside was a matt black weapon with TN-8C engraved on the side. "Teniks Neber eight mil. Hmph! And it's not even my birthday."

"I couldn't get you another P-50. That'll have to do."

"The barrel's too long." I lifted it out of the case, popped the targeting screen, tested the sighting and the weight. "It's light. Balance is good. What's it made of?"

"Something new," she replied evasively.

I ejected the magazine, counted an impressive fifteen rounds, all purple banded static force penetrators. The TNs had a good reputation, but compared to my old P-50, it was a popgun. "P-50s hit harder."

"The TNs are standard issue for I-F now. The power cells have double the charge, ideal for troops behind enemy lines. No infrared signature, and the best optics and AI in any weapon that size."

"Did the Tau Cetins help us with it?"

"No, it's all ours."

"Sonics?"

"Suppressed, but magnetic accelerators are noisy. It's the price you pay for hypersonics."

The gun's control system had options for variable muzzle velocities, infrared tracking, precision release for sniping and a bunch of other goodies I'd test out when pressurization wasn't an issue.

"It'll do, for now," I said, intending to dump it for a MAK P-50 the first chance I got.

"It's DNA locked to you, and you alone."

"Hopefully, I won't need it. I'm going to talk to my brother, not shoot him."

"We'll be at the rendezvous in the morning. You'll transfer over to the Silver Lining and I'll go with the Tau Cetins."

"Are you taking Tahl Rete?"

"Yes. The Tau Cetins will see he gets home, with a new arm."

"He's got nothing to report," I said, expecting her to be surprised he'd say anything to the Tau Cetins. Instead, she gave me a knowing look, confirming she'd already probed his mind. "Ah, but you already knew that. You knew he was working for the Tau Cetins."

She shrugged a confession.

"Huh. Did you come to rescue me, or him?"

"Sirius, when did you become so suspicious?"

"Since I started working for you."

She smiled. "I came for you both. Rescuing you was a good cover story. The Matarons would believe I wanted my top agent back, and getting Tahl Rete out was payment to the Tau Cetins." She gave me an amused look. "You don't think they'd ask the Risuleons to risk a ship just for you, do you? The Tau Cetins like you, Sirius, but not that much."

"Do you even care if my brother switches sides?"

"I do. We need those bases and we have to disrupt the Sep Fleet, but…I expect you're more likely to fail than succeed."

"That makes two of us."

"Why do you think Tahl Rete was on Kif-atah?" she asked, intensely interested in what the Tau Cetins were up to.

"You don't know?" I countered as the mind block clicked softly in the back of my mind.

"The Tau Cetins I dealt with didn't know, and I read them all." She gave me a disappointed look.

"Whatever it was, he didn't find it," I said as the clicking ramped up.

"Too bad. We could use a break."

"For a moment there, I thought you were going to leave him on Kif-atah."

She shook her head. "Never. That was in case a sensor was watching us."

"I thought you let me convince you a little too easily," I said as the clicking ebbed away into my subconscious."

"Really?" She smiled. "I thought I gave a convincing performance."

"Did you cook up this whole idea about my brother before, or after the Tau Cetins approached you?"

"After. I expected the Matarons to execute you. Using their religion against them was a nice touch."

"It was Tahl Rete's idea."

"I tried reaching you in Trel'sitar, but there was something in the way. Something I've never sensed before." She looked puzzled, not realizing it was Girutonak's telepathic madness.

"I heard you, but I was in pretty bad shape at the time."

"Hmm, that must have been it." She smiled. "It really is good to have you back. Good night, Sirius."

She returned to her room while I lay on my pressure bed dreaming of vaguely familiar stars and an inhospitable world no human had ever set foot upon. Only it was Girutonak's dream, not mine, implanted in the deepest recesses of my mind, and growing stronger by the day.

In time, it would be my dream too, and real enough to touch.

* * * *

The *Busho* unbubbled in deep space half a light year from the nearest star system, far from prying eyes. The Tau Cetins were already there waiting with three mirror-hulled ships of vastly different proportions.

The smallest was a sentinel, a needle in space about half the size of a human battleship and the fastest of the three. Astern of her was an arbiter, a top-of-the-line Ornithian super dreadnought equipped with a fearsome array of energy weapons and a tremendous shield to compensate for her lack of armor. She was spindle-shaped, with a spear-like bow and stern separated by a series of graceful curves.

Last in line was a galactic conveyor, a stretched ellipsoid twenty times longer than the arbiter and more than twelve times her mass. She was a fleet transport and mobile naval base in one, containing shipyards, immense storage holds and docking facilities to sustain the Tau Cetin blockade of the Spawn's home cluster. For twenty five hundred years, Allied fleets operating from galactic conveyors had kept the Spawn bottled up in the Minacious Cluster, sixty five thousand light years from Earth and Serris-Orn, withdrawing only after the Spawn broke the blockade several years ago. Conveyors were now relegated to more mundane duties, ferrying allied fleets and refugees across the galaxy, awaiting the day the Spawn would be driven back into their distant, extra-galactic stronghold.

"Goodbye, Captain Kade," Shilu said outside the *Busho's* airlock. He extended his tiny left hand to shake.

"This is the human tradition, is it not?"

"Wrong hand," I said, shaking his small furry paw, "but just as welcome."

"It was a pleasure, to annoy the Matarons," he said with a flutter of his eyes. "Do not lose hope. The galaxy is watching."

"They should do more than watch," Izin said bluntly.

"They fear destruction," Shilu replied.

"The Spawn won't stop at Earth," I said.

"They will not," he agreed and turned to Lena. He went to raise his left hand, recalled his mistake and offered his right. "Interesting custom, no weapon in hand. Not for us. Our ancestors never fought with hands."

"What did they use?" Lena asked as they shook.

"Ankle blades." Shilu turned and gracefully sliced the air with his foot, demonstrating how primitive Risuleons fought, swinging through the treetops of their homeworld, slashing bladed feet at each other. "Now, we use quantum blades."

"Like the Matarons," I said.

"Yes, yes. We copied them. A good weapon."

"They don't give those things away."

"They do, when they're dead," Shilu said lightly. "Safe journeys."

Shilu returned to the bridge, then Lena motioned for me to wait as the others squeezed into the tiny airlock. When the hatch sealed, she offered me her hand, but not in farewell.

"Is there something you want to tell me?" I asked dryly, taking her hand. The bionetic receptors in our palms linked and data flowed from her hand into my bunkered memory.

"If Uralo IV has fallen by the time you get there, hide in your bubble and head to Point Mylae. These are the coordinates."

Point Mylae was a code name for a point in interstellar space. "What's there?"

"You'll find out. If you're captured, do a full memory wipe." The first upload finished and a second, far more complex data stream began.

"Snowball? That's not a code name," I said, skimming the star charts pouring into my bionetic memory.

"It's an ice nebula. It looks like a snowball from ten light years away. That's where you'll find your brother. He moved his operations there after we blockaded the Shroud. These charts are the latest updates from the Tau Cetins."

"What's wrong with the old charts?"

Once the Tau Cetins had mapped an area, their prediction modules calculated the orbital drift of every object down to free molecules. Updates were routinely passed from ship to ship, but they were little more than confirmations of Ornithian computational perfection.

"The Drakes are pushing comets around inside the nebula, blocking the lanes," Lena explained.

"The Forum won't like that."

"They don't, but it's our problem to fix."

Celestial objects could be moved for mining or terraforming purposes, with a Forum license, but deliberately disrupting interstellar travel was an Access Treaty infringement. Pushing comets around would induce gravitational tides, nudging thousands of other objects off course, eventually rendering the entire nebula unnavigable. Once the star charts were scrambled, the risk of superluminal collisions would force other ships to avoid the area like the Rigellian Plague, which was the idea.

"How do the Drakes get in and out?"

"They've laid nav-markers for themselves, but they only turn them on for their own ships."

"So the Tau Cetins remapped the nebula just for me?"

"It was part of the deal for rescuing Tahl Rete."

"And me," I reminded her, then took a quick mind's eye look at the astro charts. The Drake base was deep inside the nebula, surrounded by an ocean of icebergs and a bunch of heavy weapon emplacements even Earth Navy would have a hard time cracking.

"Do the Drakes know the Tau Cetins unlocked the door?" I asked.

"No, which is why Rix will be very surprised to see you."

Considering he'd warned me not to show my face in his territory again, this was bound to be a very unhappy family reunion.

The airlock's inner door swung open and we cycled through, joining the others on a cargo platform floating inside a vast cylindrical hangar several kilometers across. It was packed with hundreds of ships from civilizations across the Orion Arm; human, Syrman, Nirisi, Lhekan, Suvoli, Gienan, along with many others I didn't recognize from beyond Human Mapped Space.

The refugee ships floated tightly together, held in place by invisible beams as securely as if they'd been maglocked to a deck. Some had scorched hulls and battle damage exposing wrecked interiors while others were unharmed and airtight. Gliding between them were small craft shuttling passengers between airlocks while Ornithian-form service bots in colored jump suits assisted alien engineers conduct repairs with flickering energy tools.

"It's crowded in here," I said.

"You should have seen it a month ago," Lena said as the platform floated away from the Risuleon ship and threaded its way through the refugee fleet.

"Where are they all going?" Marie asked

"Somewhere the Tau Cetins can protect them," Lena replied evasively.

We glided past a crippled Suvoli warship toward a familiar, human trader with a rounded bow, chunky midsection and a pair of bulging housings astern, each with three engines. The *Silver Lining II* was dwarfed by the alien vessels around her, was poorly armed and slower than any of them, yet the Tau Cetins had made her spotlessly clean and ready for space.

She was a Cabot class science ship with a heavily shielded e-plant and near silent engines to minimize sensor clutter. That made her sneaky rather than invisible, which was what had attracted me to her. Outgunned by every non-human in the galaxy, I preferred hiding to fighting, although she had teeth by human standards. I'd used Lena's EIS money to refit her as a trader, but she'd done little of that since I'd gotten my hands on her.

I gave Jase an approving nod. "She looks good."

"She's better than good," he said meaningfully.

The cargo platform came alongside the *Silver Lining's* bow airlock, then Jase entered the access code and the outer door opened.

"Good luck, Sirius," Lena said as the others filed into the airlock.

"Say goodbye to Tahl Rete for me," I replied and climbed into the airlock, feeling Earth normal gravity for the first time in months.

Knowing the Tau Cetins were going to push us into space and jump away, Izin hurried off to engineering while the rest of us went up to the bridge. The big screen, spanning the entire bulkhead forward of the crew stations, showed we were already gliding through a huge circular door into space.

"They're not wasting any time, are they," Marie said.

I climbed onto my acceleration couch, bringing my console to life. "They don't want to get caught by the Spawn, any more than we do."

"We have sufficient energy to bubble, Captain," Izin announced over the intercom.

"Already?" I said surprised, deceived by the missing hum of a living ship. The *Silver Lining* wasn't just quiet, she sounded like she was in cold storage.

"Yes, Captain, we have full power," Izin assured me.

I glanced at my console, saw every system was functioning perfectly. Better than perfect.

Jase grinned. "Look at our profile."

I switched my console to show our emissions' signature and found we didn't have one. We were producing zero particles, not even neutrinos from the e-plant.

"Told you," Jase said.

The ship had been damaged helping the Tau Cetins, and in gratitude, they'd repaired her, making her better than before, quieter than she'd ever been.

"She really is a hole in space," I said, impressed.

"We still reflect visible light, but nothing else."

"A reward for their favorite human, Captain," Izin said.

I grinned. "Well, we did kind of save their homeworld."

The Tau Cetins pushed us clear of their star drive, then all three ships streaked away together in perfect synchronization leaving us alone in interstellar space.

"Not even a goodbye," Marie said.

Jase tensed, suddenly transfixed by his sensor display. "Uh-ho. Intersecting spatial wake at vector zero nine zero, less than one thousand clicks out."

It was a ship, passing us at superluminal velocity. To come so close in the empty reaches of interstellar space was no accident.

"How fast?" I asked, summoning the autonav.

"Snakehead fast," Jase replied. He plotted the alien ship's trajectory back to its point of origin and nodded. "It came from the Matar System."

They'd followed the *Busho* all the way from Kif-atah. Being sensor blind inside their bubble, they'd have stopped frequently, scanning for the Risuleon ship's wake. It had been an easy track to follow, because the *Busho* had made no course changes.

"They don't know we've switched ships," Marie said.

"It won't take them long to realize they passed us," I said. "When they get here, they'll see one human and three Tau Cetin ships left in a hurry…Who do you think they'll follow?"

"Not the Tau Cetins, that's for sure," she said, then I entered a waypoint a few light years away and brought the *Silver Lining's* bow around to line up on our destination.

"High energy contact!" Jase announced. "Eighty five thousand kilometers."

"Already?" I said, surprised.

An optical box appeared on the bridge screen showing an unmistakable, tear-drop shaped hull lined with weapon and sensor blisters, accelerating toward us.

"They don't know who we are," Marie said, hoping they'd hold their fire.

"The hell they don't." My bionetics recognized the hull geometry immediately. "It's a scout cruiser, Griela class." She was a hunter, purpose built for wake tracking and vector analysis. That's how they found us so fast.

"They're backtracking our scan pulses," Jase said as he realized our active sensors had given away our position.

"This is the Mataron Supremacy Intercept Cruiser Riku," the bridge speakers announced. "Shut down your engines immediately or be destroyed."

"Pull sensors," I ordered.

The bridge screen went blank as Jase retracted our sensor masts into the hull, then I let the autonav have the helm. The superluminal field curved spacetime around the ship and the course simulator appeared on the bridge screen, calculating our blind progress through interstellar space. Safe for the moment, I plugged a series of random waypoints into the autonav, hoping to throw the *Riku* off.

"We'll lose them," Jase declared.

"They don't know where we're headed," Marie said.

"Don't count on it." When I saw their puzzled looks, I added, "She's a purpose built wake tracker, faster than us, better armed, and she's got our scent. She's not going to let us go."

"We did kill two of their officers getting you off Kifatah," Marie admitted.

I nodded, but that wasn't the reason they'd sent one of their most advanced warships after us. It was because I knew they'd turned a Nisk Royal into a lab rat and lied about it to the Spawn, and that terrified them. They couldn't know Girutonak had mind blocked me into silence, that I'd been unable to tell the Risuleons, or the Tau Cetins, or even my own people. They'd want to find out for themselves what I'd said, and to who, and they wouldn't give up until they knew and I was dead.

Until we all were.

Chapter Four : Snowball

Zilarov Ice Nebula
8.74 light year radius
Outer Lynx
Interstellar Space
761 light years from Sol
16,000 sentient life forms

"There's nothing out there," Jase said after we dropped the bubble for the fifth time since encountering the *Riku*. We'd made multiple course and speed changes to throw her off, although this was the first time we'd stopped long enough for her to catch us.

The bridge screen showed the nebula's outer periphery ahead, a wall of white icy mist sprinkled with dirty gray icebergs.

"It's crowded in there," Marie said, fearing a collision with millions of tons of ice.

"We'll take it slow, short hops," I assured her. "The bubble will handle the mist and we'll waypoint around the bergs."

I'd uploaded Lena's new Tau Cetin astrographics to the autonav via palm link and plotted a zig zagging course through a minefield of ice three point two light years deep. It was tricky, but with the Ornithians to guide us, reaching the Drake Base should be no problem.

I fed power to the engines, moving the *Silver Lining* toward our first bubble-out point. Tiny ice crystals bounced off the hull as an irregular iceberg took shape ahead.

"We've got company," Jase announced as an optical box appeared on screen containing a grainy, rounded silhouette. "Two million clicks astern. They've seen us."

"Our engines *are* pointed right at them," Marie said, implying we were the brightest star in their sky.

"Almost there," I assured her as the bubble-out marker loitered off to one side of the bridge screen, but her eyes were on the optical box.

"We can still jump to deep space."

"Our best chance is in there." I nodded at the white fog beginning to envelope us. "Remember, they don't know the Drakes have been moving the furniture."

"They'd be crazy to follow us in, if they knew," Jase said with a malicious grin. "Hull flares on the Riku. She's charging weapons."

A white halo began to shroud the *Riku* as she entered the nebula at high speed, her shield vaporizing ice crystals at a prodigious rate. I slid us around an irregular ice mountain to break line of sight, then let the autonav swing our bow toward the marker.

"She's in range," Jase warned and stowed the masts, losing visuals and tracking.

The course simulator appeared on the bridge screen as the *Riku* came around the berg behind us for a clear shot, then the bubble activated. The autonav threaded a needle through the ice field while the quantum effects of extremely curved space atomized the mist, dumping waves of heat onto our bow.

Marie exhaled with relief. "Too close."

"Want me to raise the shield when we drop?" Jase asked as the simulator counted down to the first marker. "They could be waiting for us."

I shook my head. "No one's that good."

The *Riku* needed time to search for our wake, to fix our bubble-out point, and if we got lucky, she'd plow into a wayward comet before she found us.

A minute later the bubble dropped and Jase ran out the masts for a look, bringing the bridge screen to life. It was whiter than before and the bergs were larger and closer, but they were where the Tau Cetins said they'd be. For that at least, I was grateful.

An optical box appeared onscreen showing the *Riku's* dark silhouette fourteen thousand kilometers ahead.

"Damn! They are that good," Jase exclaimed.

I took control of the helm, turned the *Silver Lining* hard to port as the *Riku* came around, bringing her four big energy cannons to bear. The white cloud parted as she accelerated toward us, then we ducked behind a shadowy mass of ice and dust seventy kilometers long. Four brilliant flashes lit up the nebula and the glacier exploded beside us, sending ice boulders spinning across our wake, narrowly missing our stern.

"I may have underestimated them," I said, sliding our next waypoint deeper into the dense ice zone, forcing the autonav to recompute our next vector.

"Cutting it tight, aren't you?" Marie said, eyeing a large mass close to our plot line.

"We've got clearance," I assured her, hoping the Matarons, relying on old charts, would overshoot, then Jase stowed our sensors and we bubbled toward heavy ice.

"How long?" Marie asked, taking little comfort from being inside the relative safety of our superluminal bubble.

"Three hours. Lunch anyone?"

* * * *

Thousands of tiny hammers rang through the ship as the bubble dropped and a sea of ice crystals suddenly pounded the hull. Jase ran out the sensors and the bridge screen blinked to life, revealing we were now in a thick white fog surrounded by irregular, icy mountains. None were large enough to form spheres, although their true size was disguised by the mist and the way they overlapped each other.

We started a short run through the ice field toward our next bubble-out point, then Jase declared, "Contact!... She's behind us."

The *Riku's* optical box appeared on screen, showing the fog around her flash with light as she fired.

"Shield!" I slewed the *Silver Lining* to starboard as four energy blasts flashed past our port side, illuminating the darkness ahead.

Jase silenced the tiny hammers with our shield as the *Riku* fired again. I nosed the ship down as another volley of energy blasts flashed above us, one grazing our shield topside before shattering a triangular shaped ice-roid ahead.

I banked the *Silver Lining* behind an immense glacier that absorbed the *Riku's* next bombardment without breaking apart, glowing eerily for the first time in ten billion years. We raced alongside it as flashes lit up its dark ice, then emerged into a field of ice-roids, each many times our size. I used them for cover, weaving through them as the *Riku* raced after us, blasting the big ice with her weapons and shattering the smaller pieces with her shield.

"Their shield's degrading," Jase reported, then the *Riku's* next volley shaved our shield port side, triggering a flickering overload.

"So's ours," I lamented as the white mist ahead darkened.

Marie tensed. "Sirius! I see mountains!"

"It's a planetoid," I said as its spherical outline filled the screen.

"Point one five gravity," Jase said.

Energy blasts flashed past us, striking the icy planetoid and lighting up a vast ice plain.

"Where's the Riku?" I asked.

"Port quarter, thirty degrees, and closing," Jase replied.

The black hulled cruiser closed on us rapidly as we plunged toward craters and valleys ahead. I rolled evasively as the *Riku* fired again, shaving our shield and sending energy blasts smashing into the ice plane, hurling geysers of superheated steam up toward us. I flew through the steam and levelled off, skimming the surface as the *Riku* dropped in astern of us like a lumbering beast closing for the kill.

"There!" Marie yelled, pointing at a long broken shadow across the ice.

I dived the *Lining* into the crevasse as the *Riku* fired again. Her blasts impacted the surface, sending pillars of steam jetting up into space as walls of blue ice hemmed us in on both sides. We hurtled down into a frozen darkness while the Mataron cruiser hesitated above. I thought she was going to let us escape, then she followed us down, her shield sparking and vaporizing primordial ice cliffs on either side. She fired again as I slewed the *Silver Lining* to port, grazed the ice wall with our shield and rolled clear before continuing our descent into the planetoid's frozen heart.

"Shield at twenty percent," Jase warned. "She's still with us."

The ice cliffs narrowed, then a brilliant white flash lit up the crevasse and the optical box imaging the *Riku* vanished.

"What was that?" Marie asked

"Not weapons," I said, slipping and rolling the *Silver*

Lining, hemmed in by walls of ice.

"The Riku's...stopped," Jase said puzzled. "Her shields are down."

"Are you sure?" Marie asked.

"She's not moving."

A grin slowly appeared on my face, then I laughed. "They're stuck!"

I nosed the *Silver Lining* up, climbed out of the crevasse and headed for space. Deep in the ice far below the surface, the Mataron scout cruiser lay wedged between towering walls of ice.

"The ice overloaded her shield," Marie guessed.

"That was the flash. Her armor saved her," I said. "She can't shoot her way out. The back blast would hit her."

"They could be stuck down there a long time," Marie said, relaxing.

Jase chuckled. "Someone's got some serious explaining to do, when they get back to Kif-atah."

The frozen planetoid disappeared astern as the autonav focused on our next jump, then we bubbled away through a sea of drifting ice toward the Drake base. With the *Riku* no longer in pursuit, Izin came onto the bridge.

"They won't return to Kif-atah," he said after settling himself on an acceleration couch.

"What choice do they have?" Jase asked.

"They'll try to catch us as we leave the nebula."

Jase scowled. "It's eight point seven light years across."

I sighed, fearing Izin was right. "The Riku's a tracking ship. She'll have remote sensors she can deploy."

"I don't know, Sirius, that's a lot of space to cover," Marie said doubtfully.

"She'll be waiting," I said, unable to tell her the Matarons weren't simply chasing a fleeing convict, but an eyewitness to the murder of a Nisk Royal and the betrayal of the Spawn. Faint coleopteran clicking sealed my lips and reminded me of those vaguely familiar stars I'd dreamt of. They glowed in my mind and coordinates appeared as clearly as if I was reading them off the autonav. I was suddenly filled with an urge to change course, to send the *Silver Lining* racing toward them, to–

"Sirius?" Marie shook my shoulder.

I blinked, snapping out of it, shocked by how powerful the mind block was becoming, fearing it wouldn't be long before I was unable to resist it.

"You OK?" Marie asked, staring into my eyes.

"Sorry. I had a flashback, of Kif-atah." I exhaled slowly and fixed my mind on the task at hand.

"Do you want me to take the helm for a while?" she asked.

"No, I'm good." I smiled. "It's time you met my brother, assuming he doesn't shoot us on sight."

She gave me a dubious look, then the Nisk clicking faded away, biding its time, waiting for the chance to bend me to its will. With a chill of fear, I knew it wouldn't have long to wait.

* * * *

Two days of precise navigating later, we unbubbled in a dense arctic fog thick with ragged icebergs and flooded with neutrinos radiating from many e-plants. Faint, blurry lights glowed in the distance, barely visible through the mist, forming a mosaic of light and dark amid the nebula's icy wastes.

"A lot of heat blooms in there," Jase said. "More ships and weapons than we can handle."

"Good thing we're not here to fight," I said.

"Should we activate the transponder?" Marie asked.

I shook my head. "No, that'd just tell them we don't belong, and it wouldn't stop them shooting if we did."

"They're ranging us," Jase warned. "Multiple contacts."

"We should raise the shield, Captain," Izin said.

"No, let them look."

I fed a little power to the engines, nudging us toward the fuzzy lights in the darkness ahead. Running lights on shuttles gliding through space between ships and habitats came into view, but none came our way and no one hailed us.

"Not very curious, are they?" Jase said.

"We've got their attention," I assured him. "They just haven't decided what to do with us yet."

"This was a science ship, Captain," Izin said. "They may think we're spying on them."

"They know we're here to talk."

"I'm reading a launch." Jase tensed, then as more data came in, he relaxed. "It's a low energy contact."

It came out slow and dark, no running lights, no weapons, gliding cautiously through the icy mist. It was cylindrical in shape, too small to be an anti-ship drone. At a thousand meters, it matched our velocity and heading, angled two short sensor masts at us and aimed a bi-directional comm dish at the base. They eyeballed us for several minutes, eventually hailing us with audio only.

"What do you want?" a gruff voice asked.

The odds of stumbling across a secret Pirate Brotherhood base hidden in the midst of an interstellar ice cloud were virtually incalculable. And as we were alone and outgunned, we obviously hadn't come to fight.

"I'm here to see Rix," I said, hoping they'd believe we'd been invited.

There was a thirty second delay, due to our distance from the base, then the response came through. "Who are you?"

"He knows me," I replied, hoped by refusing to identity myself, they'd assume I was on their side of the law.

There was a longer silence as they debated what to do with us, then Gruffy said, "Follow the beam."

A docking beam reached out to us from the cluster of

lights, inviting us into range of their weapons.

"Now we should raise the shield," Marie said.

"And show we don't trust them?" I grinned and eased the *Silver Lining* onto the beam.

The sensor probe escorted us in while dozens of targeting beams painted our hull. We soon began eyeballing armored turrets and drone launchers in dirty brown ice-roids. They were modern, looked almost new and followed us as we passed.

"They sure got a lot of heavies," Jase said uncomfortably.

"They're getting more than just credits for keeping the Sep Fleet running," I said.

We passed through their defensive perimeter into a zone of drifting icebergs haphazardly dotted with old and decaying prefab habitats half buried in ice and lit by grimy windows. Scattered around them were corroding resource extractors, antiquated weapon emplacements and frost covered anchoring towers, some with well-armed raiders bow-locked to their peaks.

"Getting in's going to be easier than getting out," Jase said uncomfortably.

"What makes you think we're getting out?" Izin asked.

"Always the optimist," Jase said bitterly.

Marie gave me a doubtful look, agreeing with Izin.

"The Consortium has been busy," I admitted, wondering if all Brotherhood bases had been as well fortified as this one.

A cargo shuttle slid across our path heading for blinking lights on a distant prefab, then we followed the docking beam toward an irregular glacier over a hundred kilometers across. At its center was an ancient starliner, half buried in ice and surrounded by prefabs crammed together wall to wall. Surrounding the makeshift city were dozens of anchoring towers with spider-like docking claws and flexible pressures tubes with airlock seals. Most of the ships clamped to the towers were human, although a few were of alien design.

When we approached the makeshift spaceport, we came up on a pair of long, dark silhouettes set apart from the rest of the fleet. They were secured to anchoring towers fore and aft, were identical in design and dwarfed the *Silver Lining*. Isolated pools of light on their topside hulls illuminated Drake engineers and industrial thrusterbots working on a single heavy turret for each ship.

"Those aren't Saracens," I said as we glided past them.

The mainstay of the Sep fleet were armed merchant cruisers, built by Consortium front companies and upgraded at Brotherhood shipyards. They were effective raiders, but no match for purpose built capital ships. These two, however, were almost as big as Earth Navy battleships, heavily armored and of a type I'd never seen before.

"Want me to scan them, Skipper?" Jase asked.

"No, they'd detect it. Just log the opticals."

"I don't recognize the design," Marie said.

"Neither do I." And I had them all catalogued in my bionics. Every Separatist shipyard was closely watched by Earth Navy, and any attempt to build warships was met by a precision strike from orbit. For such purpose built capital ships to have avoided destruction could only mean one thing. "The Consortium's got a secret shipyard…somewhere."

It could be hidden anywhere among millions of star systems. The Brotherhood could upgrade and repair the Sep Fleet, but they didn't build ships. They bought and stole them. Consortium front companies, however, built everything from cargo lifters to cruise liners to capital ships. All they needed was a place to do it, a place unknown to Earth Navy, where they could build enough ships for the Separatist revolt to finally shatter human civilization forever.

We glided past the first ship's cone-shaped engine

outlets, each the size of the *Silver Lining*, and moved toward the second where hullbots and Drakes in heavy engineering suits were maneuvering an oddly shaped weapon into a huge turret. The weapon had a long, cylindrical emitter protruding from the point of a triangular body.

"What kind of gun is that?" Jase wondered, zooming an optical sensor toward the weapon.

"It's new to me," Marie said.

I ran a profile match against my bionetic base, confirming it wasn't a human design, then found a Naval Intelligence sighting of a similar weapon. "It's Meropan."

Jase gave me an incredulous look. "They wouldn't give us weapons. They'd be sanctioned by the Forum."

"Their government would not," Izin said, "but their lawless factions have links with human criminals."

"Meropan smugglers would sell anything for the right price," I said.

"But their tech doesn't work with our systems," Marie said, unconvinced.

"It does now."

The Meropans were only sixteen thousand years ahead of mankind, almost a peer civilization, and only slightly ahead of the Ascellans. Their weapons were considered primitive by galactic standards, but they rendered Earth Navy's most advanced battleships obsolete at a stroke.

"I'm reading three separate neutrino sources from that second ship," Jase reported.

"Ah." I nodded with understanding. "That's why they're so big, how they can power an alien weapon. They've got multiple e-plants."

"Must be a hell of a weapon," Jase said apprehensively.

We watched the Meropan armed battlecruisers fall astern as we followed our docking beam to an aging anchoring tower. It rose from the densely packed prefabs encircling the grounded starliner. The old ship lay like a beached whale on the glacier's surface, held in place by ice mining grapples. Over the years, the ice had crept up her sides, encasing her, freezing her in place.

"She's been down there a long time," Marie observed, fascinated.

"Centuries by the look of her," I said.

View ports had been installed in her hull, letting light seep out into the darkness in a thousand places. It was a strange sight, seeing a human ship with windows. Bubble heat required thermally sealed hulls, making viewports impractically expensive, and could only mean she would never fly again.

Dozens of docking pads had been attached to her topside hull, creating a makeshift shuttle port. Some pads had hangars and cargo cranes, but most were nothing more than maglock platforms requiring cross deck marches to the nearest airlock.

"They've got artificial gravity," Jase reported, picking up the liner's acceleration field on his sensors.

Directly ahead of us, a circle of red light blinked on illuminating the center of a five legged spider clamp at the top of our anchoring tower. I eased the *Silver Lining* into the docking ring, then the spider legs magnetized to the hull and a pressure tube mated with our bow airlock.

"One of the clamps didn't lock," Marie said uneasily.

"Four's enough," I said. They were enormous electromagnets designed for ships much bigger than ours. They'd tear our hull plates off before letting us drift away. I climbed out of my couch and turned to Marie. "You have the helm."

She gave me a surprised look. "I'm coming with you."

"We're all going," Jase declared.

I shook my head. "Not this time."

"You're not going down there alone," Marie said.

"There's no reason for you to go."

"The hell there isn't," Jase exploded.

"A few more guns won't make any difference. Just

don't let them aboard. If you have to run, head for Uralo IV. Tell them the Sep Fleet is getting Meropan tech and…let Lena know I couldn't convince Rix."

"Sirius," Marie said, "he's your brother."

"That's what worries me," I replied and went to the armory to dress for the occasion.

* * * *

I floated through a zero-g pressure tube from the *Silver Lining's* airlock to the anchoring tower, then took the elevator down into artificial gravity. When the door slid open, six unwashed bottom feeders aimed an assortment of peacemakers at me.

"Hand it over," a bearded brigand ordered. He had an ugly metal breathing plate for a nose and extended a large, tattooed hand for my new Teniks Neber.

"Since when do you stop visitors carrying protection?" I asked.

"Since we don't know you, or your ship," No-Nose growled.

I sighed, unbuckled my holster belt and handed it to him. "I'll want that back."

"Where's the rest of your crew?" he demanded, slinging the gun belt over his shoulder.

"Up there," I replied, pointed up through the elevator shaft. "I wouldn't pay them a visit if I were you."

He scowled at my friendly advice, then led me through a series of poorly lit, self-sealing double-plated prefabs that smelt of old boots and vomit.

"Your scrubbers need an overhaul," I said, wrinkling my nose.

"I'll tell maintenance," No-Nose sneered. "They'll get right on it."

We passed small scale engineering workshops equipped with old, barely serviceable equipment and brand new machines freshly smuggled out from the Core

Systems. Grimy Brotherhood techs and Consortium engineers in spotless orange coveralls worked side by side, although the outsiders clearly gave the orders. The lowly greasers sullenly obeyed, although they obviously resented their highly trained overlords.

"Hey Garvie, what you got there?" a bald Drake wearing chest armor over a red silk shirt called from a workshop flashing with sparks.

No-Nose raised his hand gun, mimed firing the weapon at me, getting a knowing laugh from Baldie, then we entered a large rectangular chamber. The gently curved hull of the starliner formed the far wall and the name *Cieli Sereni Nove* was stenciled on its side. My bionetics matched the name to an Earth registered super liner, the *Clear Skies Nine*, last seen in the Liedo System almost two hundred years ago. She'd disappeared from the Core Systems without a trace, presumed lost in interstellar space.

My guide led me up a long ramp rising forty meters into the air to a high capacity airlock with both inner and outer doors removed. Inside was a grand entry with faded, blood stained carpets, vandalized naked statues and bullet-riddled chandeliers.

"Classy, " I said.

"Keep moving," No-Nose snapped, pushing his gun into my back.

We climbed a curving grand staircase with gold metal railings to a broad promenade. What had once been a glittering shopping gallery was now lined with loot merchants buying and selling booty from pillaged ships. Well-armed Drakes in bright clothes and mismatched body armor, along with a handful of Ascellan, Meropan and Carolian brigands, bartered prices with shady, mostly human merchants. The aliens all came from the least advanced Xil Pact neutrals, making me wonder how close the Orion Arm underworlds had become, and what kind of deals the Consortium had stitched up with them. They were all armed to the teeth and bartered aggressively in a variety of languages, yet were careful to keep their hands well clear of their weapons.

"Where are we going?" I asked.

"To see the Guv'na," No-Nose grunted.

"You have a governor?"

"Yeah, and he sure is eager to meet you. Recognized you right off the screen."

"Did he?" I said, hoping it was a good sign.

I knew my brother was high in the Drake hierarchy, but I figured he liked the freedom of shipboard life too much to end up running one of their major bases. His elevated status would make getting a deal with the Drakes easier or totally impossible, depending on what he thought was in it for him.

The roar of loud voices and raucous music grew, then one side of the promenade opened out, overlooking a sprawling plaza two levels below. It was crowded with people and filled with fountains, statues, bars and brothels, making it one of the largest red light districts this side of the Core Systems. There were hundreds of people down there, mostly human, throwing money and favors around like confetti, confirming the Drake Chapter of the Pirate Brotherhood was about money and pleasure and little else.

At the end of the promenade, double doors framed in tarnished gold slid apart as we approached, granting us access to the Governor's office. Screens on the side walls cycled through optical feeds from weapon turrets, anchoring towers and docking pads. In the center of the room was a high backed chair facing a screen on the far wall. Its occupant lounged back, face hidden, his boots up on a scratched banquet table with ankles crossed.

The far screen was segmented into squares displaying the faces of seven men and two women. Behind the faces were captain's staterooms or the bridges of ships, small and large. My bionetics ran facial matches on them all, identifying four Drake Captains, an escaped serial killer, two complete unknowns and Anya, my brother's auburn haired second-in-command. Her features were defined and symmetrical rather than beautiful, and her only adornment was a commband that wrapped around the right side of her forehead. Her eyes darted toward me, betraying surprise for only a moment, then all expression drained from her face, hiding she knew me.

"It was a Nirisi ship," a swarthy man my bionetics identified as Iago Suarez said. He was Captain of the *Vibora*, number eighty six on Earth Navy's most wanted list. "It was a hulk, totally destroyed. No salvage."

"You couldn't tell what hit it?" An Asiatic man, one of the unknown captains asked.

Suarez shook his head. "The hull was too cold. Couldn't identify the weapons."

The boots lifted off the table and the chair swiveled, then a tall, east African man with long braided hair stood up, and I knew I was in deep trouble. He wore a brightly colored shirt and had a gruesome plasma burn across half his face with my name on it, due to my having blown a ship out from under him at a previous, less than cordial encounter.

"Kade!" he growled through gritted teeth, fixing his eyes upon me with no satisfaction or triumph, just a look of pure hate.

On the screen behind him, Anya's face was a blank mask, warning she could do nothing for me. No-Nose and his five pet Neanderthals had me covered from three sides, as if one gun wasn't enough, which it wasn't. Five, however, guaranteed making a fight of it was a no win for me.

"I'm here to see Rix," I said.

"Rix has no say in Ice Town," Gwandoya declared.

It was a pity Tau Cetin intel hadn't extended to who was running this base, or I could have told Lena there was no chance of a deal. My only hope was to bluff or tell the truth, although Gwandoya's melted face told me he wasn't interested in either.

"It was the Spawn," I said, throwing out the only bait I had, fixing my gaze on Captain Suarez. "They did it."

All eyes focused on me, some apprehensively, some curiously, then Gwandoya grunted dismissively. "There's no Spawn here!"

"Try telling that to the Nirisi."

"You lie," Gwandoya snapped in his thick east African accent. "The Meropans told us, there was a great battle. The Tau Cetins defeated the Spawn. They sent them running back to their home beyond the Rim."

"There was a battle," I conceded, "but the Spawn have not retreated. They've regrouped."

"Why would they attack the Nirisi?" Captain Eimear Leach, the second woman on the screen demanded. She was at least twenty years older than Anya, wore no face paint and had a hardness more intimidating than most men. That's why 'Mhamo' Leach had made navy's top fifty.

"The Nirisi are Tau Cetin allies," I replied.

"So? We are not," Gwandoya declared.

"You're human. That makes you the Spawn's enemy."

"You do not scare us with your fairy tales, Kade. We are nothing to the Spawn."

"They're attacking minor worlds throughout the Orion Arm. Ask your Meropan friends to send a ship. They'll confirm what I say."

It would be months before human ships from the Core Systems got out this far, but the Meropans could get there and back in a fraction of the time.

"The Meropan supply ship is a month overdue," a Captain with a curving moustache and oversized golden earrings said thoughtfully. "The Mero dealers don't know why."

"The Arko Naris is late," Anya added. "They were coming here after their last run to Sarlo."

"Sarlo has fallen," I said.

"Impossible!" the wanted serial killer exclaimed. "The Syrmans would never surrender."

"You saw the proof," I said to Captain Suarez. "Who else would attack the Nirisi?"

"I've never seen damage like that," Suarez said uncertainly.

"He tries to scare us, because he thinks we are fools," Gwandoya said. "We are not."

I ignored Gwandoya and spoke directly to the captains. "I came here because Earth has fallen."

A shocked silence filled the room. Even No-Nose and his tribe looked stunned.

"Good!" Gwandoya exclaimed. "Now we are free to do as we please."

"How sure are you, Kade?" Anya asked.

"I was there when the Spawn landed. I barely got away with my life."

In spite of Gwandoya's protests, the Drake captains were wavering. Several had silenced their audio and were speaking to their lieutenants off screen.

"Rix will want to know. I'll tell him when he returns" Anya said to Gwandoya, for my benefit.

I nodded slightly, signaling I understood.

"Yes, tell Rix, so he can hide," Gwandoya sneered and turned to No-Nose. "Take him down to the plank room. I will make the announcement."

I caught a warning look in Anya's eyes, then No-Nose dragged me out as Gwandoya made a starport wide announcement.

"All hands! Plank bettin' begins in one hour. We got a good one for you maties, so bring your money."

* * * *

No-Nose put me in a cold storage compartment adjoining the starliner's belly hangar while the crowd gathered.

When he dragged me out, I was shivering and frosted with ice crystals, and fell to my knees when he released me. Above me were five decks with a circular transitway up through center, wide enough for a fully laden Titan class cargo lifter to pass through with ease.

Raucous crowds crammed every level of the transitway, many sitting on the lips of the circular well decks with their legs dangling precariously over the edge. They puffed fumers, drank multicolored concoctions and pumped their necks with stim guns, ripening the air with pungent, mind warping toxins. There were no safety rails, although there were recessed hand holds everywhere and they were all experienced spacers who knew how to avoid falling to their deaths.

Below the transitway was a circular space door with the words *Cieli Sereni Nove Aviorimessa B* painted across it. 'Hanger B' was crammed with tugs, space cranes and thrusterbots, wedged between equipment looted from hundreds of ships. Among the spare parts were gleaming containers shipped from the Core Systems by the Consortium, who'd dumped so much materiel on the Drakes that they were struggling to store it all.

Cheers and catcalls sounded as Gwandoya came in, waved to the crowd, and clambered onto a raised platform overlooking the space door thirty meters below. He tapped a control panel and an eight-wheeled cranebot at the edge of the transitway sent its boom arm telescoping out into the air above the hangar door.

Several of the captains from Gwandoya's screen conference stood watching. Their somber expressions indicated my warning had not fallen on deaf ears, but this was his playground and they were merely spectators.

Iago Suarez and Anya came toward me as I rubbed feeling into my arms. He was flamboyantly overdressed in a velvet short cape and dark blue silks while she was assertively sensual in skin tight burgundy leathers, high boots and a razorgun slung low on her hip.

They looked me over, saw I was shivering violently, then Suarez scowled at Gwandoya. "You left him in too long."

"Bet low," Gwandoya yelled back, triggering laughter from the audience.

Anya took my face in her hands and made a show of studying my eyes as if examining my fitness and whispered, "He's coming. Stay alive." She stood and turned to Gwandoya, "He needs time to warm up."

"He's warm enough! Warmer than he'll be out there," Gwandoya yelled to the audience, pointing down at the space door with a grin, triggering hoots of laughter.

Someone hurled a half empty drink pouch at me. It hit the deck and ruptured, splashing green liquid over me and triggering more laughter, as if they hadn't already seen that trick a hundred times.

"None of that once he's walking, or all bets are off," Gwandoya bellowed, giving them a knowing look.

He nodded as they realized it was an invitation, then a hailstorm of drink pouches pelted the deck around me. Fortunately, their aim was as bad as their looks and most missed. When the storm petered out, No-Nose forced me up a ladder onto the cranebot carriage. Its boom was just wide enough to walk on and long enough to reach all the way to the center of the transitway. One of the Neanderthals threw a shock rod up to No-Nose who drove its sparking end into my shoulder. I convulsed and doubled over, but he stopped before I fell off.

"Move!" he ordered.

I stepped cautiously onto the boom, cradling my shoulder. No-Nose came after me, using the shock rod to drive me out over the space door. He stopped, motioning for me to keep going while Gwandoya tapped the control panel again and an alarm sounded. Yellow warning lights flashed either side of the space door as it split in half and slid apart. A pressure field sealed in the atmosphere, and beyond it, an ice tunnel flanked by four lines of small white lights reached down through the ice-roid into misty darkness.

"You've got to be kidding," I muttered, staring down at the open space door. It was a sick parody of what the Brotherhood's sail-powered ancestors had done three thousand years ago. If I fell, it would be a race as to what killed me first, extreme interstellar cold or vacuum.

"Get the Inalin," Gwandoya ordered.

Two Drakes dragged a filthy spacer in tattered clothes from a cramped storage container that doubled as his prison cell. His nose was broken and blood smeared his rags, but he was big and still had some fight left in him.

"Open the books," Gwandoya yelled, then multi-armed bookiebots began moving through the crowd, taking bets and scanning credit keys.

"What are the odds?" someone called from the third level up.

"Even money on him," Gwandoya replied, pointing at me. A confused murmur rose from the audience as they looked me over, compared me to the hulking Inalin, and wondered why my odds were so bad, then he indicated the Inalin. "Cap'n Reaves you know, from Inalis Four. Winner of the plank stakes, seven times!"

Many in the audience cheered their champion while others hesitated, wary of the odds, fearing no one's luck lasted forever. The big spacer looked tired and I was fresh meat, by no means outmatched.

Gwandoya motioned to me with an open palm. "His name is Kade...He gave me this." He slid his other hand over his melted-face as if he was stroking silk.

The laughter, the chatter, the cheers vanished in an instant. In utter silence, they fixed their eyes upon me, realizing they weren't here for sport.

"I told you I'd get him one day," Gwandoya boasted. "Today is that day." He turned to the battered spacer. "Win this one, Reaves, and you win your freedom to join us!"

The crowd cheered as Reaves lifted his head as it dawned on him what Gwandoya was offering. His shoulders straightened as he sized me up, no longer fighting just to stay alive, but for his freedom, for a way out of the nightmare.

"Would you like that, Reaves? To be one of us?"

The Inalin nodded with growing eagerness, then Gwandoya faced the audience, arms wide. "Reaves, seven times champion…ten to one odds…and I'll cover all bets on the Inalin. My gift to you!"

Cheers erupted from the audience as they realized Gwandoya was letting them increase their money tenfold, to celebrate his revenge and my untimely death. Hangar B exploded in shouts as they rushed to bet against me, to back the sure thing, certain this fight was going to end only one way.

"A thousand on the Inalin."

"Ten thousand on Reaves."

"Five hundred against Kade."

The bookiebots were swamped with frenzied betting. When the fervor waned, Gwandoya sounded a claxon, closing the books, and turned to the big Inalin.

"Lash or blade, Reaves?" Gwandoya shouted.

"Lash," the spacer replied hoarsely.

A Drake handed him a black whip with three metallic rings at the end. He held it in one hand like he knew how to use it, switched it on and stepped toward me. The three rings sparked against the crane's carriage as he dragged them along its side, careful not to let them touch his boots.

"Don't I get a weapon?" I asked.

"He wants a weapon!" Gwandoya yelled to the audience, who laughed at the absurdity of my request, then he turned to the Inalin. "Kill him Reaves, and you can have his ship, and his woman."

The Inalin spacer squared his shoulders, fixed his eyes upon me and came out along the boom arm with one thing on his mind. I backed away, edging further out into the center of the transitway, glancing at the pressure field and frozen ice tunnel below.

"Sorry about this," Reaves growled, not sorry at all, and swept the lash at my chest.

I jumped back to the end of the boom as the whip cut the air in front of me and hot needles arced into my chest. I doubled over in pain as Reaves threw the whip to his other hand, letting the end slap against the opposite side of the boom. He pulled his hand back to strike again, then as he swung, I dived forward, rolled under the whip and kicked out his legs. He toppled over, grabbed one of my boots as he slid off the side and dragged me with him.

I caught the boom with one hand and we dangled above the open space door. Reaves flicked the whip at the boom, wrapping it around twice, then let go of my foot and pulled himself up. I kicked him in the head and the ribs, but he shrugged off the hits, grabbed my jacket and dragged my face toward the charge rings. My skin prickled, then I slammed my hand into his elbow, breaking the joint and driving his forearm onto the sizzling rings.

His body convulsed and he fell, screaming. His cry was cut off as he plunged through the pressure field into space. His body inflated in the vacuum and his skin cells burst as he turned to ice and spun into the tunnel wall. The top half of his body shattered into pieces, then his remains drifted away into the white fog, legs and all.

A shocked silence settled over the hangar as I pulled myself onto the boom, switched off the whip and dropped it into the ice tunnel below. An angry growl sounded from the audience as they realized they'd lost their money, believing they'd been tricked.

"Round one to Kade," Gwandoya declared. "All bets against Kade stand for round two."

Surprise rippled through the audience as they realized Gwandoya was paying the winning bets and rolling the rest, ensuring no one lost money. I glanced at Anya, who shrugged, unaware of what he had in mind. Captain Suarez saw we knew each other, gave Anya a suspicious look, but said nothing.

Gwandoya nodded to No-Nose who climbed down from the crane and opened a storage hatch in the deck. His gang surrounded the open hatch, warily aiming their weapons down into the storage compartment.

"Come out," he ordered. When no one appeared, he charged his weapon. "I won't tell you again."

He and his Neanderthals backed away as a short, hulking Syrman climbed out of the compartment, glaring at his captors. He was bare chested, rippling with muscle, shoulders double mine, with dark brown skin and small dark eyes. No-Nose motioned him to the crane as the audience buzzed with anticipation, then he thrust the shock rod into Syrman's back, forcing him up the ladder. At the top of the crane, he looked me over without animosity.

"Kill him," Gwandoya said, "and you'll be on the first Meropan transport out of here. Fail and you die in his place."

The Syrman glanced down at the guns pointed at him, and reluctantly started toward me. He was a head shorter than me, much stronger and slower, but I had no room to move, negating my speed advantage.

"Don't do it," I said as he neared the end of the boom.

"I don't have a choice."

He reached for me, then I leapt at him with ultra-reflexed speed and kicked him in the face. It was like driving my boot into a hull plate. He shrugged off the blow, snatched my ankle out of the air and swung me upside down, away from the boom. I squirmed and twisted above the open space door, but his grip was unbreakable.

"Stop!" A familiar voice rang out across the hangar.

The Syrman hesitated as a man in an armored pressure suit pushed through the crowd, followed by a squad of brutes carrying heavy weapons. The buccaneer's head was covered by a black metal skull plate that extended down over the top half of his face, hiding his burned out eye sockets. A large optronic eye was mounted at the center of his forehead, and other smaller sensors were discreetly placed around the skull plate. The audience stirred as they recognized him and those between him and Gwandoya moved back, fearing being caught in a crossfire.

"You can put me down now," I said, but the Syrman ignored me.

"This doesn't concern you Rix," Gwandoya said with irritation.

"He's mine, not yours," my brother shouted as his men fanned out, not aiming at anyone in particular, but watched anxiously by No-Nose and his gang.

"He did this to me!" Gwandoya roared angrily, pointing at his melted face. "I have right of vengeance."

"Not by our code."

"Code? He's not one of us."

"He is, by right of kinship."

Gwandoya scowled. "He's no kin of ours."

Rix clambered onto the crane, held up a DNA scanner for the crowd to see and scanned his hand. "Now him," he said and passed the device to No-Nose.

No-Nose gave Rix a puzzled looked and motioned for the Syrman to bring me in.

"Get me out of here," the Syrman whispered and lowered me onto the boom.

Not sure I could even get myself out, I promised him nothing and edged along the boom. When I reached the carriage, I held out my hand for No-Nose to scan. His eyes bulged with surprise when he saw the reading.

"They're brothers!" he declared.

"What!" Gwandoya exploded. A collective gasp rippled around the hangar as, seething with rage, he turned on Rix. "You knew! All this time! And you never told me."

"He's kin," my brother replied defiantly.

Gwandoya's face contorted with rage and his hand went to the gun on his hip. Before he could draw, Rix's men raised their weapons, filling the hangar with the whine of charging accelerators. No-Nose gave Gwandoya a worried look, warning they were outgunned, then Anya sprang on to the control platform behind Gwandoya and pressed her gun into the base of his skull.

"Right of kinship," she whispered.

"You attacked him first, and lost," Rix said, adding loudly. "You should be used to that by now, losing to me and mine."

It triggered pockets of laughter from the crowd, to Gwandoya's annoyance.

Captain Suarez stepped forward and declared, "His brother is protected by kinship." He turned to Gwandoya. "When you attack a brother or his kin, it's on you, not us." He let that sink in before bellowing harshly, "Weapons down! Now!"

No one moved, then three decks up, a man yelled, "Blood kin!"

"He's a brother of the Brotherhood," a woman yelled, and a dozen more chimed in, forcing Gwandoya to concede.

"This is not over, Rix," he said through gritted teeth and nodded to his men, who lowered their weapons.

I motioned to my gun belt slung over No-Nose's shoulder. "I'll have that back now."

He scowled and slapped the holster into my hand. With a wry grin, I buckled it on and followed my brother down the ladder to the deck.

"You took your time getting here," I whispered.

"You shouldn't have come," my brother snapped.

"Had to. Earth has fallen to the Spawn."

"Not my problem," he growled and led me out of the hangar, leaving Gwandoya standing alone on the control platform simmering with rage.

* * * *

We boarded an orbital lifter covered in an ad hoc patchwork of armored plates parked at a topside docking pad. My brother took the controls while his men strapped in around me, then we flew out through the pirate fleet docked at the anchoring towers. I cupped my eyes to a small window, recording it all in my bionetic memory, glimpsing the *Silver Lining* as she faded into the mist.

We flew away from the starliner, passed a couple of damaged Separatist cruisers hove to in space waiting to dock, and a long haul super freighter with her cargo doors open for unloading. The Consortium supply ship was clean and modern, too big to clamp up to a tower, and undoubtedly out from the Core Systems delivering Sep contraband to the Drakes.

Ice Town disappeared into the mist behind us, then we passed several space tugs and cargo shuttles with their running lights on, creeping through dark, icy space. The work boats thinned as we slid past remote prefab outposts on drifting icebergs that emerged like tiny islands of light out of the frozen, eternal night. The more successful Drake captains had larger bases and bigger ships, but such displays of wealth could not conceal the truth: they were all hunted rats hiding in a frozen hell hole.

After a while, an irregular shaped glacier loomed out of the fog. Landing lights revealed seven interconnected prefabs partly buried in ice, two docking pads and an anchoring tower holding an ugly brute of a ship, cylindrical in shape, docked side on. The *Cyclops* was a monitor, ablatively armored with a battleship-sized bow cannon, a ring of polarity guns for close-in defense and room enough for a sizable complement of cutthroats and booty. Not far from the prefab cluster was a white bunker with its blast doors closed, concealing the weapon inside.

Considering my brother's obvious fortune, there'd be other bunkers, enough to make his little hideaway more a fortress than a palace.

The lifter docked at the smaller pad beside the anchoring tower, then my brother and Anya led me through a p-tube to the elevator. I opened my mouth to speak as we rode up to the *Cyclops*, but Rix shook his head.

"Not here," he snapped, fearing his own elevator was bugged.

We cycled through a large airlock, then hurried past disciplined crew and across clean decks to his great cabin. It was lavishly decorated with deep padded chairs, synthmarble statues, colorful silks and heavy drapes that had no place on a fighting ship. DNA-locked chests with booby trapped detonators lined one bulkhead and a weapons rack with an assortment of mostly area effect weapons stood against another. A Romanesque column in one corner mounted a gelsphere containing a particularly gruesome severed head of a bearded man with face tattoos.

"A friend of yours?" I asked.

"The previous captain," Rix explained, pointing at his optronic eye. "He took my eye. I took his head and his ship."

"A fair trade. Now you keep it around to remind people what happens when they cross you?"

"You'd be surprised how effective it is." He dropped into a red velvet chair and rested his boots on a low table while Anya retrieved a bottle from behind a carved simwood panel.

"Drink?" she asked.

I waved her off. "No thanks."

She poured two amber colored refreshments for herself and Rix. He took a swig, then drilled me with a stare colder than the ice-roid outside. "Do you have any idea how much trouble you've caused me?"

"I can guess."

"Gwandoya won't let this go. He's boasted about killing you for two years. Now that he knows we're kin, he'll make it a blood feud."

"I thought he couldn't touch me. Brotherhood Rules."

"He can't challenge you in port, this is neutral territory, but he can pay someone to stab you through the heart in the middle of the night."

"Or bribe a crewman to sabotage our ship," Anya added.

"I thought your crew were loyal."

"Drakes are loyal to one thing," Rix said, "what they can spend."

I looked around his great cabin appreciatively. "You do well enough."

"Many a rich captain has died in his sleep to a loyal hand," Anya said.

"That's why this never sleeps," he said, tapping his sensor laden skull plate. "So why are you here, little brother? I know you didn't come to join us."

"No. I want you to join me. You and the Brotherhood. Maybe not Gwandoya. You'll have to kill him."

He gave me a sour look. "You came a long way for nothing."

"The Spawn are on Earth. It's only a matter of time before they come for you."

He shrugged. "We're nothing to them."

"You're human. In their eyes, that makes you Tau Cetin allies."

He exchanged uncomfortable looks with Anya, then she said, "Hear him out."

He sipped his drink, clearly annoyed. "When did they attack Earth?"

"A few months ago, and a lot of other worlds as well."

"Months?" he said doubtfully. "How'd you get out here so fast?"

"I had help."

He nodded, guessing whose help. "Who do you speak for?"

"Earth Council. The navy. Everyone on the right side of the law who wants you dead."

"Hmph...What do they want from me now?"

"Your ships, your bases, and an end to the civil war."

He grimaced. "The Brothers will never agree."

"They might, if they understand the alternative."

"Prison?"

"Extinction. The Spawn ruling Orion. Matarons killing every human they can get their hands on." I paused, letting my words sink in.

"We've survived a long time."

"Against humans. If the Spawn win, there'll be no Access Treaty. No rules. Nothing to protect you from alien interference."

He grunted. "If your Access Treaty was worth a damn, how'd you find us?"

"The Tau Cetins. They remapped this nebula, without you even knowing."

"So, Tau Cetins are no better than the Spawn."

"They could have destroyed you, but they didn't. The Spawn will. You'll have nowhere to hide."

He knew it wasn't cunning that had kept the Brotherhood hidden from Earth Navy all these years. It was the immense void of space, and millions of years of galactic law which made him and his kind a human internal problem. No one else's.

"The Tau Cetins are giving you a chance," I said.

"To help you."

"For us to help each other. They're showing you how easily the Spawn can take all of this."

"And if we don't agree, your fleet comes in and wipes us out."

"Something like that." It was a bluff. Earth Navy couldn't spare the ships to come all the way out to this rat's nest. Nor would they risk a fleet engagement with pirates while the Spawn controlled the Solar System's shipyards. But it played on his fears and I was desperate.

Rix pursed his lips, weighing his options. "Why do the Tau Cetins care what we do? We can no more fight the Spawn than Earth Navy can."

"They believe in the Access Treaty, in the right of the weak to be free, and they know if we remain divided, mankind is finished."

"If the brothers refuse, I won't be able to protect you. Any of us."

"Make sure they don't refuse."

Rix weighed the odds of the galaxy sinking into a dark age the like of which it hadn't seen in many millions of years. He gave Anya a questioning look, confirming she was much more than his pilot-navigator, and judging by her assurance in his private quarters, these were as much her quarters as his.

"Everyone has family somewhere, some on Earth," she said.

"Hmm." He drained his glass in one gulp. "Who's in port?"

She walked to a screen on the big table, summoned port control and read out the names of their allies. "El Viraz, Short, the Onuka brothers and Hu Lai's squadron are all here, but not Kaminsky or Vergolt. Thirty one captains in all."

"Only seven we can count on," Rix said apprehensively.

"Gwandoya has at least ten from his faction," she added, "and the two Sep cruisers have a couple of hundred militia."

"Do Sep cruiser captains get to vote?" I asked, assuming she was referring to the two damaged cruisers we'd passed on the way out from the spaceport.

"No," Rix replied, "but their militias are well armed."

"What about the two battlecruisers with the Meropan cannons?" I asked.

Rix gave me an irritated look, but made no attempt to deny Seps were getting alien weapons. "They've got skeleton crews, mostly engineers and techs. The rest are in training, won't arrive for weeks yet."

"If the vote goes our way," Anya said, "they'll take exception."

"Yeah," Rix agreed, "and those Meropan cannons will be live today."

"So what are we waiting for?"

"I'll call a Captain's conference under an oath of secrecy," Rix said. "The Sep commanders won't know what's happening."

"Unless Gwandoya tells them," Anya said.

"He won't know what it's about until Sirius makes his offer." He turned to me. "You are making an offer?"

"Yeah, a good one."

"I hope they like what they hear, little brother, cause if they don't, we'll be branded renegades and they'll slit all our throats."

"They'll go for it," I assured him. "They have to."

"Don't count on it," Anya muttered and poured another round of drinks, this time doubles.

* * * *

"Rix has called for a meeting with the other captains," I said, leaning close to the great cabin's communicator. "He's going to ask them to accept us into the Brotherhood."

Jase and Marie were on the *Silver Lining's* bridge with Izin. Our comm channel was open and unencrypted, leaving them in no doubt, I was speaking for the benefit of those eavesdropping on our conversation.

"Now that Earth has fallen, there'll be a lot of ships like ours looking for safe havens," I added. "We've got good weapons and, from what Rix tells me, better sensors than any of them."

"I hope they see it that way," Marie said slowly.

"Gwandoya's here," I warned, letting them know who was listening in. "He'll be against us. He may even try to take the ship."

"No one's tried boarding us," Jase said, "but we've got two drone launchers and a can opener locked on us. And that sensor barge is still floating off our stern, scanning our weapons and engines."

"We could undock and come alongside the Cyclops," Izin suggested.

"No, Rix doesn't want you giving them an excuse to open fire."

"Very well, Captain," Izin said. "I have completed the repairs we discussed before you left."

Repairs? We'd never discuss any repairs. "Good," I said with a blank face.

"I'd like to conduct a low energy power-up sequence. There will be no emissions from the engines, but they may detect a small increase in e-plant neutrinos. Do you think it is safe to conduct the test?"

After the Tau Cetin overhaul, every system was performing above spec, including our engines and e-plant. Izin was saying he could power up and have us ready to get underway, while this double talk about a test was a cover story in case Gwandoya got lucky and detected a tiny neutrino spike.

"It should be OK," I said casually. "I doubt they'll shoot you for a power test. Just keep the weapons off line."

"Of course, Captain. I'll begin the acceptance test shortly."

"The conference starts in a few hours. I'll be in touch– or not–depending how it goes."

"Good luck," Marie said then their images vanished from the screen.

* * * *

The *Cieli Sereni Nove's* grand ballroom resembled an Italian Renaissance era palace looted by barbarians and smelled like a decaying stim house. It was decorated with fractured chandeliers, stained and worn carpets, vandalized statues and gray and lifeless holographic walls that had been shot to pieces decades ago.

A raised dais for botbands and human orchestras occupied the far end of the room, and on the dance floor was the holo-projector I'd requested. Standing around the projector was a colorful collection of abundantly armed Drake captains and their first officers, whispering conspiratorially to each other.

When we entered the ballroom, they fell silent, and studied me with curiosity and suspicion. Gwandoya was there, flanked by a group of captains infamous enough to be on my bionetic wanted list, although the neutral captains were of equally ill repute.

Rix nodded to them all as we entered, allies and enemies alike. He'd sent encrypted messages to his faction leaders, warning them the meeting was not what it seemed, but hadn't risked disclosing details. Gwandoya and his supporters stuck together on one side of the room forming, according to my brother, an alliance of convenience, not conviction. The neutrals, by contrast, were careful not to place themselves between members of either faction in case the shooting started prematurely.

"This is my brother, Sirius Kade," Rix declared. "He has news that affects us all, and he has an offer to make. Captain's Rules apply, so keep your weapons holstered and your feuds to yourselves." He turned to me and whispered, "Make it good, little brother."

I stepped forward, greeted by the coldest collection of eyes I'd ever seen. "You've all heard the Ornithians defeated the Spawn at Tau Ceti. That is only partially true. They repelled an attack on their homeworld, Serris-Orn, but failed to drive the Spawn out of Orion. Since then, the situation has deteriorated."

I slid a data rod into the holoprojector's reader and said, "Lights off."

The grand ballroom darkened and a large sphere of stars several thousand light years across and dotted with orange and red lights appeared above the holoprojector. The Drake captains and their lieutenants were all experienced navigators and instantly recognized the full extent of Mapped Space and the locations of many human and alien worlds.

Seeing I now had their full attention, I plunged right in, bad news first. "Since the Battle of Serris-Orn, the Spawn have occupied many worlds in the Orion Arm friendly to the Tau Cetins, worlds incapable of defending themselves. The red markers show planets now ruled by the Spawn. The orange are those still resisting." I pointed at the large orange marker at the center. "As you can see, the people of Earth are still fighting."

The information was met with stony silence. Some captains stepped closer, reading the astrographic projection with expert eyes, picking out star systems of particular interest to them. Others seemed not to care, or hid their feelings for fear of showing weakness.

"The Spawn can't defeat the Tau Cetin fleet head on," I continued, "so they're attacking less technologically advanced worlds, trying to force the Tau Cetins to divide their forces. Once the Spawn land, they occupy the major cities, knowing the Tau Cetins won't bombard them from orbit."

"Earth's over six months away," Captain de la Cruz of the *Saker* said. "How could you possibly know all this?"

"I was on Earth when they landed. I escaped, and the Tau Cetins brought my ship out here. They told me how to find you." I glanced at my brother. "How to find him."

"Why would they help you?" Captain Bannarasee, one of Gwandoya's faction demanded.

"Ask them, next time you see them," I said, certain he never would. "What I can tell you is the Tau Cetins have given Earth Navy the locations of all your bases."

Concerned murmurs rippled around the room, then Captain El Viraz said, "The Tau Cetins do not involve themselves in our affairs."

"They do now, because billions of people on Earth are fighting for their lives."

"He's lying," Gwandoya declared. "If Earth Navy could find us, they'd be here now."

"I found you," I snapped. "I was sent here because I'm his brother." I pointed at Rix. "And because Earth Navy needs every fighting ship, every base it can get, including yours."

Captain Gale of the *Tejat* asked incredulously, "Why would they want us to join them?"

"Because Earth has fallen to the Spawn." Shocked expressions appeared on many faces, while those who'd heard the news already remained silent, not sure if it was true. "How long do you think you'll last out here with the Spawn in charge? The Access Treaty means nothing to them. You mean nothing to them. It's not Earth Navy or the Tau Cetins you should fear. It's the Spawn. If they win, they'll exterminate you all like rats."

Troubled expressions appeared on the faces of some as they realized civilization as they knew it was falling, and if it could not be saved, what was coming would be far worse than anything they'd ever known.

Sadyk Baibek, one of Hu Lai's captains, pointed at a red dot on the edge of the Core Systems. "That's Jali Naryn, isn't it?"

I checked the detailed astrographics in my bionetic memory and nodded. "Yes, it is."

"I have kin there."

Captain Tasnim, a slightly built, swarthy skinned woman studied a red dot on the far side of the sphere of stars. "They're in the Gokhale Drift?"

I checked the details again. "Yes. They took Kidarabad."

"My mother and two sisters are on Sindhala," she said softly, "not far from Kidarabad."

The captains and their first officers moved closer, seeking out worlds they knew and the fate of families they'd left behind.

"They took Rigos," the portly Captain Stojanovic of the *Korcula* said sadly. "They have good whores on Rigos."

"They haven't taken Meraya," a female first officer said with relief.

"This map is weeks old," I warned. I adjusted the perspective, expanding it to include hundreds of millions of star systems sprinkled with orange and red dots. "This is the situation for the entire Orion Arm, not just our Mapped Space. Or it was."

"It's a trick," Gwandoya sneered. "The Spawn could never attack so many worlds. It's absurd."

"It's no trick," I said. "They drop forces from orbit, overwhelm the defenders with vastly superior technology, and dig in. They destroyed Earth's regular armies in a matter of days."

"You said they were still fighting on Earth," Adeke, the younger Onuka brother declared suspiciously.

I nodded. "The people are fighting, with whatever weapons they can find. It's a guerilla war."

"You can't fight the Spawn with shock sticks and stun guns!" Gwandoya spat.

"It's what me and my boys would do, if that's all we had," Captain Mhamo Leach said belligerently.

The other captains gave her thoughtful looks. Many nodded in silent agreement. They were criminals, cutthroats and murderers all, but they were fighters too, every one of them.

I touched the holo controls again, zooming out further, revealing great spiral bands of light sprinkled with red and orange dots spanning a quarter of the galaxy. The projection now reached all the way to a cluster of red lights at the edge of the galaxy where the Spawn were strongest.

"That's their bridgehead, in the Cygnus Rim," I explained. "Their homeworld is in a cluster far beyond that."

"The Cygnus Rim!" Captain Qureshi, one of Gwandoya's loyalists exploded. "Why should we care what happens out there?"

"You may not care what happens in the Cygnus Rim," I said, "but the Spawn are here, now, and every person you ever cared about, every world, is within their reach."

"All I care about is me and my Drake brothers," Gwandoya declared, "not your war, or your Spawn, or your colored lights."

I turned angrily toward Gwandoya, raising my hand toward the great swirl of stars floating above the holoprojector. "Those lights are worlds fighting for their survival, warrior worlds that are deciding the future of our galaxy. If they fall, we all fall."

The Drake captains stared at the galaxy's great outer spirals, at billions of stars floating above their heads, so close they could almost touch them. The red and orange dots marked thousands of alien worlds no human had ever seen or even heard of, civilizations completely unknown to us, neighbors on a cosmic scale, all walking the same path, all sharing our common fate, suffering as we now suffered.

"Even if this is true," Danjuma, the older Onuka brother said, "what can we do? We cannot fight the Spawn."

"If we continue as we are, at war with ourselves, humanity divided, we won't survive," I said. "None of us will. Whatever hope we have, our chances are better united."

"What do you want from us?" Captain Short of the *Payara* asked. Rix had arranged for him to ask the question, to show an interest that might be contagious.

"Our Navy is largely intact, but Earth is in the hands of the Spawn, and the major Core System worlds still loyal could be invaded at any time," I replied. "What we want is access to your bases and for you to terminate your deal with the Separatists. That is our best hope of ending the civil war."

Gwandoya laughed. "And then they'll kill us all!"

"No." I turned to the Drake commanders, staring them down. "Any Captain, any crewman, who joins the Resistance, any base that supports Earth Navy, will receive a full pardon."

"Or we could make a deal with the Spawn," Captain Hakan of the *Ismir* said, "and be on the winning side."

"Do you really believe the Spawn will ally with you? And even if they did, how long would such an alliance last? How long before the Matarons attacked? The Tau Cetins won't exterminate you, but the Spawn will."

"He thinks we are fools," Gwandoya said, sensing the neutral captains were wavering. "He wants to buy us with hollow promises, but they will betray us as quickly as the Spawn."

"You have made fortunes beyond most people's dreams," I said, "yet…you live in filthy, frozen hovels in a remote corner of space. You are hunted everywhere you go. And one day, soon, you'll die a lonely death far from anyone you ever cared for or who cared for you, and no one will even know you're gone. Or…you can keep your riches and your freedom, live where you want, live in peace, if you join us."

"They would let us keep what we have?" Captain Iago Saurez asked.

"Yes, but it's a onetime offer. Amnesties now, or a full reckoning later."

"Next he'll be offering us commissions in their navy," Gwandoya declared with contempt.

"Not commissions," I said. "Full merc rates for any ship that fights alongside ours."

The Drakes hid their thoughts behind faces lit by the soft glow of holographic stars. Some whispered to each other, others exchanged secretive looks or gazed up at the galaxy deep in thought.

"We don't speak for the Brotherhood, just the Drakes," Rix said. "It will take time for your offer to reach all our chapters."

"The Tau Cetins will transport your couriers as far as the Core Systems," I said.

Captain Hu Lai's eyes bulged in surprise. "The Tau Cetins will take *us*?"

"If you accept our offer."

"What if individual captains accept, but not enough for this base?" Mahmo Leach asked.

"Captains and crew who join us will receive full amnesty."

Mhamo Leach looked wistful. "I got grandchildren on Denedus I ain't ever seen." She looked around at the other captains, her mind made up. "I say Captain's Privilege. The base goes with the majority. Them that wants to leave are free to set their own course."

"No!" Gwandoya snapped. "We stick together. We fight as one, like always!"

"This ain't like always," Captain Bannarasee said, signaling he was shifting away from Gwandoya's faction. "Captain's Privilege."

Gwandoya's eyes bulged with anger at the betrayal, then one by one, the other captains nodded, calling out:

"I agree."

"Free choice."

"I say no. Chapter rules."

"Not for this. Captain's choice."

Once they'd all had their say, the decision was clear.

"A privilege vote it is," Rix said while Gwandoya simmered with rage. He replaced my galactic hologram with two columns headed, Yea and Nay. He put his palm flat on the system's DNA reader, confirming his identify, and cast the first vote. "Yea."

His name appeared in the affirmative column, then one by one, the other captains placed their hands and picked their side. When it was almost over, twenty three names appeared for Yea, including several of Gwandoya's own faction. All eyes turned to the tall East African whose voice no longer mattered. His eyes bulged angrily and he stormed out without voting, followed by six naysayers, making no attempt to hide his murderous intent.

"Uh-ho," Anya whispered, exchanging a worried look with Rix.

The last few cast their votes, then Rix said, "By Privilege vote , the Chapter of Drakes accepts the offer. Our fleet and bases now side with Earth Navy. All ports are closed to Separatist ships. Any captain who disagrees has twenty four hours to clear port." The Captains nodded their agreement. "By refusing to vote, Gwandoya has broken the oath and is no longer Governor. Is there a Yea who will stand in his place?"

Most captains declined, unwilling to surrender command of their ships to run the base, then Hu Lai, the oldest of the captains with shoulder length gray hair and a long stringy beard, stepped forward.

"I'll do it." He glanced at the young man beside him. "My son's ready to take command of the Suiren."

Rix put his hand on the old buccaneer's shoulder. "Who's for Hu Lai? No better man ever helmed a ship."

A chorus of ayes rang out. Even the naysayers accepted the decision.

"Opposed?" Rix asked, finding none. "I declare Hu Lai Governor of Ice Town, Chapter Guardian and Keeper of the Oath, by Captain's vote."

The buccaneers gathered around Hu Lai, patting him on the back, celebrating his elevation while my brother stepped back into the darkness.

"That went better than I expected," I whispered to Anya.

"No it didn't," she said softly, "All our ships are in danger. Gwandoya has the firing codes."

Hu Lai turned to the assembled captains. "By breaking the Oath, Gwandoya has declared himself a mutineer. Summon half your crews to town and have your ships deploy for battle."

Rix motioned for me and Anya to follow and peered outside, one hand on his gun. Finding the corridor clear, he led us through the old starliner, past crowds yet to hear they had a new governor and a bloody fight on their hands.

"Where are we going?" I asked as I hurried to keep up with him.

"I'm putting you on your ship," he said, and spoke into a communicator. "Ikaz? You there?"

"I'm listening."

"Tell Arroyo to take the Cyclops into the blind spot with the day watch, and bring both boarding parties to the ballroom. Full weapons. Use the dropships and watch out for target locks. Gwandoya's turned."

"Aye, Captain. Don't kill them all before we get there."

Rix pocketed the communicator as we reached the long ramp down from the starliner. He drew his gun and we ran down the exposed metal ramp toward the prefabs. Halfway down, Rix turned sharply and seemed to fire blindly into a window overlooking the square. An explosion inside lit up three men with a launcher, incinerating two and hurling one through the window. The man hit the deck with his clothes on fire, didn't move as he burned, but my brother shot him anyway just to be sure.

He saw my confusion and pointed at his optronic eye. "Like eyes in the back of my head."

"Right," I said, understanding his skull plate sensors had spotted the assassins before they'd had a chance to shoot.

"There's Blacktooth," Anya said, and fired across the square at a man as he ducked into an alley.

"He's one of Gwandoya's men," Rix said. "He'll report our position."

We ran to the bottom of the ramp and into the prefabs, then two men carrying assault weapons emerged from a corridor junction ahead of us. Rix and Anya cut them both down before they could get a shot away, then we stepped over their bodies and ran to the anchoring tower where the *Silver Lining* was locked up.

"I can help," I said as the elevator door slid open.

"Our crews don't know you," Rix said. "They'll shoot you on sight." He eased me into the elevator. "Get out of here before those Sep battlecruisers figure out who you are."

"Send your couriers to Uralo IV."

"The naval station?"

I nodded. "The Tau Cetins will help them reach your other Chapters." I handed him the data rod. "Give them this. It's got the star charts on it."

"Trust you to get mixed up with Tau Cetins," he said, pocketing the device.

"I wanted you to meet someone," I said, glancing up through the transparent ceiling at the dark mass of the *Silver Lining* floating in the icy mist above. "She's up there."

"She?" he said surprised.

Anya, who was covering the corridor, stepped toward me with an interested smile. "Must be serious."

"I was going to invite you to the wedding." I smiled at Anya. "Both of you."

"We'll be there," she promised. "What's her name?"

"Marie. Marie Dulon."

"I look forward to meeting her."

My brother extended his hand. "Good luck, little brother."

"You too," I said as we shook hands. "When it's over, let the Syrman go."

"The Syrman?" Rix said surprised.

"He could have dropped me in the hangar. He didn't."

Rix nodded. "I'll send him to Uralo IV. He can find his way home from there."

"His home is occupied by the Spawn."

"Hmph," Rix grunted and stepped back as the door slid shut, then the elevator started up through the anchoring tower.

Once it cleared the prefabs, the starliner became visible, lit by landing lights and frosted windows. Small transports and gunships were racing between the anchoring towers and skimming Ice Town at high speed, heading for the starliner's topside docking pads. When they landed, heavily armed spacers in armored p-suits poured out and stormed the airlocks. Similarly dressed men holding the airlocks shot at them, then circling gunships raked the airlock defenders, clearing the way for the boarding parties. Autoturrets popped from their bunkers along the starliner's hull and fired at the gunships, turning the *Cieli Sereni Nove's* topside into a chaotic vacuum battlefield where I soon couldn't tell who was who.

I'd come to make peace with the Drakes, to bring an end to the civil war, but all I'd done was set them against each other. More humans killing humans. Even though it was Drake on Drake, it was the last thing I wanted. By the time it was over, another human faction might well have destroyed itself, along with the base and its valuable shipyard.

The elevator lost gravity and shuddered to a halt, then I pulled myself through the pressure tube to the ship, hoping it wasn't punctured by a stray shot, wondering if I'd cost my brother his life, for nothing.

* * * *

Jase and Marie were on the bridge watching the unfolding fight on the big screen.

"I take it I'm not meeting your brother," Marie said as I slid onto my couch.

"Not this time, but I told him about you."

"Oh?" She looked intrigued. "What did you say?"

"That you're a lot of trouble," I replied, glancing at the bridge screen. Bodies in punctured p-suits were drifting away from the *Cieli Sereni Nove's* topside docking pads as a low flying gunship was caught in a crossfire from multiple turrets and exploded.

"At least they're not shooting at us," Jase said.

My console indicated the *Silver Lining* had enough power to get underway, but not bubble. "Izin," I said to the intercom, "I'm going to need full power."

"Ready, Captain," he replied from engineering.

I turned to Jase. "Have the battlecruisers fired yet?"

"No, but one's waking up. The power levels on the other one haven't changed."

I activated the drones cradled in our two bow launchers, but kept the outer doors closed.

Marie saw what I was doing and gave me an uneasy look. "I thought we were running."

"We are. I'm just going to give them something to remember us by." I nodded to Jase. "Undock."

He ordered the clamps to release us, then shook his head. "The tower won't let us go."

"It's Gwandoya," I said, certain it was his doing. "We'll break the lock."

"Captain," Izin cut in. "The anchoring clamps will tear holes in our hull."

"No they won't," I assured him, and targeted the anchoring head with our cannons. They were kinetic and required no warm up. We'd shoot and scoot before anyone knew what we were doing. "Are they still ranging us?"

Jase shook his head. "No, the turrets are shooting at the transports and the launcher is tracking five ships behind a berg ten thousand clicks out."

"They think the tower's got us."

Jase winced. "One of the battlecruisers is area scanning. No target locks yet. The other's still asleep."

"They don't know who to kill." With Drake fighting Drake, all targets looked alike, but that wouldn't last. Gwandoya would see to that.

I mentally plotted a short run alongside the anchoring towers, a sharp turn away from Ice Town and a microbubble to safety. If Gwandoya was paying attention, his turrets would cut us to pieces before we got clear, but I was betting his hands were full right now.

Nisk chattering erupted in my mind, protesting my reckless plan, reminding me we had a long way to go and wanting me to jump straight out.

"Not now," I muttered irritably, trying to blank out the clicking.

Marie gave me a confused look. "What?"

I shook my head. "Nothing," I snapped and focused on my console.

"The five raiders are coming in, shields up, weapons hot," Jase announced, focusing an optical on them.

An image box appeared on the bridge screen showing five pirate ships firing beams and cannons at multiple targets. The leading raider launched a small drone that raced above Ice Town and struck one of the damaged Saracen cruisers hove to in space. An orange explosion erupted from its side, sending the cruiser rolling slowly away, venting atmosphere.

The turrets that had switched from us immediately unleashed a storm of pulse weapon fire upon the incoming ships. Their shields flashed with impacts, then the raiders hurled a concentrated barrage of heavy beams and autocannons at the armored turrets.

"Standby for full reverse thrust," I said and fired our two kinetic cannons.

The bridge screen flashed with blue light as our magnetically accelerated rail guns threw hundreds of rounds into the tower, shattering the anchoring head.

Spider clamps spun off our hull into the darkness, then I switched the k-cannons to their secondary target. They swiveled a hundred and eighty degrees and shredded the sensor barge parked off our stern. With our shackles broken, I fired the thrusters, backing away from the anchoring tower.

When we were clear, I turned the *Silver Lining* hard to port, fed power to the main engines and accelerated past a row of anchored ships. With their crews fighting in the base or guarding airlocks against boarders, they paid us no attention.

"One of the battlecruisers is pushing off its tower," Jase said. "No shield, thrusters only."

"Not bad for a cold start," I said with grudging admiration. Considering she was manned by only a few officers and a work crew, they were doing an incredible job getting her moving.

"Still nothing on the other one," Jase said, confirming the second battlecruiser was still asleep. The first now appeared on screen, drifting up from its tower. "She's got a massive heat bloom building topside."

"It's the Mero cannon," I said apprehensively.

The large triangular weapon rotated toward the incoming raiders, locked into position and fired a luminous green energy burst at the largest raider. It flashed above us, punched through the Drake ship's shield like it wasn't there and passed right through her from bow to stern. Its port side engine exploded, tearing off the stern quarter, explosively decompressing the entire ship. Glowing plasma streamed from both ends of the ship as the four other raiders turned sharply away, putting distance between themselves and the wreck.

Jase whistled, shocked. "At least they missed the e-plant."

"On purpose," I said. "They don't want to lose the shipyard."

The battlecruiser rose before us like a dark whale in

the night while her sister remained asleep at her fore and aft anchoring towers. I opened the outer doors on the bow, locked targets and released weapons. Two heavy naval drones immediately shot out into space on diverging tracks, then I rolled the *Silver Lining* hard away and poured on the power, aiming for our jump out point.

Jase split the bridge screen to fore and aft views. Ahead was darkening fog and astern, a pair of bright stars racing toward the two Sep capital ships, corkscrewing at high-gee to avoid point defense cannons, but neither battlecruiser fired. When they neared their targets, the drones launched their shield penetrators, even though neither ship had their shields up. The penetrator delivery vehicles dove into the battlecruiser's engine cones, punching through their weakest point, and detonated together. The stern of the waking battlecruiser tore off in a fiery explosion while her sleeping sister, with no energy coursing through her engines, shuddered as a jet of flame shot from her stern.

While the two new battlecruisers burned, boarding launches on the far side of Ice Town cut through the second Saracen's hull, spilling her atmosphere into space as men in fighting suits shot their way inside. Neither Saracen cruiser had fired a shot, taken completely by surprise by the sudden Drake feud. Life pods sporadically ejected from both cruisers and limped toward Ice Town, only to be destroyed by circling gunships before they could land.

The four remaining Drake raiders, seeing both battlecruisers were crippled, turned back toward the spaceport. They passed the two Saracens now dead in space, and fired at Gwandoya's defense turrets atop the *Cieli Sereni Nove's* superstructure, clearing the way for more troop transports.

The screen went blank as our masts retracted, then we bubbled for almost half a second. Safely outside the range of the Drake base's weapons, we took a final look at Ice

Town's blurry lights, now hued by the faint orange glow of superheated plasma from wrecked ships.

"At least we evened the odds," Marie said.

"Better than even," I said, hoping the loss of both battlecruisers would give my brother and his supporters the advantage. It would be a bloody, hand-to-hand fight in Ice Town's grimy prefabs, but the shipyard might yet survive, giving Earth Navy a much needed base, a safe haven the Separatists would sorely miss.

"Maybe I'll get to meet your brother, next time."

"Be careful what you wish for."

I thought of Uralo IV, of giving Lena the good news, then a whisper of coleopteran clicking reminded me I had somewhere else to go. I turned to Marie, wanting to tell her I was unfit to command, to ask her to take over, but the clicking grew louder, became stronger than it had ever been. It strangled my power to speak, insisting there was only one destination it would accept, and it wasn't Uralo IV.

* * * *

We emerged from the Zilarov Ice Nebula three days later, far from our original entry point.

"No sign of the Riku," Jase reported after a detailed sensor sweep.

"I am surprised they let us go so easily," Izin said, watching our exit from the Zilarov on the bridge.

I found the Uralo IV entry in the Tau Cetin astrographics module, but when I tried to select it, a thousand coleopteran thunder claps exploded in my mind, forcing me to robotically enter coordinates to a world no human had ever seen. I tried to stop, to transfer command to Marie, but the Nisk mind block forced me to continue. A map of unfamiliar stars appeared on the bridge screen, showing our destination, then the others gave me bewildered looks.

"Aren't we going to Uralo IV?" Marie asked.

I opened my mouth to speak, couldn't break through the crushing weight of the mind block, and shook my head, unable to function, incapable of answering.

She grabbed my shoulder. "Sirius? What's wrong?"

"Contact!" Jase said as a flashing indicator appeared on the screen. "It's Mataron."

They looked to me for an order, but I couldn't think clearly, let alone speak.

"Is it the Riku?" Marie asked when she realized I was incapacitated.

"No, it's too small. It's a picket probe, going home to mama," Jase replied as the contact marker raced away into interstellar space.

"They must have dropped them all around the nebula," she said.

I sat staring at the coordinates I'd manually entered into the autonav, unable to delete them.

"Captain," Izin said. "The Matarons will be here soon."

I nodded, paralyzed by the mind block.

"Skipper, let's go," Jase said impatiently.

The implanted memory of millions of Nisk dying in the dark depths of space screamed in my mind while Girutonak's desperate plea whispered to me.

Human-Kode-Soris... survive for me...in my place...You are me...Protector.

He was dead, yet his voice was real, and desperate. My finger hovered over the reset, but I couldn't do it. The coleopteran pleas drummed through my mind, freezing me in place.

You are me...You are me...Protector!

Marie stood beside me and glanced at my screen. "What's there, Sirius? I don't recognize the coordinates."

I opened my mouth, but couldn't find any words.

"You want to go there?" she asked gently.

I nodded.

"Why there?"

"Must...go," I whispered as millions of coleopterans screamed and the Nisk consort's face, floating in darkness, stared out at me.

"Does this have anything to do with what happened on Kif-atah?"

I nodded.

She looked at Jase who shrugged, and Izin who gave no sign at all, then she decided for all of us. "OK, Sirius. We'll go there." She studied the course plot, baulking at the duration. "Twenty two days. That's a long way."

The clicking faded as Girutonak's ghost realized it had won.

Jase checked the coordinates against our Tau Cetin astrographics and frowned. "It's uninhabited. There's nothing there."

Marie studied my nav-screen, checked the TC reference, saw the planet was a sterile bog with no microbial life, a thick unbreathable atmosphere and no oxygen. "You're sure about this?"

I nodded, scarcely knowing myself why it was so important. It was Girutonak who wanted to go there, not me, and he was dead, but his ghost would not release me.

Marie gave the others an encouraging look. "I guess we can–" A dull thud reverberated through the ship, cutting her off. "What was that?"

"Something hit us!" Jase exclaimed.

"We've been holed, port side," Izin said, studying damage control on his console. "No depressurization."

"Holed by what?" Marie asked.

"It was small, very small," he replied.

"There are no ships out there," Jase said.

An optical box appeared on screen, showing the visual feed from an emergency bot rushing out onto the hull. It mag-walked across to a small cylindrical device, half a meter long, protruding from the hull. Three rods extending from its sides speared into the hull, bolting it to the outer skin.

"The picket probe must have launched it," Izin said.

"It's not registering on sensors," Jase reported. "It's damn near invisible."

"Throw it off the hull," Marie said.

Izin tapped his console and the hullbot grabbed the trident's shaft with a claw hand. Electrical flashes enveloped the crawler's arm and its optical feed turned to static.

"What happened?" Marie asked.

"It's dead," Izin said, finding there was no telemetry coming through.

Jase oriented a mast optical toward the trident, saw it was still attached to the hull and the hull crawler was now drifting off into space.

"Izin, can we bubble with that thing out there?" Marie asked.

"I believe so."

She turned to me. "Sirius?...Do you want to risk it?"

I nodded weakly, then Jase pulled in our masts, eager to get moving.

Marie sighed. "OK, let's see what's there."

I lifted my hand to activate the autonav, but was suddenly very tired. My vision blurred and my mind went blank from the strain of the mind block. Marie took my hand and activated the autonav for me, sending us hurtling into interstellar space toward Girutonak's nightmare, now my nightmare.

Chapter Five : Galot V

Sterile World
Galot System
Outer Camelopardalis
1.46 Earth Normal Gravity
842 light years from Sol
Uninhabited

Next morning, we met Izin in engineering. He hadn't slept at all, but had spent the night studying the snakehead trident impaling our side.

"It's producing a quantum harmonic in our superluminal field," he explained as he sat in front of a bank of screens filled with data and diagrams. "It's vibrating our bubble, amplifying our spatial wake three thousand percent."

Jase whistled softly.

"We're ringing like a bell?" I asked apprehensively.

"The disturbance we are causing to spacetime makes it very easy for the Riku to track us," Izin said carefully.

"Will the bubble collapse?" Marie asked.

"No, stability is only slightly affected."

"How do we get it off?" I asked.

"That is the problem." He motioned at his screens, some showing freeze frame enlargements from his dead hull crawler's optical feed, others with columns of data. "The wake amplifier is protected by an electro-repulsion field. None of our bots can touch it, and human contact would be fatal."

"Can we blow it off the hull?" Jase asked.

"Only if you want to wreck the ship," Izin said dismissively.

"Find a way to shut it down," I said, "or we'll never get the Riku off our tail."

She would be patrolling back and forth along our wake, stopping frequently to confirm she hadn't overrun us. As soon as the Matarons realized they'd passed us, they'd double back until they picked up our trail. The *Riku* was much faster than us, able to cover vast distances in the blink of an eye. If we couldn't sneak away, we couldn't get away.

"I need more detailed scans to determine if it has a weakness," Izin said.

"Rig up a bot," I said. "Let me know when you're ready."

* * * *

A day later, we dropped the bubble and started a timer. The hull cooled rapidly, then Izin sent a sensorbot out to the study the trident. Scan data appeared on the bridge screen, along with a visual feed of the wake amplifier protruding from the curve of our hull. An orange beam reached from the amplifier straight out into space, now that there was no bubble to obstruct it.

"No contacts," Jase reported as our scanners came to life.

The sensorbot circled the snakehead device slowly,

observing it from all sides. By the time it completed one full circuit, the hull had cooled enough for the infrared display to show a bulge of heat in the device's center and a thermal sliver rising through its shaft. When it completed its circuit, the spider-like hull crawler stepped closer and began another scan.

Out in space, an infinitely long white line suddenly blinked into existence parallel to our course, and began to fade.

"Intersecting spatial wake!" Jase said quickly. "Five clicks out, reverse trajectory."

It was the *Riku*, racing back along our course, searching for our wake. Next time she dropped from superluminal, she'd pick up our trail and come back fast.

"That's it, Izin," I said. "Drop the package."

"Yes, Captain."

One of the crawler's articulated arms placed an armored box close to the amplifier. It was made of hull plates coated in the same thermal material as the ship's skin. Mag clamps locked it to the hull while its sensors kept watch on the amplifier. Data feeds and ghostly images appeared on the bridge screen when its eyes activated, then the sensorbot began ambling back to the maintenance lock.

I plugged an escape vector into the autonav and began charging the spatial disrupters, but kept helm control, giving Izin's crawler a chance.

"Mataron contact, six hundred thousand kilometers astern," Jase said and stowed the masts.

"Only two light seconds away," I said, surprised how close they were, and dismayed they'd found us in just over seven minutes. With the sensors retracting, we were blind, but knew the *Riku* was now racing toward us.

Marie's eyes were on Izin's precious sensorbot. "It's too far from the airlock."

"Sorry Izin," I said and gave the autonav helm control.

It closed the maintenance airlock and raised the

bubble, frying the sensorbot and leaving the *Riku* hurtling toward empty space while our wake echoed loudly behind us.

Marie glanced at the timer, now frozen. "Seven minutes. That doesn't give us much time."

"It'll have to do," I said. "It's all we're going to get."

* * * *

"The outer casing is highly conductive, made of a material I cannot identify," Izin said after days of analysis and a half dozen course changes. We were gathered at his engineering console, surrounded by screens filled with data from the snakehead noisemaker. "It's highly porous at a molecular level."

"It's full of holes?" Jase said.

"Millions of them, equidistant from each other," Izin replied. "It's engineered that way for a very good reason: vacuum is an excellent insulator. The holes allow the casing to vent atmosphere into space, which helps protect the amplifier's internal systems from its electro-repulsion field. The casing's interior is also lined with carbon in the form of a network solid, not a specific molecule. The basic pattern comprises five carbon atoms covalently bonded together. It's an ingenious piece of molecular engineering."

"I'm glad you approve," Jase said harshly.

"For those of us who flunked molecular engineering?" I said, having no idea what he was talking about.

"It's lined with diamonds," Marie explained, delighted she knew more than I did.

"Or a covalently bonded carbon material closely resembling diamond," Izin said. "There is no such thing as a diamond molecule. Diamond, like vacuum, is an excellent insulator."

"It's got double insulation," I said, finally understanding. "That's why it doesn't short itself out. So how do we get rid of it?"

"Contract the bubble," Jase suggested. "Shear it off."

"It extends only fifty four centimeters from the hull," Izin said. "We'd shear off the engine housings before the bubble reached the amplifier."

"Atmospheric friction might burn it off," Marie said, "but it'd take us too long to get through a planetary gravity well. The Riku would catch us."

"What about a drone, set to minimum yield?" Jase said. "Blast it off."

Izin looked at him curiously. "Why do your suggestions always involve destroying the ship?"

Jase scowled indignantly. "Well you figure it out. You're the engineer."

I stared at an image of the beam reaching off into space, racking my mind. "Can't touch it…Can't shoot it…Can't short it out." I sighed in frustration.

"There must be a way…" Marie said.

"Why is the beam that funny color?" I asked.

"It's the wavelength, Captain," Izin replied. "It's keyed to disrupt the superluminal field."

I gave him a puzzled look. "Is it a weapon?"

"It would cut off your arm, but it couldn't penetrate the hull."

I watched the beam shining into space a little longer. "The amplifier's not the problem. The beam is."

"Yes, Captain. The beam is causing the harmonic," Izin said slowly, as if I didn't understand the problem.

"So, all we have to do is stop the beam hitting the bubble. Right? So we cap it."

"Cap it, Captain?" Izin said, still overthinking the problem.

"Yeah, and you're going to build it."

* * * *

Izin created a tripod-shaped device out of a cut down hull

plate, coated it with thermal polymer skin and installed mag-locks in its feet. When it was ready, he squeezed it into a maintenance lock with his smallest hull crawler and I dropped the bubble.

"Remember Izin, seven minutes. No more."

"Yes, Captain," he replied while we waited for the hull to cool, then our mechanical spider crawled outside with the flat topped tripod in its arms and started mag-walking across the hull to the wake amplifier.

"It's too slow, Izin," I said, watching the timer.

"Any faster and it will lose its footing," he replied from engineering.

After an agonizing plod across the hull, the crawler stopped near the amplifier, placed the tripod on the hull and slid it forward. Two of the tripod's legs passed either side of the glowing trident as its flat top passed through the harmonic beam, stopping it streaming into space.

Izin activated the tripod's magnetic feet, locking the cap to the hull. "Tripod secure."

"How's it handling the beam?" I asked.

Izin studied the telemetry coming in from the hullbot. "There's photon dispersion below the cap, but it's holding."

"Good," I said, then a white line blinked on in the blackness of space as the *Riku* flashed past.

"There she is," Jase declared.

"She's early," Marie said, glancing at the timer.

"Not early enough," I said. "Izin, jump it off."

"There's still time to bring it in, Captain," he protested.

"No, there isn't."

Izin accepted my decision and ordered the hull crawler to leap into space. Its optical feed slewed around, looking back toward the *Silver Lining* as it floated away, showing the tripod cap silhouetted by the orange harmonic beam.

Leaving the hullbot to drift through interstellar space, we bubbled away, low and slow. When the *Riku* got here, she'd find our turbulent spatial wake had come to a sudden end and know we'd beaten her noisemaker. To ensure she didn't pick up our trail, I intended to tip toe through space, creating barely a ripple for a few days, putting half a light year between us and them.

"The superluminal field is producing no disharmonics, Captain," Izin reported.

"Good," I said with relief.

Marie smiled, leaned over and kissed me on the cheek. "Very low tech. If only they knew."

* * * *

Weeks of zig-zagging through space followed. We never sighted the *Riku* again, then at last, we crept up on the coordinates Girutonak had imprinted on my mind. The Tau Cetin astrographics described the fifth planet of the Galot System as a bleak, brown world, wet and cold with minimal cloud cover and devoid of life, both uninhabited and uninhabitable.

"I guess the Tau Cetins aren't infallible after all," Jase said as a blue-green, oxygen rich, subtropical world filled the bridge screen. There were no oceans, only blue-green plains, white clouds and receding polar ice caps.

"This can't be Galot V," Marie said, refusing to believe the Tau Cetin had got it so wrong.

I double checked our position against Girutonak's coordinates. "This is it. This is where it happened."

"What happened?"

I turned to her, tried to describe my implanted memories, but the mind block was too strong. I gave her a frustrated look, then she put a comforting hand on my shoulder.

"It's OK, Sirius."

"It sure is wet down there," Jase said.

"The atmosphere has a high water vapor content," Izin said from his console beside Jase. "It's warming the planet significantly." He checked the Tau Cetin description again. "There was no greenhouse effect the last time the Tau Cetins were here. It must be a recent addition."

"Planet's don't turn into greenhouses overnight," Jase said.

"Apparently, this one did," Izin insisted.

"It is very...blue," Marie said.

"That's it," I whispered, realizing what was familiar. "It's the color." I'd seen it before, but only once, on only one world. "Run a spectral–"

Nisk clicking exploded in my mind. I shuddered and fell silent as the others looked at me curiously.

Marie saw I couldn't complete the order and finished it for me. "Run a spectral analysis of the planet."

Jase nodded, ran the scan, then his eyes widened in surprise. "Huh! It's Nisk cyanobacteria. The whole planet's covered in it."

The primitive organism engineered by the Nisk was their primary food source and capable of phenomenal growth. A single cell, surviving impact, would have been enough to trigger a bacterial explosion that consumed the entire planet.

"This is about the Nisk?" Marie asked.

I nodded as clicking thundered in my mind, but the secret was out and there was nothing the mind block could do about it now.

"It does resemble Krailo-Nis," Izin said.

"No sign of intelligent life. No cities. No spaceports," Jase said, watching his scans.

"Compare," I whispered to Marie, fighting the mind block.

She to Jase, "How does it compare to Krailo-Nis?"

He put two columns of data on screen, comparing gravity, moisture, atmospheric composition, temperature, magnetic field and a dozen other variables. Not one was the same. Every habitability metric was way off.

"It may look Nisk," Izin said, "but it's not a Nisk world. They could not breathe that atmosphere."

"That's definitely their fungus," Jase said. "It's spectrally identical."

Marie turned to me, studying my face intently. "Why are we here, Sirius. What are you looking for?"

I opened my mouth to speak, but coleopteran clicking drowned out my thoughts and pain pulsed through my mind. Nisk eyes and inhuman screams filled my thoughts, fading away into the darkness as I passed out.

* * * *

I wasn't out for long, then as became aware of my surroundings, a synthetic voice sounded nearby.

"Captain Kade's front left hemisphere is registering activity two thousand times greater than human optimal in the Broca's Area region."

"What is that?" Marie asked.

"Broca's Area controls the process of turning thoughts and ideas into speech," the voice replied. "It passes information to the motor cortex which controls the movement of the mouth."

"That's why he can't speak," Izin said.

I opened my eyes to find a medbot floating beside my acceleration couch, scanning my head. I pushed it away and sat up.

"I'm all right," I croaked.

"They did something to you on Kif-atah, didn't they?" Marie said.

I blinked spots from eyes and nodded.

"Was it the Matarons?" Izin asked.

I shook my head. "Must…land."

"OK, Sirius, we'll land," Marie said gently, waving the others to their couches and sending the medbot back to sick bay.

Jase began an orbital scan, watching the results as they came in. There's a lot of biomass down there, but no Nisk."

"The Nisk are a subterranean species," Izin said. "If they're down there, we may not be able to detect them."

"There's got to be something down there," Marie insisted.

I stared at the screen, wondering where to look, then Girutonak's thought-voice sounded in my mind: *Twelve degrees north.*

"I know...where." I reached for my console as the mind block's vice-like grip loosened.

"You want me to take her?" Marie asked, doubting I was fit to fly.

"No." I put the *Silver Lining* into a low, westward orbit. "Scan twelve degrees north."

"Hmm," Jase furrowed his brow. "There's no planetary survey, no zero meridian, but based on rotation, the equator is...there. Got it, twelve degrees north. Orienting sensors. Sure is a lot of...sludge down there."

"Is that a technical term?" Izin asked.

"Yeah. It's more goopy than slime, less goopy than muck."

Izin gave him a dubious look. "Perhaps I should conduct the orbital survey."

"Haven't you got a bilge to pump?" Jase demanded.

"He's right about one thing," Marie said, "that cyanobacteria has taken over the entire biosphere. It's a...planetary extinction event."

"Except the planet was sterile when the cyanobacteria arrived," Izin said. "If the habitability parameters weren't so far from Nisk optimal, I'd think they'd terraformed the planet."

I shook my head. "No, they didn't."

We followed the curvature of the planet for more than a hundred degrees, watching a blue-green montage pass beneath us. It was more like an impressionist painting than an alien landscape, with only one form of life ruling all, from pole to pole.

"Found it!" Jase exclaimed. "It's big!"

"What is?" Marie asked.

"That," Jase said, focusing an optical on a point on the horizon.

Izin fixed his telescoping eyes on the bridge screen. "I don't see anything."

"I'll overlay the metallurgical scan," Jase said, then concentric circles hundreds of kilometers across appeared on the surface, traversed by ribs reaching into an empty center.

"It's a city," Marie said.

"Buried under thousands of meters of blue goop," Jase added.

I shook my head slowly. "It's no city."

Marie gave me a curious look, but wary of causing another blackout, said nothing, then we watched the immense circles slide across the planet's surface toward us.

"It's a nestship," Izin said at last.

Coleopteran clicking pounded my mind, still trying to hide the identity of the great skeleton buried beneath kilometers of blue-green fungus.

I nosed the *Silver Lining* down into the atmosphere, toward the concentric rings. They grew rapidly in size and detail, revealing thousands of long slender curves, tens of thousands of quadrilateral cross beams and a trail of metallic debris stretching five thousand kilometers to the north east.

"Damn!" Jase exclaimed. "It skidded a long way."

"Amazing it did not disintegrate," Izin said.

"What was a nestship doing out here?" Marie wondered.

"Maybe they were lost," Jase suggested.

"The Nisk are a major galactic power," Izin said. "They do not get lost."

We dropped through white clouds toward the largest wreck I'd ever seen. We'd heard of nestships, but human access to Krailo-Nis was strictly controlled and no human had ever been allowed near a nestship, let alone aboard one. It wasn't that they didn't trust us, just that they had no interest in us or our affairs.

Considering how densely packed together the Nisk had been, we could scarcely guess the number of lives lost. The magnitude of the disaster had driven Girutonak insane, forced him to imprint his need to return on me, to find the final resting place of his strain. Now that we were so close, I realized I was here for more than the instinctual need of a giant coleopteran to return to his nest.

It was for reasons far more human than I could have imagined.

Girutonak had been driven to return out of a sense of duty and love. Not love as I knew it, as humans experienced it, but love nevertheless, love as the Nisk knew it. Humans and Nisk appeared to be as different from each other as two species could be, yet those differences were an illusion. Girutonak had mind blocked me, had trusted me to take his place for one simple reason.

He knew what I didn't, that we were the same.

* * * *

We dropped through a poisonous, cloud filled atmosphere, passed over bleak mountains and levelled off above a vast, featureless blue-green plain.

"Twenty eight percent oxygen and lots of toxic stuff we can't breathe," Jase said as we flew toward the nestship's immense circular skeleton.

"This must be a recent event," Izin said, "otherwise the Tau Cetins would know about it."

"But it takes centuries to terraform planets," Jase protested.

"It's not a terraform, it's a bio disaster," I said. "It must have happened after the Spawn destroyed the Tau Cetin observer network."

"But that would mean this entire planet was

transformed in just two years," Marie said incredulously. "Is that even possible?"

"Nisk cyanobacteria is a controlled organism," Izin said. "The Nisk don't allow anyone access to it precisely because it could be used as a planet killing bioweapon." Izin stared at the blue-green plain filling the screen thoughtfully. "We should take a sample."

"Definitely not," I said flatly.

"But Captain," he protested, "we could use it against the Spawn."

"And they'd use it against us. We'll log the sensor reads and give them to the Tau Cetins. No one else. They'll know how to destroy this stuff."

We followed the plain toward an immense circular skeleton rising out of the fungus. The ring of structural ribs curved high into the sky before angling in toward the center. Every bone dripped with blue-green stalactites, and only where the fungus had broken free and fallen was bare metal exposed. The ribs ended raggedly, encircling a vast cavity where the center of the great ship had been vaporized.

"The debris field indicates it came down after the explosion," Izin said.

I reduced speed as we glided between a pair of towering ribs so large they made the *Silver Lining* look like a tiny insect hovering over the skeletal remains of a gigantic dinosaur.

"Now that we've found it, what do we do with it?" Jase asked.

I stared at the soaring ribs stretching away through the blue-green haze of a spore filled atmosphere. Close to the horizon, the nestship's back had broken under its own weight, cracking the symmetry of the ring. The mind block projected a ghostly image of the nestship overlaying the wreck into my mind revealing an immense spire rising from the center. It was surrounded by vast galleries teaming with Nisk, and ringed by a circle of towers evenly spaced around the periphery. The nestship was as much an organism as it was a flying city, with a beating central heart and many limbs. It all seemed vaguely familiar, yet completely alien as Girutonak's memories merged with my own, leading me on.

"It's over there," I whispered, and steered to the west.

"That fungus is deep, nine thousand meters," Jase said, reading his sensors.

"If it was damaged in space, how'd it get here?" Marie asked.

"It's a shell," I explained, "like the Nisk themselves. Its strength comes from the skeleton. That's why it could still fly even when the center was destroyed."

"It's tough all right," Jase said, scanning the wreck. "I'm reading tungsten, iridium, carbon and...a bunch of elements I can't identify."

"I never knew nestships were this big," Marie said.

"We're the first humans," I glanced at Izin, "and the first tamph, ever to get this close to one."

The Nisk were 'insular', not xenophobic like the Matarons. They preferred limited contact with other species because of introspection, not fear. It was a natural consequence of their immense numbers, looking inwards rather than out. A single Nisk world contained a hundred billion or more coleopterans, living in subterranean galleries carved throughout a planet's crust, hiding their civilization from sight. It was why we knew so little about them. To sustain such populations required a regimented way of life that made them extraordinarily industrious, especially for a society that relied on their worker caste rather than robotics.

I eased the *Silver Lining* a little to the south, matching the curved ribs to the ghost image in my mind. When we neared the outer periphery, we came upon a large circular shaft reaching down through the algae into darkness.

"Someone beat us to it," Marie said.

"It can't be," I whispered as I felt a pang of fear, both

mine and Girutonak's. Whatever I was searching for was hidden below an ocean of Nisk fungus, where no one should have been able to find it.

I brought the *Silver Lining* to a hover above the borehole, then Jase angled an optical at it. The shaft was perfectly circular with a smooth wall swirling with blue and green and no structural supports to shore up the sides.

"There are no signs of regrowth," Izin said. "Considering the bacteria's capacity for exponential cell division, this hole has only recently been excavated."

"How recent?" I said surprised and turned to Jase. "Scan everything!"

Jase fixed his gaze on his console as he searched every micron within range. He shook his head, finding nothing, then his expression changed from disappointment to confusion to alarm. "We've got company."

"The Riku?" I asked.

"No." He put an optical feed of empty air off our port side on the bridge screen. "It's out there, six hundred meters."

Marie peered at the screen uncertainly. "It's invisible? Are you sure?"

"There's a dead spot out there, soaking up our wide area scans. I'm getting no returns, no reflections off the nestship, not even background radiation. It's a sensor sponge. It can't be natural."

"They must be hostile, Captain," Izin declared, "otherwise they'd hail us."

I shook my head. "If they were hostile, we'd be dead already. Give me a marker."

Jase painted the sensor dead spot on the screen. I turned the bow toward it and hailed them on all channels.

"This is the Earth ship Silver Lining. Can I help you?"

There was no acknowledgement, then the contact marker began to shift slowly to port.

"They're circling," Marie said. "Testing us."

I turned our bow, keeping it angled toward the contact

marker.

"We could put a burst across their bow, just to say hello," Jase suggested.

"And get us all killed," Izin snapped.

"No weapons," I said and hailed them again. "You can hide all day, or we can talk."

The contact marker stopped moving while I eased the *Silver Lining* toward them. At a hundred meters, I stopped and held position.

"What are they doing?" Marie wondered.

"Scanning our offensive capability, most likely," Izin said.

"Any ship advanced enough to hide in broad daylight knows we're no match for them," I said, then the air wavered as a white hulled ship appeared.

She was twice as long as the *Silver Lining*, narrow at the bow and broad at the stern. On both sides, angled slightly down, were long thin blades whose sharp outer edges curved gently from far ahead of the bow to well aft of the stern. A third blade stretched over the top of her hull like a dorsal fin, as long as the two underside blades, forming a triangular configuration. The blades were held several meters out from the hull by slender pylons molded into the hull, giving her a sleek, racer look. It was a drive technology I'd never seen before, which made me more than a little uncomfortable.

"Still getting no readings," Jase warned. "We can see her, but that's all. She's invisible to the rest of the spectrum. I can't even tell if they have weapons."

I ran a profile match against my bionetic base and drew a blank. "Izin, you ever seen a ship like that?"

"No, Captain. I recommend extreme caution."

"They wouldn't have shown themselves if they intended to destroy us," I said, and spoke on all channels. "Thank you. I don't recognize your ship, or your technology."

"I would be surprised if you did, Captain Kade," a

cultured, recognizably female voice sounded inside the bridge.

"That did not come through our comm system, Captain," Izin said quickly. "I don't know where it came from."

"You know me?" I asked in surprise.

"I saw you once," the voice replied, "before the war."

"Really? Where was that?"

A spherical, three dimensional image appeared in the air halfway between me and our big screen. It contained a brown, fur covered face, elliptical in shape, with a high forehead, green eyes, round nose and a broad mouth with impressive teeth. His only ornamentation was a silver collaret around a short, thick neck that fanned out across sloping, furry shoulders more muscular than a man's.

"I am Gastillion Kalantropis," she said. "Do you remember me now, Captain Kade?"

I blinked in surprise. "I do. It's been a while." She'd been the number two D'kol ambassador on Centralis the day the Spawn attacked. She'd been fair to me and had made the snakeheads squirm, which considering the entire galaxy was watching at the time, had left me with a positive impression. "You're a long way from home, Ambassador."

Her ears twitched. "This is not a formal meeting, so please, address me as Gastillion." She turned and the spherical image expanded revealing another D'kol behind her, a male, and beside him, a feminine Uvo. They were standing in a forest with a blue sky above and sunlight breaking through the canopy. It was a neat trick, hiding their ship's interior from us.

"This is Prince Valtonarsi Dasilonius of the Imperial Household," Gastillion said, motioning toward the other D'kol.

He wore an opulent gold and bejeweled livery collar around his neck, indicating his high office, and acknowledged me with a slight incline of his head and a twitch of his ears.

Gastillion then introduced the Uvo humanoid, "And this is his advisor, Laleya Rohal, High Seer of the Sibylline Sisterhood and a member of the Emperor's Personal Retinue."

Laleya was tall and graceful, like the only other Uvo I'd met, and had the same piercing blue eyes that seemed to bore through your very being. That first Uvo I'd met had been an empath who'd hinted that some of her sisters had far greater abilities than she. This Uvo was a High Seer and advisor to a Prince of D'kol, which made me wonder if she was–?

"Yes Captain Kade," Laleya Rohal said, "I am."

I froze, feeling uncomfortably naked before her.

"She's what?" Marie whispered to me.

"Spooky."

"I prefer Supreme Telepath," Laleya said, "but spooky will do, if you prefer."

A chill ran down my spine as I wondered what a Supreme Telepath was capable of, then I started to introduce the others, turning first to Marie "This is–"

"Marie Dulon," Gastillion said. "Yes we know. Laleya has already identified you all."

"Of course she has," I said. "So, what are you folks doing this side of the galaxy?"

"Gathering information," Gastillion replied.

"I take it that's your hole back there?"

"Yes, it is."

"I don't suppose you'd care tell us what's at the bottom?"

Gastillion hesitated, but before she could respond, Laleya interjected. "He knows." She said with conviction. "Captain Kade already knows everything, remembers everything, he just doesn't realize it yet."

Marie and Jase gave me questioning looks while fearful Nisk clicking sounded softly in the back of my mind, preventing me from explaining.

"We should meet," Gastillion said.

"We'll come over there," I said. "You can show us around your ship."

"We will come to you," she countered firmly.

"I should warn you, there's a Mataron cruiser looking for us. If they show up–"

"That would be most unfortunate…for them," Gastillion assured me.

"Right," I said and the D'kol image sphere vanished. "In that case, I hope they get here soon."

* * * *

Jase took the helm while I went with Marie and Izin to greet our visitors from the other side of the galaxy at the bow airlock.

"I can see them," Jase said. "They just…came through the hull. No airlock that I can see. And they're not wearing p-suits."

"There should be a shaped field linking our ships," I said.

"It's not showing on sensors. They're floating over now."

They cycled through our airlock then the two D'kol stepped out wearing collarets of rank, dark sarongs and sandals while the Uvo was dressed in a fine white robe. The physically impressive D'kol were more than half a meter taller than me with large heads that grazed the overhead while the slender Uvo was only slightly taller. The D'kol were covered in thick fur from head to foot while the Uvo was hairless with a gently ridged head almost as large as Izin's.

Laleya Rohal extended her hand to me in the Earth custom. "Captain Kade."

"Laleya," I said, taking her delicate hand. "Welcome to the Silver Lining."

She greeted Marie with a hand shake and Izin without

touching. "You are the first of your kind I have met."

"I am not of the One Spawn," he said icily.

"I know. You are a terrestrial amphibian from Earth. I have met Spawn before. You are biologically identical, but you are not like them."

He relaxed, surprised by her response.

"Most people don't realize he's different," I said.

"He has learned trust," she said, "a necessary first step to brotherhood. The Spawn have not."

"It only took two thousand years," I said with a grin.

"The tamphs of Earth are proof how rapidly one can evolve, when rightly motivated."

She obviously knew mankind had given the tamphs a choice, co-exist with us or be exterminated by a species as warlike as their own. The tamphs chose to survive, to adapt and we eventually took our finger off the trigger and gained an unlikely friend.

Gastillion eyed Izin curiously. "I would not have thought it possible."

Laleya looked into Izin in a way no one ever had, not even Lena. "I am certain. His kind now follow a different path to the One Spawn."

Gastillion and Prince Valtonarsi inclined their heads forward slightly in greeting, keeping their eyes on us. Their ears angled toward us while they raised their hands with palms and finger tips facing back toward their chests in the standard D'kol greeting of peace and parlay; claws in, ears open. Considering their size and physical strength, claws forward and ears back would have been intimidating millions of years ago, before technology.

I chose not to emulate their greeting, but merely bowed curtly, maintaining eye contact, and motioned them to the ward room. "This way."

They declined refreshments, then because the D'kol were too large for human chairs, we all stood.

"Now that we're all acquainted," I said, "would you like to tell us what you folks are doing so far from home?"

"In time, but first…" Gastillion motioned to Laleya, who stepped forward and peered into my eyes, stripping me bare and making me feel at ease at the same time.

"As I suspected, he has an overlay," she said.

"Something happened to him on Kif-atah," Marie said.

"The overlay is Nisk," Laleya explained. "It is coercive. A mind block. The Nisk do not normally impose their will on others. They know the dangers, but…he…was desperate." She gazed at me in silence and added. "Girutonak. He also was a prisoner."

Fearful clicking thundered into my mind at the mention of his name, at the prospect of the mind block's secrets being laid bare by this Uvo mind reader. I winced, unable to speak and pressed my hands to my head.

Marie saw I couldn't speak and turned to Laleya, "Can you help him?"

"I can remove it," she replied, raising her hand to my temple.

"No!" Gastillion said sharply, pulling Laleya's hand back. "You must not change him."

Marie turned to the D'kol Ambassador angrily. "Let her help him!"

"A Nisk gave him the mind block. A Nisk must remove it."

"But he needs help now," Marie declared.

"You do not understand," Gastillion said gently, releasing the Uvo's hand. "His mind block proves he shared a cell with a Nisk on Kif-atah. A Nisk consort. If Laleya removes the overlay, she destroys the proof that the consort survived the crash."

"I don't care," Marie declared. "Get that thing out of his head!"

"That would be…unwise," Gastillion said.

"The overlay has the quality of the one who created it," Laleya explained.

"So?" Marie demanded.

"It matters," Prince Valtonarsi said meaningfully. "It

matters to the one who awaits below."

Marie's eyes widened in surprised. "There's another Nisk below, at the bottom of your hole?"

"Not just any Nisk," the Prince replied.

"Who's down there?" Izin asked.

All three aliens hesitated, then the Prince's ears twitched permissively to Gastillion, who said, "A Nisk Royal of the Iskeratul Strain. This nestship, the Iskeratix, was hers."

"Irukoochati," I whispered, surprised that for once, there was no Nisk chatter to silence me.

"You see? He knows," the Uvo Supreme Telepath said. "That's why you're here, to free her."

I nodded as a coleopteran face filled my mind, horribly alien, yet the object of Girutonak's love and devotion.

"She's in stasis," Gastillion said, "barely alive."

"You've been down there?" Marie asked.

"I am aware of her presence," Laleya said, "although she sleeps too deeply to be aware of mine."

"You sensed her from the other side of the galaxy?" Marie asked incredulously.

"No. I only became aware of her after we discovered the wreck, when we were close."

"Why did you come?" I asked weakly as the coleopteran clicking and Irukoochati's face faded from my mind.

"The Emperor sent me to discover how the Spawn Fleet reached Centralis without being detected," Prince Valtonarsi explained. "He fears the Spawn will use the same method to attack the Empire if the Tau Cetins are defeated."

The Spawn's surprise attack on Centralis had shattered the Forum's ancient meeting place and plunged much of the galaxy into war while the D'kol Empire and its dependents had remained neutral on the far side of the galactic core.

"We have been retracing the Spawn Fleet's course for

many months," Gastillion said.

"Spatial wakes don't last that long," Izin said suspiciously.

"We do not follow spatial turbulence. We trace microtessalons."

"Are they particles?" Izin asked.

"A microtessalon is a long lasting energy filament produced by the Spawn star drive. They are millions of times smaller than any particle. It is a technology unknown to the One Spawn, or the Tau Cetins."

I lowered my hands from my head. "So the Spawn came here, two years ago?"

"The Spawn Fleet gathered in this system, before its attack on Centralis," Prince Valtonarsi said. "When they arrived, the Iskeratix was gathering material for a colony the Nisk are constructing not far from here."

"So the nestship was in the wrong place at the wrong time," I said.

"Unfortunately so," Prince Valtonarsi replied "The Spawn believed this system was uninhabited, which is why they chose it. The need for secrecy meant the Spawn could not allow the Iskeratix to leave."

"But the Nisk are neutral," Marie said.

"The Nisk choose not to involve themselves in galactic affairs," the Prince said, "but they are a lawful race. They would have warned the Galactic Forum of the impending attack, as required by the Access Treaty."

"So the Spawn killed them all," I said as Girutonak's memories of the entire Spawn Fleet descending on a solitary nestship flooded my mind, unlocked by Prince Valtonarsi's revelation.

"The Spawn Fleet knew when the Galactic Forum was meeting," the Prince said. "They could not delay their attack or risk dividing their fleet to dispose of the wreck, so they left the Iskeratix adrift in space. They asked the Matarons to remove the evidence because Kif-atah is nearby."

"But how could they hide something so big?" Marie asked.

"The Matarons were supposed to tow the Iskeratix into this system's star where it would have been destroyed," the Prince replied. "However, by the time they got here, the Iskeratix had crashed onto this planet. It was too large for the Matarons to lift, so all they could do was ensure there were no survivors. That's when they found the Nisk consort who coerced Captain Kade."

"They were meant to kill him," I said, "but they took him prisoner instead."

"Nisk consorts are fitted with technology far more advanced than anything the Matarons possess," Gastillion said, "and consorts are highly intelligent. The Matarons tried to force him to help them understand his technology."

"That's why they tortured him, drove him mad."

"He told them nothing," Gastillion added. "Even we could not force a Nisk consort to speak against his will."

"The Spawn would never have agreed to let a witness live," Izin said.

Gastillion gave Izin a long, thoughtful look. "The Matarons lied to the Spawn about their prisoner and about the Nisk technology they recovered. We may be sure that whatever the Matarons stole from the Nisk is now well hidden, even from us."

"I still don't see why you can't take that thing out of his head," Marie said, then the D'kol exchanged furtive looks.

"They're here to rescue Irukoochati," I said.

"In a manner of speaking, although our plans have now changed. We shall not rescue her." Prince Valtonarsi fixed his gaze upon me. "You will."

I blinked. "Me? Why?"

"Because when you revive her," Laleya explained, "she will clear your mind block and know who put it there. She will see, as I did, how Girutonak suffered to protect her. She will remember who destroyed her strain, and most important of all, she will be grateful to you, Captain Kade. You, who rescued her on behalf of her consort, who took his place as her Protector. And she will trust you, only you."

"But...I had no choice."

"The Nisk are lawful, rational," Gastillion said. "They think in terms of what is, and is not. They do not see shades of gray. They will consider only what you have done, and what the Spawn have done."

"What the Spawn have done..." I whispered, realizing Gastillion was thinking far ahead.

"The Nisk Myriad do not yet know the Spawn destroyed one of their nests," she continued, "killed millions of their kind, billions of their eggs. When a Nisk Royal returns to them, relates what happened, passes on the memories of Girutonak which you carry, Captain Kade, the entire Nisk Civilization will be enraged in a way they have never been before in their entire history. Trillions of Nisk all across the galaxy will rise up as one and strike the Spawn down with all their might, and they will be grateful to you, Captain Kade, a human, for bringing Irukoochati back from the dead."

We all stared at Gastillion Kalantropis in stunned silence as the enormity of what she was saying sank in. I'd been so tormented by the mind block, so distracted fighting it, obeying it, I'd never considered the consequences of it. Girutonak's mind block wasn't my enemy, it was our deliverance.

"The Nisk are not as advanced as the Spawn," Prince Valtonarsi said. "They are peaceful by nature, inward looking by temperament, and have played no part in galactic affairs. That is why the Spawn did not hesitate to attack them. However, their numbers are immense, their industrial power beyond measure, and their warrior caste utterly fearless. The Nisk are the sleeping giant of the galaxy, and you are about to awaken them."

I stared in astonishment at the D'kol Imperial Prince as I realized the magnitude of the Spawn's miscalculation. "You're handing them...to us?"

"To you, Captain Kade," he declared, ears fluttering with anticipation, "for the greater good of the galaxy and for the freedom of Earth."

* * * *

The *Silver Lining* hovered above the vertical shaft as I moved out onto the levelled stern door-ramp in a p-suit with a booster pack. The D'kol ship floated silently to starboard while a blue-green haze filled the air as far as the eye could see. The algae covered bones of the *Iskeratix* curved into the sky, making me feel incredibly small and alone in their embrace. I paused, remembering the millions of Nisk who'd perished within this vast expanse, then my exterior mike picked up the clatter of metal feet as four heavy-lift thrusterbots marched out of the cargo hold onto the door-ramp. Multiple articulated limbs extended from central bodies containing high impulse thrusters. Their arms were equipped with powerful, jointed fingers; their feet with maglocks for hull walking; and their knees and elbows all had built-in stabilizers for attitude control.

"Watch that first step, Skipper," Jase's amused voice sounded inside my helmet. He was holding the ship steady above the D'kol borehole, watching the optical feeds with Marie.

"Be careful of those bots, Izin," I said apprehensively. "I don't want one of those things landing on my head."

"Make sure you don't get underfoot, Captain," Izin replied unsympathetically from engineering.

The four big thrusterbots lined up either side of me, each one big enough to crush me in Galot V's heavy gravity, then I stepped off the end of the ramp and dropped into the hole. I plunged into darkness, falling blindly for several seconds before the booster pack's stabilizers fired, keeping me in the center of the shaft while my main thruster remained silent. My suit's floodlights activated, lighting up the blue-green shaft walls flashing past me so fast, they were a blur. One light angled down into the shaft below, but it was still too deep to see the bottom.

When I was well below the surface, Izin jumped the four thrusterbots off the door-ramp five seconds apart, each at one corner of a square formation with me at the center. The entrance faded to a point of light while the big thrusterbots twinkled like fiery stars as their retros feathered, ensuring they didn't overtake me.

"Your descent vector is good, Sirius," Marie reported, overseeing the telemetry. "The bots are holding formation."

"Looks dark down there" Jase said.

"Dark and blue," I replied, trying to relax as I dropped like a stone.

After almost five minutes, Marie said, "Standby for breaking sequence."

My suit's proximity sensor detected the approaching deck and fired the thruster as my floodlights lit up scorched metal below. After a short burn to break my fall, my feet settled gently on blackened and heat-buckled metal. The floodlights reoriented to the horizontal, giving me all round visibility, then the four big bots thudded onto the deck in sequence, forming a square around me.

"Bots are down, boosters are off," Izin announced.

"Nice job," I said and studied my surroundings.

The air was thick with a blue haze that glowed in my floodlight beams. Breaking through the borehole's curved side was a dark metal wall with a circular vault door at its center. A film of cyanobacteria was already spreading across it from the spore filled atmosphere.

I wiped a finger across the door and held it up to the light. "This stuff is aggressive. We're going to need to sterilize the lower cargo deck. Maybe the entire hull."

"I'll synthesize additional decontaminates," Izin said.

"How do I open it?" I asked, looking up at the vault door. It was an immense slab of armor seven times my height with no control panel in sight.

"There is a circular engraving in the center of the door, Captain." Gastillion replied from the D'kol ship. "Turn it left and press."

I activated my thruster and floated up to a decorative pattern with indentations matching Nisk antenna-manipulators. I tried turning it with both hands, but it wouldn't budge.

"Izin, this is yours," I said and floated back from the door.

One thrusterbot took up position below the lock while a second climbed onto its back and reached into the indentations. It strained hard, then the locking mechanism groaned and turned slowly until it clicked, but the door didn't move.

"It's stuck," I said.

"It needs power," Gastillion said. "The door is conductive. Your machines should be able to energize it."

I floated down onto the buckled deck while Izin maneuvered all four thrusterbots up to the door. They put their arms on it and pumped electricity into it. Sparks flashed where thrusterbot hands pressed against the Nisk door, then the massive armored slab swung in. The bots shone their floodlights into a dark, dome-roofed chamber illuminating a large, rectangular sarcophagus. It was half as high and twice as long as the vault door, and pinpoints of light glowed from it in several places indicating it was still functioning.

"That is her stasis chamber," Gastillion said.

"Skipper!" Jase said. "I'm getting energy readings. They spiked when you opened the door."

"You sure?" I asked, peering uncertainly into the floodlit darkness. "Looks dead in there."

"I'm reading something."

I stepped back from the doorway, played my floodlights over the deeply shadowed domed roof, then tossed a compression tester from my suit's utility kit at the sarcophagus. Three red beams flashed from the walls, vaporizing the small tool in midair.

"Hmph!" I grunted. "No power for the door, but plenty of juice for weapons."

"You are in a royal citadel, Captain," Gastillion said. "They are the most protected points in the entire ship, placed as far from the central energy source as possible to ensure the royals survive even a catastrophic system failure. It has its own organic defenses."

"Now you tell me."

"They only activated once you opened the door. The sarcophagus is powering them."

"Can you shut them down?"

"One moment, Captain Kade."

My floodlights and suit HUD blinked out and the thrusterbots shut down leaving me alone in the darkness listening to my breathing. Uncomfortably aware my suit's life support was dead, I felt blindly for my wrist control and tried to restart my suit, but nothing happened. There was no air coming through and the cold outside began to penetrate my suit.

"I have a slight problem down here. Hello?...Can anyone hear me?"

I calculated how much air I had inside my suit, didn't like the answer, then the bot floodlights blinked back on and my suit's air began to flow again.

"You could have told me you were going to shut me down," I said, relaxing.

"Apologies, Captain Kade," Gastillion replied. "We underestimated how fragile your technology is. The citadel's defenses have been deactivated. It is now safe for you to enter."

I took a calibration wrench from my utility kit and tossed it into the chamber. It sailed through the air and clattered harmlessly onto the deck in front of the sarcophagus.

"Don't you trust me?"

"Sure I do," I replied, glancing warily up at the dome as I cautiously entered the chamber. When I wasn't incinerated, I retrieved my wrench and walked around the sarcophagus. "It's bigger than I expected."

"It is a fully self-powered survival unit, shielded against all forms of radiation," Gastillion explained. "You will have to move it into your ship, decontaminate your cargo hold and provide a breathable atmosphere before it will open."

"Looks kind of heavy," I said uncertainly. "What do you think, Izin?"

He didn't reply. Instead, the four thrusterbots moved into the citadel, took up positions at each corner, and lifted it off the deck.

"Alright," I said optimistically, thinking we were now in the Nisk rescuing business, then the four thrusterbots set the sarcophagus back down. "Izin? What are you doing?"

"I'm sorry, Captain. The sarcophagus is extremely dense, more than double the mass of the Silver Lining."

"Double?"

"Our thrusterbots can lift it, but they cannot fly with it."

"Now that's a problem. Gastillion? We need some D'kol magic down here."

"We are scanning it." After a long silence, she said, "The shell is constructed of molecularly compressed karsinium-359, an extremely dense material."

"Can you lift it out of here?"

"No, Captain. The Parsiphilius is an Imperial star yacht. She is not equipped for salvage."

"A yacht?" I said surprised. "You came all this way in a yacht?"

"The Spawn are watching our every move. If we sent

a large ship, they would detect it. Such a move could start a war."

"They've already started a war."

"Yes, but not with us," she said, indicating the D'kol were prepared to meddle in secret, but not actually fight.

"We need a ramp, Captain," Izin said, "with a forty degree incline. That will allow the thrusterbots to walk the sarcophagus to the surface."

"Gastillion?" I said. "Can you dig us a ramp?"

"Yes. It will take several days. We will need to fuse the molecules to a sufficient depth to ensure your robotic devices do not sink into the bacteria."

"OK. Start drilling. I'm coming up."

* * * *

While the D'Kol ship cut a sloping access tunnel down to the royal's citadel, Gastillion invited me to the *Parsiphilius* for a meeting. I was floated from our airlock through Galot V's poisonous atmosphere directly into their ship.

Gastillion and Laleya greeted me as I stepped onto a tiled terrace perched atop a high cliff. On one side, an Imperial Palace soared above me, all white marble, curved balconies and graceful towers. On the other was verdant farmland, a tranquil lake circled by slender blue and yellow birds, and in the distance, snowcapped mountains and a high waterfall.

"Nice trick," I said. "No pressure tube. No airlock. No p-suit."

"We use transit fields and matter manipulation," Gastillion explained.

"Hmm. Shame about the view."

"You're disappointed," Laleya said.

"I was hoping to see your ship, not a hologram" I glanced back over my shoulder, searching in vain for any sign of the hull.

"This is not a hologram, although it is an illusion," Gastillion said. "The interiors of our ships are not the cold corridors and cramped compartments you are used to. What you see is the interior of the Parsiphilius. It is designed to eliminate the psychological stress of confinement associated with long duration voyages."

"Where do you hide the stuff that makes it go? At the bottom of the lake?"

Her ears twitched with amusement. "They are built into the hull, and very small by your standards."

I nodded. "Ah, super miniaturization."

"To the limits of atomic compression within the laws of this universe. One day, millions of years from now, this will be as commonplace for you as it is for us."

"Can't wait," I said dryly, turning toward the valley. "Is this a real place?"

"It is Seliseoshara, one of our designed worlds."

"Designed? Not terraformed."

"Engineered to our specifications, as is the star it orbits."

I glanced at the soft yellow sun high in the sky. "You build stars?"

"We modify them to suit our needs, and when necessary, to protect other civilizations."

"Right. No one likes pesky supernovas going off all over the galaxy."

"It is simply a matter of managing gas and gravity." The ursidaen ambassador motioned me to a round table with three chairs by the terrace wall. "Please."

I glanced over the edge, saw a dizzying drop to farmland below, then sat where I could watch the waterfall. "Cracking the limits of atomic compression gets you a good view."

"Among other things," Gastillion replied. "Would you like some tea? We are quite fond of brewed drinks. Or would you rather something stronger. We have a drink similar to your coffee."

"Coffee's fine, thanks."

An ornately carved silver tray floated out a doorway and settled on the table. It contained three fluted silver cups, several plates of D'kol delicacies and four small bowls of what appeared to be different colored sugars.

"You will like the light green crystals in your drink," Laleya said, "and the banisimala are very tasty." She took a small round cake to demonstrate and bit into it.

I dropped a green cube in the coffee, was shocked by how good it tasted, and found the banisimala equally delicious. "I could get addicted to these."

"I assure you, Captain Kade," Gastillion said, "we would never serve you addictive substances."

"Any chance of getting the recipe, for my galleybot?"

"Unfortunately, you lack the ingredients to produce these substances."

I finished another D'kol delicacy, sipped my non-addictive coffee substitute and gave them both a questioning look. "So, why am I here?"

"You think we have an ulterior motive?"

"I may be a simple hominid from a backward world, but even I know you didn't invite me here for coffee and cake. Not that the cakes aren't great by the way. They are, really." I selected another and bit into it appreciatively.

"You are correct, Captain Kade. We did not invite you here for coffee and cake." She glanced conspiratorially at Laleya. "We want to ensure that no one ever discovers we were here."

"Why? The Nisk would be grateful. So would the Tau Cetins. Maybe you two could patch things up."

"Any gratitude the Nisk may feel toward us would be discovered by the Spawn, who would know we had interfered in their war with the Ornithians."

"If you'd rescued the royal, they'd have found out."

"We never intended to rescue her ourselves," Gastillion explained. "We dug the shaft so Laleya could get close enough to be sure who was down there. In a few weeks, the Nisk bacteria will fill in the shaft as if we were never here."

"You were going to leave her down there?"

"No, she would have been rescued, but not by us. Or you."

"Who then?"

"The Tau Cetins."

I baulked in surprise. "What? But you two aren't exactly on good terms." The D'kol had accused the Tau Cetins of technological espionage and had almost had them kicked out of the Galactic Forum literally days before the war began.

Gastillion hesitated, choosing her words carefully. "We were preparing to leave when you arrived, but Laleya suggested you should perform the rescue."

"You see, Captain Kade," Laleya said, "the Spawn would never believe the D'kol would help humans, so the risk to the Empire is minimal, providing they do not find out the truth."

"If you rescue the Nisk royal," Gastillion added, "we would be above suspicion and the Nisk would look favorably upon you. We would both benefit from the agreement."

"There's one thing I don't understand," I said, considering a third cake. "The D'kol Empire is huge. From what I've heard, you're a little ahead of the Tau Cetins technologically and the big power on the far side of the galaxy. So why are you tip toeing around the Spawn? Why don't you drop the hammer on them?"

"The Empire is old–very old–and tired," Gastillion said. "The only war we have fought in four million years was against the Spawn, two and a half millennia ago, to help our Ornithian friends. We sent our best ships, which were technologically superior to Spawn, and also…they were the only ships we could send. The Spawn did not know it at the time, and still do not. Today, we could not send even that."

"But you have an enormous fleet. You helped the Tau Cetins blockade the Spawn after the First Intruder War."

"The Tau Cetins provided most of the ships for the blockade, and of the few we sent, most were lost when the Spawn broke out of the Minacious Cluster. Not only have the Spawn closed the gap technologically with the Tau Cetins, at least militarily, the advantages we once enjoyed are now greatly reduced." She paused, letting that sink in. "We have a few extremely powerful ships which protect a vast area. Most of our fleet is ancient and barely serviceable, kept operational so our fleet numbers appear large."

"How come the Spawn don't know this. I thought they were watching you."

"They are, and we shadow them with our most advanced ships, ensuring that is all they see."

"You're bluffing them."

"There are many young civilizations dependent upon us for protection," Gastillion explained. "We must consider their safety, as well as our own."

"Maybe you should start building more ships."

"When one spends eons promoting interstellar brotherhood," Laleya said, "one does not prepare for war."

"So the whole falling out with the Tau Cetins on Centralis, that was…staged?"

Her ursidean ears twitched, as if ensuring no one was listening before answering. "Yes, to conceal our weakness and protect the many civilizations we are responsible for, without fighting. We knew the Spawn were preparing for war, but we did not anticipate they would attack so soon. We underestimated how quickly they would exploit breaking the Tau Cetin blockade."

"They are very aggressive," Laleya lamented.

"Yeah, they are that," I agreed. "So the Tau Cetins really are on their own?"

"They have many friends, although the truth is, their

fleet is all that stands between the Spawn and disaster for us all."

"That's why they didn't complain about getting censured by the Forum. They were protecting you. All of you. They never stole your technology did they? You gave it to them."

"To spy on the Spawn, yes," Gastillion admitted. "The Ornithian Consociation and the Empire of D'kol have been allies for millions of years. Neither of us would throw that friendship away. The Ornithians know we will do what we can, when the time is right."

"Who else knows?"

"A few senior members of the Forum Council, enough to ensure the Forum vote went against the Tau Cetins, but not enough to undermine their capacity to fight the Spawn."

I sighed. "You people really know how to pull a galaxy-sized con."

Gastillion realized it was as much a compliment as a characterization. "We knew the Xil were trying to convince the weaker civilizations to sign their Neutrality Pact, to isolate the Tau Cetins and divide the Forum membership, so we gave the Xil what they wanted."

I smiled. "You encouraged the minor civilizations to join."

"We merely indicated we were not opposed to them looking to their own security," Gastillion said. "Their self-interest did the rest."

"Hmph, and the Tau Cetins knew all along."

"Of course. That is why they were silent on the matter."

"And here I thought I was uncovering a plot against the galaxy." I shook my head in dismay. "I nearly screwed the whole thing up."

"On the contrary, Captain Kade, your unexpected involvement proved very convincing. We realized afterwards if there had been no attempt to disclose the Xil

Neutrality Pact, to disrupt their plans, the Spawn might have become suspicious. Instead, they believed they had succeeded in spite of your interference."

"As a result," Laleya said, "billions of lives on thousands of worlds have been saved."

"Well, seeing as you put it that way," I said, feeling better about my blundering.

"We are building new ships," Gastillion assured me, "but our ships are extremely complex and we have few worlds able to construct them."

"Meanwhile, the Tau Cetins are buying you time."

"And for that, we are grateful."

"You do understand, time is running out. The Tau Cetins nearly lost their homeworld."

"Yes, and thanks to you, it was saved, which is why we are speaking to you now. Our Tau Cetin friends trust you, and so do we." Gastillion sipped her brewed tea, then put her silver fluted cup down. "The truth is, we are not here because we fear the Spawn will attack us using the same approach they followed to Centralis. We are here because we knew a nestship had inexplicably disappeared shortly before the attack."

"You suspected the Spawn destroyed it?"

"Nestships do not go missing, Captain Kade. That is why we have carefully retraced the Spawn Fleet's movement, hoping to discover the fate of the Iskeratix."

Finally, something that made sense. The galaxy was big and the Spawn were too smart to pull the same trick twice. If they were going to hit the D'kol, it would be from a different direction to their attack on Centralis.

"We knew the Matarons were aligned with the Spawn. When we tracked the Spawn Fleet to this part of the Orion Arm, we naturally searched the Matar System for any sign of their passing, although the Matarons did not detect us.

"When we entered orbit over Kif-atah," Laleya explained, "I sensed a Nisk presence on the surface."

"From orbit?" I wondered what Lena would make of

that.

"We could not rescue him without revealing ourselves, and we knew there was no way the Matarons could have captured a Nisk Royal, unless..."

I nodded. "He was a survivor."

"To conceal our presence, we had no choice but to leave him there," Gastillion said. "So, we told the Tau Cetins what we had discovered."

"Ah...And they sent Tahl Rete to Kif-atah. Only they couldn't risk telling him what he was looking for, so they sent him in blind, because....he was expendable."

"Tahl Rete had to discover the Nisk on his own, so the Spawn would not learn of our involvement. All we needed was for the Kesarn to hear of the Nisk prisoner's presence and escape. That would give the Tau Cetins a reason to rescue Girutonak."

"That'd put the snakeheads and the Spawn in the soup and you'd be in the clear."

"Fortunately for all of us, Tahl Rete failed. He never found Girutonak, never even heard of his existence, but you did. And Girutonak forced you to come here, to do what he could not."

"Rescue Irukoochati," I said with understanding, "and prove to the Spawn the Matarons got greedy, and lied to them."

"The Mataron Supremacy will, of course, deny ever having taken Girutonak prisoner," Gastillion said.

"But the Spawn won't believe them, because the Nisk will believe me, and the more the snakeheads deny it, the more the Spawn will know they're lying." It was elegant and flawless, and its consequence was obvious. "It'll break their alliance."

"The mind block will prove to the Nisk royal that Girutonak sent you," Laleya said, "that the Spawn and the Matarons conspired against the Nisk, and your memories will show her the Matarons murdered her consort."

"Which is why I'm stuck with it."

Gastillion fixed her eyes on me. "There is, however, one problem."

"What problem?" I asked suspiciously.

"You have seen us," Laleya said. "When the Nisk royal removes the mind block, she will see your memories and know we were here. Once the Nisk know, the Spawn will know."

"I'll ask her to keep it a secret? She'll owe me."

"She will not understand," Gastillion said. "The Nisk are rigidly truthful. In a species so crowded together, subterfuge is unknown. Even if she agrees to your request, the secret will get out."

"So what are you suggesting?" I asked warily. "You want to wipe my mind?"

"Nothing so severe," Laleya said. "I merely wish to ensure the Nisk royal will not see your memories of us."

"What's the catch?"

"You must agree with your heart and soul, without reservation," Laleya replied. "It must be a conscious decision, an application of your free will to allow me to affect your mind. And your companions must also agree."

"Suppose they refuse?"

"That is their choice and I will respect it," Laleya said. "I cannot coerce you in any way."

Lena would coerce her own mother, anywhere, anytime, but not Laleya. The Uvo seer had the power to do it, and the moral restraint Lena lacked.

"I believe you," I said. "I think you're nuts, but I believe you."

"One does not become a Supreme Telepath, Captain Kade, if one does not respect the freedom of others."

"What about the tunnel you're digging to get her out, how will I explain that?"

"You will believe it was here when you arrived, excavated by the Matarons and chemically treated to prevent the spores from filling it in," Gastillion replied. "She will assume they used it to capture Girutonak, and intended to use it to break into her citadel, once they had devised the means to do so."

"They'll deny it," I said and smiled, "but no one will believe them."

"No one," Laleya agreed, "especially not when the Nisk royal confirms your memories."

"She won't know they came from you?"

"No. They will be as real to her as to you."

"We've had very little interaction with your crew," Gastillion added. "That is why we invited you here, instead of going to your ship, to limit our contact."

"And I thought I was getting the ten credit tour."

"Speak with your crew," Laleya said. "Obtain their wholehearted agreement. Understand, you cannot order them to agree. It must be their choice. I will know if it is not. When next they sleep, I will make the necessary adjustments."

"What if I'm captured by the Spawn? Will they be able to recover my memories? They have some nasty interrogation techniques."

"They will be unable to penetrate your mind."

"At least I'll have one secret from them."

"You misunderstand me, Captain Kade. After I am finished, the Spawn will never again be able to penetrate your mind."

I blinked. "Wait!...Never?"

"It is necessary for me to shield your entire mind. It cannot be partial, nor will it prevent the Nisk royal from dissolving the mind block, because you will want her to free you."

I whistled slowly, thinking Lena would be pleased.

"Lena Voss will not know," Laleya said, reading my mind, "unless you tell her, which would be inadvisable."

"So, even Lena won't be able to..." I pointed a waving finger at my head and whistled eerily.

Laleya leaned toward me conspiratorially. "She will see only what you want her to see. Nothing more."

I smiled. "Well, seeing as you put it that way."

"Remember, your companions must also agree. You cannot speak for them."

"They'll agree. Trust me. Even Izin. Especially him."

"We will await your confirmation," Gastillion said.

I emptied my coffee thoughtfully. "The Matarons wouldn't be happy if they knew you parked a ship over their homeworld, and they never even knew it was there."

"We were careful to avoid their sensors," Gastillion said, "something we neglected to do when you arrived."

"I wonder what the Spawn will do to them, when they realize they lied."

"If they attack Kif-atah," Laleya said, "the Tau Cetins will protect the Matarons."

"What!" I exploded. "Are you crazy?"

"The Tau Cetins are a very advanced people," Gastillion said. "They will do everything in their power to prevent genocide."

"Will they stop the Nisk taking revenge for the murder of Girutonak?"

"The Nisk will deal with that Mataron crime through the Forum, a possibility that does not exist for the Spawn, who are guilty of far worse."

"So all they'll get is a rap across the knuckles?" I said. "They deserve more than that."

"You despise the Matarons and they despise you," Laleya said, "but they have merely taken a wrong turn. They are trapped by their own fears, but in time they will overcome them. One day, they will stand with us as brothers."

"You're an optimist," I said, not believing a word of it.

"All intelligent life in the universe eventually finds its way onto the same path," Laleya said.

"Oh yeah? When was the last time you had tea and cake with a snakehead?"

"Never. No Uvo has ever set foot on Kif-atah, not in seven hundred thousand years."

"Because you scare them," I said, a little scared of her myself.

"We make no attempt to hide our abilities. The Matarons fear us because they are a very secretive people. They do not realize the more awakened one is, the fewer secrets one has. On Uvona, there are no secrets."

"It seems to me you have a lot of secrets."

"Between the Uvo, there are none," Laleya insisted. "How can there be? Every thought, every impulse, every unkind word, every good deed and bad is instantly known to us all."

"It's not that way on Earth, or on Kif-atah."

"You would be surprised how alike we all are. We are at different stages of development, but essentially, all intelligent life is the same. The Totemic Trials prove that."

"They tried to kill me, three different ways."

"Their Totemic religion is built upon the journey all intelligent life in the universe follows. Each trial represents mastering a plane of perception, a stage of unfolding consciousness, a dimension of reality. Call it what you will. These dimensions interpenetrate the entire cosmos, which is why we all walk the same path, face the same challenges, master the same lessons. They are as ubiquitous as gravity or spacetime. Did you not recognize the symbolism of the Mataron totems?"

"I was too busy staying alive."

Laleya exchanged a knowing look with Gastillion and said, "The plains of Magrod are the burning ground of physical purification, the experience of being born into a higher way.

"The seething sea is the battleground of the emotions, the struggle to overcome the fears and illusions represented by the shrieking varidons. When the emotions are mastered, the watery plane ceases to exist, because it was of your own creation.

"The third trial symbolizes the disciplining of the mind. The Felrum's spitting fires are the critical thoughts that burn one's self and others with their harshness. Defeating the Felrum makes one immune to the fiery tongues of thought and frees the consciousness.

"You see, Captain Kade," she concluded, "the Totemic Trials are the Mataron symbology for mastering the three aspects of one's lower self. They correspond to the physical, emotional and mental dimensions of the universe that challenge all intelligent life. No matter how outwardly different we may appear, no matter how peculiar our cultures, our languages, our histories, eventually we all master ourselves, expanding our consciousness through these universal dimensions."

"Is that what the Uvo did?" I asked.

"That and more. It has been this way since the beginning of time and will be until the end of the universe. On your world, you call the trials by different names; birth, baptism, transfiguration. Every culture in the universe has its names, its teachers, its great exemplars, but they are all the same. We all learn to overcome the outer illusions of form and discover the inner reality, the true self, what humans call the soul."

"I guess the Spawn missed that lesson."

"One day, even they will understand," Laleya insisted. "For now, the Spawn define themselves by the characteristics of form, and that separates them from us. But they have the same magnetic seed of Life that is within us all. One day, they will define themselves by higher qualities, unrelated to form, to appearance. Only then will they emerge from their present delusion, and know we are the same."

"The same," I whispered, recalling my impression of Girutonak, a hideous insectoid alien possessing strangely human qualities of love and duty. "Maybe."

"It's what makes the Galactic Forum possible," Gastillion declared. "If it weren't true, we could never have come together the way we have."

"I saw the statues on Centralis," I said, recalling the

crumbling, ancient monuments at the center of the galaxy, commemorating the first great civilizations that had founded the Galactic Forum and created the Access Treaty millions of years ago. The Original Signators had all been wildly different in appearance, utterly alien to each other, and yet they'd founded not an interstellar empire, but a galactic brotherhood.

"There are many monuments like those, on many worlds," Laleya said. "What humans achieved on Earth is in its own way a monument, one that gives us all hope."

"What did we do?"

"You proved the Spawn can be redeemed."

"Ah, at the point of a gun."

"Survival is a great motivator," Gastillion said. "Your friendship with Izin Nilva Kren proves there is hope, even for the Spawn."

"That's not going to save us in this war."

"No, it is not," Gastillion Kalantropis agreed somberly. "The Spawn will not be redeemed for a very long time. Until then, we must guard ourselves against them, and those like them, painful as that may be."

* * * *

I discussed Laleya's proposal with the others after returning to the *Silver Lining*. Once they realized they'd be protected from Spawn mind probes, while retaining their memories, they readily agreed. I informed Laleya of their acceptance, and next morning we awoke feeling like we'd slept for only a moment, recalling no dreams. After breakfast, Gastillion confirmed everything had gone as planned although none of us were entirely convinced.

Two days later, the *Parsiphilius* finished drilling the access tunnel down to the Nisk royal's sarcophagus. They then strengthened an area in front of the entrance where the *Silver Lining* could land for loading while our thrusterbots hauled the stasis chamber to the surface, one laborious step at a time.

Continuous optical feeds filled the ship's screens with monotonous images of the heavy lifters crab walking the massive chamber to the surface. We all quickly lost interest in their progress, except for Izin who barely slept for the week it took to get the stasis chamber to the surface.

When the thrusterbots emerged into sunlight, Izin and I went outside in p-suits to supervise the loading. The *Parsiphilius* was no longer visible, keeping our memories of her to a minimum and permitting the Nisk royal unobstructed access to our recollections of her rescue.

Izin used a thruster pack to hover over the sarcophagus as our big hull crawlers crept onto the ramp in perfect synchronization. The ship's landing gear sagged into the D'kol hardened fungus under the weight as they eased it into the cargo hold with very little room to spare. The big bots set it down on the deck, I sealed the door-ramp and Jase purged the cargo deck's atmosphere. Smaller bots emerged and began decontaminating every surface, then Gastillion's voice sounded in my p-suit via a private link.

"We'll be returning to Harlingara soon."

"Is that your homeworld?"

"No. The D'kol origin world has been uninhabitable for a very long time. Harlingara is the Emperor's private residence. He is waiting for news of our expedition."

"Before you go, could you do us a small favor? There's a Mataron device on our hull. Could you remove it?"

"Ah yes, the wake amplifier. Have you tried washing it off?"

"With what?"

"Water. It is a primitive device sensitive to conduction, and the casing is highly porous. Water inside the vacuum layer would cause unintended electrical flows."

"It'll short circuit!" If I wasn't wearing a helmet, I'd have slapped myself in the head for not thinking of it myself. "Thanks for the tip."

"I shall not contact you again, Captain Kade, although we will remain in this system until you leave, ensuring the Matarons do not interfere with your departure."

"Will we meet again?"

"Perhaps. After Harlingara, we will return to the Orion Arm to advise the Tau Cetins of our success. Goodbye, Captain Kade."

I sidled up to Izin, who was now busily supervising his fungus scrubbing bots. "I want you to put a hose on that snakehead gizmo on the hull."

"A hose, Captain?"

"Yeah, give it a good bath. The water will short it out."

"Hmph!" Izin grunted thoughtfully. "That is an ingenious idea, Captain."

"Yeah, it is, isn't it," I agreed, wishing I'd thought of it.

* * * *

Six hours of scrubberbot decontamination later, the lower cargo deck was habitable again. Nisk clicking was running softly through my mind, a gentle touch compared to its earlier, oppressive stranglehold over my thoughts. A series of pictograms floated before my inner eye in a specific order, identical to symbols engraved on a circular plate at one end of the sarcophagus. They were meaningless to me, as I couldn't read Nisk, but their purpose was obvious.

I turned to Izin, who stood cradling his sniper rifle on the other side of the transverse bulkhead dividing the lower cargo deck in two and waved him back. "Shut the door."

He hesitated, not wanting to leave me alone, then tapped the wall panel. The big airtight cargo door slid across the deck, stopping before it fully sealed, leaving a gap just wide enough for the barrel of his sniper rifle.

"No shooting," I said, regretting have agreed to let him

arm himself.

"The Nisk may not understand, Captain. It might give you no time to explain."

"No matter what happens, Izin, don't kill her. I mean it."

Her life was more important than mine, although Izin didn't see it that way. He said nothing and aimed through the narrow gap, making me wonder if I should lock him out of the cargo hold, but there was a chance he was right. The Nisk royal wouldn't be expecting to be revived by a human in a strange ship. She might be disoriented from stasis sleep, frightened or angry at what had happened to the *Iskeratix*, and simply rip my head off. Izin had loaded his most powerful stun round, but if it bounced off her shell, his next shot would be an armor piecing detonator that would splatter her intestines across the cargo hold.

"Sirius, we should get a hullbot to open it," Marie said, watching from the bridge.

"No, she's got to see me." She had to sense Girutonak's mind block before she'd trust us.

I stepped up to the pictogram display as the gentle rhythm of Nisk clicking painted the sequence in my mind, guiding my fingers through the symbols. The outline of each engraving glowed with white light once selected until every symbol was lit.

"That's the last one," I said, then a circle of light appeared around the display and the top of the stasis chamber cracked apart with a hiss of air. Two long rectangular doors slid out over the sides as soft yellow light spilled from the interior.

I backed away, eyes fixed on the top of the sarcophagus. When no Nisk emerged, I scrambled up onto the chamber and spied an enormous coleopteran sleeping inside. She had a dull golden shell flecked with red, was fitted with silver attachments and covered by a thin yellow mist. Her six legs were folded up against her sides and both antenna-manipulators were crossed in front of her huge head.

"What do you see, Captain?" Izin asked.

"A very...big...bug," I replied slowly as the yellow mist drained away like water and the claw-tip of one manipulator twitched. "She's alive."

Her dead black, compound eyes stared ahead, unblinking, showing no sign of consciousness. Slowly, an antenna-manipulator unfolded and her legs stretched.

"Hey!" I yelled, waving both hands. "Up here."

She seemed not to hear me, then one of her manipulators flashed through the air and swatted me like I was the bug, hurling me off the sarcophagus. I landed hard, slid across the deck and lay stunned, wheezing to breath. A manipulator claw caught the top of the sarcophagus and her head lifted above the sides and looked around. She spotted Izin pointing a gun at her through the gap in the doorway and leapt out of the sarcophagus toward him.

I got to my feet, realizing she thought he was Spawn, and raised my arms. "No! Here!"

She ignored me and charged at Izin who pulled his rifle back and closed the airtight door as her head slammed into it with a heavy crack. She turned toward me as I took the translator from my belt, but she charged again, forcing me to dive with ultra-reflexed speed. She snatched at me and missed, then I rolled to my knees as she slid across the deck, trying to stop.

"Girutonak sent me!" I yelled at the translator, the first time the mind-block had let me speak his name. The translator clicked Nisk at her and she froze, confused. "We were in a Mataron prison together."

I couldn't tell if she understood, but she fixed her eyes upon me and came closer. I fought the urge to run, listening to the metallic clink of her footfalls.

When she towered above me, I said, "Girutonak sent me in his place, to protect you."

She scooped me off the deck with one manipulator-

antennae and clicked at me.

"You are human," my translator announced.

"Yes. I am a friend."

Her hideous dead eyes studied me suspiciously. "You serve Spawn."

"No." I pointed at the airtight door. "He's from Earth, like me. Not Spawn. Terrestrial amphibian."

She clicked again and the translator declared, "All Spawn are enemies."

"Yes, they are." I started to relax. "I can prove Girutonak sent me. He did something to me, in here." I pointed at my head.

She looked at the airtight door, ensuring it was still closed, then gently touched my head with her other antenna-manipulator. Her touch revolted me, but I forced myself to remain still, giving her a chance. I stared at the tiny black bristles on her black arms, recalling how Girutonak had held me that close, forcing his will upon me. She had the strength to crush my head like rotten fruit, but her touch was delicate and precise.

After a long silence, she clicked, "Iskeratul-consort-Girutonak is dead."

"Yes. The Matarons killed him. Can you see what happened?"

"I see...everything," she clicked softly. " All are dead." She shuddered, making a wailing sound my translator could not interpret.

"I'm...very sorry," I said, sensing sadness behind her cold, emotionless black eyes. "Can you remove what Girutonak did to me?"

She gazed at me for a long time, holding me close to her eyes, silently probing my mind.

"Hello, Irukoochati?" I said gently, trying to get her attention. "Can you remove the mind block?"

Her head tilted slightly, aware of me again. "I understand, Human-Kode-Soris...Protector in his place."

I was so close now, I could have stuck my fist in one

of her big black pool eyes, then pain exploded in my head and I passed out. When I came to, I was lying on my back on the cargo deck and she was standing over me. When she saw I was conscious, she gave me a burst of clicking.

"Iskeratul-consort-Girutonak mind-impulse gone from Human-Kode-Soris," the translator announced from the deck beside me.

The airtight door opened a crack and the barrel of Izin's rifle slid out.

"It's OK, Izin. She's friendly. Put it away. Stay there until I call you," I yelled, then the rifle barrel withdrew, but the door remained ajar so he could listen in. "You are friendly, right?"

"Iskeratul-royal-Irukoochati friend to Human-Kode-Soris."

"That's good to know." I scooped up my translator and looked up at her, finally matching the coleopteran face Girutonak had forced into my dreams with the real thing. "I'm pleased to meet you, Irukoochati." I motioned toward the airtight door. "Now I need you to go through there. I have to depressurize this end of the cargo deck so I can get your stasis chamber off my ship."

"Why you must?"

"We can't take off while it's on board. It's too heavy."

"I cannot leave my eggs."

"Eggs?" Girutonak said nothing about eggs. "In there?" I pointed at her sarcophagus. "How many eggs?"

"Thousand-two-millions."

My eyes bulged in surprise. "You've got two billion eggs in that thing?"

"Iskeratul Strain, to start world-new-Nisk."

"No wonder it's so damn heavy," I muttered. "Izin, get out here. Leave the gun."

The airtight door opened a little more and Izin stepped into plain view, unarmed, but didn't approach.

"His name is Izin," I said slowly, looking up at her. "Don't hurt him. He's a friend. OK?"

"Iskeratul-royal-Irukoochati not harm Earth-tamph-Izin."

"You hear that, Izin? We're all friends here. No one's ripping anyone's head off today."

He approached warily, glanced at the massive stasis chamber, then adjusted his vocalizer to speak Nisk. "Can your eggs be frozen?"

"Yes," she replied. "They are in preservation."

Izin turned to me. "We can jettison the frozen foods, Captain, clear out the med freezer, the cryogenic chemicals. It'll leave us short of supplies, but we can live on freeze dried ration packs for months."

I turned to Irukoochati. "Do you understand? We'll put your eggs in our freezers."

"Acceptable, Human-Kode-Soris."

"I'll have the bots start jettisoning the supplies immediately, Captain," Izin said, and took the elevator up to engineering.

"Are you hungry?" I asked Irukoochati.

"I am in need," she replied. "Stasis chamber has no food."

"There's a planet full of your cyanobacteria outside."

"It will be contaminated."

"Yeah," I said thinking fast. "You like sugar, right?" It was the only thing we could sell to the Nisk, who happened to have a massive sweet tooth, or would have, if they had teeth.

"Human-sugar? Yes, very much."

"Good. I'll get you–"

"Skipper," Jase's voice sounded from the intercom. "Something just went into orbit overhead. Right above us."

"A ship?"

"It's about seventy kilos and actively scanning. It's got to be another sentry probe."

"The snakeheads will be here soon," I said, certain the probe was already reading Nisk technology and life signs.

With the sarcophagus on board, there was no way the *Silver Lining* could launch, which made us a sitting duck. And if the *Riku* got here before we could fly, the *Parsiphilius* would have to destroy her, revealing the D'kol to Irukoochati and any Mataron survivors.

"Izin, get those eggs into the freezers fast. We've got to dump the stasis chamber and get off the ground before the Riku gets here."

"I'm issuing task assignments now, Captain."

I opened the airtight door to the forward section and turned to Irukoochati. "I'm going to have to seal you in here for a while. After we dump the sarcophagus, we'll decontaminate the rear section in space. Until then, this will have to do."

She marched up behind me and looked into the forward section. "Acceptable." She stepped through and turned to me. "Thank you, Protector."

"We have a naval base on Uralo IV. I can take you there."

She turned toward me. "Talib-Nis is closer."

"I don't know where that is," I said, puzzled. There was only one Nisk system in all of Mapped Space and it was a long way from here.

"Common designation, Yentauri System."

"I'll look it up."

"Thank you, Human-Kode-Soris. I have one question."

"What is it?"

She folded her legs and settled her shell on the cold deck plates. "What are snakeheads?"

* * * *

"Not the ice cream," Jase complained as we watched a cargobot on the bridge screen dump a thermal container from the topside hull.

The rectangular box bounced off the ship's side as it

fell, split open when it hit the ground and scattered ice cream packs over the pile of frozen foods, medicines and cryo-chemicals growing port side. The mechanical spider immediately scuttled back across the hull to an access port to collect another load. Inside the ship, other bots were busily ferrying frozen supplies from cold storage to the small access locks, which ran full decontamination cycles every time after opening to Galot V's toxic, bacterial atmosphere.

The corridors outside the access ports were now stacked high with frozen containers, packs, satchels and cases waiting to be jettisoned, while our few precision engineering bots were carefully filling cold storage with Nisk egg sacks from Irukoochati's sarcophagus. The sacks were synthetic, translucent spheres, cloudy inside and frozen into solid balls of ice that steamed vapor in the ship's warm air.

"Have we got enough room for them all?" Marie asked.

"Izin says we'll have one freezer to spare." I replied.

Jase frowned. "That's where we should have put the ice cream."

"Stims and cryo-chems get priority," I said.

Marie watched another container crash onto the growing trash heap alongside the ship. "We're making a hell of a mess out there. The Matarons are going to know we made room for something."

"No time to hide it." I ignored the jettisoned containers and watched an optical box showing Izin supervising the egg transfer in the lower cargo hold. "Izin, how much longer?"

"We're moving the last egg spheres now, Captain," he replied as a precision bot crept past cradling a frozen egg-ball like it was carrying unstable novarium. "It'll take at least another five hours to finish jettisoning the frozen stores."

"Just get the stasis chamber off the ship. Any frozen

stores we haven't unloaded by then, we'll dump in space."

"As you wish," he replied.

When all of the eggs had been moved into the freezers, I dropped the stern door and the four big thrusterbots crab-walked Irukoochati's sarcophagus off the ship. They set it down just beyond the ramp and ambled back inside, then the scrubberbots began another laborious sterilization of the cargo hold.

"The satellite's still up there," Jase said, "and the water's not working."

Two hoses running from a maintenance airlock had been spraying the wake amplifier for hours, but it was still firing its beam into the tripod cap.

"We can't sit here waiting for it to short," I said, regretting not insisting the D'kol remove it, but it was too late now. "Izin, dump the hoses."

"But the wake amplifier is still functioning."

"I know. Seal the hull. We're leaving."

"Very well, Captain."

"It's moved," Marie said, staring at the tripod. Both it and the snakehead noisemaker were both dripping and electricity was arcing between them.

"It can't move. It's clamped." I took a closer look, thinking it was a little off center. "Izin, is the tripod OK?"

"The water is conducting energy from the wake amplifier onto the tripod legs, Captain," he replied. "It's weakening the magnetic clamps."

"Will it survive launch?"

"I don't know. I could bring it inside and replace the clamps."

"We don't have time," I replied, hoping it would work long enough for us to slip away.

While we raced through prelaunch, the hullbots dumped whatever freeze packs they were carrying, threw the hoses over the side rather than waste time cleaning them, and clambered into the maintenance locks to be decontaminated. Finally, the bridge screen reoriented for forward flight, giving us a panoramic view of *Iskeratix's* monstrous skeleton, then we lifted off and climbed vertically between the ribs toward space.

"Give me a marker on the sentry," I said, keeping the acceleration low so the air pressure would not buffet the weakened tripod.

A red hostile indicator appeared on screen as the sky darkened to space. The sentry probe was in range, so I launched a drone just to get it off our tail. The drone leapt from the bow, turned in a graceful curve to starboard and climbed rapidly away.

"Technically, that's an act of war," Marie said wryly.

"I doubt they'll complain to the Forum," I said, certain the last thing they wanted was to draw attention to Galot V.

The drone faded to a point of light, heading straight for the hostile indicator, although the sentry itself was too small and dark for an optical.

"The sentry's evading, still tracking us," Jase said, then a white flash appeared in the sky followed by an orange white bloom.

Jase studied his sensor scans uncertainly. "No direct hit. No sign of the probe. Looks like a proximity kill," he said as Izin joined us on the bridge.

"One of the tripod magclamps has shorted out," he said. "And the beam's energy is degrading the cap. It won't hold for long, Captain."

"How's our passenger doing?" I asked as we accelerated through vacuum toward the edge of Galot V's gravity well.

"She wants more sugar."

"Give her all we've got. Break down the ration packs if you have to."

Jase frowned. "No ice cream. Now no sugar!"

"Yentauri's not far," I said. "A couple of weeks, then we'll head to Uralo IV to resupply."

Jase swept space for the *Riku* while I plotted a zig-zag

course to the Yentauri System. The Tau Cetin astrographics indicated it was uninhabited, although there'd been an unchallenged Nisk claim on it for over three hundred thousand years. With no sign of the *Riku*, we jumped out as soon as we reached flat space, then a field stability warning flashed onto the bridge screen.

"The cap is gone, Captain," Izin replied. "Two magclamps failed when we bubbled."

"And we're ringing like a bell," I said bitterly.

"Yes, Captain. If the Riku arrives in the Galot System any time in the next thirty hours, they will be able to track us."

"Make another cap. Cannibalize your bots if you have to."

"We need those bots, Captain."

"The Matarons know there's a Nisk on board. If we can't lose them, they'll track us all the way to Yentauri and destroy us in sight of Talib-Nis."

And if that happened, the sleeping giant of the galaxy would remain forever in its slumber.

Chapter Six : Talib-Nis

Nisk Myriad World 283
Yentauri System
Outer Camelopardalis
0.94 Earth Normal Gravity (Nisk Optimal)
796 light years from Sol
Planetary Nest Surveyors

"Exoskeletal-attachments-Nisk are brain-reptilian-Mataron incompatible," Irukoochati said as she scooped brown sugar out of an open storage container and spooned it into her mouth. Three separate tongue-like appendages wiped the manipulator clean with rapid, slithering movements that made my skin crawl.

"The snakeheads wanted to understand your technology, to use it for themselves. That's why they took Girutonak."

"Science-reptilian-Mataron too primitive for exoskeletal-attachments-Nisk." Irukoochati crossed her manipulator arms and tapped her claws against her upper arm-segments in irritation.

The forward section of the lower cargo deck had been set aside for her use, there being no cabin or passageway large enough to accommodate her. Izin had assigned two bots to ensure she always had food and water, to clean up after she defecated, and to allow him to watch her every move. We'd installed a large screen for her use and given her access to the ship's library, although all she watched was the bridge screen feed. Mostly she consumed copious quantities of sugar, hummed to herself and crapped on the deck.

"Does Iskeratul-consort-Girutonak's mind-impulse-effect cause Human-Kode-Soris pain?" she asked, watching me with her dead insect eyes.

"The headaches are fading and the nightmares have stopped."

"He was himself not."

"It wasn't his fault."

"Reptilian-Mataron-snakeheads learn nothing from him."

I smiled at how neatly she'd adopted my nickname for the Matarons. "They tortured him, drove him mad."

"Consorts are loyal," she said absently, convinced Girutonak had told them nothing.

"Do you have many consorts?" I asked.

"For my needs, enough." She stopped tapping. "Humans have one only, do they not?"

"Yeah, and that's more than most men can handle."

She shoveled more of our rapidly shrinking stockpile of sucrose molecules into her triple tongued mouth, forcing me to suppress a shiver of revulsion and look away.

"Why is there no record of a Nisk colony on Talib-Nis?" I asked.

"None exists. Planetary-nest-surveyors prepare, ship-nest-Iskeratix build."

"So there's only a survey team on the planet?"

"Planetary-nest-surveyors will be where crust rock is

hard, surface is wet, air is warmest."

"At the equator?"

"Yes, in galleries."

"Will there be a landing beacon?"

"Not for ship-human-Silverlining."

"We'll ask them to show themselves when we arrive."

"Planetary-nest-surveyors not listen for human signalers." She tapped one of the gray metal casings on her carapace. "They hear me, when close."

"How close?"

"Near surface, if Planetary-nest-surveyors remain."

"Why wouldn't they still be there?"

"Ship-nest-Iskeratix did not arrive."

"How long before they consider you overdue?"

"Nisk on time. Always."

"Will they wait?" I asked, suspecting impatience drove their punctuality.

"Once all tasks complete, Planetary-nest-surveyors seek new tasks."

"In that case, I hope they had plenty to do."

* * * *

"Captain, are you awake?" Izin's voice sounded from the intercom a few days later.

"I am now." I yawned wearily, finding the post mind-block headache had faded to a dull ache behind my eyes.

"The superluminal field's harmonic has changed."

I sat up, fully awake. "I'll be right there "

"Doesn't he ever sleep?" Marie complained drowsily beside me.

"He might, but his mind never does."

I gave her a peck on the cheek, dressed and hurried down to engineering where Izin was sitting in front of his bank of screens staring at numbers and graphical diagnostics.

"There's a recurring instability in the bubble every two

point six seconds." He pointed at a frequency diagram on one screen illustrating the oscillation. "Each cycle, the wake amplifier's effect drops away to almost nothing, then pulses back to three hundred percent above baseline."

"Above?" I said with a sinking feeling. "It's louder?"

"Three times louder. The ship's wake is pulsing intermittently through spacetime. Because we haven't sighted the Riku in weeks, the amplifier may have changed modes, making it easier for them to reacquire us."

"We've got to cap it again. I don't care where you get the parts from."

"I'll have to cannibalize our hullbots. It will limit my capacity to maintain our hull mounted systems in space. If we lose spatial distorters or shield emitters, it will be impossible to repair them."

"Better that than have the Riku find us."

"Very well, Captain," he said unhappily, then I went back to bed.

* * * *

"Captain, did you alter our superluminal field settings?" Izin asked over the intercom the following day.

"No change," I replied from the bridge. "Why?"

"Our velocity just increased zero point two percent."

Marie looked surprised and studied her console. "He's right."

Izin projected a complex graphic onto the bridge screen and said, "The disharmonic has vanished, Captain. The amplifier may have concluded we escaped the Riku and has entered a terminal phase."

"It's going to blow up?" Jase said anxiously.

"I want eyes on that thing, fast," I said. If we took major damage now and couldn't bubble, it would take centuries to reach the nearest habitable world, leaving us trapped in interstellar space.

"I have a hull crawler heading to the nearest maintenance lock, Captain."

We sealed all airtight doors against a hull breach, then a bot optical feed appeared on the bridge screen, showing the inside of an access port.

"Ready, Captain," Izin said.

I dropped the bubble and set a new waypoint while the hull cooled. Soon, a small sensorbot crawled out onto the skin and mag-walked toward the snakehead noisemaker. It was still harpooned to the hull, but was emitting no radiation of any kind. When the bot got close, Izin zoomed its optical until the microscopic holes in the amplifier's casing appeared, ringed by tiny black circles.

"The interior is fused, Captain," Izin said at last. "It short circuited."

Bubble heat would have vaporized any water inside as soon as we went superluminal, but the drenching we'd given it on the ground had been enough, even if it had taken days for the device to fail.

"The hoses worked," I said with relief. "It just took a while."

The hullbot activated a laser cutter and began severing the amplifier's hull clamps. When it began cutting through the third leg, a white line blinked into existence, parallel to our course.

"Superluminal flyby, one forty five degrees off axis," Jase announced. "It's the Riku. Damn! Those guys just don't give up."

"Izin, we're going to have company," I said.

"I need two minutes, Captain," he replied, then we sat on the edge of our seats while the bot continued cutting.

"Contact!" Jase said after the timer passed six minutes. "Eighteen million kilometers astern. They've seen us."

"Izin, tear it off and jump," I said.

The hullbot's laser cutter winked out and it grabbed the amplifier with two arms. It wrenched it hard enough to break the partially severed third leg and sprang into space with the amplifier in its arms.

"Riku's spiking!" Jase warned as the Mataron ship's energy level suddenly climbed. "She's jumping in."

A line of light blinked onto the screen as the *Riku* performed a sub-second micro bubble toward us, then the bridge screen feeds vanished as Jase stowed our masts. The sensorbot's optical feed was still visible on the bridge screen as I fired our port thrusters at full power, pushing us sideways. The Mataron scout cruiser appeared directly above our previous position, watched by our drifting sensorbot. Yellow energy bursts flashed down past our starboard side as the *Riku* fired blind, blasting the space we'd occupied a moment before, then we bubbled away.

Jase exhaled slowly. "Too close."

"How'd you know they'd shoot without a target lock?" Marie asked.

"They're scared. The amplifier's dead and they know we have a Nisk on board. They've got no choice. They have to kill us now."

"I wouldn't want to be them," Jase said, thinking they wouldn't catch us and would have to return empty handed to Kif-atah.

"Now we'll see how good they really are." I decreased power to the bubble to barely ten percent, increasing our flight time to the Yentauri System and cutting our wake to a mere ripple in spacetime.

"Slow and sneaky," Marie said appreciatively.

"We're going to need more sugar. A lot more."

* * * *

"Human-Kode-Soris, I must be closer to establish contact," Irukoochati's synthesized voice sounded on the bridge. She'd been patiently watching the bridge screen feed on her viewer for hours while we loitered outside Yentauri IV's gravity well and had finally decided there was nothing to be gained by waiting any longer.

"Still no sign of the Riku, or the Nisk," Jase said, in silent agreement with our coleopteran passenger.

"Doesn't mean she's not out there," I said, wary of committing to insertion and getting trapped in curved space where we couldn't bubble away.

"Human-Kode-Soris?" Irukoochati pressed, waiting for an answer.

I killed the intercom and glanced at Izin. "You could have set her translator to say my name right."

"I like the way she says your name, Captain," Izin replied. "I'm thinking of calling you Human-Kode-Soris myself."

"Hmph. What does she call you?"

"Kren-Nilva-Izin."

"So you taught her to say your name correctly, but not mine?"

"Chief Engineer's prerogative."

Marie smiled. "She's waiting...Human-Kode-Soris."

"Don't you start," I said and reactivated the two way. "OK, Irukoochati, we'll survey the planet for your people."

"They will not reveal themselves to you," she said, "and your sensors are incapable of detecting them."

"We'll scan for what they're looking for. If we find a suitable site, we'll go down for a closer look."

"Acceptable."

We began an equatorial survey of the planet from the edge of the gravity well, finding no sign of intelligent life. It was a cold world with enormous ice sheets at both poles, swampy continents dotted with thousands of lakes, and oceans supersaturated with calcium carbonates over more than half the surface area. Dead forests blackened by ancient fires covered every continent, giving the land a gray to black appearance.

"I'm not reading any life signs," Jase said. "Not now anyway. It was carboniferous, before everything died."

"Are you sure?" Marie asked.

Jase shrugged. "That's what it says."

She arched her brow, surprised. "The Carboniferous Era was Earth's greenest period."

"Now we know why the Forum agreed to let the Nisk dump their fungus here," I said. "Can't kill a world that's already dead."

"What killed the planet?" Marie wondered.

"The atmosphere," Izin replied. "The carbon dioxide level is too low for photosynthesis. That's why all the plants died out."

"What happened to the CO2?" I asked.

"CO2 is the gas of life, Captain. The trees, the phytoplankton, the sea creatures with exoskeletons, they consumed it all."

"Right. No CO2, no photosynthesis, no food chain."

"Yes, Captain. The same thing almost happened on Earth thousands of years ago. Only the industrial revolution saved mankind from a similar fate."

"There are massive carbon readings below the surface and on the ocean floor," Jase said. "It's thousands of meters deep. Must have been a lot of sea life down there once."

"We will excavate the carbon rocks to make way for our galleries," Irukoochati explained, "and mine the calcium carbonates from the ocean floor. The carbon dioxide will be recycled into the atmosphere allowing us to restart the food chain."

"For your fungus?" I asked. "It eats CO2?"

"Of course. Our cyanobacteria is the most efficient carbon-organism-photosynthetic in existence."

"Will it eat the dead forests?" Marie asked.

"They will be consumed," Irukoochati replied. "We have been waiting for this planet's ice age to end."

I gave Izin a puzzled look. "Ice age?"

"Oceans contain many times the CO2 of the atmosphere, Captain," Izin explained. "In an ice age, the oceans cool and absorb carbon dioxide. The Nisk were waiting for the ice age to end so the oceans would warm and release CO_2 back into the atmosphere, thereby allowing plants to grow again."

"Kren-Nilva-Izin is correct," Irukoochati said. "In a century, Talib-Nis will have ten times the CO_2 required for photosynthesis, enough to sustain us."

"Well there's no fungus down there yet," Jase said, watching his scans.

"Planetary-nest-surveyors do not seed," she explained. "Biosphere adaptation occurs after nest construction. The ship-nest-Iskeratix was the seed ship."

"Where's the survey ship now?" I asked.

"The ship-nest-surveyor does not stay. It gathers supplies."

"So your survey team could have evacuated with the last supply drop?"

"It is possible, Human-Kode-Soris."

Jase gave me a shake of his head indicating there were no Nisk on the planet. Considering the *Iskeratix* was more than a year overdue, I tended to agree, but Irukoochati had not given up hope. With my doubts growing, we continued on around the planet searching for any sign of the Nisk.

"There's a volcanic plain ahead," Jase said. "I'm reading giant batholiths containing quartz, feldspar, silica and alkali metal oxides ten to thirty kilometers underground. Solid granite."

"High hardness and toughness, structurally strong, but not brittle," Izin said. "That section of crust also appears to be tectonically stable."

"Ideal for tunneling," I said.

"If they are anywhere, Human-Kode-Soris, they will be there," Irukoochati said.

"Any sign of the Riku?" I asked.

Jase shook his head. "No, but she could be outside sensor range, waiting for us to take the bait."

"Irukoochati, does your survey team have weapons that could destroy a Mataron cruiser?" I asked.

"No, Human-Kode-Soris, only personal protection," she replied, confirming even if her planetary engineers were down there, they'd be no help if the *Riku* showed up.

I cut the intercom. "My gut tells me not to do it, but we can't sit out here forever."

"We could wait for the supply ship," Marie suggested.

"If it's coming. There's always Uralo IV, but we barely have enough to keep Irukoochati fed all the way there."

"The Nisk are our best hope of liberating Earth, Captain," Izin said. "If they are here, we should try to contact them."

"What are we waiting for?" Jase asked with a reckless grin.

Marie nodded her agreement, then I reopened the intercom link. "Irukoochati, we're going down to the surface. If the Matarons are out there, we won't be able to get back out to bubble."

"I understand, Human-Kode-Soris."

I turned to Jase. "Put a marker on those batholiths and watch for snakeheads."

When the indicator appeared on the bridge screen, I nosed the *Silver Lining* down into the planet's gravity well. We made a slow run to the atmosphere, watching for the *Riku*, then began a long glide toward a swampy plain covered by scrawny, lifeless trees and huge gray rock formations. When we reached the troposphere, I levelled off and followed the equator.

"All channels open, Nisk translator on," Marie said.

"This is the human ship, Silver Lining. We are transporting a Nisk Royal–"

"Skipper!" Jase said urgently. "It's the Riku."

"What?"

"She was hiding behind the fifth planet. She's jumping in."

"They were waiting for us," I said, certain we were in too deep to get back to flat space.

"How'd they know we were coming here?" Marie asked.

"This is the only world in Orion with a Nisk claim on it," Izin said.

"Yeah," I agreed, "they gambled we'd bring her here, and got lucky."

"The Riku's at the edge of the gravity well, coming down fast," Jase warned.

The *Silver Lining* shuddered as explosions tore through both engine housings at once. Five engines died and the sixth sputtered while our thrusters fought to keep us airborne. Our speed fell sharply, then a damage control optical box appeared on the bridge screen, showing the stern. Both engine housings were a burning mass of tangled metal, belching thick black smoke that blotted out the sky behind us.

"Stern quarter fire suppressors have failed, port and starboard sides," Izin reported. "Thermal doors forward of the engines are sealed. We cannot reach orbit." It was a terse death sentence delivered without a trace of emotion.

"Only one way to go," I said and nosed the *Silver Lining* down for speed while the AI did its best to maintain our trim as engine debris spun off into our smoky contrail.

"Blow the cargo door," I said, looking for water ahead. We were far from the coast, but there were shallow lakes all around us.

Marie triggered a soft boom of exploding bolts that reverberated through the ship while the optical box showed the stern door-ramp fly off into the smoke trailing astern.

"There's no fire in the cargo hold," she said, "but the bulkheads are getting hot."

I opened the airtight door dividing the lower cargo deck in half. "Irukoochati, when we land, you'll have to run through the flames. It's the best I can do."

"Acceptable, Human-Kode-Soris. Thank you for trying."

Izin put an optical feed from the lower cargo deck in one corner of the bridge screen showing Irukoochati peering from the forward section. Her coleopteran eyes were fixed upon the open cargo door and the smoke, flames and debris pouring from our disintegrating engines.

"The Riku's forty clicks out, thirty degrees up, following us down," Jase said.

"The atmosphere is breathable, but cold," Izin reported, not that we had time to don p-suits.

We slowed to subsonic and began to go down by the stern as we raced above dead treetops. I nosed the bow down, trying to keep her level and our speed up, hoping to reach a lake ahead.

"Izin, shut her down," I said, not wanting to risk the e-plant detonating on impact. "I'll ditch using backup power cells."

We dropped toward the spiny branches, then a wrenching metallic thud sounded as the underside sensor mast smashed through the trees and sheared off. The bridge screen wide angle view adjusted for the loss of our belly optics as we passed over a narrow lake, still too fast to ditch. There was a blur of movement in the hold as Irukoochati charged cross the cargo deck, leapt out into the smoke and vanished from sight.

"Did she make it?" Marie asked.

"I couldn't see," I replied as our underside hull began shattering treetops like matchsticks.

The screen flickered as our lateral masts tore off, leaving me only the topside dorsal to steer by. Flames pouring from our wrecked engines set the bone dry corpse trees alight, leaving a path of fire and destruction in our wake. Our remaining thrusters began winking out as the trees hammered the hull while the glimmer of blue water appeared through the spindly forest ahead.

"The e-plant is sub-critical, Captain, and cooling," Izin said, relieving me of one fear, then the *Silver Lining* began listing to port.

"Impact positions," I ordered.

The others lay back, pressing their heads into their head rests while I tried to stop the *Silver Lining* turning over. We crashed through dead trees standing in shallow water, listing further to port, then the dorsal mast tore off and the bridge screen filled with static. With the controls now unresponsive, I lay on my couch.

"Activate crash fields," I said.

Emergency pressure fields pinned us onto our couches, as we smashed through the dead forest and fell into shallow water. The *Silver Lining* bounced, rolled to starboard, and flopped into the swamp with a shattering metallic scream as hull plates were ripped away. The ship vibrated wildly, sliding through trees like a wrecking ball. The bridge lights went out and the red emergency glow tubes activated as the shuddering slowly faded. When we finally came to rest, the crash fields deactivated and Marie reached out to me. We clasped hands briefly in the dim red light, glad to be alive.

"Fires have broken through the starboard thermal barrier, but the e-plant is dormant," Izin said, now poring over his console. "All emergency hatches are open, Captain."

Jase jumped off his couch, grinning with relief. "You know what they say, any landing that doesn't vaporize you instantly…"

I climbed off my couch. "Get what you need and be at the bow airlock in two minutes. Not a second more," I said, then Marie and I ran to our cabin and dressed for sub-zero temperatures.

I went to the armory while she went to the galley for supplies. When we met at the bow airlock. Jase was already there waiting for us, wrapped in arctic gear and humping a full survival pack from the lifeboat.

"Where's Izin?" I asked.

"Haven't seen him."

"He'll have to find his own way out." I distributed assault rifles and peered through the open airlock. The air was icy and the emergency chute was down with its end on dry ground. "At least we won't get our feet wet."

Marie went first, then Jase followed while I turned back to the companionway. It was lit by soft red light and eerily quiet.

"Izin?" I yelled, but got no response. "Damn," I muttered and dropped onto the chute.

At the bottom, I gazed into the lifeless forest, searching for any sign of the *Riku* or Izin. There was no movement anywhere, just gnarled trees, shallow murky water and dome-shaped, gray monoliths as far as the eye could see.

"I bet the nights are cold," Marie said with a shiver, exhaling steam with every breath.

"No clouds," I said apprehensively. The sky was barely blue, confirming there was only a little water vapor in the air, not nearly enough to warm the planet.

I turned back to the *Silver Lining* for one last look. Her hull was a patchwork of smashed thrusters, torn sensor masts, missing hull plates and skin scratches from bow to stern, but she was still intact. Both engine housings were burning furiously, spreading fires to the surrounding trees. The entire forest would soon be ablaze and us with it if we couldn't find protection fast.

I raised a comm unit from the armor to my lips. "Izin? Where are you?...Izin!"

"Yes, Captain," he said, emerging from behind the *Silver Lining* riding a thruster bot and wearing his heavy engineering p-suit with the visor up. It gave him the best protection of any of us; a good thing considering tamphs had a low tolerance for cold. He carried no food or medical supplies, just his sniper rifle cradled in his arms. Behind him were three more big bots flanked by eight small hull crawlers carrying laser cutters. "There's one for each of you."

"Good. I hate walking," Jase said.

We scrambled up onto the thrusterbots, then Izin asked, "Which way, Captain?"

Irukoochati had jumped out a long way back and the forest between us and her was now ablaze. Even so, if the snakeheads weren't coming for us, I'd have tried to find her in case she'd survived the fall, but searching for her now would only lead them to her.

"That way," I said, pointing in the opposite direction. We'd lead them away from her, buy her time to hide, and maybe survive until the next Nisk ship arrived.

Izin used his suit controller to instruct the bots to begin loping through the trees. Our mechanical mounts spread out side by side, using their articulated arms to surround us like safety railings, protecting us from low hanging branches, while the smaller machines scouted ahead. The bots galloped through the spindly, corpse trees faster than a man could run, occasionally shattering their dead and brittle limbs.

I peered up through naked branches, searching the sky, yelling to the others, "Anyone see the Riku?"

"She was circling to the south when I came out of the ship," Izin replied over the crunching of metal feet on gritty soil.

I kept looking back toward the pyre of black smoke rising into the sky from the *Silver Lining*, searching for our pursuers. I soon glimpsed lanky reptilians in body armor far behind us. They were almost as fast on foot as our bots, faster with jump packs that allowed them to leap through the trees, gobbling up the distance. The snakehead soldiers carried bulky, rifle-sized energy weapons and were surrounded by faintly glowing skin shields. Snakehead shields weren't as advanced as the Spawn variant, but they'd stop anything but static force penetrators, ensuring the coming fight would be short and one sided.

The others saw them too, then I pointed to a granite batholith ahead and Izin ordered our bots toward it. By the time we reached the rock, several dozen Mataron soldiers were in sight, spread out in a skirmish line behind us. The nearest soldiers started firing from extreme range, sending energy blasts flashing between us, shattering tree trunks and slamming into the granite wall ahead.

The dead trees offered little cover, so Izin kept the bots at a full sprint, following the base of the batholith, looking for a refuge. Energy blasts cut through the trees around us, but the snakeheads' aim was hampered by their need to fire while running, then as we came around the side of the batholith, we saw the *Riku* floating ahead, dropping more troops.

The snakeheads behind us had been herding us into a trap.

Izin ordered the little scout bots to charge back through the trees with their laser cutters glowing. Within moments they were at the feet of the reptilian soldiers, slashing and stabbing at their skin shields with the glowing tools. The Mataron force fields flashed, repulsing the laser cutters while the snakeheads blasted the bots at their feet. There was a flurry of slashing and shooting that lasted barely a minute and left Izin's little toys in pieces.

Our four mechanical mounts darted into a narrow cleft in the rock that gave us protection on three sides, but offered no way out. The big bots dropped to the ground to let us off, then we took cover behind granite boulders while they formed a protective wall in front of us.

"Here, use these," I said, pulling penetrator ammo boxes from my pockets and throwing them to Marie and Jase.

Jase saw the purple banding and grinned. "I'll take a thousand."

I shook my head. "That's all there is. Don't waste them."

A squad of lanky snakeheads jogged into view, saw us

holed up in the cleft, and formed a cordon through the trees ensuring we didn't escape. More soldiers streamed in, then when the entire force had arrived, a Mataron emerged from the forest with his skin shield glowing. He walked confidently forward and hissed into a translator.

"Surrender humans and you will not be killed."

I put a penetrator between his eyes, sending his body flying back into the trees, demonstrating to the other snakeheads that their contour shields were no protection.

"So it's a fight to the death?" Jase said wryly.

"I'm not doing those trials again," I replied.

"At least we'll get to take some of them with us," Marie said, slamming her magazine into her gun.

"I want five," Jase declared.

I turned to Izin. "Send the bots."

"Yes, Captain."

The four big machines charged and the Matarons opened fire, tearing them apart. We picked off a few snakeheads with penetrator rounds, then with our mechanical mounts reduced to burning wrecks, the snakeheads unleashed a withering fire on us. They saturated our position with energy blasts, melting the boulders shielding us and the rock wall behind us. We fired back sparingly, picking our targets and ducking for cover, but there were too many.

"I don't suppose you got one of those fancy N-grenades?" Jase asked, pinned down behind a disintegrating granite slab.

I ducked behind a smaller rock, unable to get a shot away. "If I did, I'd have used it by now."

Izin fired a detonator from his SN6 sniper rifle. It exploded on contact with a skin shield, hurling the snakehead soldier back, but doing no harm, then an energy blast shattered the boulder he sheltered behind and another struck his shoulder, spinning him around and knocking him face down onto the ground.

"Izin!" I yelled, unable to reach him through the heavy

snakehead fire.

"I'm alive, Captain," he wheezed, and rolled onto his back. His heavy engineering suit had taken most of the blast, but there was still blood and burnt tissue visible through a gaping hole in its upper chest plate.

Marie was forced to crawl from a melting boulder to a cleft in the rock wall. None of us could get a shot away, then the firing suddenly ceased. I stole a look and saw the *Riku* slowly descending into the forest, crushing the trees beneath her with her armored hull. When she settled onto the ground, one of her weapon blisters fired a single blast over our heads, melting fifty square meters of granite behind us and sending a river of lava flowing down the cliff face.

"WHERE IS THE NISK?" a synthesized voice bellowed from the *Riku*.

"I just need one more," Jase said, focused on his body count.

"I got six," Marie said, checking her weapon. Jase and I turned to her, equally surprised, then she smiled smugly. "Count them."

"IF YOU WANT TO LIVE, THROW OUT YOUR WEAPONS NOW."

"They'll hand me to the Spawn," Izin said weakly, preferring death to what his hated cousins would do to him.

"You could escape," Jase said.

"Has a human female ever survived the trials?" Marie wondered.

"You'll be the first," I replied. "Izin?"

"Very well, Captain," he said and pushed his SN6 toward me.

I grabbed his rifle and threw it and my pistol out into the open. Jase and Marie did the same, then we stood with our hands in the air, except for Izin who lay bleeding on the ground.

Mataron soldiers stayed behind the trees, keeping their

weapons on us as a hatch on the *Riku's* underside opened and a ramp extended. More armored snakeheads came out carrying prisoner restraints. As they reached the base of the ramp, the ground shook violently. Rocks broke free of the cleft walls and rained down around us as trees cracked and toppled. Mataron soldiers struggled to keep their balance, some clutched at trees for support as others lost their footing.

"It's an earthquake!" Jase exclaimed as a geyser of rock and dirt erupted from the ground between us and the *Riku*.

"No, it isn't," I said as more geysers exploded into the air, showering us all with gritty soil.

Clouds of dust filled the air, then orange beetles streamed up out of the holes, each carrying a large weapon. They fanned out, firing energy blasts through the Mataron skin shields and splattering reptilian body parts and blood through the trees.

The snakeheads blasted the swarming coleopterans in return, raking them with energy bursts that shattered their unprotected carapaces. It was a frenzy of flashes and blood, but no matter how many Nisk died, more kept coming, pouring up out of the holes in an unstoppable tidal wave that overwhelmed the Matarons and trampled their corpses.

The orange-shelled horde flowed like a river up the ramp into the *Riku* and swarmed up the sides of the ship, planting devices on the weapon blisters that suppressed their ability to fire. The scream of energy weapons and dying snakeheads filled the air, almost drowned out by a cacophony of Nisk clicking.

The *Riku's* engines hummed softly as she lifted off the ground in a desperate attempt to escape, but she only rose a few meters, wobbled briefly and slewed sideways into the forest, knocking down trees with her hull. She righted herself, then as the roar of battle faded, the *Riku* settled onto the ground and her engines powered down.

Scores of orange beetles ambled toward us, although none aimed their weapons our way. They were only a meter and a half tall, the smallest Nisk I'd seen, although their heads were larger than the drone-worker class suggesting substantial intelligence. They stopped a few meters away, hemming us and fixing their empty black eyes upon us, clicking softly among themselves.

"This must be the place," I said.

"Did you bring a translator?" Marie asked.

"There wasn't time."

The Nisk clicking suddenly stopped and the orange coleopterans shuffled quietly aside, clearing a path for a large Nisk with a golden shell flecked with red streaks. She came forward, looked down at me with chilling, alien eyes that never ceased to make my skin crawl.

"You have no need of translators here, Human-Kode-Soris," Irukoochati said through a device newly attached to her mandible. "On behalf of the Myriad-of-Strains, I welcome you, Protector, to Talib-Nis and thank you all, Friends-of-Nisk, for saving my life."

* * * *

"Did you recover your eggs?" I asked Irukoochati when we met next day in a hemispherical chamber tiled with black hexagons far below the surface.

"Yes, Human-Kode-Soris. My planetary-nest-surveyors saved your ship," Irukoochati's mandibular attachment replied with the same female voice Izin had created for her. She rested on a circular metallic heat mat with her legs drawn up beside her carapace, sweeping slender wands through the air with her antenna-manipulators, drawing colored patterns that passed for art among the Nisk.

"Can you repair her?"

"Not on Talib-Nis."

"What about the Mataron prisoners? What are you

going to do with them?"

"There are no prisoners."

"They fought to the death?"

"The planetary-nest-surveyors knew reptilian-Mataron-snakeheads executed Iskeratul-consort-Girutonak and sought to harm me," she replied, dabbing her three dimensional artwork with soft pastels.

"They killed them all?"

"The Nisk value order, Human-Kode-Soris. Rigid order. Each has his place. Each serves in his way. Disorder is unknown to us, and not tolerated from others."

"Hmm?...What's the punishment for destroying a nestship?"

"It has never happened before." She dabbed a splash of red over the pastels. "The Myriad-of-Strains will decide. The planetary-nest-surveyors have sent a report."

"What about us?"

"A ship will come. They will take you wherever you wish to go."

"We've got emergency rations. We can survive for a while."

"Do not concern yourself with survival, Human-Kode-Soris. My planetary-nest-surveyors are builders. They will synthesize whatever you require."

"What about Izin?" I hadn't seen him since an orange beetle had carried him away after the Nisk captured the *Riku*. "He needs specialized medical care."

"Kren-Nilva-Izin is being restored."

"You have medical facilities for tamphs?"

"My builders have synthesized what he needs."

I doubted Izin would enjoy being fussed over by creepy coleopteran care-givers, but I figured he was in no danger.

"How many builders did you lose?"

"Seventy six killed, one hundred ninety two harmed."

"That many? I'm sorry."

"Order is restored," she said simply, adding a series of

concentric blue curves to the colored mess floating in the air.

"With so many casualties, I guess that's the end of the survey mission."

"It continues. Planetary-nest-surveyors number thousands-hundred-five."

My eyes widened in surprise. I'd been thinking we were looking for a handful of bugs digging holes and taking core samples. "Half a million? That's a colony."

"Ship-nest-Iskeratix was the colony, Human-Kode-Soris."

I realized coleopteran thinking was on an immense scale, reflecting the size of their civilization. "Will you still build a colony here?" I asked, thinking the more Nisk in our backyard, the better.

"My seed is here. The Myriad-of-Strains will send another nestship. And Talib-Nis will proceed."

She reached into the floating kaleidoscope of color and carefully added a series of black and gray squiggles in one corner.

"If you don't mind me asking, what are you painting?

"My story." She pointed to different parts of her masterpiece. "This is the enemy-fleet-Spawn, the destruction of the ship-nest-Iskeratix, the killing of Iskeratul-consort-Girutonak, my rescue by you, the crash of your ship, the saving of my seed."

"All that in one picture," I said, not seeing it.

She pointed to a tiny doodle in a glowing triangle. "This is you, Human-Kode-Soris."

I leaned forward for a closer look. "Hmm...uncanny resemblance."

"It is an abstraction," she said simply. "Royals, consorts and attendants across the Myriad-of-Strains will see its meaning."

"I should be taller."

She stopped painting, studied her work seriously then looked down at me. "A wildly incorrect interpretation,

Human-Kode-Soris."

She clearly didn't appreciate human humor, but she was a giant beetle after all.

"Is that really how you see me?" I asked.

"I depict what you are as an immortal life, Human-Kode-Soris, not a container."

"If you say so," I replied, straightening. "You know, it would have helped if you'd told me you had an army down here."

"Builders are not fighters."

"Are fighters another type of Nisk? Another caste?"

"Fighters are strong. Builders are resourceful. Workers are disciplined. Attendants are efficient." She dabbed a little yellow into a random swirl of color. "Not so many fighters would have died."

I'd never heard of a Nisk fighter caste, no human had even seen one, but the prospect of a Nisk whose sole purpose was combat had my attention.

"Do you have many fighters?"

"None on Talib-Nis, but they will come, now."

"What about on other worlds?"

"All have their place," she replied, seemingly unaware I was trying to gauge Nisk military power.

"Place in society, like a social status?"

Irukoochati shifted her attention from her artwork to me. "Not status, Human-Kode-Soris. Place, evolutionary place."

"Oh. Is that because you have physical castes?"

She lowered her wands. "Most intelligent life in the universe is protean: one container serves many purposes," she said patiently as if addressing a child. "Humans are protean, versatile. Nisk are immutable: many containers, each with one purpose, for one level of consciousness, for one stage in our evolution. Workers work, builders build, fighters fight, attendants organize, consorts serve, royals inspire." She motioned to her artwork as if her creation was proof of her words. "Nisk consciousness evolves through our different containers, from small self to large. Human consciousness evolves through one container, from small self to large. Same. Protean or immutable. All is consciousness. Containers are nothing."

"One human container? Hmph. Makes us one big unhappy family."

"Humans of high and low ability, of varying intelligence, creativity, morality, immorality, all use the same container. Protean. Versatile. Many humans focus on the characteristics of the container, rather than what is contained. Nisk do not. We focus on the quality of the life within the container."

"I guess genetics means more to us than you."

"Genetics controls the characteristics of the container, not the life within. The life has its own qualities which cause the container to evolve. Without life, the container is nothing, has no use, ceases to be. The life precedes the container, uses it for a time, then discards it and continues until a new container is required. It is obvious, life is greater than the container."

"Right. And royals are the most advanced, the most evolved of all the Nisk?"

"We are the oldest and have the greatest responsibility. We appear when needed to guide the Myriad-of-Strains. My container reveals what I am to all Nisk."

"What you are?" I said slowly, recalling what she'd shown me of herself. "You're a Nisk Uvo, aren't you?"

"The Uvo are profoundly wise, as are royals. We are the flower of our race. Our purpose is to see all Nisk grow. That is why we are valued, why the loss of one is a tragedy for all."

"The loss of one?" I said thoughtfully. "Were there other royals aboard the Iskeratix? Other than you?"

"Seven royals. Seven consorts. Seven citadels. I am the only survivor."

Suddenly it hit me. The Spawn hadn't simply destroyed a colony ship, killed millions of Nisk, destroyed billions of eggs, or even slain six kings. They'd done something far worse. Irukoochati was called a royal, but she was no hereditary ruler. She was a spiritual leader of the Nisk, the apotheosis of their evolution, revered by their entire civilization, as were the six other royals slain with their eggs in cold blood by the Spawn.

Laleya and the D'kol had known what Irukoochati and the other royals were, what they meant to the Nisk. That's why they'd been so certain of the Nisk reaction, why they'd insisted I rescue Irukoochati. They knew the Spawn had provoked an enemy whose numbers were vast, whose vengeance would be implacable, and once roused would never relent.

"Will every Nisk see your painting?"

"Every Nisk on every world. The attendants will explain its meaning to the young."

"What then? What will the Nisk Myriad do?"

Irukoochati dabbed her painting, scarcely realizing how I hung on her every word, how the hairs on the back of my neck were tingling, how the knot in my stomach was gut wrenching. When she answered, she did so absently, unaware how her words would resound through the stars, from rim to rim, as the slumbering peaceful Nisk unleashed a holy war upon the galaxy's greatest enemy.

"We will restore order."

* * * *

Twenty three days later, we returned to the surface of Talib-Nis. They'd fed us well, healed Izin and shown us around an immense tunnel network that would soon become the center of planetary seeding operations. In a few centuries, there'd be a hundred billion Nisk down there, scurrying through a network of galleries that would reach into every part of the planet's crust, creating a second nestworld in Orion.

The thousands of civilizations inhabiting the Orion

Arm would normally have hardly even known they were there. The inward looking, inherently peaceful coleopterans would have gone about their business, disturbed no one, barely spoken to their neighbors, occasionally traded with them through one tiny entry point and quietly tended their planetary fungus garden.

But these weren't normal times and the Nisk were angry.

Since our arrival, the half a million builders had switched from crust surveying to producing anti-orbital weapons that were rapidly turning Talib-Nis into a fortress that even the Spawn would have a hard time cracking. In a matter of weeks, the industrious builders had mined and smelted metals from across the planet, built fabrication plants, fortified their galleries, constructed an array of formidable weapons and deployed them around their post-glacial world with a speed and efficiency that even Izin found astonishing.

When we emerged into Yentauri's sunlight for the first time in weeks, a builder led us through a small cluster of trees to where Irukoochati and her fighter escort waited. It was my first sight of the fighter caste. They had green and black dappled shells thicker and heavier than any Nisk carapace I'd seen, and were substantially larger than Irukoochati. Their mouths were horizontal blade-like strips that reminded me of a guillotine and each carried a single barreled weapon that could have passed for field artillery on Earth. Unlike other Nisk, their eyes were recessed back into their heads for protection.

"The little ones get out of their way fast," Marie whispered as a fighter marched past us.

"I noticed."

"They are physically impressive," Izin observed, "but they lack armor and shields."

"When you can bite someone's head off," Jase said, "you don't need armor."

"You do if you want to get close enough to the Spawn

to bite off their heads," Izin replied, unconvinced.

"At least they're on our side," I said, "and they can make armor, if they need it."

In the distance, thousands of builders with liquid tanks on their backs were spraying blue-green mist over a plain filled with dead trees, turning the gray landscape blue. Beyond the sprayers was a granite batholith surrounded by scaffolding and swarming with Nisk. Its center had been drilled out and a ship killing energy weapon was being lowered into place, while sheets of armor were being bolted to the exterior, turning the batholith into an armored redoubt. And it wasn't the only one. Thousands more were being installed across Talib-Nis, and many others would soon be installed on planets and moons throughout the Yentauri System.

"Welcome Human-Kode-Soris," Irukoochati said as we came up beside her. "It is time for us to leave."

I'd seen her several times since our first meeting, although she'd been unable to shed any light on what the Myriad had decided.

"You're coming with us?" I asked.

"The Myriad-of-Strains have asked me to go to a place of your choosing."

"My choosing?" I said surprised. "Uralo IV."

"No. The secret place, known only to you."

She meant Point Mylae, where Lena had told me to go if Uralo IV was destroyed. I'd checked the coordinates back on the *Silver Lining*, but as far as our all-knowing Tau Cetin astrographics were concerned, there was nothing there but empty interstellar space.

"How do they know there's such a place?" I asked, not that I didn't trust the Nisk, but someone had gone to a lot of trouble to hide what was there.

"Ambassador-Avian-Ornithian to the Myriad-of-Strains said you would know."

"Did he…"

There'd been enough time for Laleya and Gastillion to

brief the D'kol Emperor and update the Tau Cetins, and for the Tau Cetins to instruct their ambassador to the Nisk. If the Nisk couldn't keep a secret, having me give them the coordinates was a clever way of getting them to the right place without risking a security breach.

"Do you know of the secret place?" she asked.

"I do. I'll give you the coordinates once we're underway."

"Acceptable."

"So, when does your ship arrive?"

"They are here," she said, motioning to the sky behind us.

"They?" I turned to see five circular nestships floating silently in the sky. They were each hundreds of kilometers across, dark hulled and ringed by vertical towers that extended above and below their outer circumferences. At the center of the nestships were clusters of spires reaching high into the air and down toward the surface. They nearly blacked out the sky and seemed to reach from one horizon to the other. Glowing bands of light radiated out from the underside spires and across the hull, ionizing vast expanses of atmosphere as they held the massive ships aloft.

Jase looked from one to another and whistled softly.

"I guess the Myriad's made its decision," I said.

"They're flying cities," Marie said, awestruck.

"It is a mistake to judge an adversary by his size," Izin warned, implying the small stature of his kind was no indicator of their abilities.

A white beam flashed down from the central nestship to the ground, then a tiny, teardrop-shaped object rose out of the forest. It was the *Riku*, now a Nisk trophy and proof of Mataron duplicity.

"You're keeping it?" I asked as the snakehead cruiser entered the Nisk leviathan.

"For now," Irukoochati replied.

A second beam flashed down and the broken wreck of

the *Silver Lining* floated up into the sky.

"She doesn't look so bad from here," Jase said.

Izin studied her with his telescoping amphibian eyes and came to a different conclusion. "The damage is extensive. She may not fly again."

"Your Tau Cetin friends will fix her up," Marie assured me.

"Maybe," I said doubtfully as a small craft landed nearby.

We followed Irukoochati and her fighter escort aboard, then were transported up to the central nestship. Moments after we docked, the five nestships left the Yentauri System for Tau Ceti. Safely isolated in space, I gave an attendant the coordinates to the secret place and the Nisk fleet altered course for Point Mylae carrying three humans, a tamph and millions of angry coleopterans on a crusade to restore order.

Chapter Seven : Orsalee-M29

Ornithoid Consociation Clandestine Possession
Earth Council classified sub-mandate
Rogue gas giant moon
Inner Hydra
7.27 light years from Sol
COTEF and civilian personnel

The Nisk put us in a compartment with four biped friendly beds and basic amenities they'd created just for us. It gave us privacy from the Nisk masses, insulation from their incessant clicking, and food and drink arrived like clockwork every six hours, but there were no data screens or amusements and boredom quickly set in.

After fourteen hours of staring at the walls, the door opened, filling the compartment with coleopteran chatter. A chestnut colored attendant entered and introduced himself as Chokutalik.

"It is time, Human-Kode-Soris." We all got to our feet, eager to escape our tiny cell, then he added, "Not them. Only you."

"Why does he get to go, and not us?" Jase demanded.

"He is the Protector," Chokutalik said and led me into a corridor wide enough for two large Nisk to comfortably pass each other.

It was dead straight for a hundred kilometers, periodically intersecting corridors laid out in concentric circles around the center of the ship. Ramps led off to other levels and spaced along its length were large, recessed pressure doors that could instantly seal the ship in the event of an emergency. Either side of the arterial corridor were deck-galleries crammed with Nisk of different colors and sizes, squeezed together in ordered ranks, clicking incessantly, flooding the ship with an annoying buzz.

I had to hurry to keep up with Chokutalik, who led me into a seven sided chamber. He clicked rapidly and a wall dissolved, then we were instantly transported to a much larger heptagon-shaped waiting room containing small groups of coleopterans chattering softly to each other. Chokutalik clicked again and we were swept up through the central tower to a large circular deck hundreds of meters across. It was filled with light brown attendants whispering to each other, making the room sound like a beehive. Irukoochati sat on a raised dais at the center surrounded by an inner ring of yellow consorts. There were no screens or consoles typical of the bridges of human ships because the attendants and consorts were networked together into a single guiding intelligence.

Chokutalik led me between the attendants and consorts to Irukoochati, who turned her dead black eyes toward me. "Greetings, Human-Kode-Soris. Is your accommodation acceptable?"

"Yeah, its ah…acceptable. Thank you."

"We are about to arrive at the secret place. You will speak for us."

"Me? Why?"

"They know you, not us."

"But the Tau Cetins told you to come here. They're expecting you."

"Very few know we are coming, or when. You must tell them not to fear us."

"How do I do that?" I asked, looking around for a comm panel.

"A device-communications-human has been fabricated for you."

An orange-shelled builder ambled forward and placed a dull metal visor over my eyes, momentarily blinding me.

"It's not working," I said, then suddenly I was looking down at all five nestships flying together in one immense fleet-bubble. Lightning radiated continually from the central and outer towers of all five ships, feeding directly into the glowing superluminal sphere that surrounded us.

"Wow!" I exclaimed. "You're all in one bubble. How is that possible?"

"The Myriad travel as one," Irukoochati explained.

"Even the Tau Cetins can't do this," I said, finding I could turn my head, seeing in any direction from the central tower of her nestship.

"The Tau Cetins could travel as one, but choose not to," she replied, then the Nisk fleet-bubble dissipated and was replaced by a field of stars.

I swiveled my head, finding we were alone in interstellar space. "I don't see them."

"Look lower right," the builder supervising my introduction to Nisk attachments instructed.

I shifted my gaze, saw nothing but starry blackness, then noticed a tiny, dark blue orb in the distance. "Oh there it is...I think."

It was a gas giant, gravitationally ejected from its birth system eons ago, just one of billions of non-luminous objects that made interstellar travel so perilous. Dark matter was impossible to detect at a distance for all but the most advanced civilizations, and they shared their astrographics only to those who obeyed Access Treaty rules. In the Orion Arm, the Tau Cetins were responsible for interstellar navigation, yet their astrographics showed no hint of this rogue world. That could only mean the Ornithians had doctored their star charts to conceal its presence and ensured their calculation modules kept all interlopers well away from this isolated island in space.

Nine streaks of light flashed out toward us from unmapped space, dropped their bubbles and locked weapons on us. The long, mirror-hulled spindles accelerated instantly, orbiting us at high velocity as clicking sounded in my ears. It was the Tau Cetins, hailing us in the Nisk's own language, then my headset translated the signal.

"Attention Nisk Myriad. You have entered Ornithoid Consociation exclusionary space. Withdraw immediately. Under Article Nine of the Access Treaty, we assert the right to use offensive force to preserve life. Signal your intention to comply."

"Don't shoot!" I said. "We're on your side."

"Identify yourself," the Tau Cetin voice ordered, no longer using Nisk clickity-clack.

"Sirius Kade, Earth Intelligence Service. Lena Voss gave me these coordinates, and your ambassadors to the Myriad told the Nisk to come here."

The Tau Cetin arbiters continued circling at high speed, ready to slice and dice us if they didn't like what they heard, then a familiar human face appeared before me. He had close cropped hair, steel gray eyes and a scowl that was hard coded into his DNA.

"Kade, is that really you?" Admiral Joran Talis demanded.

"Yes, sir."

"You're supposed to be dead. What are you doing on a Nisk ship?"

"I thought you might need help, so I brought some friends."

"They're neutral."

"Not anymore."

Talis eyes narrowed. "Are you saying the Nisk are going to declare war on the Spawn?"

"They already have, Admiral." I smiled. "The Spawn just don't know it yet."

"Hmph...First good news I've had in months." He turned, nodded to someone I couldn't see and his face disappeared.

All but one of the Tau Cetin arbiters streaked back toward the dark blue gas giant, then the Tau Cetin commander said, "Nisk Myriad vessels, you have been granted approach authorization. Follow us to your orbital assignments."

The arbiter moved slowly off toward the rogue world, followed by the nest fleet. Soon, I began receiving Nisk scans of an enormous world, eight times the mass of Jupiter. It was big, but not quite big enough for nuclear fusion, narrowly missing becoming a star in its own right.

I found out later the Tau Cetins called it Orsarlee, had kept its existence hidden for millions of years, until a nosy prospector had noticed a hole in her charts and came out for a look see. It had been a reckless move, but she'd been in search of the mother lode, although instead of riches, she stumbled onto a different kind of treasure. The Ornithians could have silenced her permanently, but they hadn't used the rogue system in a long time and decided to give it to Earth instead, as an exclusive, secret concession. It was in our backyard after all, and it tied us ever closer to our mighty neighbor, which suited them–and us–just fine. For Earth, getting an invisible world for free, a world no one even knew existed, thanks to Tau Cetin trickery, was a great deal. And an even better deal for the prospector, who received the largest secret finder's fee in human history, and never breathed a word of it again.

Orsarlee resembled Neptune on a dark night, cold but not dead. Nisk bio-scanners sensed bizarre psychrophilic organisms that thrived in the rogue giant's freezing hydrogen-helium atmosphere, alongside the water ice crystals that gave the planet its bluish tint. Orbiting the frigid ice giant were more than thirty moons, mostly small in size and irregular in shape, although four had enough gravity to produce spherical worlds. The largest was Orsalee-M29, a barren, earth-sized rock with a primitive, cryotic atmosphere so cold it made Pluto look like a tropical island.

Orbiting M29 were thousands of ships, mostly human. Every type of vessel man had built in the last two centuries was there, many damaged with bots of various kinds patching their hulls with flickering energy tools. Earth Navy's home fleet was there too, evacuated from the Sol System and reinforced by other naval units brought in by the Tau Cetins from across Mapped Space. Guarding our fleet and a sorry collection of old and decaying ships were just fifteen Tau Cetin arbiters and four of the smaller sentinel reconnaissance cruisers.

There were human life signs on M29, along with Tau Cetin, Nirisi, Syrman, Suvoli, Gienan, Fenari and even Lhekan. They were crowded into a cluster of military bases on the planet-facing side, as well as on the ships in orbit, and in far greater numbers than might be expected for the available habitats.

"We're all here," I whispered. It wasn't the invincible battle fleet I'd hoped for, but a disorganized gaggle of demoralized refugees.

The Nisk fleet entered high orbit above M29 as an enormous elongated sphere flashed in from interstellar space, appearing at the edge of Orsalee's gravity well. Huge circular openings appeared in the galactic conveyor's hull, then Syrman and Suvoli civilian ships glided out into space. The biosigns indicated the ships were overflowing with passengers, straining their life support systems to the limit and soon to increase the woes of the base on M29.

This was Point Mylae, named for the Roman Empire's first great naval victory in 260 BC. Earth Navy had picked the name to inspire optimism, not realizing it would become a haven for the bedraggled survivors of the conquered worlds of Orion.

"There are many ships here, Human-Kode-Soris," Irukoochati said.

"Too many."

They were so numerous, they seemed to fill all of space above M29, yet there were not nearly enough Tau Cetin arbiters to protect them all. And now the Ornithians had the nestships to guard as well. If the Spawn ever found this place, they'd descend upon it with flame and fury, crushing the last hope of the wretched warrior worlds of Orion.

I turned to the starry sky, followed the constellations to a small yellow star now only a stone's throw away. It was so close and yet, it might as well have been on the far side of the universe for all the help we could offer. Unless the Tau Cetins had something more up their sleeve, the Nisk had come a long way for nothing.

* * * *

"Our underworld contacts told us the Drakes killed you in a shootout at the Zilarov base," Lena said when we met in her tiny office two days later. "And the Meropan embassy on Kif-atah reported a Mataron cruiser had destroyed the Silver Lining in deep space. That's why Talis thought you were dead, killed twice over."

"He seemed disappointed I was still alive," I said, shifting uncomfortably in the metal chair in front of her small desk, ignoring the fact that she obviously hadn't read my report.

Lena's office was a shoebox, although it came with secure data links and three assistants in an even smaller room next door. I stood up, giving the chair and her office a disparaging look. "Is this the best they can do for an EIS regional commander?"

"I'm lucky to have it. COTEF has four times more people than it was designed for. There are three star admirals sharing closets smaller than this."

"How come I never heard of this place?"

"You and me both. Talis knew, but that tight lipped bastard wouldn't tell me it was daytime with the sun overhead." She smiled. "That's why I like him."

"What's COTEF stand for?"

"Combined Operations, Training and Evaluation Facility. We got half a million people crammed in here. We had to dock two troopships just to process the air."

"I saw. It's still damp and sweaty in here." I walked to her grimy, oval-shaped window and looked out over a barren plain sprinkled with sensors. A white flash appeared on the horizon, bloomed momentarily lighting up buildings sprawling off in both directions, then fading away. "So it's a test facility?"

"More than that. We've got firing ranges and military bases here, but also laboratories, food processors, refineries, every kind of industry, even a small shipyard. And out there," she nodded toward space, "we've got resource extractors going non-stop on seventeen moons and a fleet of atmo harvesters over Orsalee."

"No wonder it's cramped."

"Everyone's here. Earth Navy, troops from all four collectives, and our best scientists and engineers. Most of it's underground."

"I heard Iron Fist have a sim-shooting range all to themselves."

"Yeah, although no one knows they're zygote constructs. They get final training here, from an old friend of yours." I gave her a curious look, then she added, "Dietz is Chief Instructor of the Spawn Close Combat Course."

I smiled wryly. "Ah. I wouldn't want to be those

grunts."

"Larsen and Shen are here too. Both instructors."

All three had been with me before the occupation and had given the Spawn a nasty surprise. "What about Parekh and Riley?"

"Parekh's leading an I-F combat team on Earth. I don't know where Riley is. They all trained here. Dietz even fired the first N-grenade on the far-side range two years ago."

"And the Spawn still don't know about this place?"

"Not as far as we know."

"They can map dark matter."

"Yeah, but they're not. According to the Tau Cetins, the Spawn are using Forum astrographics from the Matarons and the Xil. They've tried bringing their own mapping ships in, but the Tau Cetins hunted them down. Top priority."

"So we're safe for now."

"Orsalee is still a secret, as far as we know. The Tau Cetins used it as an inner perimeter defense station about a million and a half years ago. All their stuff was gone by the time we got here, of course. We built all this from scratch, except the tunnels."

I watched a test craft blinking with nav lights fly out over the firing range. It launched a glowing light that streaked away over the dark horizon, then a red-orange curtain of energy poured out into space as a tremor shook the floor beneath my feet.

"What was that?" I asked when the furniture stopped rattling.

"Don't get excited," Lena said, joining me at the window. "It's not ready yet. Won't be for years."

"Novarium based?"

"A derivative," she said evasively. "Our problem isn't making bigger bombs, it's getting close enough to use them."

If all it took was a big bomb, we could have tossed

multi-gigaton crust crackers at the Spawn, but primitive fusion weapons were easily detected and destroyed at range.

I watched the glow on the horizon fade, then asked the question that had been burning in my mind since I got there. "Are we going back, in my lifetime?"

"The Tau Cetins are stretched thin, and Spawn reinforcements have arrived from the Minacious Cluster." She gave me a grim look. "They're fortifying Earth with orbitals and more ships, and turning Mars spaceport into a fleet base. To attack now, the Tau Cetins would have to leave every other world defenseless. They won't do it."

"So they're just sitting around watching?"

"No. They're rebuilding Serris-Orn's defenses, protecting hundreds of billions of lives on many worlds, building new ships and trying to stop the flow of supplies from the Minacious Cluster. They've taken a huge risk dividing their fleet, but any major world they leave unprotected, the Spawn drop and run. Once the Spawn are on the ground, the Tau Cetins can't dig them out."

"We have the Nisk now."

"Yeah, the Nisk," she said, glancing uncertainly at the data link on her desk.

"What?" I asked, following her eyes.

"They're tough, very tough, but...I don't know how useful they'll be. Dietz is putting them through the ringer. We'll know more in a few weeks."

"Weeks!"

She sighed. "The Tau Cetins don't have the ships to destroy the Spawn Fleet holding Sol, and we can't send in transports until they do. We're lucky to have any TC ships here at all. It's more than they can spare."

"So we're sitting here on our asses while they grind our cities into dust."

"We train. We prepare. I-F are still fighting on Earth, coordinating a planet-wide guerrilla war."

"Just like you planned."

She shook her head. "No. The civilian casualties are...far worse than expected."

"How high?"

"Fifteen percent."

"Three billion!" I said shocked. "Dead?"

She nodded. "And climbing. Now there's starvation. Everywhere. They can't grow enough food and we can't supply them."

"There'll be nobody left to liberate," I said bitterly. It was just like the Kesarn.

Another bright light appeared over the firing range, flew toward the horizon, then suddenly veered off course and crashed in a fiery explosion, turning the rogue moon's eternal night into day. We shielded our eyes from the flash as hundreds of pieces of glowing debris rained over Orsalee-M29's frozen wasteland.

"We're just not ready," Lena said sadly.

"It's all been for nothing. Escaping Kif-atah, the Drakes, the Nisk, all for nothing."

"Not nothing, Sirius. Just not for Earth."

* * * *

"We should have stayed on the nestship," Marie said disheartened, dangling her feet off the top bunk in our cramped corridor dormitory forty levels below the surface.

We'd been living there for three weeks surrounded by refugees crammed into a human warehouse. We all had our own bunks, breathed putrid air and faced a two hour wait for the washing facilities. Three times a day, service bots trundled along the corridor handing out ration packs and recycled water. With nothing to do, the boredom was more choking than the air, sapping the spirits of everyone trapped down there.

I lay on the bunk below Marie, skimming the portable commlink Lena had given me for news of Earth and the war. The reports told a sorry story of defeat and retreat, of Tau Cetins evacuating survivors from across Orion, of besieged and bloodied worlds, and of inferior allied fleets wiped out by the Spawn in one sided ambushes. Only Earth Navy, the most numerous and weakest of all Ornithian allies, had survived the onslaught, and only because they'd avoided battle rather than allow themselves to be annihilated in a futile gesture of defiance.

There were endless lists of casualties, of ships lost, of worlds occupied, of new arrivals–not all human–brought in by galactic conveyors and dumped here for their own safety. There were even a handful of ships from devasted Rim systems that had come seeking Ornithian protection, although none were Kesarn.

Izin watched me impatiently from the bottom bunk on the opposite side of the corridor, waiting his chance to use the reader while Jase playfully scared refugee children.

Marie looked down at me. "Can't Lena get us a ship?"

"Let's go to the outer colonies," Jase suggested. "Anywhere would be better than here."

"There are no ships," I said.

"Have you looked out the window lately?" Marie asked. "If we had a window."

"There are thousands of ships out there," Jase added, then lowered his voice. "We could steal one."

"No one can leave," I said. "They can't risk the Spawn finding this place. And besides, all those ships are full."

I switched to COTEF's schedules and rosters for the day, using my EIS security clearance, and searched for a familiar name, barely noticing footsteps approaching.

"There he is," a deep voice declared close to our bunks.

A dozen disheveled men wearing worn boots and dirty coveralls eyed Izin angrily. The leader, a large brute with a loader tag grabbed Izin by the collar and dragged him to his feet. "This is what we think of your kind."

"What exactly would that be?" Jase demanded,

leveling his twin fraggers at the men.

"What do you care what happens to this Spawn scum?" the man asked, eyeing Jase's guns warily.

"He's not Spawn, he's a tamph," Jase declared icily, "and I'm the only one who calls him names."

"You're not allowed to have those guns in here," another man barked.

"Try taking them off me," Jase said belligerently.

"I'm not your enemy," Izin said, placing his small hand on the man's wrist, unable to push it away.

"I say you are," the brute growled, then I rolled off my bunk and pushed through the men.

"Let him go."

"You a toad-lover too?"

"We're all in this together, friend" I said.

"I ain't your friend, toad-man."

"That's too bad, because my…Orie…companion over there is kind of trigger happy, especially around unfriendly people."

Jase primed both guns, filling the corridor with the hum of charging magnetic accelerators, making everyone nervous, including me.

"He's from Oresund?" The load operator asked, glancing apprehensively at Jase.

"We don't want to fight no mercs," another man said, backing away, clearly aware of the Orie reputation for casual violence.

Jase scowled at me. "What do you mean trigger happy? I ain't killed no-one since Tuesday!"

The load operator glanced at the barrels of Jase's twin fraggers, then pushed Izin away roughly. "I'll be watching you, toady," He snapped and stomped off down the corridor with his gang.

Izin adjusted his crumpled jacket, glancing at Jase as he holstered his weapons. "That wasn't necessary."

"They were going take turns stomping on your face," Jase said.

Izin opened his hand, revealing a thin, shiny blade with a square hilt. "No, they weren't."

"Where'd you get that?"

"From the Nisk."

"They made you a knife?" I asked.

"No, Captain, I stole it from their medical bay when they were treating me."

"Hmph." I handed him the commlink. "Here. I'll be back in a few hours."

"Where are we going?" Jase asked, eager to get out of our musty confinement.

"You don't have clearance."

"Skipper, I'm climbing the walls. I got to get out of here."

"I know," I said, "but they won't let you through."

I gave him a sympathetic pat on the shoulder, then made my way to the surface, through more than twenty security checkpoints to the north range weapons depot. I sat where I could watch the hatch and settled in to wait. Two hours and four ground tremors from nearby detonations later, a man in a pressurized fighting suit entered. His visor's glare shield was down, hiding his face, but his name was stenciled on the suit. He didn't acknowledge me, so I followed him into equipping and waited while he peeled off his armor and began locking away his weapons.

"What do you want, Kade?" he asked with his back to me.

He was my size with a shaved head, lean muscles and gaunt features. My super reflexed gene mod should have made me physically superior to him in every way, except he was I-F, a zygote construct with intuitive combat abilities that gave him eyes in the back of his head and a sixth sense for survival. If we went hand-to-hand, I'd be lucky to land a blow, because he was engineered to anticipate my every move.

"It's good to see you too, Dietz. Is there someplace we

can talk?"

He peeled biometric patches off his skin, tossed them down a chute for sterilization and gave me a long look. "Sure." He glanced at three grunts gearing up for a training op nearby, then motioned for me to follow him into the showers. He stripped naked and began scrubbing as hot water blasted his skin.

"I hear you're testing the Nisk," I said.

"The what?" he replied, pretending not to know what I was talking about.

"Are they any good?"

"I can't discuss it." He turned toward the wall, closed his eyes wearily and let hot water beat down on his shaved head.

"Do you want to get off this rock and go liberate Earth, or spend the rest of your life nursemaiding grunts?"

He turned off the water and straightened. "Dumb question."

I nodded, certain he was itching to fight. "So...how good are the Nisk?"

"They're tough and stupid."

"Stupid how?"

"Swarm mind. They see a threat, they attack, head on. Frontal assault. No regard for casualties or tactics. Gets them killed every time."

"Right," I said thoughtfully. "They protect the nest."

"That might work in bug world, but not against the Spawn." He sighed with frustration. "The Nisk have no concept of close quarters combat as we know it. Flanking, ambush, evasion, feign, retreat, cover. No matter how many times I tell them, they don't get it. They're just not wired that way. They're bug-heads, all of them. They have courage and numbers. That's it."

"They're highly intelligent, Dietz. You can train them."

"You don't think I've been trying? When the shooting starts, they fight like bugs. Swarm attack every time.

Totally predictable. I've run sixty eight battle simulations, Nisk verse I-F." He shook his head. "Sixty eight to zero. The Spawn will annihilate them." He walked across to the dryer and began turning slowly as warm air blasted his skin.

When the dryer fell silent, I asked. "What can they do?"

He considered my question, eyes downcast. "They're the most disciplined warriors I've ever seen, and totally fearless. Crazy, stupid fearless. When they get the order to attack, they don't stop for anything or anyone. But that's not enough. To beat the Spawn, you need tactical awareness, flexibility, adaptability. You need to be able to read a situation. They can't do it."

"Dietz, we've got to get them into this fight."

"Don't do it, Kade. You'll just get them killed."

I sighed, demoralized. "What can they do?"

"Use them as garrison troops. Defend what we have."

"That's not enough," I said, unwilling to consign the Nisk multitude to guard duty. "There's got to be a use for them." I turned to go, but Dietz caught my arm.

"If you figure it out, Kade, make sure I'm in the first wave."

I nodded. "You and me both."

* * * *

"I wonder where they're sending us?" Jase said a couple of weeks later as he lay on his bunk taking his turn with the commlink.

"Who said they're sending us anywhere?" I asked.

"They just announced it." Jase held up the commlink as proof. "They're meeting today."

"Today?" I sat up on my bunk with a puzzled look. There was a meeting scheduled, but it was weeks away.

"Yeah, they brought it forward, cause we're low on supplies." He showed me the commlink as proof.

Since I'd met Dietz, I'd read every classified COTEF report for the last two years. He'd also been sending me everything he could on the Nisk, even material I wasn't cleared for. I'd stopped paying attention to the unclassified dailies, which were little more than morale boosting propaganda, and I had no access to classified diplomatic traffic.

The commlink headline for today was 'Decision Expected'. The Tau Cetins, the D'Kol, Earth's government in exile, our top brass and representatives from various non-human refugee groups were meeting to plan our next glorious retreat.

"The D'kol are offering to resettle us in the Empire," Izin said.

"On the far side of the galaxy?"

Marie nodded, confirming I was the only one who didn't know. I got to my feet, took the reader and scrolled through the news reports for confirmation. "They're out of their minds."

"They're giving us a seventy nine percent match for Earth," Jase said.

"They've promised to raise its suitability to ninety three percent within a century," Izin added. "It is a very a generous offer."

"They say it's the best we're going to get," Marie added.

"Well they're wrong," I snapped, and called a restricted number on the north range. "You still want to be first wave?"

"Hell yeah," Dietz growled.

"Be at COTEF HQ in ten minutes," I said and switched off.

Jase dropped onto the deck from his bunk with an expectant look. "About time!"

"You don't even know what I have in mind."

"It's got to be better than this."

"I can do this alone."

Marie stood and smiled, "Yes, but we're not going to let you, not this time."

"If it doesn't work, they'll lock us up," I said, saw their minds were made up and turned to Izin. "You better wait here."

"I'm sure I speak for all terrestrial amphibians, Captain, when I say, I will choose where I live. No one else," he declared, determined not to be left behind.

Marie smiled. "We'll ask for adjoining cells."

"Don't say I didn't warn you," I said, expecting to be in the brig by lights out.

With rising spirits, we hurried through dark and crowded passageways, teeming with desperate humanity, toward the sprawling COTEF headquarters where the fate of mankind was about to be decided by the great and powerful–unless we could stop them.

* * * *

Entry to the COTEF red zone was through a security checkpoint manned by Union Regular Army Military Police in dress black and gold uniforms. It was in a large lobby with windows overlooking the crowded spaceport on one side and pictures of three hundred years of COTEF commanding officers, mostly Earth Navy admirals, on the other.

One look told me there was no way the MPs were going to let us in, so I called Lena five times until she eventually answered.

"I can't talk now, Sirius," she whispered.

"I want to speak."

"Call me tonight."

"Not to you. To them."

There was a stunned silence. "Are you crazy?"

"You wanted me to talk to Earth Council a year ago."

"And you blew them off for your Sep girlfriend."

"I had nothing to say then. I do now."

"It's impossible. Even if I wanted to, I couldn't get you in here."

"Talk to Talis."

"He can't either. It's too late for that. I've got to go, Sirius, and please, stop calling me."

She broke the link. I immediately called her back and found she'd blocked me. Across the room, the URA security detail was eyeing us suspiciously. We were armed and they were more than a little suspicious of Izin, but they refrained from aiming their weapons at us.

"Wait here," I said and approached the master sergeant, whose metal work was so shiny I could see my reflection in his belt buckle.

"No weapons allowed in here," he snapped.

"I'm here to address the conference."

"What's your name?"

"Sirius Kade."

He checked his portable data screen. "You're not on the list."

"I'm a last minute addition."

"Not to my list."

"They're with me," Dietz's grizzled voice sounded behind me.

The master sergeant made a show of checking his screen and shook his head. "You're not on the list either, Dietz."

"I wouldn't be here without a good reason." Dietz glanced at me curiously. "There is a good reason, right?"

"Well…" I said uncertainly.

He turned back to the sergeant. "Good enough for me."

The MP shook his head. "If I let you in, they'd use my head for a target drone."

Dietz sized up the security detail as if about to put them to the test. Jase took up a flanking position to the left while Izin and Marie moved to the right. The tension in the room went orbital as we prepared to draw weapons, then the double doors behind the checkpoint slid open and a fur covered ursidaen wearing a silver collaret and a sarong emerged. The security detail snapped to attention, then Gastillion Kalantropis stopped in front of the master sergeant.

"These are my guests," she said evenly.

The sergeant stiffened uncomfortably. "They're not on the list, Ambassador."

"Are you sure?"

"Yes, Ma'am."

"Perhaps you should look again…Please."

The master sergeant reluctantly checked his screen once more, just to placate her, and blinked in surprise. "I…don't understand."

"I trust everything is in order?" Gastillion said.

"This list was security locked ten hours ago," he stammered. "It can't have changed."

"Are you denying the Empire of D'kol the right to select its own delegates?" She looked down at the stripes on his arm. "Sergeant?"

He straightened. "No, Ambassador. Absolutely not."

"The Emperor will be glad to hear that." She turned to me. "Leave your weapons here. The sergeant will take good care of them."

I nodded to the others, then we placed our weapons on the table. Jase deposited his gun belt on the table and looked at the master sergeant's screen.

"There it is! Jase, with a J." He tapped the screen, smiling with satisfaction. "You need those eyes re-lensed, Sarge."

"Izin," I said sternly, seeing there was one weapon missing.

He reluctantly deposited his stolen Nisk shell-scalpel alongside the guns. The master sergeant glanced curiously at the oddly shaped knife, then we followed Gastillion into the entry hall.

"How'd you know we were out there?" I whispered.

"Laleya told me," she replied softly.

"She's here?"

"She's above us, aboard the Parsiphilius."

"Ah, listening in. You know, breaking into our top level military security system, in real time, is going to raise eyebrows."

"It's unwise to be complacent," she said as we entered a large amphitheater.

Concentric rings of terraces with seating, commlinks and holoscreens for several hundred surrounded a sunken central stage. Earth Council leaders flanked by top level brass from all services occupied the inner ring facing Ornithian and D'kol ambassadors while representatives from various alien refugee groups sat behind them in order of importance.

The members of Earth's government in exile looked toward us with confusion as we entered, while Lena frowned apprehensively and whispered a warning to Admiral Talis. Talis nodded slightly, more thoughtful than alarmed.

Lena fixed her eyes upon me, sending her mega-psi thoughts into my mind: *This better be good, Sirius.*

I gave her a not so reassuring smile, then Gastillion motioned to a row of empty seats at the back. "Sit here." We stepped toward the seats, but she caught my arm. "Not you. Laleya says you wish to speak."

Gastillion led me down to the sunken stage and turned to face the human delegation. "Before the Council of Earth votes on whether to accept the Empire's offer of resettlement, I wish you to hear from this human, Sirius Kade, whom we know and trust."

Puzzled looks rippled across the human faces. Some had read my name once or twice in classified EIS briefing reports, but most simply saw a sloppily dressed outsider with no status, except for the ear of the esteemed ambassador of the largest and oldest empire in the galaxy.

"With respect, Ambassador, this is quite irregular," the Chairman of the People's Federation of Asia said. "No time has been allotted for…unscheduled presentations."

"I wish to hear from Captain Kade," Grand Fleet Commander Siyarn, leader of the Tau Cetin delegation said softly. "He is also known to us."

A five star general in the second row looked me up and down curiously, and asked his aide. "Who is he?"

Talis turned and said loudly, "He's the one who destroyed the spawnship at Serris-Orn."

"Oh," the general said with understanding, studying me with renewed interest.

"If he's got something to say, I want to hear it," Talis added firmly, turning to the Council Members. "With your permission, of course."

President Giannelli of the Democratic Union, current president of the Earth Council in Exile, looked puzzled but nodded. "He may speak."

Gastillion Kalantropis leaned down and whispered, "I trust you will not embarrass the Empire of D'kol, Captain Kade." Her ears twitched with amusement, then she took her seat beside Prince Valtonarsi.

I shifted uncomfortably under the impatient gaze of the most important eyes within ten thousand light years. My mind went blank, then Marie gave me a reassuring look from the stalls and ideas that had been whirling through my mind for weeks coalesced.

"You're here today to decide if mankind should abandon its homeworld and everyone trapped there," I began. "You believe we can't go back because the Spawn are too strong, because the Tau Cetins can't spare enough ships to take control of the Sol System and because our armies on Earth have been destroyed and we have nothing left." I paused to study their faces, seeing many resigned looks of agreement. "No one can blame you for that. It's all true." I paced slowly, gathering my thoughts. "The Spawn are strongest on the ground, where our Tau Cetin friends are weakest. We all know that. The Spawn know that. That's why they drop and run. It's their strength, and if we retreat now, they'll keep on doing it until there's nowhere left to run to."

The military types nodded soberly, the politicians looked disheartened and the non-humans, who had as much to lose as we did, looked on without hope.

"I understand," I continued, "why a resettlement world on the other side of the galaxy seems like our only way out, even if it means abandoning the people of Earth. We could send our survivors to the Empire, millions of them, abandon the Core Systems and start again. But for how long? How long until the Spawn decide to attack the Empire? And they will. By the time it happens, the people still alive on Earth, starving and resisting the Spawn, will be dead. Make no mistake. They will be dead, and the Spawn will have done to us what they did to the Kesarn."

"What choice do we have?" an Indian Republic general asked.

"There's nothing we can do," the anointed leader of the Second Caliphate declared.

"He wants us to commit suicide," a member of the People's Federation of Asia delegation said.

"No." I glanced up at Irukoochati who sat in a special area set aside for her and three consorts. Terraces had been removed and the floor leveled to make room for them, unintentionally isolating her group from the other representatives. "When I arrived here with the Nisk, Tau Cetin ships came out and threatened to destroy us."

"We did not know they had joined the war," Siyarn explained.

"Yes, but your ships said something that got me thinking. They said they had the power to destroy the Nisk under Article Nine of the Access Treaty. Article Nine?" I said thoughtfully. "When mankind signed the Access Treaty, we were told we were joining a rules-based, galactic civilization that had existed in peace for millions of years according to universally recognized laws. That's why we had a chance; why we were allowed to settle so many worlds; why we weren't wiped out fifteen hundred years ago by the Matarons; why even though we were the weakest, we had an opportunity and a right to survive. The rule of galactic law was the silver lining in an otherwise impossible situation. I actually named my ship after it, the Silver Lining. It really means hope, hope for the future."

I smiled, recalling one ship with that name had been destroyed and the latest one crippled, but I didn't tell them that.

"I've been wondering what Article Nine really means. Why could the Tau Cetins have blown the Nisk to pieces, killed millions, according to an obscure and ancient law? So I looked it up. I found thousands of words explaining its meaning, interpreting its nuances, citing precedents and exceptions going back millions of years, but it boils down to just a few simple words. I memorized them."

Many in the audience leaned forward, hanging on my every word, although not knowing why. Even Siyarn and Gastillion seemed intrigued.

"Article Nine. The Preservation Principle. Civilizations are always free to act to Preserve Life, irrespective of all other restrictions." I let that sink in, then repeated the key point. "...irrespective of *all* other restrictions."

I turned to Siyarn. "That's why you could have blown the Nisk to pieces. And if you had, galactic law would have been on your side, because you were preserving life, the lives of millions of refugees from all across Orion and as far as the Cygnus Rim. All hiding in all those ships and in this base. Not just human life, but all life, the most precious thing in the universe. The only thing of any real value. Life."

"The preservation of life is the galaxy's most sacred law, Captain Kade," Gastillion agreed.

"Every other article in the Access Treaty has restrictions," I said. "Those restrictions have kept mankind bottled up in our tiny little corner of the galaxy for thousands of years. We call it Mapped Space, mapped not by us, but by the Tau Cetins, the D'kol, the Yhinsar, the Ovani, the Girria and others I've never heard of, some of whom were out here before dinosaurs walked the Earth.

"The Access Treaty is the basis of all galactic law. It gives us the right to access interstellar space, to do our thing, but it also stops every other civilization in the galaxy transferring technology to us. Why? Because we have to make our own way, step by step, learning and growing as we go. There was no need to give us military tech because the Access Treaty, and the Tau Cetins, protected us. Well, they're not protecting us now, are they? Or the seventeen billion survivors on Earth, many of whom are soon going to die."

"We did our best, Captain Kade," Siyarn said.

"You did, and we're grateful. Believe me, we are. But now we need more. We need you to help us save ourselves."

"Your ships are too primitive to utilize our technology, Captain Kade," Siyarn said anticipating my request.

"Yes, so you've said many times, and it's true. Your tech is too advanced for us, and for most of your allies, all of whom are on their knees. Their fleets are destroyed, their armies annihilated, their worlds conquered. Even the Nisk, who have the biggest ships I've ever seen, can't stand up to the Spawn Fleet. They have nestships, which are transports, not warships. Only two battle fleets have survived." I turned to Siyarn. "Yours…and ours, the most advanced and the most primitive."

"I do not wish to offend you, Captain Kade," one of the few Lhekan representatives said, "but human ships, while numerous, are fragile."

"Yes, fragile and slow. Our shields are weak, our armor thin, our weapons hopelessly ineffective against the Spawn. We fail by any measure, except one."

Puzzled looks appeared on every face, wondering what could possible redeem our many failings.

"The human factor. Our fleet survived because our crews are disciplined, professional, and adaptable. We have more ships than anyone else in Orion, some say more than everyone else combined. Far more. We build a lot of ships. All we need are the right weapons." I turned to Siyarn. "Not your weapons. Our ships could never power them, or your shields or your star drives. I don't want any of that. What I want is for you to make our weapons better."

I reached into my pocket, pulled out a small eight millimeter slug with a purple band around its base and tossed it to Siyarn. He caught it with one hand, opened his palm to study the Ornithian designed, human made penetrator. Every eye in the auditorium strained to see the tiny projectile in his hand.

"Like you did with that," I said.

"Large static force projectiles will not harm a spawnship," Siyarn replied.

"I figured that one out myself, but that's not what I want." I stepped over to the holoprojector and slid a data rod into the slot, then the lights dimmed automatically and a dark, cylindrical object with an armored nose, oversized engines and fold-out sensors appeared above the sunken stage. It had 'EN-VI-ASD' inscribed on its side, and was recognized by most of the human military types.

"This is a Type VI heavy naval drone, Earth Navy's principle antiship weapon. Every capital ship, all our cruisers and some of our escorts can fire this weapon." I turned to Siyarn, who was studying the sleek black drone with interest. "I want you to make it better. Redesign what goes inside that shape. It must be able to talk to our systems the way our drones do. It's got to be fast and able to think for itself, because once we start shooting, our ships are dead. And most important of all, it must be able to destroy a spawnship. Give us a weapon like that and we'll put it on thousands of ships. Not just Earth Navy ships, but anything that can fly. And we'll hide it on every planet, asteroid, nebula and comet in Orion. By the time we're done, no spawnship will dare come within a thousand light years of Earth. You want Article Nine? Well there it is."

Stunned silence settled over the room as every eye, human and alien, lenticular and compound, was mesmerized by Earth Navy's pride and joy.

"Is such a weapon possible?" a Syrman diplomat asked.

Siyarn hesitated. "No projectile weapon that small could destroy a spawnship."

"We'll settle for crippling them," I said, "and you finish them off."

Siyarn straightened, surprised by the concept. "That...might be possible."

"Admiral," the President of the Democratic Union said, "how many ships do we have that can fire this type of weapon?"

"Over two hundred here," Talis replied. "Hundreds more at our various naval stations."

"How many civilian ships could take launchers?" I asked.

"Thousands have drone bays, mostly small, but they could be modified. And portable launchers can be fitted to cargo bays."

"Your ships would be destroyed as soon as they fired," a Fenari said.

"One of ours for one of theirs," I said, fixing my gaze upon the Fenari. "That's a good deal, for you."

The Fenari straightened, considered the implications and accepted my words in silence.

"You want to create suicide ships," a Nirisi diplomat said aghast.

"Not suicide," the Indian Republic Prime Minister stated calmly, "sacrifice, for the good of all."

"Even if we could design such a weapon," Siyarn said, "you could not build it, and we are restoring Serris-Orn.

We have no capacity."

"We will build it," Irukoochati said from the back of the auditorium. "Whatever Human-Kode-Soris requires."

The assembly looked up at the four coleopterans in surprise, then realized Irukoochati had just committed the Nisk's immense industrial might to the scheme. Gastillion Kalantropis stood, immediately gaining the full attention of the audience.

"The D'kol Empire, speaking on behalf of the Galactic Forum, considers the human request satisfies the requirements of Article Nine. Further, any civilization attacked by the Spawn may lawfully utilize the Ornithian-human weapon to preserve life."

The Syrman Ambassador jumped to his feet. "If this weapon is effective against the Spawn, we want it for our ships."

A Lhekan, one of the few who'd escaped the Niedarim disaster said, "The Lhekan League also desires access to this weapon."

Other ambassadors began to chime in, shouting over each other.

"Gienah humbly requests the weapon."

"Nirisi too wants this."

"Suvol still has ships. Give us the weapon. We will fight."

The amphitheater exploded with voices, clamoring for a weapon the Tau Cetins hadn't even designed yet, then the Union President stood and motioned them all to silence.

"On behalf of Earth's government in exile," he said, "we will provide all our launcher designs to the Nisk, for them to copy and share with any who want them."

Siyarn stood, immediately commanding their attention. "The Ornithian Consociation agrees. Article Nine applies. We will design Captain Kade's weapon to the best of our ability and send specialists to assist the Nisk to produce it."

The delegates jumped to their feet cheering wildly, banging on the consoles, stamping their feet and hooting in many languages, suddenly filled with hope. When the euphoria died away, they returned to their seats, while Gastillion remained standing.

"We are yet to address the question of resettlement," she said. "The Ornithian-human weapon may help protect the free worlds, but it will not defeat the Spawn Army." She turned to me. "Or do you have a solution for that also, Captain Kade?"

I knew from the look in her eye, she knew I did. Laleya was feeding her information, making sure I got my chance.

"I believe there is a way to liberate Earth, and all other conquered worlds." I glanced up at Irukoochati, watching intently from her rear terrace, hoping she wasn't about to be offended. "Chief Instructor Dietz runs the Spawn Close Combat course here. He has been assessing the Nisk's combat effectiveness. Instructor Dietz, what are your conclusions?" I met his eyes. "The truth."

He scowled and stood, uncomfortable in the spotlight. "The Nisk are tough, disciplined and predictable fighters. They lack the tactical skill necessary to defeat the Spawn Army. They are brave, obedient...cannon fodder."

The harshness of his assessment shocked the audience. Some were incensed that he'd insulted the Nisk. Others who hadn't read his reports doubted they were true, and those who knew better couldn't hide their disappointment. Just when it seemed Dietz would be lynched, Irukoochati spoke.

"The Myriad-of-Strains agrees with Instructor-Chief-Dietz," she said with no trace of resentment, silencing the dissenting voices.

I gave Lena a curious look, who shrugged: *We didn't tell her.*

"You do?" President Giannelli asked.

"Our fighters-swarm-leaders confirm failure against

fighters-intuitive-human." She fixed her eyes upon me. "Does Human-Kode-Soris have a solution?"

"Our intuitive soldiers have proven they have the instincts to defeat the Spawn," I replied, "but they are few in number. Too few to win a planetary war. I propose we put our Iron Fist in a Nisk glove. Have them work together. Put the Nisk under human I-F command."

"Nisk under human command!" A Syrman said incredulously, followed by other non-human protests.

"Insane!"

"The Nisk are an ancient race!"

"Human arrogance."

Siyarn and Gastillion exchanged calculating looks, then Irukoochati said, "Human-Kode-Soris, explain."

"If our intuitive fighters command the Nisk, anticipate the enemy's moves, decide tactics during the heat of battle, tell the Nisk where to move and when to attack, I believe together, they will defeat the Spawn. Something they cannot do apart."

"What are intuitive soldiers?" a Syrman asked, getting no answer.

"The proposal has merit," Irukoochati said. "Fighters-intuitive-human are small in size, "but formidable. Our fighters-swarm-leaders acknowledge their place. Human-Kode-Soris is correct. We are stronger as one. The Myriad-of-Strains agrees."

The tests we'd put the Nisk through had worked both ways. We'd seen what they could and couldn't do, and they'd seen the same of us. And the Nisk way of thinking, that each 'container' had its place, made it natural for them to recognize the best use for our precious I-F soldiers.

The Union President conferred with the other Earth Leaders then turned to Gastillion. "Ambassador, the Council of Earth wishes to defer deciding on the Empire's generous offer of resettlement, for now. We trust this meets with your agreement?"

"Our offer will remain open indefinitely, Mr. President," she replied.

Irukoochati stood, towering over the assembly, and offered her parting remarks. "It is decided. Fighters-swarm-Nisk and fighters-intuitive-human will swarm as one. Together, we shall restore order."

* * * *

It was quietly announced that resettlement had been deferred for the time being although no reason was given as to why. Refugees continued to trickle in, increasing the overcrowding in COTEF's subterranean passages and its orbital parking zones while morale fell steadily, and unseen by all but a few, I-F and Nisk began training together in secret.

I-F teams from across Mapped Space were quietly brought to M29 by the Tau Cetins, expanding the number of combined human-Nisk units, but it wasn't enough. There were simply too many Nisk fighters and too few I-F soldiers, so elite infantry units from the four major militaries were tested with the Nisk with considerable success. Eventually, at the request of the Nisk themselves, regular infantry units were integrated as well, creating a hybrid force whose numbers and capabilities were kept a closely guarded secret.

Dietz became very tight lipped, would send me no more reports about the training and when I did see him, all he would say was the Nisk were improving. In saying nothing, I knew he now believed they'd be ready to fight one day, and keeping that a secret was more important than keeping me informed.

After several months, Lena invited me to the Rykander Proving Ground on the far side of M29. Talis was there, along with a bunch of Earth Navy admirals and representatives from the allied civilizations at Orsalee. Only the Nisk were absent, too big for the cramped corridors, although Irukoochati and her consorts watched from a nestship via an impenetrable Tau Cetin security feed.

The proving ground was sparse; just one rectangular building flanked by landing pads and connected to the firing line by a simple monorail with a three carriage, unpressurized flatbed train. It was all very low-tech, looked like it had been there for a couple of hundred years and was surrounded in all directions by thousands of kilometers of empty, barren land. Down range were a bunch of sensor towers. Some had been blown to pieces and never repaired, and beyond them was a plain of craters stretching to the horizon. We were on the windowed observation deck of the control center, and on the roof above us was a forest of sensor towers and downlink receivers taking real time feeds from observation satellites in geosynchronous orbit.

Even though Izin was as loyal as any of us, and in spite of I-F combat teams on Earth reporting the entire tamph population was in full revolt, he was barred from attending. Even Talis agreed with the decision. It seemed the military could not get past the idea that because tamphs looked like Spawn, they couldn't be trusted.

"He'll get over it," Lena assured me as we watched the train move out along the monorail. Two of the flatbeds were empty, while on the third was a cylindrical block house that served as a firing platform.

"Don't worry about Izin," Jase said mischievously. "He loves being stuck down there. No air, no bots to play with, surrounded by hordes of sweaty humans, most of whom want to beat him to death. He's fine!"

"Don't joke about that," Marie said. "They might hurt him."

Jase shook his head. "Nah, he's got my fraggers."

"That's all we need, a tamph running amok, slaughtering humans," Lena said.

"He won't shoot more than two or three," I assured her

with a grin, then a Tau Cetin wearing a metallic body suit and a fancy headset entered the room. He was followed by an Earth Navy munitions bot carrying a shiny black Type VI naval drone with the Earth Navy crest on its bow.

"This is Hirseya," Talis said, introducing the Tau Cetin. "He's the design lead for our new weapon."

"It looks like a Type VI," one Earth Navy admiral observed.

"It's anything but," Talis assured him.

"Welcome to the first test firing of this prototype projectile weapon," Hirseya said through a small disk on his collar that translated his thoughts into speech. "It was designed and constructed on Ansara, there being no capacity on Serris-Orn. The Nisk have fabricated the required infrastructure to produce both the weapon and a variety of launch solutions. If you confirm it meets your requirements, large scale production will begin immediately."

The expectant crowd stepped closer, eager to inspect the weapon, even though there was nothing new to see externally.

"It is powered by a dark energy micro-siphon," Hirseya continued, "a miniaturized version of the power source we use on our ships. It is designed to withstand high acceleration and extreme inertial forces while evasively maneuvering. The drone-projectile has the capacity to penetrate Spawn shields and armor–"

"It's not a projectile," Jase said. "That's what we put in guns."

Hirseya looked puzzled. "You are confusing size with function."

"It's not really a drone either," Marie said thoughtfully.

"It is designed to simulate the autonomous mission profile of human drone weapons with greatly enhanced tactical performance," Hirseya said.

"It might look like a drone, but it's not a drone," Lena

agreed.

"It needs a name," I said, receiving nods and equivalent alien gestures from the audience.

"A name?" Hirseya asked with growing irritation. "This is a weapon to destroy the Spawn."

"Exactly!" I exclaimed. "It needs something...catchy."

"It's a torpedo," Talis said, delving far back into ancient naval history.

"It's way beyond any torpedo we ever invented," another admiral muttered.

"It's a hyper-torpedo," I said, "A spawnship killing, ass kicking, hyper-torpedo."

"As Grand Fleet Commander Siyarn warned, this projectile weapon is incapable of destroying a spawnship," Hirseya declared.

"But it'll mess them up good, won't it?" Jase asked with a grin.

"A single weapon has the potential to cause severe localized damage," Hirseya replied. "Multiple synchronic detonations will generate a cumulative, dark energy tremor that will–"

"We'll call it the hyper-torpedo, mark I," Admiral Talis decided. "HT1."

"But admiral," Hirseya protested, "it is not hyper-, it is sub-relativistic."

"We don't care," I said impatiently. "Show us what the...HT1 can do."

"HT1," a massive Syrman said thoughtfully, glancing at the humans in the room. "Human...torpedo... one. We call it that."

"But we designed it," Hirseya said, "and the Nisk built it."

"Yeah, but we made it sexy," I said, motioning to its distinctive black curves.

"Call it what you want," Hirseya snapped irritably. "You should know that any attempt to open the casing will cause the weapon to self-destruct."

"Don't you trust us?" Lena asked silkily.

"It is a precaution to prevent the Spawn from reverse engineering our technology should they capture one of these devices."

"What if it runs into one of their null fields?" I asked. It was a Spawn trick for draining space of dark energy, disabling the Tau Cetin's energy source.

"It has a sensor to avoid null space," Hirseya replied.

"I thought you couldn't see their null fields."

"We can now. All our ships have been equipped with null space detectors, and we have given priority to attacking null space generator ships. Those that have not been destroyed have been withdrawn to the Spawn cluster."

"That is good news," a uniformed Nirisi said.

"What else do we need to know about the hyper-torpedo?" a Lhekan officer asked.

Hirseya thought for a moment. "They will be most effective in large numbers, and will only attack chromodynamic targets."

"Chromo-what?" a human vice admiral asked.

"Spawnships use ultra-dense, chromodynamic armor," the Tau Cetin engineer replied.

I frowned, suspecting we'd been short changed again. "So we can't shoot snakeheads with it? Or anyone else?"

"That is correct."

"What if the Matarons attack us?" Lena asked. "Or the Xil?"

"Neither will attack you while our fleet is operational," Hirseya replied.

Talis gave Hirseya a harsh look. "Suppose your fleet is destroyed?"

"We can reset targeting parameters, but that would occur only under special circumstances."

Lena and I exchanged dubious looks. There was always a catch when dealing with the Tau Cetins, even with the Spawn trampling Earth into oblivion.

I sighed in frustration. "Any other little nasties we need to know about?"

"It has unlimited range, but it will self-destruct if it does not acquire a chromodynamic target within sixty minutes of launch."

"What about tactical weaknesses?" a human admiral asked.

"It is a projectile," Hirseya said simply. "It is highly evasive, but the longer the Spawn have to track the weapon, the greater the chance of them destroying it."

"Wait," I said, smelling another avian rat. "You're saying to get a kill, we have to fire at close range. How close?"

"Fifteen light seconds," Hirseya replied, puzzled by the audience's growing dissatisfaction. "We thought it was understood, if projectile weapons were effective against the Spawn, we would be using them."

A somber mood settled over the room as naval officers from human and alien commands digested the limitations of our new—not so super—weapon.

Admiral Talis' eyes narrowed as the implications sank in. "We'll have to bubble in to close range."

"You cannot, Admiral," Hirseya said. "Their ships are parked well inside Earth's gravity well."

"You'll have to lure them out," I declared.

"Impossible. You know we cannot concentrate our fleet against the Sol System."

I shook my head. "Not your whole fleet, just enough for bait."

"We have no ships for such a mission."

"Sure you do. You've got fifteen arbiters here. They'll do."

"That would leave M29 undefended," Hirseya protested.

"We'll evacuate the base before we attack," Talis decided.

"Even if we could lure the Spawn Fleet out of Earth's gravity well, Admiral," the Tau Cetin argued, "they will destroy your fleet the moment it appears."

"No if we don't send warships," I said, turning to Talis. "Send the refugee ships loaded with hyper-torpedoes, and offer to surrender."

Jase grinned. "Yeah, and blast them at point blank range."

"That is suicide," Hirseya declared. "Your entire fleet will be annihilated."

Talis fixed his eyes upon me, mind racing. "I'll put navy crews on every ship. No civilians. And launchers in their cargo holds. We'll only get one shot, so we'll need to know exactly where they are before we jump in."

"Even if we could draw their ships out of the gravity well," Hirseya said, "the moment we signal their location, the Spawn will know it's a trap and withdraw."

"Someone else has to send the signal," I cut in. "Someone they won't suspect."

Talis eyes narrowed on me. "Like who?"

"Their loyal snakehead allies. There's a Mataron cruiser aboard one of the nestships. We could send her in first, alone. She could signal our fleet with the coordinates."

"Fleet Commander Siyarn will never agree to such a plan," Hirseya said.

"He will," Talis insisted. "Ask him."

"As you wish, Admiral," Hirseya replied stiffly. He received a message via his private communicator, adding, "The test weapon is ready."

We went to the windows as the launch count ran down to zero, then a bright light streaked away from its launch platform on the train carriage. It was so fast, it looked like a beam weapon had been fired, except it curved over the horizon and was gone in the blink of an eye.

A brilliant flash illuminated the moon's curvature as it struck a mountain range two thousand kilometers away, sending debris hurtling out into space. It wasn't the biggest explosion I'd ever seen, but it put hope on the faces of everyone watching.

"What do you know," Talis said slowly, "the goddamned thing works." He turned to me. "We're going to need someone to fly that Mataron cruiser, someone who can talk his way in. Someone expendable."

"I figured you would." I glanced at Jase and Marie, who nodded. "We'll start flight training in the morning. With Izin."

* * * *

The Tau Cetins cracked the *Riku's* security lockout that night and had an instructor ready for us next morning for on-the-ground familiarization. It took several days to label snakehead interfaces so we could read them and another week to learn how to work with the *Riku's* highly intelligent control systems.

To us, the snakehead cruiser was a leap into the future. For the Tau Cetins, it was a tedious journey back into the distant past. Much to Lena's annoyance, the Tau Cetins sealed off the *Riku's* systems before she could sneak engineers aboard to see what they could steal.

By the time we'd learned enough to actually fly the *Riku*, the Tau Cetins had modified the environmental systems to our liking and installed a bio-simulator that made it appear as if she was operated by a full complement of snakeheads. Apart from air and gravity, everything else felt off and out of proportion. The reptilians were one and half times taller than humans, with longer arms and legs that put everything out of reach when we sat on their tail friendly, segmented flight couches. The back, seat, arm rests and foot supports were all separated, held in a skeletal cradle that individually adjusted the pieces to the Mataron form. The Tau Cetins couldn't improve the feel much because we were too small for them, especially Izin. Worse still, their two meter wide, curving consoles were simply beyond our reach while seated. The Tau Cetins installed narrow platforms in front of the couches for us to stand on, and Izin, with his shorter arms, had to use small wands to reach the control surfaces, making him look like he was conducting an orchestra.

Circular light projections appeared above our consoles with context sensitive data feeds decided by the ship based on rank, priority and situation. With only four of us aboard, the Tau Cetins assigned us the most important roles and sent everything else to the *Riku's* AI. We focused on flying, snooping and fighting while the AI handled the rest.

Five weeks into flight training, we received a Mataron picket probe, reworked by the Tau Cetins to make it idiot proof. All we had to do was launch it with our coordinates and it would jump toward the Matar System so as not to alarm the Spawn, then at the edge of the system it would change course for the refugee fleet.

One day, while practicing high-g sling shots and barrel rolls in the *Riku*, a sixth nestship arrived bearing gifts from the gigantic Nisk industrial machine. It was carrying enough hyper-torpedoes and launchers to equip every ship that needed them, along with a wealth of specialized equipment for the humans serving in the coleopteran army. The nestship had been given Orsalee's location by a Tau Cetin emissary only after it was in space, and instead of returning to Krailo-Nis, it went on to Serris-Orn to help with reconstruction, ensuring no word of our preparations got out.

Over a million human refugees and base personnel, along with tens of thousands of non-humans, were evacuated in that nestship. They were told it was only temporary, because supplies were running low and life support systems on both the base and the ships in orbit were critically overloaded. Once the refugees had been removed from their decrepit vessels, skeleton navy crews began refitting them for flight, with help from Irukoochati's highly efficient builders.

Talis refused to allow the *Riku* to be armed with hyper-torpedoes because he and the Tau Cetins insisted it was too big a risk. The launchers were sensor shielded, but if the Spawn saw through the deception, the game would be up, so we agreed to go in toothless.

The Tau Cetins tinkered with the *Riku's* energy plant, rigging it to leak non-lethal particles to fog the Spawn's sensors. It would start low and slowly increase in intensity as we got closer. Talis called it laying smoke, an old wet navy strategy for blinding an enemy at sea, only this version was designed to help the refugee fleet get close to the Spawn, not hide their retreat.

With the refugees gone, the ships over M29 were moved into three marshalling areas. The largest was for the refugee fleet, almost a thousand worn out human ships and some sixty alien ships, all with cargo holds large enough to take heavy drone launchers. Navy engineers overseeing the installations nicknamed them the Scrap Metal Armada, as most were fit for nothing but the breaker's yard. Each ship was commanded by a junior Earth Navy officer, usually an ensign, supported by a few ratings and, if they were lucky, volunteers from the ship's original company. The civilians offered the chance to stay behind were told they'd likely be killed for their trouble, but most opted in, sensing something big was in the works.

The second fleet was smaller, comprising Irukoochati's five nestships, a flotilla of other alien warships and six hundred and fifty Earth Navy warships and troop transports, many brought in from outlying bases by Tau Cetin conveyor. They were all armed with HT1s, even the nestships which could carry thousands of them, a sign of their determination not to allow a repeat of the *Iskeratix* disaster. This was the invasion fleet, carrying the human-Nisk landing force, and it would only appear once the way to Earth had been cleared.

The third fleet was the smallest, and the most powerful. It was the bait, containing Tau Cetin and Fenari warships only. They'd go in first, lure the Spawn Fleet out of Earth's gravity well and, outnumbered and outgunned, try to survive long enough for the Scrap Metal Armada to launch its attack. If they failed, our fleets would withdraw to Serris-Orn until they could be used to liberate other, less well defended worlds.

Earth Council had wanted Admiral Talis to command the invasion force, but he argued the fight would be over by the time they arrived, if they arrived at all. He insisted on leading the Scrap Metal Armada, and had threatened to resign his commission and go as a deck hand if they refused, so he got his way.

"He meant it," Lena told me one night. "He was ready to throw his stars in their faces."

"Old school. He wants to be in the fight, not nursemaiding troop transports. Are you going with him?"

She frowned. "I had a seat on the Artropis, but someone told the Union President and he wouldn't allow it. I threatened to resign too, but..." She shook her head.

"They can afford to lose a fighting admiral, but not a mega-psi." We had more admirals, but there were only four mega-psi humans in all of mankind.

"He was going to lock me up until it was all over," she said with exasperation.

"Who ratted you out?"

"I think it was Mallory." He was the director general of Earth Council Security. "He knows I'm mega-psi. He's a sneaky bastard, politician, deal maker. I don't like him, but he's good at his job."

"You weren't tempted to...?" I pointed to my head and whistled. "You know, make him let you go."

"I was tempted, but...Lord Geoffrey would have had a fit."

"Is he still alive?"

"Oh yes, still on Earth. The Spawn know he's important. Not why, but they've tried to kill him several times." She smiled appreciatively. "He's a slippery old fish."

"Are you in touch with him?"

"Not from here. I ride along with the Tau Cetins sometimes, when they go to the edge of the Sol System for a look. They always take a few human observers. I go just often enough to stay in touch with him."

"How bad is it on Earth?"

"Civilization has collapsed. There's cannibalism now, in some parts." She shook her head grimly. "They won't survive much longer."

* * * *

When the assault on the Sol System was only weeks away, we took the *Riku* out for our routine practice run, flying solo now without our Ornithian instructors. Just as we were about to put back to M29 a galactic conveyor flashed in from interstellar space. The immense Tau Cetin base ship appeared a few hundred clicks away, opened its huge space doors and proceeded to disgorge a motley collection of haphazardly armed and armored human ships.

They were fighting ships, with their transponders off and their registry markings removed to conceal their identities. Their hulls were scarred and patched, making them the ugliest collection of ships I'd ever seen, then a large cylindrical beast, black hulled with a battleship sized naval gun on its blunt bow glided out into space.

"It's the Cyclops!" I said, hardly able to believe my eyes.

Marie immediately reached for her console. "Hailing them."

My brother's face appeared in light projection above my console. "Hello little brother," he said, staring at me with his optronic eye, showing no surprise I was flying a

Mataron cruiser off his port bow.

"What are you doing here?" I asked.

"We've come to fight. It's what you wanted, isn't it?"

"I see you bought your friends."

"It turns out everyone's got a mother, and some of them are on Earth. I've got a hundred and eighty two ships for you: Drakes, Vipers, Falcons, Celts, even Demons. Ugly as hell and tough as they come."

"We can use them all," I said, hardly able to believe for the first time in our lives, my brother and I were finally on the same side.

The pirate fleet poured out of the Tau Cetin conveyor, past hundreds of refugee ships they would have hunted down and looted only a year ago. They took up position midway between the Scrap Metal Armada and the Earth Navy Invasion Force, watched in disbelief by smartly dressed navy crews, puzzled aliens and the human-Nisk legions awaiting their chance to liberate Earth. Almost immediately, support ships full of Nisk builders, human engineers and hyper-torpedoes came out to meet them, while admirals and aliens debated how best to use them.

The Pirate Brotherhood's scarred, battle worn hulls were ugly and brutish, straggling through space without formation or discipline, some sorely in need of repair, and yet to all who saw them, they were beautiful to behold, every last one of them.

* * * *

Rix and I met several days later in a dark corner of a crowded COTEF bar. It was overflowing with hard drinking, noisy revelers who fought each other, and anyone else, for no particular reason and who seemed to never sleep. They looked with suspicion upon anyone in uniform, intimidated the quieter patrons and had caused two deaths and more than a dozen hospitalizations since their arrival.

"I didn't like leaving you like that," I said, referring to the fight in Ice Town.

"You did enough." He sat with his back to the wall and scanned the room with his optronic cyclops eye, trusting no one. "We'd have lost if you hadn't hit those Sep battlecruisers." "It took a couple of days to clean out the Sep militia. By then, Gwandoya had escaped."

"Will he come after you?"

"Bound to," he grunted, watching the raucous crowd. "He's put a price on my head, not as big as the one I put on his, but big enough."

"They've doubled the guard on the bars since you arrived."

"That's comforting," he muttered, not at all reassured. He emptied his drink in one gulp and ordered another. "Well, you got what you wanted. Ice Town needs patching, but the towers, the engineering works, the spares, it's all there. And three other bases besides."

"Earth Navy will be pleased."

"I've got good captains heading to the other chapters. You won't get them all, but you'll get some."

A new round of drinks arrived, then I said, "They'll be well paid."

"They didn't come for your money or your amnesty. They came for their families, or because they figure the Spawn will kill them first chance they get. Some came because they like to fight, and drink."

"We can use them all."

"I was hoping for more. The Skulls heard me out, but they don't come from the Core Systems. A pity. They're good fighters. Falcons and Celts joined straight away. They're mostly Earther types, ex-cons, deserters, killers on the run. Amnesty extends to them, right, no matter what they've done?"

"Absolutely."

"Hmm, that's what I told them." He sipped his drink thoughtfully. "The Vipers let each crew decide. Split them right down the middle. No shooting. Those that wanted out just up and left. Word's spreading. Anyone who wants in is heading for Uralo IV. Ships will be coming in for months, I expect."

He motioned to a server bot and held up his small, shot glass. "We want bigger glasses, and two more rounds." He emptied his drink while I took a deep breath and followed suit, doubting I could keep up with him.

"Them navy boys on Uralo IV didn't know what to make of us. They wouldn't even let us land. Kept us locked up in orbit the whole time, then the Tau Cetins showed up with some of your EIS people. Told them there really was a deal." He grinned slyly. "You should have seen their faces."

"They'll all get their pardons," I assured him. "They'll be free to do whatever they want."

His jaw tightened. "They're free now."

"To roam the backwaters of space, constantly watching over their shoulders, hunted everywhere. That's not freedom."

"It is to them." An attractive young woman, not a bot, brought us more drinks in larger glasses. She set them down quickly and backed away, trying not to stare at Rix's cyclops eye. "Don't get me wrong, little brother. Some'll take the pardons, the older ones who want to retire. Most will go back to what they know, once their families are safe, and they know the Spawn won't be coming to exterminate them."

He glanced at the noisy buccaneers crowding out the other patrons. They wore mismatched, garishly colored armor, some painted with chapter crests, and all armed to the teeth. They didn't fit in with the base personnel, with scientists and engineers or military and naval officers, only with each other.

"Don't tell Talis, or he'll stop arming your ships."

Rix scowled, unimpressed with the new weapons. "From what I hear, those fancy torpedoes of yours are only good for one thing; killing Spawn. The way I see it, he's disarming our ships."

Talis had allocated the Brotherhood ships to the Scrap Metal Armada because they could fight and pass for armed refugee ships. To make full use of them, they were being stripped of much of their existing armaments to make way for HT1 launchers.

"The launchers are designed for heavy drones," I said.

"Too bad our suppliers aren't selling us weapons anymore. Every Consortium arms dealer I know has us blacklisted."

"Will any captains rejoin the Separatists?"

He shook his head. "They don't trust us anymore, and we didn't like the way they thought they were better than us."

"If you take the pardon, you won't need weapons."

"We've talked about it, me and Anya, but...it'd be dangerous for us, for me, to stay in one place too long."

"I can help you." I could get him false identities, security systems, a new life somewhere.

"I figured you could," he said, showing no interest. "Hell, we'll be dead in a week." He motioned for five more drinks each, then we clinked glasses. "To a quick death."

"To a great victory."

He smiled sourly. "You always were an optimist, little brother, one of your least endearing qualities. Only you'd call your ship Silver Lining."

"It's better than Cyclops."

"I only have one eye."

"We're both one eyed, in our own way."

He grunted agreement. "It's a family trait."

We began drinking in earnest, catching up on lost years and putting old differences behind us. I struggled to match him for the first few hours, but it got easier as the night wore on. By M29's black dawn, barely able to stand, we took comfort in the possibility we were going to die together in a fight worth having, just as our hard bitten old father had always intended.

* * * *

Two days before the *Riku* was scheduled to leave, the Scrap Metal Armada departed Orsalee-M29 with over twelve hundred mostly human refugee and Brotherhood ships. Having the slowest vessels, the Armada was the first to leave for the short run to the Sol System, along a route carefully scouted by the Tau Cetins.

Admiral Talis had hoisted his pennant aboard the seventy five thousand tonne liner *ISL Aruna*, a large ship with excellent comms and six pleasure craft hangars that made excellent drone launcher bays. The Armada would arrive at its rendezvous point in the Kuiper Belt just minutes before the *Riku* appeared in the Sol System. It would hide there until our Mataron sentry probe reached it with the Spawn fleet's coordinates, then it'd jump in and the fun would begin.

Under the pretense of training, I took the *Riku* out to see them off, taking up a position ten thousand clicks astern of their bubble out point. Not far away was the *Solar Constitution*, Talis' Third Fleet flagship. She was one of many capital ships quietly brought in from distant outposts by the Tau Cetins, to enable Earth Navy's greatest ever fleet concentration. The navy's top brass were aboard her, along with political leaders and alien diplomats, all anxiously watching the launch of the largest, most important fleet operation in human history.

Beyond the *Solar Constitution* was the mirror-hulled *Rillesium*, Fleet Commander Siyarn's flagship. Her presence was a sign that a victory now would mean almost as much to the Tau Cetins as it would to us. If successful, massed hyper-torpedo attacks and human-Nisk landing forces might become the formula for liberating worlds from Orion to the Outer Rim, bringing an end to the

Spawn Army's planetary supremacy.

Because no signals of any kind could pass through superluminal fields, the Armada ships would not see each other again until they unbubbled fourteen billion kilometers from the Sun. Only then would they know if all ships had arrived safely. Thirty two days later, light from the Kuiper Belt would reach the inner planets, revealing their arrival at the edge of the Solar System to the people of Earth; by which time it would be all over, one way or the other.

To eliminate the risk of collision, the Armada was laid out in a grid pattern, twenty five rows wide. The ships were ten kilometers apart, had their own unique pre-computed courses and would take turns jumping, one every five seconds. The Brotherhood and alien ships were slightly in advance of the rest because the pirate ships had the best fighters and the heaviest armor and the alien ships the best shields. When the shooting started, they'd draw the initial Spawn bombardment, buying the more fragile human ships astern time to release their weapons.

It had taken the Armada more than fifty hours to form up, with each ship moving in turn to its assigned grid position. The navy ensigns and lieutenants did a good job of holding formation, giving their decaying vessels some semblance of fleet discipline and keeping comms chatter to a minimum.

The *Cyclops* was near the center, close to the *Aruna*. Talis had noticed her heavy armor and had notified my brother that if the *Aruna* was destroyed, he would transfer his flag to her. The idea of his ugly, one eyed brute becoming flagship of the fleet amused my brother, who promised me he'd rescue Talis if the liner was shot out from under him.

I wanted to send a private message to the *Cyclops*, wishing my brother luck, but strict comms silence was imposed, and for once we followed orders. He knew I was in the *Riku*, although not why, and would know I'd come to see him off and that was enough.

Down on the surface of M29 in the COTEF complex, in the Invasion Force ships in orbit, and in the small Tau Cetin-Fenari fleet, thousands watched mesmerized as the silent vacuum of space filled with ships. When every place on the grid was taken, there was a long silence as final checks were made, then a steely voice sounded out of the darkness.

"Attention all ships," Admiral Talis said, "standby for fleet staged deployment. Initiating synchronization." There was a long pause as every ship's navigation system verified time keeping with the flagship. "Confirmations received...Automatic countdown activated...See you on the other side."

Every ship pulled sensors and buttoned up, then the first ship streaked away. The rest followed one by one, on parallel courses. It took almost forty one minutes for them all to leave, peeling off into space like a cloth unraveling from one end to the other. When they were gone, only one ship remained, an old water tanker that had broken down at the last minute and missed its window.

"That's it," I said. "We're committed."

"Finally!" Jase exclaimed.

Marie sighed apprehensively. "I hope this works, for all our sakes."

"Hope has nothing to do with it," Izin declared. "Either the Spawn will be deceived or we will fail."

"Never underestimate the human factor," I said, turning the *Riku* toward M29, thinking we'd survived when many, far more powerful than us, had not.

Shuttles launched from the *Solar Constitution* carrying the brass and civilian dignitaries back to the COTEF complex while the battleship moved off to its bubble-out position with the Invasion Force and Earth Navy's finest. They would go in a few hours, making a slightly faster crossing than the refugee ships. The Invasion Fleet would take up position much further out in the Oort Cloud and wait for the all clear from the Tau Cetins before approaching Earth. Fifty hours from now, the Tau Cetin-Fenari Decoy Force would leave, crossing to the Sol System in under a minute to lure the Spawn out into flat space.

And then it would be our turn, the last to leave.

If all went according to plan, we'd arrive in the midst of a battle raging near the orbit of Mars, where we hoped to destroy the spawnships defending Earth. If they weren't there, if there was no battle, if the Spawn had not taken the bait, the entire operation would be abandoned, but it was too late to worry about that now.

We were going, risking it all, and there was no turning back.

* * * *

The night before we were due to bubble out, we went to the officer's mess for dinner. The Invasion Force was long gone, the Tau Cetins and Fenari were in their ships conducting last minute battle drills, and all but a handful of volunteers remained on the ground, the rest having been taken off to Serris-Orn by a conveyor. The normally overcrowded mess was deserted, except for a solitary PFA officer sitting alone in a corner reading a data screen while bots scrubbed spotless floors and tables, unaware the base was now empty.

"Lucky they could squeeze us in," Jase joked as we took our seats and three serverbots jostled each other to get our order. "Four of your most expensive drinks, and keep them coming. We have credits to burn."

"Nothing intoxicating," I said to the service bot, then turned to Jase. "No hangovers, not this time."

Jase gave me a deflated look. "In that case, bring us the best food you have, six courses, whatever the admirals eat."

"We have freeze dried, vacuum sealed, irradiated type

K ration packs only," the servicebot replied.

"K?" Jase wrinkled his face. "No meat?"

"All other supplies have been requisitioned by Logistics Command."

"I hate K-packs," Marie said.

"So does Logistics Command," I said dryly and turned to the serverbot. "Four K-packs with all the trimmings."

"And bread," Jase added, "to go with the water."

Marie put her hand on my arm, gave me a reproachful look, and turned to the servicebot. "Do you have...champagne?"

Jase saw I was being overruled by a higher authority and hung on the bot's response.

"We have Scintilli Bianchi."

Marie frowned. "What's that?'

"Double fermented, carbon dioxide infused, pressurized grape substitute from the waste recycling facility on Nuovo Sicilia."

"Any Merayan reds?" Marie asked hopefully, not enticed by recycled Sicilian waste.

"No Merayan products are currently listed in inventory."

Marie sighed. "In that case, bring four glasses of your best Scintilli Bianchi."

The drinks came almost immediately, more gray than white, and bubbling like cheap Carolian fizz-bombs.

Marie raised her glass. "To friendship."

We clinked glasses, sipped cautiously, then Izin slid his glass across to Jase without a word.

"Now that's friendship," Jase declared, threw the first drink down and grabbed Izin's full glass before I could intervene.

Marie wrinkled her nose. "Hmm...And I thought I could drink anything with bubbles."

Jase turned to the servicebot, holding up his glass. "Have them load whatever's left of this stuff aboard the Riku. Tonight." We gave him surprised looks, then he added. "For after the war."

The K-rations came, as disappointing a last meal as any condemned man ever had. When we rose to leave, I took Marie's arm in hand.

"We'll see you in the morning," I said to the others. "We're sleeping on base tonight."

Marie gave me a surprised look. "We are?"

"Have fun." Jase grinned, then he and Izin went back to the *Riku* while I led Marie through officer country, up into the rarified air known only to God-like beings of flag rank and above.

"Where are we going?" she asked.

"It's a surprise," I replied mysteriously, leading her past the base commander's quarters to an impressively oversized door. "It's a present from Lena."

I palmed the DNA lock which had been reset to my sequence, then the door slid open revealing a large suite with a bar, central lounge, several eager-to-please service bots and picture windows with a view of the deserted south side of the spaceport.

"Nice," Marie said appreciatively, surprised COTEF had such luxury.

"It took a bit of arm twisting, but considering the Spawn might destroy it all tomorrow, we might as well put it to good use tonight."

"A little better than corridor bunks," Marie said as we stepped into the central lounge.

"Lights, five percent." I guided her to the picture window where we stood in the soft glow of the spaceport. "It was the Flag Officer Commanding's quarters, but he got bumped by the Union President and the PFA Chairman."

"They shared? How inconvenient for them."

We looked out over landing pads glowing with light beneath a sea of stars to Orsalee's great dark blue sphere descending beyond the barren horizon.

"It's a ghost town," she said softly, taking in the view,

then turned to me. "Thanks Sirius. Those bunks on the Riku hurt my back."

"Mine too, but I didn't bring you up here just to show you the stars, or get a good night's sleep, not that you'll be sleeping much tonight."

"Hmm, I worked that out all by myself," she said sensuously.

I reached into my pocket for the small black cube I'd had her hold for me in Paris. "I've been carrying this for a long time."

"I know," she said, hinting she'd been waiting a long time too.

I flipped open the lid, revealing the dazzling Witari diamond inside. It sparkled in the starlight, tinted blue by Orsalee's faint glow. "I couldn't give it to you before now, because..."

"I was the enemy," she taunted.

"Something like that."

"How do you know I'm still not?"

"Lena would have shoved you out an airlock by now if you were."

"Ah, so I have Lena's blessing." She smiled. "How romantic. Just you, me and a scheming, cold blooded, mastermind."

"And ruthless. Don't forget that."

"Now that we're on the same side, and there really are no more secrets," I took the ring out of the box.

"Aren't you getting on your knees?"

"Are you kidding? In this gravity?"

"Well, I wouldn't want you straining anything...not before we fight the Spawn for the future of mankind. But you can only use that excuse once."

I grinned and peered into her eyes for a long time. "I do love you, you know. Always have, even when you were the enemy."

"I was never really the enemy," she said as I slipped the ring onto her finger. She held her hand up to the light, admiring it sparkle. "It is beautiful." She gave me a sideways look. "You didn't get this from Ameen Zadim, did you?"

I froze. "What does it matter where I got it?"

"Did he steal it?" she demanded.

"I...didn't ask," I replied awkwardly, certain Zadim had pulled a shady deal to get me such a ring. I couldn't have afforded it otherwise.

She grinned at my discomfort. "I'm just playing with you, Sirius. I don't care where he got it. It's perfect." She put her arms around my neck and whispered, "And I love you too, more than you'll ever know." She sighed. "I just hope I don't get arrested for wearing stolen property."

We chuckled together, certain Zadim had covered his tracks well, then I kissed her as if we'd be together for the rest of our lives, however long or short that might be.

Chapter Eight : Luna

Sterile asteroid
Sol System
0.165 Earth Normal Gravity
Terrestrial Moon
Depressurized cities
No survivors

Next morning, we took up position astern of the Tau Cetin fleet. Reinforcements had arrived from Serris-Orn during the night, bringing their number to twenty one arbiters and four sentinels. They were accompanied by ten Fenari ships; long, four bladed arrowheads slightly smaller than Earth Navy battleships that would fight alongside the escorting sentinels. The combined force was arrayed in two circles; an inner ring of arbiters that would make high velocity strafing runs against the Spawn Fleet, and an outer formation of weaker sentinels and arrowheads that would fight at extreme range. If the Spawn took the bait, the fleet would fight defensively, trying to survive long enough for the main blow to fall. If it didn't, the escorts would destroy the naval facilities on Mars and withdraw to Serris-Orn with the arbiters.

"Would it have killed them to give us another twenty ships," Jase complained.

"They sent all they could," I assured him.

"More than they promised," Marie said, then Jase saw the rock on her finger and jumped off his couch.

"So! You finally got some backbone." He shook my hand and grinned at Marie. "Does this mean you're Captain now?"

"I always was," she replied mischievously.

Jase gave her a kiss on the cheek. "Does Izin know?"

"Know what?" Izin asked as he came onto the bridge.

"Marie's giving the orders now," Jase said, pointing from his finger to hers as he returned to his station.

Izin saw the ring. "I understand. You are now matriarch."

"Captain Matriarch to you," she said lightly.

Fleet Commander Siyarn's head and shoulders appeared in the light projection rising from my curving console. "Captain Kade, we are about to depart. Synchronizing now."

Siyarn's ship made an infinitesimal adjustment to the *Riku's* chronometer, putting our ships on the same nanosecond.

"We'll see you soon," I promised and his face disappeared.

"They really like calculating to a gazillion decimal places, don't they," Jase said.

I nodded. "I just hope the Spawn are on our timetable."

The concentric rings of the Tau Cetin-Fenari bait fleet appeared in the curved light projections rising from our consoles, there being no central bridge screen. They floated silently in space, then without a formal countdown, suddenly flashed away as one, travelling at the Fenari's top speed. It would take them only a few seconds to reach the Sol System, even with a mid-course adjustment to hide their point of origin, then they would go straight in to attack.

"They're making their run now," I said as my light projection began counting down for our jump.

I imagined the arbiters diving into Earth's gravity well, raking the spawnships with their energy weapons as they sped past at high velocity, goading the enemy. There was no possibility of taking the Spawn by surprise, only of inflicting enough superficial damage to tempt them out to fight.

"You think they fell for it?" Jase wondered aloud.

"We'll know soon enough," I replied.

The *Fersiyon*, the fifth Tau Cetin sentinel assigned to the operation, but temporarily detached from the bait fleet, raced up astern of us, then a broad, dappled face with a small mouth and closely spaced, green almond-shaped eyes appeared in my light projection.

"Captain Kade, we are synchronized to follow ninety seconds behind you," Commander Ruyeen said. "Same velocity."

His job was to convince the Spawn we were genuine, by shooting at us. If the Spawn bought it, the *Fersiyon* would join the Tau Cetin fleet. If not, she'd leave us to our fate and run for Tau Ceti.

"That's not much of a head start," I said.

"It will be sufficient for our purposes."

"Just be careful where you hit us."

"Do not be concerned, Captain Kade. We will do no serious damage to the Riku."

"Should I fly straight?" I asked, not sharing his confidence. "Make it easier for you."

"No. Push your ship to its limits. Anything less will make the Spawn suspicious."

"You do realize I'm still learning how to fly this thing?"

"Rest assured, Mataron technology is so primitive, your lack of skill will not be a factor in our attack."

Commander Ruyeen's face disappeared, then Jase asked, "When did they decide to shoot us for real?"

"Right after they agreed to risk their own ships," I replied.

"A single hit from a Tau Cetin energy weapon will collapse our shield," Izin warned, "and penetrate our armor."

"One hit?" Marie said surprised.

"They know what they're doing…I hope," I muttered.

We buttoned up to bubble, watched the sync timer count down to zero, then the *Riku* leapt away into the void. After almost a minute, we unbubbled in interstellar space and altered course for Sol, hiding our departure point.

"Here we go," I said as we jumped again.

The snakehead course simulator tracked our passage into the Oort Cloud, through the Kuiper Belt and past the outer planets toward the orbit of Mars. When the snakehead bubble dropped, I poured on the power, not waiting for the hull to cool or the sensors to deploy, sending the *Riku* hurtling blindly through space for the benefit of the watching Spawn, and to get a good start on the *Fersiyon*.

The exterior temperature dropped and the *Riku* opened her eyes revealing a rust colored orb with gravity less than a quarter of Earth's to starboard. The ugly scar of Valles Marineris was visible showing no lights anywhere along its length. Marineris City, mankind's largest pressurized habitat, was a blackened uninhabited ruin, a tomb for millions, confirming the red planet was once again a dead world.

Directly ahead was Earth, a bright point of light in the blackness, and beyond it to port was the Sun's weak golden orb. The Spawn Fleet was supposed to be right in front of us, but there was nothing ahead but empty space.

"Oh-ho," I said, knowing we had very little time to figure out what was happening before the *Fersiyon* arrived, beams hot.

"Where are they?" Marie asked.

"They cancelled the war and forgot to tell us," Jase quipped, trying to make sense of the Mataron scanning information before him.

"There!" Izin pointed to a tiny point of light floating close to Earth, seeing changes in color and intensity with his powerful eyes that we could not.

"That's the Moon!" I exclaimed, realizing its light was obscuring the flash of energy weapons.

"They're still in the gravity well," Jase reported.

"How close to flat space?" I asked, turning the *Riku* toward Luna and rolling and weaving her wildly like our lives depended on it, because they did.

"Close," Jase said uncertainly. "What do you think Izin?"

Mars fell rapidly behind us as the Moon grew to a gray orb. Energy flashes and shield flares sparkled against Luna's light as the battle became visible to human eyes. Spawnships appeared, formed in three parallel lines firing at arbiters circling so fast they were glowing streaks in the darkness, desperately avoiding a barrage of Spawn energy blasts. Further out at the periphery of battle, Tau Cetin sentinels and Fenari arrowheads painted high velocity circles in space, shooting from extreme range, doing minimal damage and drawing little Spawn fire in return.

The arbiters strafed the spawnships, turning their shields white hot in places before banking away through space crisscrossed by streams of white Spawn energy pulses. No spawnships had been destroyed, while adrift between Earth and the Moon was the slowly tumbling wreck of a Tau Cetin arbiter leaking glowing orange plasma from blackened holes in its mirrored hull.

"Izin?" I said urgently, trying to decide if we should abort.

He studied the data carefully, then said, "They're in Luna curvature, Captain, at the top of Earth's gravity well."

"I'm reading sixty two spawnships," Jase added.

"They've been reinforced," I said, fearing we were the ones in the trap.

A brilliant light bloomed close to Earth, hurling an energy blast at the arbiters. The Tau Cetin ships scattered as it flashed between them, then another star bloomed in a different part of Earth's sky and a second energy blast hurtled out toward the Tau Cetin fleet.

"That fire's coming from Earth orbit," Marie said surprised.

Jase focused a sensor on a pinpoint of light high above Earth, then an armored ovoid with a dark hole at one end appeared. Contrarotating rings of faceted armor ran along its length, revolving slowly as the orbital oriented itself toward its target. A brilliant flash erupted from the hole as a white energy blast burst into space, then the station fell silent as it began a long, slow recharge of its weapon.

"Damn! That's a big gun," Jase exclaimed.

We'd assumed the orbital defense stations were to prevent landings on Earth, but their reach extended far across the Solar System.

"They're siege weapons, Captain," Izin said. "Look at the surface."

I'd been so focused on the battle, I hadn't even looked at Earth. It was pockmarked by thousands of craters large enough to be seen from space. They were on every continent and shoreline and reached out through the shallow seas to the edges of the continental shelves, confirming the Spawn were bombarding man and tamph with equal ferocity.

Jase winced. "They're not taking the bait, Skipper."

"The Spawn are staying in range of the orbitals," I said, "using the Earth-Moon gravity well to disrupt our bubbles."

It was a smart move, forcing the Tau Cetins to fight their fleet and Earth's defense stations at once while disrupting superluminal flight into and out of the battle zone. We should have expected nothing less from the Spawn.

"Should we abort?" Marie asked.

I studied the scene in frustration as more orbitals fired, scattering Tau Cetin arbiters already contending with a tremendous barrage from the spawnships.

"Captain, at this range, the Tau Cetin ships have one point two eight seconds to evade fire from the orbital battlestations," Izin said.

"Yeah, so?" Jase said, thinking it was no more than the blink of an eye.

"Their ships are very fast, Captain," Izin added. "They have a chance."

"That's why they're still here. They can outfly them," I said and turned the *Riku* toward the spawnships above Luna.

Marie smiled. "I guess that means we're not aborting."

I nodded toward the beleaguered Tau Cetin fleet. "While they stay, we stay," I said, then a brilliant blue beam flashed above us, skimming our topside shield.

"The Fersiyon's behind us!" Jase warned.

I began rocking the Mataron cruiser from side to side like a fighter as we raced toward the Spawn Fleet. The *Fersiyon* sent another beam burst at us, this time passing through our shield port side. Our console's light projections distorted momentarily as overloaded power systems reset, then a Mataron symbol flashed in front of me.

"Our shield has failed, Captain," Izin said, removing the warning symbol.

An orbital blast struck an arbiter amidships ahead of us, causing a brilliant yellow-white flash as the Tau Cetin ship broke in two. It lit up the other ships and the surface of the Moon and confirmed the arbiters couldn't always evade the orbital siege cannons.

"Mataron ship, identify yourself," a challenge came in as snakehead hiss and was automatically translated by our

Tau Cetin tweaked comm system.

I corkscrewed the *Riku* through a pair of blue beams from the *Fersiyon* that seared our hull, then said, "This is the cruiser Riku requesting your protection. Our shield is down and the Tau Cetins have us locked."

Before the Spawn could reply, the *Fersiyon* raced up above us and fired down into our topside hull from two thousand meters away. Her blue beam punched through the *Riku* like she was naked, triggering decompression alarms throughout the ship.

"They ain't kidding," Jase snapped angrily.

"They're making it look too good," Marie said.

I threw the *Riku* hard to port, dodging the *Fersiyon's* next shot, surprised how well she maneuvered after having been holed from top to bottom.

"She feels the same," I said surprised.

A fusillade of beam blasts from four spawnships targeted the *Fersiyon*. She evaded with a tremendous burst of acceleration, rolled half a turn and streaked away toward the allied escorts.

"Riku, approach second rank," the Spawn commander snapped, then Marie closed the channel.

"The door's open," I said, aiming the *Riku* for the middle row of spawnships.

"Thirty one sections decompressed, no critical systems damaged," Izin reported. "Activating particle generator."

I sputtered the engines pretending to be crippled, hoping the Spawn wouldn't realize we were messing with their sensors. We sped through the center of the battle, ignored by both sides, and banked sharply in behind a massive spawnship where we hid like a goldfish sheltering behind a whale.

"They're scanning us," Jase announced.

A Tau Cetin arbiter made a high speed flyby, strafing the spawnship, giving the Spawn something else to think about. We waited, but no challenges came through

"I think they bought it," Marie said hopefully.

My console's light projection showed spawnships and spawncarriers all around us. The first were heavily armored superdreadnoughts, much larger than Tau Cetin arbiters, but not as fast or as well shielded. Alongside them were the almost as formidable spawncarriers, purpose built planetary conquest ships that carried the Spawn Army's full panoply of war. An ancient ancestor of the spawncarrier had crashed on Earth thousands of years ago, bringing Izin's ancestors with it, although this latest version was vastly more powerful.

"It sure is crowded out there," Jase said uneasily.

There were far more Spawn leviathans here than we'd expected. They must have been rushed to Earth, confirming Tau Cetin suspicions that the Spawn intended to turn the Sol System into their Orion fleet base and hold it like a dagger to the throat of the Ornithians.

"Izin, how close can our fleet get?"

"Close, Captain, but they won't get through the Earth-Moon gravity well."

"They'll need time to come in," Marie said, "enough time for the Spawn to wipe them out."

"They've only got to be close enough to launch their weapons," I said. "And we still have surprise on our side. The Spawn don't consider us a threat. They might ignore our ships until it's too late."

"And they might not," Izin said evenly.

I watched the Spawn Fleet all around us, weathering the Tau Cetin onslaught, determined to hold its position, to hold the Sol System, and feared this chance would never come again.

"If we leave now, we're never coming back," I said.

Marie nodded and smiled encouragingly. "What are we waiting for?"

"Load our coordinates," I said.

Jase's fingers played over his console, fed our sensor readings and location into the Mataron sentry probe, then nodded. "Done."

I hovered my hand over my console, my mind racing, heart beating. Admiral Talis would see the Spawn Fleet was not where we wanted it to be, that our ships would be dangerously exposed as they moved to their firing positions, that our entire Armada could be lost in a heartbeat, and I knew, he'd come anyway.

"Roll the dice, admiral," I said and tapped launch control. The sentry probe streaked from the stern launcher, raced alongside the spawnship and hurtled out toward flat space. "Message away."

We held our breaths as the sentry probe cleared the Earth-Moon gravity well and bubbled toward the Matar System. A moment later, at the edge of the Sol System, unseen by the Spawn, it dropped its bubble, made a sharp course correction and jumped to the Scrap Metal Armada hiding in the Kuiper Belt.

"Mataron ship Riku," the spawnship alongside us signaled. "What did you launch?"

"I ahh…sent a signal…" I stammered, "to the Mataron fleet, requesting reinforcements. To help you." I waited anxiously, exchanging uncertain looks with the others while they considered my reply.

"When your fleet arrives, instruct it to focus its attack upon the enemy escorts."

I relaxed. "Sure thing. They'll get right on it. Happy to help. Loyal allies and all that."

"Your responses are...strange for a Mataron."

"I'm new. This is my first Mataron ship."

"Improve your signals discipline when communicating with us."

"Yes sir. I will, right away…I promise.. Next time," I waited for a reprimand but none came, then Marie cut the commlink.

"Did you have to say it was your first Mataron ship?" she asked.

"A little truth makes a big lie go a long way."

"Watch out!" Jase said as the spawnship veered across

our bow, almost running us down.

I banked the *Riku* hard away, narrowly avoiding a collision, then the Spawn Fleet spread out into a circular formation. The outer edges advanced, making the circle concave, forcing the Tau Cetins into a killing zone at the center.

I eased the *Riku* toward the spawnship's stern while Izin erratically increased our jamming particles, raising our smoke screen to a level the Tau Cetins had indicated would disrupt Spawn sensors. The change did not go unnoticed.

"Mataron ship Riku," the Spawn bellowed. "Disable your kyronic particle emissions immediately."

"We're trying," I replied. "We've taken heavy damage. We may have to abandon ship."

"Move two million tessakons from our fleet immediately."

"Yes sir. Two thousand…tessa-cans. Right away." When Marie confirmed they weren't listening, I asked, "How far is that?"

"A tessakon is a Mataron spatial unit equivalent to zero point zero four light seconds," Izin replied.

"How'd you know that?" Jase asked.

"It was in the Tau Cetin familiarization manual."

"You read that thing? It was twenty thousand pages long."

"I read it twice."

"I looked at the pictures," I said.

"There were pictures?" Jase asked.

Concentrated fire from a group of spawnships on the far flank struck a Fenari arrowhead, triggering a massive explosion, then I eased the *Riku* away from the spawnships while arbiters made high velocity strafing runs against them. Their radiant blue beams laced space, crisscrossed by white Spawn energy beams and pulses. A supernova bloomed against the blackness as an arbiter was caught in a withering crossfire and disintegrated before our eyes.

"Talis better get here soon, or this'll be over," Jase said, watching glowing debris from the vaporized arbiter spin off into space.

"The Tau Cetins saw us launch the probe," I said. "They know he's coming."

Three arbiters dived through the spawnship ranks, firing at close range and flashing past us at incredible speed.

"Attention Spawn Fleet," Admiral Talis' voice sounded in the *Riku's* bridge. "We surrender. I repeat, we surrender."

There was no response from the Spawn. The black leviathans continued to focus upon the Tau Cetins who attacked with renewed vigor, deliberately risking their ships to distract the Spawn.

"Where are they?" I asked.

"Eighty thousand clicks out, and closing," Jase replied.

My console's light projection expanded in size, almost touching the overhead, while scrolling in scale revealing a dense cluster of contact points beyond the Earth-Moon gravity well.

They seemed to be crawling toward us, moving painfully slow as they fanned out, giving all ships clear firing trajectories and forming a cone whose apex was aimed at the Spawn Fleet. They looked like a disorganized rabble, not worth the Spawn's attention, clawing their way toward the mighty superdreadnoughts from beyond the Galactic Rim.

"The particle generator is at full power, Captain," Izin reported.

"Keep it there, no matter what."

"We are in need of food and medical supplies," Talis said. "We request permission to land on Earth."

Marie gave me a wry smile. "He's almost as good a liar as you."

"Almost," I conceded.

The Spawn Fleet ignored the feeble human ships, focusing on their vastly more powerful Ornithian enemy, giving the Scrap Metal Armada valuable seconds to close the range. Out in front was the *Aruna*, flanked by the *Cyclops* and some of the faster ships. Strung out behind them was a cloud of decrepit refugee vessels, seemingly unaware of the battle raging before them.

The Tau Cetin ships formed up and made a combined dash at the Spawn's opposing flank, drawing the enemy's attention away from the human ships limping toward them. For the first time, the escorts joined them, risking all to give the motley Armada a glimmer of hope. One sentinel was caught in a crossfire from two spawnships and exploded. Two Fenari ships were hit by siege guns and spawnships then an arbiter's shield collapsed, forcing it to streak away into space while the rest of the fleet hugged the enemy leviathans, using their size against them. Finally, when the *Aruna* was more than halfway to the battle zone, the Spawn responded.

"Human ships. Landing permission denied. Enter Solar Orbit and await instructions."

The Armada was deliberately slow in responding, drawing ever closer, then Talis said, "You don't understand. Our ships are barely functional. Our people are starving and in need of medical attention. We must be allowed to land."

Tau Cetin arbiters began weaving and rolling through the Spawn lines, firing in all directions and using the spawnships to shield themselves from the siege guns. One misaimed orbital blast struck a spawncarrier, punching through its shield and impacting its massive armor, then another arbiter was hit, lost control and crashed at high velocity into a spawnship. The immense explosion vaporized one side of the spawnship, leaving it a glowing wreck adrift in space. Distracted by the ferocity of the Tau Cetin attack and partially blinded by our smoke screen, the Spawn paid scant attention to Talis' ramshackle fleet straggling toward the Moon's shadow.

"Human ships, withdraw immediately," the Spawn said at last. "This is your final warning."

A sentinel and another arbiter were destroyed while a Fenari arrowhead withdrew trailing glowing plasma, and still the human Armada kept coming.

"What are they waiting for?" Jase demanded.

"It's Talis," I said. "He's going to ram this down their throats."

For another half a minute, the Tau Cetin and Fenari ships swarmed the Spawn, battering the enemy's shields, but unable to sustain any one attack long enough for a kill, then a steely voice reverberated through the vacuum of space.

"Talis to all ships. Open fire. Fire at will."

Six tiny stars leapt from the *Aruna's* pleasure craft docking bays and shot toward the Spawn Fleet, accelerating faster than any human weapon ever had. Behind them, thousands of tiny lights poured out into space from over twelve hundred broken down ships and flowed toward the Spawn Fleet. For vital seconds, the spawnships and orbitals continued firing at the Tau Cetins, unable to believe human ships posed any threat to them.

"Wow, those things are really moving," Jase said as the torpedo cloud filled the blackness of space like a plague of fireflies hurtling toward the massed might of the One Spawn. The Tau Cetins veered sharply away, retreating toward open space, desperate to get clear of the weapons they had created.

"Sirius," Marie said nervously, eyeing the glowing cloud about to envelop us. "We need to get out of here. Now!"

"We're still jamming their sensors."

We'd achieved complete surprise, launched our weapons and still the Spawn fired at the retreating Tau Cetins, unaware of the danger.

The first hyper-torpedo glowed with a blue Tau Cetin energy aura, punched through a spawnship's shield and dived into a weapon turret, avoiding the ship's heavy chromodynamic armor. The hyper-torpedo bored deep into the great ship's interior, then a weak flash lit up the entry point, but there was no catastrophic explosion, no devastating tear in the spawnship's hull. Nothing.

"It didn't work," Jase said, shocked.

"It'll work. It has to," I insisted.

"Captain, we've done all we can," Izin said as space filled with hyper-torpedoes.

"Yeah," I agreed and dived the *Riku* toward the surface of the Moon.

Behind us, massed hyper-torpedoes picked their targets and rolled through the Spawn Fleet like a tidal wave. Thousands of thin white defense beams flashed from the spawnships, striking at the angry fireflies which jinked sideways with incredible agility. Some torpedoes were destroyed, but many dodged the beams and struck their targets. Thousands of light points twinkled against prodigious shields, smashed through weapon turrets, sensor domes, docking pads and fighter bays, avoiding the Spawn's near-impenetrable armor. A mass of human spears plunged into the hearts of the great beasts, hit after hit, pounding the black monsters from all sides, but not one spawnship exploded. Only muted flickers of light marked interior detonations that had no effect on the mighty Spawn behemoths, all of which continued firing unabated.

"They're too big," Marie said, horrified by our failure.

I levelled-off the *Riku* above the Moon's dark craters, watching the twinkling lights around the spawnships fade as the last of our fireflies vanished. I felt a pang of fear as I wrestled with the possibility that we still lacked the power to harm such gargantuan war machines.

"They're duds!" Jase exclaimed. "All of them!"

"It can't be," I said, wondering how the Tau Cetins had

got it so wrong.

Jase cursed, studying his sensor scans. "The torps are gone. All of them!"

I slowed the *Riku*, skimming the moonscape and turned to Izin. "Why didn't they work?"

"Wait, Captain," he said, transfixed by the monstrous black leviathans floating above us.

We followed his eyes, saw a spawnship fire into the Armada, instantly destroying three human ships, then others followed suit, intent on wreaking a terrible vengeance for our impertinence, and our failure.

"Oh no," Marie cried. "They're going to be destroyed. Tell them to retreat."

"Open all channels," I said.

"No, Captain! Wait," Izin snapped as more of our ships were obliterated by the Spawn.

"For what?" I demanded.

Izin's gaze was fixed upon the spawnships. Their bombardment began to falter and, one by one, the Spawn leviathans fell silent. Suddenly, the first spawnship to be torpedoed shattered like an egg. Brilliant blue light poured through cracks in its hull as the interior dissolved and thousands of chromodynamic armor slabs came apart at the seams.

"For that," Izin said.

I leaned forward, astonished. "What is it?"

"A dark energy tremor."

The broken eggshell kept its spawnship outline, expanding like a slowly disintegrating jigsaw puzzle. Brilliant light and plasmatic gases flooded through the ever-widening cracks into space, forming a luminous aura around the gigantic wreck. Another spawnship shattered, and another, as a ripple of destruction passed from one end of the Spawn Fleet to the other. Every one of the gigantic ships broke into pieces, emitting blinding light more brilliant than the brightest sun through their fracturing hulls.

"Oh yeah!" Jase yelled. "Mess with us, will you!"

I turned to Izin. "Why didn't they tell us?"

"They did, Captain, but you weren't listening. No one was."

"Except you."

"The Tau Cetins demonstrated one hyper-torpedo, not ten thousand working together. Hirseya tried to tell you, multiple synchronic detonations would generate a dark energy tremor inside the spawnship. That is the true power of this weapon."

"Yeah, I skipped that part," I said, making a note to read more Tau Cetin books.

"The HT1 is a mass attack weapon," Izin added. "Its power is amplified by each additional detonation. The synchronized effect of multiple dark energy attacks on spacetime itself is an immense, localized energy release. Tau Cetins do not use such weapons because they could never fire enough, close to the target, to have the desired effect."

"But we could."

Jase grinned. "We did."

"We surprised them, this time," Izin said.

A brilliant flash streaked across the sky and slammed into a human ship, destroying it instantly. Suddenly, the sky filled with energy comets, streaking into the Armada from Earth.

"It's the battle stations," Jase said.

I brought the *Riku* to a hover above a dark crater while bright exploding ships filled the sky. The blasts were coming from Earth at the speed of light, too fast for our ships to evade, far too powerful for their shields to withstand.

"All channels, plain language," I said, then Marie switched off the snakehead translator and nodded. "This is Kade to all ships. Rendezvous on the dark side of the Moon. Put the Moon between yourselves and those defense stations. Talis, confirm."

Some ships changed course immediately, not waiting for confirmation, and raced for the shelter of the Moon while others tried to accelerate away to bubble.

"Do as he says," Talis ordered. "All ships, make for Luna. Flank speed. Save yourselves. Sending my authentication now. And well done, everyone."

The Scrap Metal Armada accelerated toward the Moon's shadow under constant bombardment from the Earth orbitals. Every human ship struck was instantly destroyed, littering space with glowing wreckage and luminous gases, but no life pods.

One blast narrowly missed the *Cyclops*, whose shield collapsed from an overload, leaving her naked as she ran into the sanctuary of Luna's shadow. The *Aruna* also made it to safety, although two ships close to her were both destroyed. While the Armada retreated under fire, the Tau Cetin and Fenari ships returned and tried to distract the battle stations with long range attacks, but the siege cannons were intent on avenging the loss of their fleet. They rained terrible destruction upon the Armada, until one by one, the survivors reached safety and the orbitals ceased fire.

I put the *Riku* down on the cratered landscape and watched the refugee ships come in to land. Over seven hundred survived, including the *Cyclops* which set down in a valley several hundred kilometers away. The *Aruna* landed at the old observatory, the only large structure still standing on the dark side, which the admiral commandeered.

By the time the last stragglers had got down safely, the black sky above Luna's dark side was a sea of wreckage. Hundreds of thousands of slabs of glowing chromodynamic armor along with the unrecognizable remains of five hundred human ships and a handful of Tau Cetin and Fenari wrecks formed the greatest debris field the Sol System had seen in two and a half thousand years. Not since the First Intruder War, before mankind had developed interstellar travel, had such been seen in our home system, only this time, it was of our doing, not theirs.

In sheer numbers of ships lost, it could have been mistaken for a defeat, but the ships lost were expendable and we had many more. And while the Spawn had vast resources, it would take them time to recover from the defeats at Serris-Orn and Sol III. Long before then, they would know the second defeat had been at the hands of humans, the galaxy's youngest interstellar civilization, wielding a deceptively powerful weapon in a very human way.

It had been a victory, but only half a victory. The siege orbitals standing guard over Fortress Earth remained operational, capable of destroying any ship, human or alien, with a single shot. We'd risked everything to defeat the Spawn Fleet, had lost hundreds of ships, expended all of the Armada's spawn-busting hyper-torpedoes, and all we had to show for it was a drab gray hiding place on the dark side of the Moon.

* * * *

The Lutke Observatory was over fifteen hundred years old. It had been built during the Forum Embargo on human interstellar travel, using the Moon's mass to shield its sensors from signals radiating from Earth. Over the centuries, it had grown to more than a hundred pressurized buildings scattered across Lutke Crater's south rise, linking sensors from all across the solar system, making it the largest telescope mankind had ever built.

Having survived the Spawn, Admiral Talis selected its stellarium for a council of war to be attended by human and alien political and military leaders. Every seat was taken, or cleared away to make room for the Nisk, while floating beneath the center of the domed ceiling was a vibrant, real time holographic Earth. Spawn orbitals circled the planet, their locations beamed in from Tau Cetin sentinels loitering beyond the range of the mighty Spawn siege cannons.

We took our seats at the back, well away from the great and powerful. My brother sat with a contingent of Armada captains comprising junior naval officers and a handful of senior Brotherhood and alien commanders. He acknowledged me with a nod, now aware of the role the *Riku* had played in infiltrating the Spawn Fleet and signaling its position to the Armada.

Lena and Admiral Talis were in front with the brass, whispering busily to the various leaders, debating what to do next. When Lena saw me, she excused herself, came up the stairs to the cheap seats and whispered to me.

"Good job out there, Sirius. I heard the Riku was hit."

"Yeah, by the Tau Cetins."

She gave Marie, Jase and Izin a calculating look, making no attempt at a greeting then asked for my ears alone, "Is she still serviceable?"

"The Riku? She's holed top to bottom, but she can still fly if that's what you mean."

"Good," she said absently. "Very good."

Without another word, she returned to her seat and resumed whispering to Admiral Talis who occasionally glanced up at us.

Marie leaned over to me. "Why's she asking about the Riku?"

"She's got something in mind," I said suspiciously. "I've seen that look before."

"She cares more about that ship than us."

I nodded, then Fleet Commander Siyarn walked to the center of the room and stood beside the holographic Earth.

"Thank you all for coming," the Tau Cetin said slowly. "As you are aware, the Spawn fortification of Earth has proceeded rapidly. The weapon platforms above Earth are far more formidable and in much greater numbers than we anticipated."

"You can say that again," one of the Brotherhood captains growled bitterly.

Siyarn ignored the comment and looked up at the siege weapons orbiting Earth. "Our tactical simulations indicate a direct attack on Earth with our existing forces would fail. The civilian fleet has already taken heavy damage, expended all of its weapons and cannot be resupplied by the Nisk for many weeks. Earth Navy's ships have considerable stockpiles, however, if they launch at long range, the orbitals would destroy the hyper-torpedoes before they could reach their targets. If the human ships attempted a close range attack, they would be destroyed before they could launch their weapons. As for our ships, the closer we approach, the less time we have to evade, dooming any direct attack by us to failure."

He glanced at the stony faces of the mostly human audience, seeing many had come to the same conclusion.

"There must be a way to destroy those things," a Syrman diplomat said, fearing the orbitals would soon be guarding his own conquered homeworld.

"This is the first time the Spawn have used such weapons. We have sent our scans to Serris-Orn for analysis, but it will take time to devise an effective counter. You must understand, they were designed specifically to defeat us."

"What if your ships fire our torpedoes at close range?" Admiral Talis asked.

"Our ships are not designed to launch projectile weapons, admiral. Opening a hull portal would destabilize our shields. To use your torpedoes, we would need to build new ships."

"Can you make the torpedoes faster?" a Fenari commander asked.

"To withstand higher acceleration, the hyper-torpedo would have to be redesigned with more advanced technology," Siyarn replied.

"The torpedo-human-one is already very complex,"

Irukoochati said. "We cannot produce a more advanced weapon."

"We would have to construct it," Siyarn conceded. "Considering the demands on our resources, we could only produce a tiny quantity."

"We don't want that," the President of the Democratic Union said. "We want the Nisk to make millions of them."

"As do we," Siyarn said. "Clearly, we cannot approach Earth, and we cannot stay here. Our only option is to withdraw."

"Retreat?" The Second Caliphate Emissary said indignantly.

"We have won a great victory, the first in a year," Siyarn replied. "We should withdraw to Tau Ceti before our gains are lost. Allow us time to devise a counter to the orbital siege weapons and for the Nisk to produce more hyper-torpedoes."

"We caught them napping once," Talis said. "We won't be so lucky again."

"We have considered every possibility, Admiral," Siyarn said.

"Not every possibility," Lena said, standing up. "Not sabotage."

Siyarn gave her a puzzled look with his large green almond-shaped eyes. "Sabotage what?"

"The orbital battle stations are automated, controlled from the Spawn's central stronghold on Earth. If we infiltrate that stronghold, we could deactivate the orbitals and land our forces unopposed."

"Uh-ho," I whispered, guessing why Lena was so interested in the *Riku*.

"We have received no reports of a ground-based control center," Siyarn said.

"My information comes from Earth Resistance," Lena said.

"How is that possible?" Siyarn asked. "Spawn ground forces are jamming all communications with the planet."

"Not quite all." She walked to the center of the room and stood beneath the Earth hologram. "The orbital defense system's command center is there." She pointed at a narrow island chain reaching north east from Australia toward the equator. "In Tamph City."

A murmur of surprise rippled around the room, then everyone squinted to make out the aquatic home of Earth's terrestrial amphibians.

"It was once the most heavily fortified concentration camp in human history, and a natural fortress," she continued. "Ten million tamphs lived there before the Spawn landed. It was designed for their species. That's why the Spawn made it their planetary capital."

"How many tamphs live there now?" the Gienan admiral asked.

"None. They abandoned the city when the Spawn attacked. The entire population scattered into the sea, where they have proven to be effective allies."

Jase grinned at Izin and whispered, "We could have told them that! Right Izin?"

Izin stared back in silent agreement.

"We are aware the Spawn are using Tamph City," Siyarn said. "They have put millions of humans in prison camps there, to prevent us destroying it from space. It is the most heavily defended location on the planet."

"There are ways in," Lena insisted. "All you need is a guide and a way to pick the lock. And we have both."

"Even if that were true, any ship you send to Earth will be destroyed by the orbital weapon platforms before it could land."

"Not any ship, just any human ship," Lena replied meaningfully.

"Here it comes," I whispered.

"We believe the Spawn will allow a Mataron ship to land. And we have just such a ship, and a crew trained to fly her."

"The Riku is damaged," Siyarn said, guessing her

intent.

"She can reach Earth," Lena said, "and the orbitals saw one of your ships shoot at her. They saw her take cover with the Spawn Fleet. We believe the Spawn on Earth will consider her an ally. They might even protect her, from you."

"And if they don't, the Riku will be destroyed," Siyarn said surprised.

"We'll take that risk."

"Nice of her to ask us," Marie whispered.

"We have a combat team ready to go," Lena continued, "a tamph who grew up in the city to guide us in, and thanks to our people on the ground, a way to break into the orbital control system."

"What way?" Siyarn demanded.

"Leave that to us," Lena replied secretively.

"It's worth a try," Admiral Talis said.

"It's our world and we have the right to decide its fate," the Democratic Union President declared.

"You do," Siyarn said.

The Union President turned to me, under no illusions who Lena was referring to. "Captain Kade, when can you leave?"

I swallowed uncomfortably as all eyes turned toward me, glanced at Marie and Jase, who nodded and Izin who didn't object, then stood up and cleared my throat nervously.

"We're ready now, Mr. President."

* * * *

After the council of war, Lena summoned Izin and me to the *Solar Constitution* while Marie and Jase remained on the *Riku* to oversee the combat team's arrival. The Earth Navy battleship had bubbled in behind the Moon after the battle and landed without incident. She was now parked on a large apron north east of the observatory's main building cluster with her stern hanging out over gray regolith and an atmo-bridge sealed to her bow airlock.

When we stepped from the airlock, a Union Regular Army trooper showed us to the ship's medical bay where Lena, two doctors and a host of medbots were waiting.

"A bit late for a physical, isn't it?" I asked.

"That's not why you're here," Lena said, turning to Izin. "We want to scan him."

"For what purpose?" Izin asked.

"We want to check your implants, the ones the Spawn Queen implanted in you last year."

"They are functioning perfectly."

Lena handed Izin a data screen displaying two columns, one filled with serial numbers, the other containing abbreviated descriptions. She pointed to a serial number a third of the way down the display. "Do you have that one?"

Izin glanced at the screen. "Yes. It's an auxiliary subsystem interactive."

"Good," she said with relief. "I have a twenty million character Spawn symbolic I want to upload into it. You can use it to take control of their orbital defense system."

"How did you get such a code?"

"Tamph resistance fighters captured a senior Spawn officer two days ago. It was in one of his implants."

"A Spawn male of any rank is incapable of betraying his matriarch, even under torture. It is impossible for them to reveal any information, and you do not have the technology to extract it from an implant directly."

"My counterpart on Earth found a vulnerability in Spawn security." She tapped the screen several times, then it filled with Spawn characters. "That's it."

Izin studied the screen with increasing astonishment. "This symbolic appears genuine, although its usefulness is time limited."

"Yes, that's why we're in a hurry." She motioned him to the medbed. "Please. We have the required interface."

"That will not be necessary," Izin said. "I can load the interactive optically, via my eidetic memory."

He began scrolling rapidly through the twenty million characters, committing them to memory by sight. When he was done, he handed the screen back to her.

"That's it?" she asked.

"What did you expect? A physical data transfer?"

Lena and I glanced at each other, recalling how often we'd held hands to link our bionetic systems for data transfers, then she summoned a map to the screen and showed it to Izin.

"You recognize this?"

"It's Tamph City."

"And this?" she asked, pointing at a structure on one of the larger islands.

"The global-net communications hub."

"Now it's the Spawn Occupation Forces' comm center. Their equipment, our building."

"I understand," he said. "We have twenty hours to reach the hub and disable the orbital defenses before the symbolic resets with a new sequence."

"That doesn't give us much time," I said.

She nodded. "You can make it, if you start now."

"If we're late and it resets, can we get another code?"

"No, this is a one shot deal. The only reason they haven't triggered a reset already is because they believe there's no way an imprinted male can betray his matriarch." She gave me a knowing look, confirming there was one way, the mega-psi way.

"Does Talis know we have this key?" I asked.

"Yes, although not how we got it. And he knows we're on the clock, which is why he helped me steamroll the Tau Cetins. They think we're out of our minds, that you're going to be killed and we're all still going to Serris-Orn."

"Who's in the combat team?" I asked.

"Four combat engineers to help you break in, and a four man I-F team led by Dietz in case you get into trouble."

"Make sure Dietz knows I'm in command. I want to sneak in there, not start world war nine."

"He knows. As soon as we detect the siege orbitals go down, Talis will bring the fleet in and start the invasion." She turned to Izin. "We'd still like to scan you, to catalogue what you've got."

"Very well," Izin said reluctantly and followed a medbot to a bed where they began a microcellular scan of his body.

"So Lord Geoffrey melted a Spawn officer's brain to get the key?" I whispered.

"Something like that."

"And he sent it to you, from Earth?"

"Don't let his age fool you. He's not just the oldest mega-psi, he's the most experienced, the most gifted. And Earth isn't far from here."

"You and him have something in common with the Uvo."

"Except we're engineered. They're naturals."

"Is he going to meet us?"

"No. He's with Republic Forces in south Asia, helping hide tamph females. The Matriarchs see them as rivals. They want to exterminate them all. They don't like our females imprinting tamph males, protecting them from Spawn females."

"Our females," I said thoughtfully. "You wouldn't have said that a year ago"

She smiled. "Earth's oceans weren't full of tamphs fighting the Spawn a year ago."

"Why don't our tamphs break into the command center?"

"No Spawn implants. Izin's the only one that can do it."

"Lucky him."

"He's uniquely valuable to us now. Make sure he survives." She smiled. "It's ironic, isn't it, that after all these years of distrusting tamphs, of holding a gun to their heads, of threatening to exterminate them, the liberation of Earth comes down to just one tamph."

"Ironic," I agreed sourly. I'd been trusting Izin with my life for years, because I knew what he was made of, even though one look at him was enough for most humans to treat him with suspicion. "Never judge a tamph by his container."

"His what?" Lena asked.

"It's a Nisk thing."

The medbots finished scanning Izin and he rejoined us.

"Good luck, to both of you," Lena said, then we were escorted off the *Solar Constitution*.

We hurried back through interlocking pressure tubes to the south side landing ground where a navy shuttle was waiting for us. It flew us out over dozens of Armada ships parked on the gray moonscape to the *Riku*. Once aboard, Izin went to the bridge to start preflight with Jase and Marie while I greeted the combat team in the cargo hold.

A tanky black-hulled armor-plated dropship stood in the center of the deck. Four army engineers in heavy lift suits were loading ammo into its pylon-mounted kinetic cannons and containers into its payload bays while Dietz and three I-F grunts in light assault suits performed last minute gear checks prior to boarding the troop compartment. Two of them, Larson and Shen, I knew from a previous mission. The fourth, a powerfully built West African named Nwibo had gone lone wolf in Kinshasa after its fall, leaving a trail of death and destruction in his wake before eventually escaping Earth. That had got him Dietz's attention.

The dropship had mine. "What's that thing doing on my ship?" I demanded.

"Got to land in something," Dietz replied. "Might as well have teeth."

"This is a stealth mission."

"So I heard." He watched an engineer wearing two

tonnes of power armor hoist a robo-gun container like it was a toy. "Put it near the drop gate," he yelled, "in case we have to shoot our way out."

"Roger that," the engineer replied and stomped up the ramp into the troop compartment.

"They'll scan us going in," I said. "If they see a human dropship on board, the mission is blown."

"The Tau Cetins cleared it. It's masked, like the rest of us."

I relaxed, realizing I was wound a little tight. "We'll land close to the city. Shouldn't have far to go."

"I can handle the dropship if you want."

"No, I'll do the flying."

"You're the boss. There's a recon suit in your cabin. Got them for Logan and Dulon as well. The tamph will have to take his chances in a p-suit. Didn't have his size."

An engineer bumped a canister painted with chemical hazard symbols. Dietz's eyes flared. "Hey!" he bellowed furiously. "Watch those corrosives. You want to melt the whole goddamned ship? I want them single stacked and maglocked."

"Yes Sarge," the engineer replied.

"You got your wish," I said. "First wave."

He scowled. "I thought we'd be going in with more than this, but I'll take it."

I left Dietz and went up to the bridge to get the *Riku* into space. We now had just nineteen hours until key reset. If I couldn't get Izin into the Spawn command center by then, this was going to be the shortest invasion in the history of galactic war.

Chapter Nine : Sol-III

Spawn Occupied World
Sol System
16 Billion insurgent hominids
9 Million Spawn renegades
Resistance Level: High
Reinforcements requested

I donned the light armored, all-environment recon suit Dietz had left in my cabin and went to the bridge. Marie and Jase were at their stations, similarly attired, while Izin, the one irreplaceable member of the team, wore only a thin unarmored p-suit over his clothes.

"The combat team's strapped down in the dropship," Jase said as I climbed onto my Mataron multi-segmented couch.

"Dietz," I said over a direct link to the dropship. "Keep your ears open. If they don't buy it, the dropship will be our lifeboat."

"Roger that," he replied.

"Izin, how's the damage?" I asked.

"The Tau Cetins have adjusted our e-plant emissions to radiate high intensity neutrino bursts. It will appear to the Spawn as if we have been critically damaged."

"I hope they buy it," I said, activating the launch sequence.

The light projections radiating from our consoles glowed with Luna's gray and cratered surface, now crowded with ships all the way to the observatory. Above us, space was littered with mostly human and Spawn wreckage still glowing hot amid thinning gas clouds.

Jase whistled softly. "What a mess."

"We'll need our shield to get through that," Marie said.

"We're not going through it," I replied. "We're going under it."

"So no shield?" Marie asked apprehensively.

"Keep it at twenty percent, so we look weak."

We lifted off, skimmed the bows of the grounded fleet and followed Luna's curvature toward the light side. Stars climbed above the horizon, then Earth appeared beyond the white hot hulk of a Tau Cetin arbiter adrift in space. I nosed up, climbing the *Riku* away from the Moon's gray surface as Snakehead symbols appeared beside pinpoints of light in Earth orbit, indicating the positions of Spawn orbitals.

"Let's make this look good," I said and put the *Riku* into a clumsy, rolling spiral around our approach vector, feigning a lack of control.

"Opening all channels," Marie announced as we raced across the Earth-Moon narrows.

"This is the Mataron Supremacy cruiser Riku requesting landing coordinates," I said through the snakehead language synthesizer, then nodded to Marie to close comms.

"We've got their attention," Jase declared. "Ninety target locks, and counting."

We raced on toward Earth, watching it expand before us, receiving no response.

"They're giving us the silent treatment," Marie murmured.

"They're making up their minds," I said as the orbital pin points began to take shape.

"A hundred and seventy three stations tracking, everything this side of Earth," Jase reported tensely.

The oceans and continents grew rapidly in size, revealing widespread bombardment cratering and still the Spawn did not respond.

Marie gave me an apprehensive look. "They're not buying it, Sirius."

"They will," I assured her, certain if the orbitals opened fire now, we wouldn't have time to evade.

A warning indicator appeared showing hostile contacts astern as three arbiters came up behind us fast. A group of orbitals fired together, sending energy blasts flashing past us, forcing the Tau Cetins to turn sharply away and retreat, then the Spawn broke their silence.

"Mataron ship Riku, land at forty two point seven nine degrees north, one hundred five point zero three degrees east."

"Understood," I replied. "Be advised, we have limited flight control."

"Minor deviations from optimal approach will be tolerated," the Spawn replied without defining what they considered minor.

"Where are they sending us?" I asked.

"The Gobi Desert," Izin said, translating the latitude and longitude with his encyclopedic mind.

Jase furrowed his brow. "There's no spaceport there."

I nodded. "That's why. If we blow up, all we'll kill are the scorpions."

"At least it's in the eastern hemisphere," Marie said, relieved.

I put the *Riku* on a heading for North East Asia, following the optimal approach vector, then pretended to have trouble staying on track, drifting and correcting constantly. Each feign took us a little further off course, carrying us out over the Indian Ocean and pushing the 'minor deviations' warning to its limit. Earth filled the forward half of the bridge imager and the siege orbitals became ovoids of contrarotating armored rings, turning to keep us target locked all the way down. Soon our underpowered shield began smashing atmospheric molecules as we executed a clumsy insertion.

"The shield's weakening," Marie reported.

"Let it bleed," I said as we glowed like a flaming meteor, coming in too fast, kept cool by the failing shield. We plummeted into thick air, drifting further off course, then I nodded. "OK, drop it."

"Are you sure?" Marie asked uneasily.

"Snakehead armor can take it."

She exhaled nervously and killed the shield, letting the atmosphere cook our hull. We began aerobraking, slewing back and forth as we fell toward the ocean, and even as the exterior temperature soared, the reptilian armor didn't ablate.

"If we don't land in the Gobi," Marie warned, "they'll blast us from orbit."

"Not if we crash first."

"Crash?" she said alarmed.

I grinned as we plunged toward the great watery expanse south of Asia mimicking a ship out of control while the hull glowed from friction. "Have to. They're tracking us. We'll ditch in the sea and swim out in the dropship. Got that Dietz?"

"Affirmative."

"Izin, set the Riku to blow. She'll flash their sensors while we escape underwater."

"There'll be a shockwave, Captain" Izin warned.

"Mil-spec dropships can fly through fusion explosions. Right Dietz?"

"Yeah, air blasts," he replied uncertainly. "How deep are we going?"

"Right to the bottom."

"The water density at that depth will amplify the shockwave, Captain," Izin said.

"I only want to blind them, not trigger a tsunami."

"We could limit the blast radius with a partial shutdown, and detonate close to the surface," Izin suggested.

"Do it."

He began powering down the energy core, adding, "Once the surrounding water is vaporized, most of the energy should radiate into the atmosphere." He did some complex math in his head. "Two hundred meters should be enough."

"Dietz, I'm going to open the cargo door just before we hit. You'll be underwater by the time we reach you."

"Understood. We're all sealed up here. The drop gate's down. I'll raise the pressure field when we hit."

"We won't have much time, Captain," Izin said. "The hull damage will cause the ship to flood rapidly."

Jase scowled. "She's going to sink like a rock."

"Make it four hundred meters, Izin," I decided, searching the widening blue expanse below. "We need somewhere deep."

"Sunda Trench is over six thousand meters deep, Captain," Izin said. "It's a subduction zone between two tectonic plates."

"You've been there?" I asked.

"I've hunted there many times. You can follow it to the east."

"It's perfect." I got the bow up, reducing our rate of descent and aiming for the long island chain to the north. "Open the airtight doors between here and the dropship. Seal the rest."

"You might have to swim," Marie warned, wary of my aquaphobia.

"We'll be in a dropship," I said emphatically. "I won't even get my feet wet."

She smiled. "If you do, I'll save you."

"Hmph," I grunted, praying she wouldn't have to.

"We're getting ground scans from Asia and Australia," Jase said. "They know we're coming. And the orbitals are still on us."

"Not exactly stealthy." I nodded to Marie to open all channels. "This is the Riku. We have lost helm control and core stability. Surface impact imminent," I said, trying to sound like a snakehead officer about to die.

Marie cut comms for the last time, then I fluttered the engines, decelerating erratically as we entered the tropics. The bow came around to the north east and a vast cyclonic spiral of white cloud came into view, obscuring the Arafura Sea all the way to Tamph City.

"The Spawn are hailing us," Marie said.

"Ignore them." I let the *Riku* drop toward the sea, her armor now burning so hot, microns were boiling off its surface. "Izin, time for you to go to the dropship."

"I should remain until we are in the water, Captain."

"Not in that p-suit. I want you in the dropship before we hit."

Izin glanced at his flimsy suit and relented. "Very well." He climbed off his perch and hurried below. The *Riku* began to shudder from buffeting, then as the ocean filled the bridge imager, Izin announced, "I'm in the dropship, Captain."

"Opening cargo door," I said, decelerating erratically, letting the *Riku* nose into a dive. I rolled her completely over for the benefit of the Spawn, righting her moments before we slammed into the ocean.

A giant waterspout shot into the sky as internal acceleration fields absorbed the impact. The cruiser's superheated hull boiled the sea around us, sending steam billowing into the air as the *Riku* fell. When her hull had cooled for the sea to catch us, the ocean rushed in to fill the void above us.

"How deep are we?" I asked, not having counted on

the sea vaporizing so fast.

"Forty meters and...rising," Jase replied, then the *Riku* bobbed to the surface. "We're floating, sort of."

"Not for long." I jumped down from my station. "Let's go."

We ran out into the companionway where the lights were blinking from seawater flooding into the ship, shorting out systems. The vertical transit shaft aft of the bridge was lit by flickering green emergency lights and at the bottom, water was already flooding in through the open cargo hold, sending a roar of rushing air through the *Riku*.

Jase stuck his hand into the shaft, feeling for the acceleration field. "It's dead."

Marie looked over the edge. "We'll have to jump."

I eyed the dark waters apprehensively, recalling my Kif-oyene nightmare in the subterranean cistern.

"It's not swimming, Sirius. It's a spacewalk."

"I can do this," I said, trying to still my beating heart.

"I know you can." She fixed her eyes on the sloshing water at the bottom of the shaft as a big ocean swell rolled the *Riku* to one side. We held onto handholds as she rocked and slowly began to come back, then Marie took my hand. "We'll go together, when she levels."

"Right," I said apprehensively. We sealed our visors, switched to suit air and waited.

"Now," Marie said as the *Riku* righted herself.

We jumped out into the vertical shaft, fell between green emergency lights and speared into the water in a cloud of bubbles. Our recon suits sank to the bottom, two decks below, watching each other's faces in the soft glow of our head-up displays. When our boots touched the deck, we pushed through a strong current toward a faint light spilling through the cargo hold doorway.

Jase splashed down behind us in a swirl of bubbles, then the shaft's lower lights winked out. He dropped to the deck and followed us into the cargo hold, now lit only by a dim rectangle of light coming from the dropship's open jump gate. Beyond the dropship was the open cargo hatch framing an endless blue sea.

The dropship's ramp was down and a pressure field held back the water while the eight man team and Izin sat inside looking out at us. We marched up the ramp and pushed through the pressure field into the troop compartment as the *Riku* sank below the swells into calmer, deeper water.

When Jase stepped in after us, Dietz sealed the jump gate and said, "They'll send autacs to search the wreck."

"I hope they get here when she blows," I said, dripping water on the deck.

Marie strapped herself in beside Izin while Jase and I cycled through the internal airlock to the flight deck. The *Riku* was now down fifty degrees by the stern and sliding backwards into the Sunda deep.

"Depth seventy meters," Jase reported when his console illuminated.

My fingers skipped over the controls, then the dropship hummed to life and I released the deck clamps. I gave her a little push and we slid out through the cargo door into the vast blue expanse of the Indian Ocean. I turned the dropship back toward the *Riku*, getting a glimpse of her through the narrow slit windows. She was sliding silently into the depths beneath a thinning column of bubbles.

Jase peered at her curiously. "Her armor's hardly damaged."

"They build them tough on Kif-atah," I said, and dived the dropship under the *Riku*.

Using the snakehead cruiser's growing energy signature to mask our escape, I put the dropship into a vertical descent into darkness. After several minutes, I switched on the exterior lights, levelled off over the sandy ocean floor and headed for the great tectonic rift to the north. Our progress was slow through the highly compressed water, but I didn't dare risk using the particle field in case autacs were above us scanning for survivors.

"Want me to check the Riku's depth?" Jase asked.

"No. They'll detect our ranging signal, and she's going to blow when she blows."

We continued on through the blanketing darkness at the bottom of the ocean, a darkness pierced only by our floodlights, then a great valley running east to west appeared before us. We passed over the edge and followed a ragged cliff down into the tectonic trench, dropping a thousand meters without sighting the bottom.

Suddenly, a brilliant flash shattered the ocean's eternal night. The cliff face and the trench bottom far below lit up as if in daylight while the dropship's armored windows darkened to absorb the flash.

"Brace for shockwave," I warned over the intercom, knowing the troops sealed inside their compartment hadn't seen the flash.

The cockpit windows cleared as a dull boom reverberated through the hull and silt exploded from the cliff face. We were tossed against the trench wall as it crumbled and became an avalanche of rock. Giant boulders thundered against our hull, driving us down into the abyss while I fed power to the engines, forcing the dropship away from the cliff as the shockwave passed.

"Good thing we were in the trench," Jase said with relief as the avalanche rolled away into the depths.

"Everyone OK back there?" I asked.

"We're alive," Dietz replied, unfazed.

I dived the dropship deeper into the Sunda Trench and turned east toward northern Australia. We continued on for more than an hour while I watched the bionetic timer in my mind's eye count the seconds to key reset, to the moment the grand alliance sheltering in Luna's shadow would abandon Earth and its people to the Spawn. At reset minus seventeen hours, I activated the particle field, pushing the ocean clear of the hull, and accelerated the dropship to high subsonic velocity six kilometers below the surface, hoping the sea would mask our energy signature.

"If there are autacs up there..." Jase said warily.

"They'll see us and it'll be over," I declared, deciding it was better to risk all and fail, than risk nothing and lose everything.

* * * *

Hours later, the continental shelf rose like a gray wall, forcing us into the shallow waters of the Timor Sea. Visibility was limited as the cyclone's thick clouds had almost turned day into night and high gale force winds lashed the surface.

Jase peered at the mountainous waves rolling above us and whistled softly. "It's rough up there."

"Too bad the storm won't blind their sensors," I said.

We crossed the Timor Sea, skimming the bottom inside our particle field below the speed of sound to keep our signature down. By the time we reached the Arafura, the storm's driving rain and howling winds had whipped the surface into a white capped fury, blinding us to the sky. We continued on for a while, then I turned the dropship toward northern Australia and activated the intercom.

"Tamph City's an hour away," I announced. "Eat now. You won't get another chance once we make land."

Jase and I cracked open our ration packs, then I called Marie by direct intercom patch. "How is it back there?"

"No inflight holograms, no bar service, and the food is terrible," she replied.

I chuckled. "Yeah, but the seats are good."

"If you like high-gee combat clamps."

"We'll be there soon," I said. "Send Izin up."

"Will do."

Moments later, he cycled through the airlock from the

troop compartment and peered through the cockpit's slit window into the darkening water.

"See anything?" I asked, knowing his telescoping amphibian eyes saw further than our weaker, human equivalents.

"No. Are there any acoustic contacts?"

"Nope," Jase said. "We're all alone out here."

"We are not alone," he said absently, then stood between the two piloting couches and checked our position on the nav display. "There are ancient sea towers ahead. None were operational when I was last here."

"They are now, according to the Tau Cetins," I said.

"That explains why the sea is silent. My brothers know the Spawn are listening. Otherwise, the sea would be echoing from these." He tapped the sonar lobe bulging from his forehead. "Humans selected the tower locations best placed to detect our biosonar. That is why the Spawn now use them."

"There used to be sensors on the sea floor."

"Many centuries ago, Captain. Any devices the Spawn put down there, my brothers have destroyed by now. The only operational sensors will be on the towers, where the Spawn can protect them."

"OK," I said doubtfully. "We'll tip toe in between the towers. Hopefully, no one will see us."

"My brothers will be watching, Captain."

"They don't know we're coming," Jase said.

Izin gave him a long, knowing look. "Rest assured, every tamph in every ocean on Earth heard the Riku explode. Their deep ocean scouts are now wondering what a human craft was doing inside a Mataron cruiser."

"Will they help us?" I asked.

"Perhaps. Spawn acoustic sensors will be focused on our biosonar frequencies, which are much higher than the noise generated by our turbulence. Once we're through the sea towers, we'll land in the shallows and approach on foot, along the bottom."

I winced. "More water walking."

"It's not the walking you'll find difficult, Captain, it's the climbing."

"Climbing?"

He didn't explain, then we hugged the bottom for the run toward Tamph City. Before the sea towers appeared on the horizon, I cut our speed, lowering our sonic signature as the ferocity of the cyclone increased, blasting the sea and drowning out the sound of our approach. Sometime later, a blinking red light appeared in the underwater gloom to starboard and I throttled back to a crawl.

"That's the underwater base of a sea tower," Izin explained, motioning for me to give it a wide berth. "Steer one twenty degrees."

The blinking light was on an immense circular foundation that rose above the water where giant waves crashed against it. The tower itself was hidden from sight above the gray sea. Its kind had been constructed millennia ago and rebuilt many times since. They formed a ring of fortifications designed to keep our uninvited tamph guests bottled up on desolate rock and sand islands, proving so successful that none had ever fired in anger. Now the Spawn had given the towers another purpose, to keep the tamphs out of the island chain that they'd transformed over the centuries from a prison into a home.

The first blinking light began to pass into the distance as another appeared far off to port. Moving more slowly than a swimming tamph, we slipped between the two towers as the mighty sea battering their sides drowned out our sonic signature. Once past the sea towers, we entered the shallows, passing only meters beneath the troughs between the big swells.

"I'm going to have to put her down soon, Izin, or we'll breach," I said.

"Almost there, Captain," he replied, peering intently with his telescoping eyes through the dropship's slit windows.

We groped our way forward, being slowly forced toward the surface by the shelving sea floor, then huge dark metal doors appeared out of the gloom. They stretched from the sandy bottom, high into the air, standing immovably against the pounding waves. Either side of the doors was a massive, steeply sloping sea wall running south west to north east. It was as high as the gate and ran fully around the Wessel Islands, sealing them off from the Arafura Sea to the north and the coastal channel to the south. The northern sea gate allowed supply ships to enter Cumberland Straight, the waterway passing between two northern islands to a second gate at its southern entrance.

"Hell of a place for a prison," Jase muttered.

"That's why they picked it," I said.

Izin pointed to the north east. "Follow the sea wall, Captain, that way."

I turned the dropship as instructed, fighting a surging current to stay close to the barnacle encrusted wall. The ancient structure was cracked with age, and vast schools of colored fish darted back and forth along its base as if it were a gigantic reef. Just visible through the churning waters and sleeting rain were circular watchtowers, widely spaced along the top of the wall.

I peered up at the nearest one, seeing no lights. "Anyone in those towers?"

"I don't know," Izin replied. "They haven't been used in centuries."

"Doesn't mean there aren't Spawn up there," Jase said.

We continued on alongside the sea wall, leaving the giant black gate to fade into the rain lashed gloom astern. In the turbulent shallows, we almost breached the surface several times, but the dropship's high mass saved us, sinking like a rock whenever I cut the power.

"This is it," Izin said at last, peering out into featureless greyness. "Land here, Captain."

With a sigh of relief, I killed the thrusters and let the dropship settle to the bottom, then we went back into the troop compartment. Dietz and the team were already on their feet, visors locked, lining up in front of the open drop gate. The pressure field was holding back the sea and the ramp was down to the sand outside, although the rear lights were off, leaving the seabed gray and shadowed.

"Izin will show you the way," I said to Dietz.

He nodded, stepped through the pressure field and walked down onto the sea floor. His three I-F team mates followed in their light assault suits, then the four combat engineers stomped after him in their two tonne power armor, weighed down with heavy containers on each shoulder rack. While they stepped into the sea, Izin stripped down to a skin tight body suit, dumping his pressure gear on the deck.

"What are doing?" I asked.

"Don't worry, Captain, I won't let you drown."

His amphibian feet fanned out into fins that could propel him through the water faster than a dolphin. He took a deep breath, compressed air into his quad-lungs, and pushed through the pressure field. Instead of walking down the ramp like the others, he swam away at great speed, very much in his element.

"Show off," Jase said, then we followed him into the water.

I grimaced. "Now he's got no protection."

"Swimming out there, he's safer than any of us," Marie said.

We sealed up our visors and pushed through the pressure field. The troops stood on the sandy bottom watching the giant swells rolling barely ten meters above their heads while Izin circled and came to a floating stop in front of us. He pointed through the gloomy water at the sea wall and glided toward it, stopping to ensure we were following.

We marched in comms silence through a strong current

to a rusty ladder that ran up the side of the sea wall to a circular drainage outlet. Waves crashed over the entrance, filling me with trepidation, then I stepped up to the ladder and began to climb. When I reached the surface, a wall of water rolled in and tried to tear me from the ladder. I wrapped both arms around it tightly and hung on until the wave receded, then clambered up into the drain. It was three times my height, with steps and railings on either side and centuries of green slime coating the curved floor.

I lost my footing on the slick surface, fell on my face and started to slide back out when a big wave struck me from behind and carried me to the stairs. I caught the hand rail and hung on as the wave drained away, then pulled myself up and turned for my first look back out to sea. Halfway to the horizon, barely visible in the heavy rain, were three red blinking lights marking the locations of the nearest Spawn controlled sea towers.

They were tapering rectangular structures that reached high into the sky, with a flat top where artillery emplacements and a landing pad were located. The aquatic fortresses were impossible for tamphs to climb and used their fear of heights against them, putting the heavy weapons and aircraft out of their reach.

Another big wave flooded the entrance, then Marie climbed up. I pulled her onto the stairs and motioned for her to go to the landing above where heavy metal gates barred the way. By the time she was safely beyond the reach of the sea, Jase climbed up, caught my arm and followed her up through the sloping tunnel. Dietz was next, taking up a position on the other stairs. He was followed by his three I-F super soldiers, who came between waves.

Corporal Haines, the first of the combat engineers was next. He took one step inside the tunnel and slipped on the slime. Dietz and I grabbed him, but he was much too heavy and was torn from our arms. He clawed the floor with one servo powered hand and grabbed a hand hold with the other, then rode out the next wave on his face. When it drained away, I gave him my place so he could help the other combat engineers while I acted as spotter a few steps above him.

Izin's head was visible bobbing in the water below, gliding back and forth, completely at home in the violent sea. When the next big wave came in, he let it carry him up into the tunnel, then effortlessly leapt out of the water onto the stairs above Dietz.

"You've done this before," Dietz yelled through his visor.

"Many times," Izin replied. "If not for the Spawn, there'd be hundreds of juveniles playing here now."

There was a long delay as Corporal Deung struggled up the ladder, pounded by the waves. When he finally climbed into the tunnel, he was too slow and a big roller slammed into his back, driving him helmet first into the stairs on Dietz's side. The surging water dragged him back out of the tunnel and over the edge. He bounced off the sea wall as he fell and crashed into the sea. I caught a glimpse of his bloodied face and red smears inside his visor as he sank out of sight.

I opened my helmet and shouted over the screaming wind to Izin. "He's out cold."

Izin jumped onto the green slime, skated effortlessly to the entrance and dived into the sea. The two remaining combat engineers climbed to safety while Dietz and I waited for him to reappear.

"He shouldn't have gone," Dietz yelled. "We can't do this without him."

"I know," I said, fearing I'd made a terrible mistake.

We sealed our visors and braced as several waves broke over us, then a big one crashed into the tunnel. When the water drained away, Izin and the combat engineer were left clinging to a hand hold. Deung was groggy, but conscious, and crawled up the stairs on all fours.

I gave Izin a relieved look. "You had me worried."

"About what, Captain?" he asked.

Another wave surged into the tunnel and four tamphs leapt onto the stairs below us. They were dressed in skin tight body suits similar to Izin's and carried a variety of weapons. One even wore a Spawn energy weapon on his hip. Izin removed his vocalizer, then they sang to each other in frequencies partially above my audio range.

When they finished, Izin replaced his vocalizer and turned to me. "They are scouts, Captain. They've been watching us and want to help."

None wore vocalizers, although they listened as if they understood our every word and showed particular interest in the soldiers higher up in the tunnel.

"Did you tell them what we're here for?"

"I told them nothing." He pointed at the white capped sea. "There are many others, out there."

"So close to the Spawn?" Dietz said doubtfully.

"We are of the sea," Izin declared. "The Spawn are crèche-born. They have not permitted storms on their worlds for millions of years. Their seas are tranquil and they learn nothing. That is why they hide in the coastal shallows while we control the ocean deep."

I turned to the four tamphs, certain they understood me. "There's a fleet coming to liberate Earth, but we need to get to the comm center. Can you draw the Spawn away from us?"

The tamph with the Spawn energy weapon spoke in rapid, high frequency squeals which Izin translated.

"He says they've been waiting for the humans to return. Now they will make the Spawn pay."

"They're motivated, I'll give them that," Dietz said with approval.

"Thank him," I said.

Izin bid them farewell, then they slid down the tunnel and leapt into the sea the way he had done. They didn't appear again, so we climbed to the platform where the others were waiting. Shen was patching a cut above Deung's forehead while Haines produced a laser cutter from his kit.

Izin pointed to the bars beside the gate. "Cut here. The bars have no sensors, but if you touch the gate, they'll know."

"Yes sir," Haines replied and set to work.

While he cut, I watched the sea for tamphs, hoping the crèche-born Spawn from beyond the galactic rim were no match for our poorly armed, ocean-bred, terrestrial amphibians.

* * * *

The last metal bar fell with a clang onto the floor, then Izin led the way up through the sea wall to a tunnel blocked by rectangular columns. They were so close together, not even an adolescent tamph could have squeezed through, although foul smelling, brown liquid trickled between them and drained into the sea.

"How'd you get past this when you were young?" Jase asked.

"I did not," Izin replied. "We swam up to the entrance from the seaward side." He turned to Sergeant Guerrero, the combat engineer squad leader. "The column sensors have not worked for centuries, but anyone outside the wall will hear an explosion."

"Won't be a problem," Guerrero said, then the engineers placed circular devices on folding stands against the two central columns and motioned for us to move back.

"Thermal mines," Dietz explained. "Watch your eyes."

We lowered our light filtering visors while Izin turned his back, then Guerrero activated the devices. Harsh orange-white light radiated from the two mines as they liquified the masonry columns, sending steaming lava trickling over the damp green slime on the floor.

"Your suits can handle the heat," Guerrero said when the mines winked out and we opened our visors again. "I'll carry the tamph." He offered Izin a servo-powered arm, then carried him across the molten lava into a large metal pipe on the other side.

Izin pointed to a ladder leading up to a maintenance hatch above us. "We can reach the recycling plant through there."

"I'll have to widen it for the heavy suits," Guerrero said, producing a pair of metal slicing power shears. He cut away the ancient lock and gave the hatch a servo-powered push, forcing it open with a creak of rusted metal. The howl of the wind exploded into the pipe and heavy rain beat down through the open hatch.

"This way," Izin said and scrambled up the ladder.

"Izin, no!" I yelled. "Dietz first," but he was gone before I could stop him.

Dietz and I exchanged frustrated looks, then I climbed the ladder in time to catch a glimpse of him running through wind and rain along a rusty walkway beside the pipe. He disappeared into a gray building at the edge of a sprawling industrial complex woven with stained pipes, metal walkways and grimy storage tanks. It resembled a drilling platform, standing high above the coastal shallows on thick metal legs with only the outlet pipe connecting it to the sea wall.

Beyond the recycling plant was Marchinbar Island, the largest and most northerly of the Wessel group. The islands had once been windswept slivers of sand and rock, but were now completely covered by sun bleached buildings reaching into the shallows on all sides. Tamphs hated heights, which was why the structures were only two and three stories high and why the once restricted recycling plant was on stilts.

I climbed out and ran along the rattling walkway to a blown out doorway. The wrecked door lay on the floor inside and Izin stood beyond it, gun in hand, studying four cylindrical waste processors, only one of which was humming.

"Hear anything?" I asked as I came up beside him, assault rifle level, knowing his sonic lobe could detect Spawn far beyond the reach of my senses.

"No," he replied, then we moved cautiously between the waste processors to a tamph skeleton lying on the floor.

"He's been here since they landed," I said, eyeing the charred hole in the back of his bloodied overalls.

"They had no warning the Spawn were coming."

"How can you tell?"

"He was unarmed."

Dietz joined us, glanced at the skeleton and said, "Haines is cutting open the pipe. They'll be here soon."

Jase arrived wiping water from his face and giving Izin an irritated look. "Not the tropical paradise you said it was."

"This is the wet season," Izin replied.

Jase scowled. "Yeah, wet."

The others arrived in a trickle, then when everyone had caught up, Shen and Larson scouted ahead, clearing each room in turn while Nwibo went forward to cover the far side entrance.

"How many run the plant?" Dietz asked.

"It's fully automated. Just a few inspectors like him," Izin replied, motioning to the skeleton.

Larson appeared, signaled the building was empty, then we joined Nwibo at an open doorway overlooking the waste storage tanks. Outside was a metal grate landing and stairs leading down through several levels of piping to the work deck.

Tamph City was clearly visible from the doorway. It was crisscrossed by swimways linking thousands of pools, wet ramps and weirs that emptied directly into the coastal shallows. Scattered through the ruins were human prison camps, put there to stop the Tau Cetins bombarding the Spawn stronghold from orbit. The Spawn had chosen it as their capital because of all Earth's cities, it was the only one that offered them the kind of habitat they desired.

Parts of the city had been reduced to blackened ruins and skeletal frames where the tamphs had put up ferocious resistance, while other areas were relatively untouched and were now inhabited by the Spawn. Surrounding the islands was a patchwork quilt of abandoned sea farms and tamph nurseries and pockmarking both land and sea were craters blasted by the orbital siege cannons in response to intrusions by tamph raiders. The onshore craters now overflowed with rainwater, flooding the streets and draining into the swimways, turning tranquil weirs into gushing waterfalls.

"They really pounded it," I said.

"We always knew the Spawn would treat us more harshly than the humans," Izin said.

"Because you look like them, but are really like us," Jase said with a wry smile.

Izin grunted in disgust. "No need to be insulting."

I exchanged an amused look with Jase, then studied the promontory to the east where Tamph City's shuttle port was located. Hundreds of flying autacs, strike craft and transports sat on a black landing apron. Beyond it, Spawn earth movers bulldozed buildings into the sea, expanding the landing ground, turning the once modest shuttle port into a global strike base.

Sleek winged autacs, barely visible in the beating rain, glided low over the city-islands to the south, effortlessly resisting the fierce winds. They patrolled the city and the shallows, never venturing beyond the sea wall, sometimes shining search beams at the ground hunting for infiltrators.

"Look out, Captain," Izin said, pulling me back into the shadows as two flanker-elites with glowing contour shields and shoulder cannons strode into view. They crossed the work deck, shone search beams down into the sea and started up the stairs toward us. We backed away into the shadows, aiming our weapons at the doorway as the metallic footsteps grew louder.

"If you destroy them, others will come," Izin whispered.

I winced, fearing we'd have no choice, but they stopped outside on the landing listening to the robotic squeal of their comms. The soft boom of a distant explosion sounded over the roar of the storm, then the elites suddenly broke into a run and leapt across the plant.

Relieved, we edged forward as they launched themselves off the work deck toward the promontory. They landed in waist high water, vaulted to the shore and began bounding over the rooftops toward Guluwuru Island to the south where Earth-tracer and autac energy weapons crisscrossed through the ruins.

"Their comms reported my brothers were attacking the e-plant," Izin said.

"Got a Spawn implant for that too?" I asked.

"Yes, Captain."

The e-plant was the only structure still intact down there, surrounded on all sides by the flashes of battle, and used by the Spawn to power a sprawling military base sewn with human concentration camps.

"We must hurry," Izin said.

He led the way through howling wind and pelting rain, down the metal grill stairs to the work deck, then between storage tanks into another building. The door was clamped open and soft light spilled out. Larsen and Nwibo went ahead, then flashes from their guns lit up the entrance. By the time we got there, a recon-flanker lay on the floor with four penetrator slugs in its torso.

"They know we're here now," I said.

"Did either of you touch the flanker?" Izin asked.

"Nah, just this," Nwibo said, patting his assault rifle.

Izin reached down to the wrecked autac, deliberately

cut his finger on its torn metal and smeared blood on it.

"Tamph blood," I said, guessing his intent.

"And our ammo," Dietz added, doubting the Spawn would be fooled.

"When they scan it," Izin said, "they'll believe what they want to believe, that we are their equals, and you are not."

"Right," Dietz said.

Wiping blood on his jump suit, Izin led us through the pumping station, but rather than head toward the city, he went through a door opening onto the north side of the platform. The processing plant hid us from the Spawn base and the narrow walkway gave us our first look toward the comm center.

"There it is," Izin said.

It was a curving spire that became a needle rising thousands of meters into the cloudy, gray sky. Beyond it, a high wall crossed Marchinbar Island, cutting it in half, isolating the northern Female Zone from the densely populated male zones to the south. The tamph matriarchs had been sequestered north of that wall for millennia, permitted to imprint only enough males for reproduction and barred from all contact with the rest, preventing the females using them to make war upon each other, or worse, on us. To the tamph matriarchs, it had been the most galling of the peace treaty restrictions, but it had saved them from a fiery extinction. Ironically, the arrival of the Spawn had ended their isolation. The tamph females had fled the Female Zone and imprinted all tamph males to protect them from the Spawn Matriarchs, breaking the ancient treaty with us in order to make war upon their far more dangerous cousins from beyond the Galactic Rim.

"How do we get there?" I asked.

Izin pointed at the causeway below. It ran from the base of the platform all the way into the city, north of the shuttle port. Pipes connected it to the treatment plant's legs and a road ran along the top to the city.

"We'll use the sewer inside the causeway," Izin said, then motioned to the doors behind us. "We'll take the elevator down."

"No, too easy to get trapped," I said.

"There's no other way."

"There's one," I said, guiding him to the edge of the platform.

Izin's fear of heights froze him in place. "Tamphs do not jump, Captain."

I glanced at Jase, who sealed his visor. "OK Izin. We'll wait for you at the bottom."

"Thank you."

Izin relaxed and Jase charged, wrapping both arms around the little tamph and leaping off the platform. Izin screeched in terror, then they separated in midair and crashed into the water.

Marie grinned. "He's never going to forgive you for that."

I chuckled. "It wasn't me."

We spread out along the edge of the platform, sealed up our suits and jumped together, splashing into the sheltered water between the sea wall and the island. By the time we settled to the bottom, Izin had recovered his composure and motioned us toward a barnacle encrusted metal dome beneath the causeway. It was windowless and circular, standing several meters above the sea floor with two ladders reaching down to the sand. We climbed up through a pressure field that kept the sea at bay into a pool surrounded by a broad ledge. Beyond the ledge was a path beside a large sewer that fed a shallow stream of effluent into the recycling plant's intake pipes.

"We'll get out before we reach the shuttle port," Izin explained.

The combat engineers activated their suits' floodlights, illuminating an ancient tunnel of stone and concrete. Jase took one sniff, winced and resealed his visor, then we followed Izin toward the city. The combat engineers stomped in their heavy suits through the sewerage channel while the rest of us used the path. When we reached Marchinbar Island, Izin stopped at the foot of a stone stairway beneath a rusted metal door.

"Open it," Izin said to Sergeant Guerrero who climbed out of the sewer and sprayed the door frame with a squirt gun.

Smoke hissed from the door as the corrosive spray dissolved rusted metal. The engineers switched off their floodlights and Guerrero gave the door a servo-assisted push, sending it falling back with a reverberating clang. Inside was a large basement with a collapsed ceiling allowing torrential rain to pour in, flooding the floor.

We waded across to a ramp, then Izin led us up to the ground floor. It was littered with tamph skeletons lying among cracked data screens, overturned chairs and small tables strewn with fallen masonry. Thick gray clouds flashed with lightning above the broken ceiling as wind screamed through the ruins.

"This was the city library," Izin explained.

"They're just bones," Jase said, eyeing the skeletons.

"This is the tropics," Izin said, reminding him how quickly heat and insects consumed the dead.

We scrambled through the debris to a covered swimway overflowing with stormwater. It was flanked by flooded paths and spanned at regular intervals by arched footbridges. The canal was surprisingly deep and lined with swim up platforms and tamph-sized benches.

"This leads to the comm center," Izin said.

I turned to the others. "Remember, Izin's got the key. If he dies, the invasion dies with him."

"His life's worth more than all of ours put together," Dietz added, ensuring the I-F super soldiers wouldn't hesitate to sacrifice themselves to keep Izin alive. Nods from the combat engineers indicated they were prepared to make the same sacrifice, if needed.

"Your team's on point," I said to Dietz. "Engineers take the rear. Izin and the rest of us in the middle."

"I know the way," Izin protested, wanting to lead.

"You stay with me. Give Dietz directions. He'll find the way."

"Very well, Captain," Izin said reluctantly. He turned to Dietz and pointed into the dark swimway passage. "It's that way, two kilometers."

Dietz nodded, then Shen and Riley took one side of the swimway and he and Nwibo the other. With thermal and motion sensors probing the darkness ahead, they crept along the waterway searching for trip sensors, booby traps and ambushes. When they were some way ahead, we started after them, all on Dietz's side of the swimway.

"Stealth mode," Guerrero instructed his team, then the engineers moved forward in slow motion. Their servo-powered legs carefully placed each metal foot on the ground, replacing their mechanical clanking with a soft crunching sound almost lost against the roar of the wind and the drumming rain.

Distant explosions boomed sporadically as we crossed several intersecting swimways, then Dietz signaled to us and the I-F troopers took cover. We followed their lead, melting away behind broken walls into abandoned shops and eateries where we waited in darkness. After a long silence, a soft humming reached us. Soon, a faint green light appeared floating above the swimway. A lightning flash from the storm revealed a flattened sphere surrounded by rotating sensor spines above a gimbaled energy weapon. Green light from the tips of the sensor spines cast ghostly hues into our hiding place as the probe glided by. It continued on past the engineer's hiding places and turned off into an intersecting swimway.

Jase was eager to get moving, but I motioned for him to wait for Dietz's all clear. I'd learned the hard way to trust the I-F squad leader's intuition, so we sat in silence waiting for Dietz's gut to tell us it was safe to proceed.

After a while, I stole a look toward him sitting motionless in the dark, eyes fixed on a point behind us. He gave me an emphatic shake of his head, warning it wasn't clear.

I followed his gaze, saw nothing in the shadows, then after a long wait, he fired a three shot burst into the darkness. A yellow flash lit up the swimway as the Spawn sensor probe exploded and its remains splashed into the water. It had come back with its active scanning off and been waiting for us to show ourselves.

"They'll be coming," Izin warned, eager to get moving.

Dietz emerged from the shadows and we continued along the swimway. It led into a circular chamber with a round pool filled with masonry blocks that had fallen from the bombed out building above. A wall had been blown out revealing a two lane road outside and tamph skeletons littered the water, some crushed beneath masonry slabs, others charred black from energy blasts. Unlike the other skeletons we'd seen, these all had weapons, mostly hunting rifles and sports pistols. Food and drink dispensers sat on the ledges, all inoperable after more than a year without power, and open weapons lockers were visible beneath the water.

"We hid weapons here," Izin explained.

Dietz took in the building's structural damage at a glance. "They hit it from orbit, then assaulted."

"They were betrayed," Jase said.

"No, the snakeheads would have told the Spawn about this place," I said. "They've been scanning the planet for centuries, waiting for their chance."

An explosion boomed on the road outside, sending us scrambling for cover as three armed tamphs ran to a break in the wall. They fired back down the street then started to climb through the broken wall, but Izin stood and pinged them with his sonar lobe. The tamphs saw us hiding inside, listened momentarily to Izin, and without hesitation, ran across the road away from us.

Energy bursts flashed down the street, striking one tamph in the chest, killing him instantly while the others darted into a wrecked building. A moment later, four flanker-elites charged into the ruins after them, firing into the darkness. They were followed by two spawnwarriors in battle armor and glowing contour shields. Flashes of human tracer, chemical grenades and Spawn energy weapons sporadically lit up the darkness until distance and the roar of the storm drowned out the din of battle.

"If they make it to the sea, they might survive," Izin said.

"Maybe," Dietz said doubtfully and led us around the pool, along another swimway to a large crater full of muddy rainwater.

"It was a siege orbital," I said, eyeing the flooded crater, certain no one could have survived such a blast.

"Damn, took out a whole city block," Jase said.

Beyond the crater lake were more burned out ruins, and looming above them was the undamaged, windowless comm center, glowing with light. Rising from its roof was the tower, supported by three guy-wires anchored to strongpoints at the edge of the ruins. Recon-flankers patrolled the streets bordering the comm center and a pair of winged darts orbited the tower, oblivious to the cyclonic winds sweeping around them.

"They're airblasters," Dietz said. "Flying artillery. Don't let them see you."

We moved around the lake and through a series of burned out buildings toward the comm center. Wrecked vehicles littered the roads and a handful of tamph skeletons lay on the streets and in the ruined buildings.

"There's a way in," I said turning to Guerrero, "but you'll have to cut through a wall."

"They won't hear our acid guns," he said, then we crept around to the side of the comm center, hiding each time the airblasters approached.

Once in position, I studied the building's plans in my

bionetic memory and indicated a point on the wall well away from the main street. "There's a locked room on the other side."

We watched flankers patrolling the streets, got a sense of their timing, then Guerrero and Deung fired corrosives at the wall from a wrecked doorway. Acrid smoke boiled into the air and was swept away by high winds as the wall silently dissolved.

We hid again as the airblasters made another pass, then Dietz led the I-F squad across the laneway into the comm center. When he waved it was clear, the rest of us crossed into a storeroom filled with spares the Spawn used to keep the human comm system running for their own purposes.

I compared the room to my bionetic floor plan and pointed to a tamph ramp leading to the level above. "The main entry's up there."

Dietz motioned for the I-F team to follow him up to the door. They charged weapons while Larson placed a six legged insect smaller than an ant on the floor. The optical hexapod scurried under the door as all four lowered their visors to watch the feed.

"Guards inside and out," Dietz whispered.

"No heavies," Larson added. "Lot of shields."

Dietz pointed to each member in turn. "Left side, right side, front doors. I'll take the back pair and the ramp to the control room. Larson, follow me up." He turned to Nwibo and Shen. "You two kill anything that comes in from outside."

They nodded curtly, then he silently counted down from three, pushed the door open and charged through. The whine of magnetic accelerators, the boom of hypersonic projectiles and the scream of Spawn energy blasts sounded amidst breaking glass, followed by a long silence.

Finally Dietz appeared in the doorway above. "Clear!"

We hurried up to ground level to find six recon-flankers in pieces inside, two more outside and the sensiglass front wall reduced to shattered fragments. None of the lightly armored I-F troopers had been hit due to their intuitive survival instincts and speed of attack.

"The control room's intact," Dietz said to Izin, and pointed at the ramp. "Up there."

"Go with him," I said to Jase.

They jogged up the ramp together while the engineers unhitched the containers from their shoulder racks.

"Where do you want it?" Guerrero asked Dietz, who paced to the center of the room, studying the angles.

"Mine the entire floor and the ramps. Put a gun in each back corner, there and there, one on the landing and the other one outside the control room."

"You got it," Guerrero said.

"And blow the elevators," Dietz added.

Naidu, the fourth combat engineer, set one of his shoulder containers in a corner and stepped back. He clicked a remote, then the sides opened and a robotic autocannon unfolded behind sharply angled, deflective armor. When it finished self-assembly, it began scanning back and forth, auto seeking targets.

"Alpha is armed," Naidu announced.

"The Spawn will be shielded," I said to Dietz, expecting the roboguns wouldn't last long.

"No kidding." He gave me a knowing look. "You think we lugged that stuff all this way for nothing?"

"They fire penetrators?"

He nodded. "Armor piercing, static force, heavy cal. Ten thousand rounds a piece."

"Ah huh," I grunted appreciatively.

Naidu unloaded the container from his other shoulder rack and began laying thin, flat squares in front of the entrance. He backed toward us, activating them as he went. Each time they came to life, they took on the appearance of the surrounding floor tiles, disappearing from sight.

"And those?" I asked.

"Camouflage mines."

"Tau Cetin?"

"We adapted their static force tech." Dietz nodded with satisfaction. "We haven't been sitting on our asses all this time."

"Won't the Spawn detect them?" Marie asked.

He shook his head. "They're shielded, like our ammo."

"Another thing we adapted from the Tau Cetins," I said.

"They ain't complaining."

"Let's hope they hold them."

"They'll hold, until the ammo runs out and the mines are gone." He grimaced. "Then they're going to come charging in here like a plague of death and kill us all."

I gave him an astonished look. "If you thought that, what are you doing here?"

"Where else would I be? This is what they made me for." He made a fist, glanced at the small Iron Fist insignia on his suit's shoulder. "We're the shield."

"Right." I-F were engineered from single cells to fight the Spawn, not gene modded like me. I was changed after I was born. He was changed before. We were both human, but different.

"Now get out of my kill zone," Dietz snapped. "I'll meet you in the control room."

Marie and I left Dietz to his work and went up to the control room. It was two stories high with floor to ceiling screens on every wall, rings of consoles around a four camera holostudio in the center and the remains of two recon-flankers on the floor with Dietz's name tattooed on their chests.

The room had once been the beating heart of Tamph City's global communications center, taking feeds from every source on the planet, rarely sending any in reply. Now it was the only source of global news, with Spawn propaganda on every screen beamed in all languages to the world. Images of defeated humans and triumphant autacs, of spawnwarriors patrolling Earth's cities, of unbroken victories on many alien worlds relentlessly saturated Earth's demoralized people, all sent from this one room. It was the only news they saw, proclaiming the Spawn as rulers of the known universe, crushing all hope.

Alongside the holostudio was a black surfaced Spawn console glowing with the light of geometric patterns swirling inside. Izin stared into it, reading the patterns with the complete understanding only his Spawn implants could give.

"Two hundred and ten siege orbitals are fully operational," Izin said. "Four are undergoing self-diagnostic cycles and six newly deployed stations are awaiting activation sequences."

"Can you pull their plug?"

He placed his hands onto the solid shiny surface which dissolved, allowing his hands to sink into it. He reached down into the swirling geometries, spread his fingers and let the console connect with his Spawn implants. The colors and shapes morphed around his hands, forming symbolic patterns that changed shape each time Izin issued a new command. His bulbous blue-green eyes reflected the colors within the console, mesmerized by them, becoming one mind with the Spawn system.

"I have access," he said slowly. "The orbitals cannot be disabled remotely. Once armed, they can only be deactivated by physically entering them in orbit."

"Screwed again," Jase muttered.

"The siege network is designed to prevent centralized sabotage," Izin said.

"How come Lena's EIS contact didn't know that?" Marie asked.

"He retrieved the code," Izin replied, "but not an understanding of its use, or limitations."

"If you can't switch them off," I said, "crash them into the atmosphere."

Izin became absorbed again by a kaleidoscope of

morphing shapes and colors, then said, "Safety overrides prevent remote de-orbiting."

"There's got to be something we can do," Marie said.

I studied the wall screens with rising frustration. The Spawn used their own tech to communicate with the orbitals, and our comm system to flood every channel on Earth with propaganda to brainwash mankind into submission.

"At least turn that garbage off," I said, motioning to the propaganda feeds.

Izin dragged his hands through a kaleidoscope of colored light, then the screens went blank, silencing Spawn propaganda for the first time since the invasion.

"Do you think anyone noticed?" Marie asked.

I nodded. "Every man, woman and child on Earth knows something is happening."

Izin continued staring into the Spawn console, then the wall screens filled with images of the Earth and the Moon sliding through space, watched by the siege stations.

I turned to Izin. "What happened?"

"I have purged their spatial designators, Captain." Izin looked up at me. "They are unable to identify a contact by its emission's signature."

I blinked. "They can't tell friend from foe?"

"Correct," he said slowly. "And Captain, Spawn targeting protocols prevent firing upon unknown signatures for fear of hitting friendly targets."

"They can't shoot?"

"They won't shoot," he corrected.

"Will the Tau Cetins see it?"

"I cannot predict what the Tau Cetins see, Captain."

Marie pointed at one of the screens. "Look!"

A Tau Cetin sentinel emerged from beyond the Moon and raced toward Earth. Its image appeared on every screen as the orbitals tracked it. The sentinel came in straight and fast, then made a long curving sweeping run past the siege orbitals, daring them to open fire, but none did.

I smiled. "They know!" I slapped our little tamph on the back. "Izin! The Tau Cetins know. You did it!"

The sentinel turned away from the siege orbitals and streaked away toward the Moon, informing the allied fleets hiding beyond it that the way to Earth was now open.

"Captain, the siege orbitals could disengage from safe mode at any time," Izin warned.

"Keep an eye on them," I said, then Dietz hurried up the ramp from the entrance, followed by the combat engineers dropping camo mines behind them.

"It's a good position," Dietz said. "Thick walls, only one way up."

"Those roboes can hold off an army," Guerrero added.

"They may have to," I said as the orbital feeds focused on Luna's solitary gray orb.

"What's happening?" Dietz asked, his eyes jumping from screen to screen.

Tiny lights rose from beyond the Moon, a few at first, then many, many more. They spread out through space like a cloud, growing brighter with every second. Only it wasn't cloud, it was ships, thousands of them: Earth Navy battlewagons of every class, refugee ships from the Armada, combat scarred privateers from the Brotherhood, troop transports, assault ships, arbiters, sentinels, gigantic nestships, Fenari arrowheads and ships from all our alien allies, all streaming toward Earth while the siege orbitals slumbered.

"They're coming," I said with relief. "All of them, with everything they've got."

* * * *

The Alpha robogun roared, shredding a multi-legged spotter as it landed in front of the shattered sensiglass entry on the ground floor. At the rear of the control room, we watched the robogun's optical feed on one of four control screens set up by the engineers.

"It saw our roboguns," Marie said.

"They can't hit them from the road," Haines assured her. "They have to come inside."

"Unless they fry the whole building," Jase added pessimistically.

"They won't do that," Izin said. "They need orbital comms intact."

Bipedal flanker-elites glowing with contour shields appeared on both Alpha and Bravo gun feeds. The autacs charged the entrance, firing energy weapons blindly, trying to suppress the roboguns which opened up together, tearing the lead flankers apart. They crashed through the remains of the sensiglass wall, detonating camo mines beneath their feet, then the roboguns went full auto. They swept left and right, pouring withering, overlapping streams of heavy caliber penetrators into the attacking flankers. Some autacs exploded, others were cut to pieces, scattering metallic arms and legs across the floor.

Two heavily armored rhinos charged through the entry after the flankers, triggering multiple camo mine detonations before they could target our roboguns. The rhinos were hurled into the air, giving the roboes a chance to blast their rear mounted field accelerators, the rhinos' only weak point. One exploded before it hit the ground. The other got off a shot as it landed on its side, melting Bravo's deflective armor and turning its gunsight feed into hissing white noise. Alpha gun raked the rhino as it tried to right itself, then the big autac's short, thick legs folded as it rippled with static energy and died. Alpha immediately finished off the two remaining flankers as they leapt over the camo mines and crashed onto the foot of the ramp, detonating a mine that ripped their metallic bodies apart. With no targets left, Alpha fell silent and resumed scanning, sweeping its barrel slowly from side to side.

"It's a scrapyard down there," Larson said, impressed by the autac torsos and limbs spread across the floor.

"Round one to us," Dietz said.

"Bravo's dead," Guerrero declared grimly. "Alpha's at thirty percent. Charlie and Delta are still full."

I glanced at the orbital feeds. The fleet was now almost halfway to Earth, fanning out toward its assault positions. "It's going to be a while before they get here. We need a fallback position."

"The tower is the strongest part of the structure," Izin suggested.

"Haines," Dietz said, "you and Deung rig some nasties on the roof, but don't arm them until we get there. Set up a defensive position in the tower. Larson, Nwibo, go with them. We'll hold here as long as we can."

"On it," Haines said, then he and Deung went up to the roof, escorted by the I-F troopers.

"The guns won't hold them," Dietz said grimly. "They'll be up here soon."

He and Shen took up positions where they could cover the ramp while the rest of us used the rear consoles for cover. Only Guerrero was behind us at the robogun controllers, covering our escape route.

I watched the wall screens as our fleet formed into five distinct squadrons, each with a nestship at its center, each maneuvering for orbital insertion above a different continent. "Izin, if our satellites are dead, how'd the Spawn send their propaganda?"

"They relayed our signals off their orbitals, Captain."

"Can we do that? Send our own message?"

"A message, Captain? To who?"

"To every human and tamph out there. To anyone still alive on Earth."

Izin considered my request. "We could ride the Spawn uplink."

"Set it up. Hurry."

Izin sank his hands into the Spawn console, preparing

to send the biggest surprise in history. It would be a message to sixteen billion desperate humans and millions of tamphs, a call from the dark for them to set the entire planet on fire.

* * * *

"People of Earth, I speak to you on behalf of our Government in Exile. A great fleet is, even now, approaching orbit. Look up and you will soon see our ships. They will fill the sky. They have defeated the Spawn Fleet and are bringing a vast army to free you. Now is the time for you to rise up and attack the enemy wherever he is. Attack with everything you have. Every Spawn you tie down now, every enemy you distract, will help our forces land. They will be here soon. And remember, the tamphs are on our side." I glanced at Izin operating the control console nearby. "One is helping get this message to you now. Others are fighting and dying nearby to make this invasion possible. Help us. Strike now. Strike hard. Liberation is coming."

I nodded to Izin, who sent the message to the siege orbitals, instructing them to play it continuously.

"You're on every channel, Captain, visible everywhere on Earth."

"Now lock out comms so the Spawn can't take it down," I said.

Izin gazed into the Spawn console's swirling geometric patterns briefly. "Done. They will be unable to break my encryption until long after the invasion has begun."

"That's it then, there's nothing more we can do."

"I guess your days as a deep cover agent are over," Marie said. "You just became the most famous man in human history, the man who announced the liberation of Earth."

"She's right," Jase grinned. "Every human in the

galaxy's going to see that message, and your face."

"Lena won't be happy," I said, not caring.

Marie grinned. "She'll make you wear a disguise."

"Or get surgery," Izin said. "I've always thought you could do with an improvement."

"I like him just the way he is," Marie said, then gave me a thoughtful look. "Although, you could be taller."

"Nice," I said and turned to the screens tracking our ships entering Earth orbit. "They'll start dropping troops soon."

"Captain!" Izin exclaimed, watching morphing geometries in the Spawn console. "The orbitals have reinitialized their spatial designators. They're reactivating."

I turned to the screens, saw the orbitals begin scanning for targets again. "Our ships are inside Earth's gravity well. They can't bubble out!"

The screens filled with images of allied ships as the first orbitals opened fire. A human supply ship exploded, then a Syrman troopship was cut in half, sending a cloud of bodies and venting atmosphere spilling into space. Suddenly, every orbital was firing, destroying allied ships with every blast.

Earth Navy warships launched their hyper-torpedoes in response as Tau Cetin arbiters and sentinels accelerated to high velocity, rolling through space, evading energy blasts as they laced the orbitals with their glowing white energy beams. The siege cannons began to focus on the Tau Cetins, whom they assessed as the greatest threat, while their rapid fire self-defense weapons targeted the incoming torpedoes.

Ships exploded like novas, hurling waves of energy onto the shields of their nearby companions and destroying our torpedoes en masse. Many ships broke formation and began to run toward the edge of Earth's gravity well, trying to escape the slaughter, while others held steady, steering for their invasion positions. The five big Nisk ships were hit many times, but their enormous shields weathered the storm, firing hundreds of hyper-torpedoes as they approached their assault positions.

"Izin!" I yelled.

His eyes were fixed upon his console, ignoring everything but the three dimensional geometry flowing around his fingers. "The kill list cannot be modified during combat."

"They're getting massacred out there."

Ships and torpedoes exploded on every screen, then Izin said, "Tell them to stop shooting."

"The orbitals won't listen to me."

"Not the orbitals, Captain. Our fleet. Tell them to stop firing."

I furrowed my brow in confusion. "What?"

He looked up at me. "It's the only way." He made an adjustment in his console. "They can hear you, Captain. Tell them. Tell them to stop."

I winced and looked ahead, hoping someone could see me. "This is Sirius Kade to all allied ships. Ceasefire immediately. I repeat, ceasefire immediately. Admiral, if you can hear me, order them to stop firing, now!"

The message went straight out to every ship, then Admiral Talis' face appeared on one screen.

"This is Talis to all ships, ceasefire. Sending my security code now." He shook his head. "I hope to God you know what you're doing, Kade."

Every ship stopped firing while the torpedoes in flight continued toward the orbitals. Most were destroyed by exploding ships and orbital defense beams, but a few reached their targets, although not in the numbers needed for a kill. The Spawn battle stations continued to blast our ships, now gliding through space without returning fire.

"Izin, it's not working!"

He seemed not to hear me, then suddenly the orbital weapons ceased firing. The screens were still filled with images of our ships, confirming they were being tracked, but they were no longer under attack. It seemed like a miracle, then one orbital opened fire. And another.

"They're shooting again!" I exclaimed.

"Yes, Captain, they are," he agreed, "but not at us."

He looked up at a screen now showing a siege orbital. It was struck by an energy blast, immediately rotated toward its attacker, and returned fire. Images of egg-shaped battle stations firing or being hit blinked onto every screen, replacing images of our ships, as the Spawn battle stations targeted each other.

Energy blasts flashed harmlessly between our ships, then a great explosion bloomed as the first orbital exploded. One by one, others detonated, filling the sky with igniting stars that could be seen everywhere on Earth. Our ships reformed and hurried to their invasion positions while the orbitals tore each other apart, turning the screens in the comm center to static as one feed after another died. New feeds from other orbitals replaced the static until there were no more new feeds and, one by one, the wall screens filled with static until only a few stations remained, separated from each other by Earth itself. The Tau Cetin fleet then swept in with massed beam assaults, turning all our screens to white noise.

"How?" I asked.

"I couldn't remove our ships from the kill list, so I switched list designators," Izin replied. "I made friends the kill list."

"That's why we had to stop shooting, to keep our ships off the new kill list."

"Yes, Captain. Foes became friends."

"Give me the fleet," I said, moving back into the holostudio.

Izin's attention returned to his console briefly. "They're receiving you."

"Admiral, this is Kade. You're clear to land. There's a lot of people down here eager to see you. Don't keep them waiting."

Talis' face appeared on every screen, every channel. "You heard the man. All ships, attack," he ordered, then the screens went blank, leaving us blind to the approach of the invasion force.

"We did it," Jase declared, hardly believing it.

"Izin did it," Marie said, taking his large face in her hands and kissing the top of his oversized amphibian head. "With a little help from his friends." He squirmed, uncomfortable with human contact as she looked down into his large bulbous eyes. "Sirius will be famous, but you saved the day."

I spread my arms expectantly. "Don't you like famous?"

"Sure I do," Marie said and kissed me.

I winced. "You smell like fish."

She grinned. "I did just a kiss a tamph. My first."

The whine of automatic fire sounded as the Alpha gun on the ground floor opened fire, sweeping the entry on full auto.

"We've got company," Guerrero said, watching Alpha's gunsight feed.

"Positions!" Dietz yelled.

We took cover behind the consoles, aiming past Delta gun at the top of the ramp. The roar of Alpha shredding autacs and the boom of detonating camo mines thundered through the building, then the robogun's magnetic accelerator fell silent and its optical feed died.

"Alpha's down," Guerrero shouted.

The clatter of metal feet charging the ramp echoed up to us as Charlie gun opened up from the first landing, felling autacs in the narrow rampway. The flankers behind leapt over the wrecked autacs and charged the autocannon, blindly shooting the ramp, trying to hit our camo mines. Some were destroyed, others detonated beneath their metal feet, blowing them to pieces. The second rank fired at Charlie, ablating its armored shield, but in the confined space, the autocannon's hypersonic wall of charged metal shredded them almost instantly.

"It's wall to wall down there," Jase muttered, glancing at the gunsight feeds.

"Charlie's at sixty percent," Guerrero warned, eyes locked on the ammo counter. The robogun kept firing at a tremendous rate, piling up wrecked autacs at the base of the ramp. "Forty percent."

A flanker leapt over the carnage at the bottom of the ramp and blasted Charlie while still airborne, grazing the gun's frontal armor and smashing its interior.

"Charlie's down."

"Zero mines on the lower ramp," Naidu added over the rattle of metal feet.

The flankers reached the landing, then Delta opened up as they charged around the corner, cutting them down before they could shoot. Flankers behind hurdled Delta's merciless fire, leaping high and springing off the far wall. They landed on camouflage mines and were blown to pieces. D-gun poured a constant stream of tracer down the ramp, blue light flashing from its barrel as it held the autacs at bay, chewing through its ammo. Elites and recon-flankers charged together, running, leaping off walls, shooting blindly at the ramp mines. Explosions boomed as mines shredded the autacs and the robogun whined, hurling metallic arms and legs through the air.

"They're not shooting the gun," Marie said.

"They want the comm system intact," Izin explained.

"But the orbitals are dead," Jase said.

"They still need to coordinate their forces against the invasion, with this," Izin said, withdrawing his hands from the Spawn console.

"Guerrero, blow that thing," I said, pointing at the Spawn terminal.

"No," Izin said. "Let them capture it."

"What! Why?"

"Their communications array is in the tower, Captain. They won't destroy the tower if there's still a chance they can use it."

Dietz glanced back, nodded to me, then I shrugged. "OK. Leave it. We'll blow the array instead."

"Delta's dry!" Guerrero declared, watching his screen.

"Here they come," Dietz bellowed as flankers charged up the ramp. He and Shen opened fire, picking off flanker sensor heads with accurate bursts.

"There's too many," I yelled. Seeing we were about to be overrun, I pumped the under barrel launcher of my K-8 and stood. "N-grenade!"

Dietz turned to me with alarm. "No! Not in here!"

"Oh crap," Jase muttered and threw himself onto the floor.

I fired the novarium grenade over the useless D-gun onto the ramp. Dietz cursed and he and Shen dived away from the door. The rest of us ducked for cover as the grenade bounced down the ramp, struck the landing wall and detonated amid densely packed autacs.

A brilliant white flash flooded the control room as the building shuddered. An air blast blew out the doors, tore the screens off the walls, and sent the outer ring of consoles skating across the floor. The ramp well's thick walls funneled the blast upwards, blowing the roof off, then as the thunderous novarium detonation faded, a black cloud billowed into the comm center.

"Fallback," I yelled.

Dietz got to his feet angrily. "You could have killed us all."

"Not through those walls."

He scowled, glanced at the ragged cavity where the ramp well had been, saw it was now empty, and activated his suit comms. "Haines, we're coming up."

"Be advised, we got flyers circling the tower," the engineer replied.

"Understood."

I helped Marie to her feet as she held her ringing ears. "An N-grenade, in here?" She shook her head in dismay, then we ran up the back ramp.

The flat roof was awash with wind and rain, although it wasn't as strong as before. The clouds were thinning and the northern horizon was noticeably brighter as the eye of the storm approached. The comms building had partially collapsed behind us while the tower curved skyward before us, its needle point piercing the gray clouds.

Halfway up the needle was a circular observation deck showing no lights, and above it, the three thick guy-wires still anchored the tower, unaffected by the N-grenade or the cyclonic winds. The two airblasters beyond the observation deck saw us spill out onto the roof and came toward us. They were ground strike units with twin belly-cannons, not air combat units, but could still easily outfly and outfight any human interceptor.

With no way to deal with them, we ran across the roof toward the tower entrance. Streams of tracer licked out from the observation tower, raking the flyers, trying to buy us time, but the flyer ignored the attack and aimed at us.

"Look out!" I shouted.

We scattered as they hurled a stream of energy pulses at us, punching ragged tears through the roof. The dark storm clouds above them glowed white as if from lightning, then two brilliant white beams flashed down and struck both airblasters, destroying them instantly. A moment later, a mirror-hulled sentinel dived out of the clouds at high speed and passed directly overhead.

"Yeah!" Jase roared, fists pumping excitedly as the sentinel made a fast, low altitude sweep over the ruins of Tamph City.

Its beams carved a swathe of destruction through the Spawn flyers on the ground, turning the base into an inferno, then it banked away over the sea before anyone on the ground could return fire. The sentinel accelerated away in a streak of light toward Asia, where great land battles would soon be fought, and vanished into the clouds.

"Keep moving!" Dietz ordered, running past me, waving everyone on.

Larson appeared in the tower entry, covering us with his rifle. When we were all inside, Deung attached a mine to the door and armed a camo minefield.

"The tamph was right," Larson said to Dietz. "It's a solid position." He nodded at the thick columns forming the tower's spine. "They're carbon reinforced perdurium. They'll hold the tower up even if the cables are cut."

"The foundations go deep," Haines added, looking up. "The cross beams will give us good cover if the Spawn get inside. The bad news is the outer skin is thin. It won't give us much protection."

The thick girders above fanned out from the four central columns like spokes on a wheel and walkways ran along them, linking platforms at the junction points. An elevator ran up between the massive pylons and a ramp spiraled around the outside all the way up to the observation deck. Nwibo was riding the elevator down from the observation deck where he'd fired at the flyers.

"How many ways in?" Dietz asked.

"Only four rooftop doors," Larson replied. "All mined."

"The tower is sensor suppressed to stop background noise disrupting the comm signal," Haines said. "It'll hide us from EM and thermal scanning."

"What about those hatches?" I asked, pointing at the metal doors in the tower skin at the end of each girder.

"Don't have enough mines for the bot access points," Haines replied.

"We'll use them as sniper positions," Dietz said.

I turned to Izin, who was acrophobically eyeing the access hatches. "Not exactly tamph friendly, are they?"

"Human engineers and maintenance bots did the high work, Captain," Izin explained. "I will stay close to the central pylons."

"We can't let them get above us," I said, looking up at the base of the observation deck. "That'll be our last fallback position."

Larson winced. "There's no cover up there. It's a thin floor and all windows."

"We can move the signal amplifiers up there, and weld deck plates over the windows," Guerrero said. "It won't be a bunker, but it'll be defensible."

I nodded. "Do it. The rest of us will hold the first level of cross beams."

"Just one thing, Kade," Dietz said. "No N-grenades inside the tower. The walls will funnel the blast into our faces."

I chuckled. "Agreed."

"I've rigged the elevators to explode," Haines said, "and there are demo charges on the ramps."

"We'll blow them as we go," I said. "Give the detonators to Izin. He'll be in the center."

Guerrero and two of the engineers went off to build the observation deck bunker while the rest of us climbed onto the lowest level cross beams. There were bot charging stations up there, but not a bot in sight.

"Tamph snipers destroyed them whenever they showed themselves," Izin said.

"The scouts told you that?" I asked.

"No." He pointed at tiny bullet holes near the hatches. "They did. Near misses."

"I didn't think tamphs missed."

"Strong winds, Captain," he said, carefully avoiding looking over the edge of the landing.

"Are you going to be able to shoot down?"

"I will try," he replied, choosing a place beside one of the pylons.

The rest of us split up and moved out along different walkways to the bot maintenance hatches in the skin. I took the south west hatch where I could see along the coast toward the burning Spawn base. The winds were rapidly falling away, although the tower still creaked and swayed from strong gusts. Beyond Cumberland Straight, fires burned across Guluwuru Island as tamphs, autacs and spawnwarriors fought ferociously for control of rubble strewn streets and wrecked buildings.

Armored transports were now ferrying Spawn reinforcements from the burning base to the ruins surrounding the communications center. There was already movement all around us as autacs and spawnwarriors moved to their assault positions.

"They're massing for an attack," I said over suit comms.

"Yeah, looks like it," Dietz replied. He'd taken the most southerly position where he expected the weight of the Spawn attack to fall.

"There's a big fight down south," Nwibo reported from the south east side.

"Too bad they don't have our ammo," Jase said.

"They have what they need," Dietz declared meaningfully.

I-F units had hidden stockpiles of static force ammunition to wage guerilla war for years if necessary, but Dietz's tone indicated something else.

"I-F doesn't have authorization to arm tamphs," I said.

"Says who? Earth Council Special Directive, in the event of planetary invasion, I-F units have complete tactical discretion."

"I know, but that doesn't mean–"

"It means whatever the hell we want it to mean."

"What makes you think I-F shared?"

"I told them too, before the invasion," he replied. "I had a feeling."

"Your intuition."

"I wasn't the only one. We all had it. We knew the Spawn were coming, tried to warn Earth Navy, but no one would listen. So we made our own plans."

"How? You weren't even on Earth."

"I told Master Sergeant Dietz how to contact my brothers, Captain," Izin said. "I'm sorry I couldn't tell you, but it was necessary for their survival."

"You would have told that Voss woman," Dietz said. "I trust her about as much as I trust the Spawn."

"Maybe I would have. Maybe not," I said.

He'd done what he'd been designed to do, used his intuition to outsmart the enemy before the battle had even begun. And as usual, he guessed right.

A pair of Spawn transports dropped squads of autacs and battle armor clad spawnwarriors a few blocks away and flew off toward the Spawn base for more.

"Sure is a lot of them out there," Marie said from the access port next to mine.

I searched the sky for any sign of the invasion, but it was empty. The eye of the storm was almost over the islands now, the wind dropped to almost nothing and the rain stopped.

"Wouldn't you know it," Jase said bitterly, "good weather for the Spawn to attack."

"I got midgets and tin heads forming up, north side, two hundred meters out," Larson reported.

I looked out across the calming water to the sea wall and its fortress-like artillery bastions. "The eastern sea wall is clear."

"They're going to hit us on three sides," Dietz said.

"Izin, don't wait for my order. When they reach the ramp, burn them."

"I will, Captain," he replied with his usual calm, knowing Spawn hell was about to break loose on us all.

* * * *

"Small flyer, hovering east side. Looks like a probe," Shen reported over comms, then the crack of a single shot sounded. "It's out of range."

"There's another one to the west," Marie said as a spiny sphere ringed by bands of light rose from behind the sea wall. It floated in sunlight, beneath blue skies, as the eye of the storm began to pass over Tamph City. Far off on the horizon, a wall of black cloud reaching high into the sky rolled toward us.

We had our hatches open, watching movement in the ruins surrounding the comm center, but no autacs tried to get onto the roof or approach the tower.

I nodded reassuringly to Marie, who was to my right, covering the shallows between us and the sea wall. It was the least likely line of attack for the Spawn, and with Jase to her right, she had the safest position of any of us.

"Heads up!" Nwibo called. "Flankers crossing the road."

"Same here," Shen said. "They're jumping."

"They're on the roof," Larson said.

The tower rang with the whine of our magnetic accelerators charging, then Dietz and Shen fired single shots at autacs on the east side, conserving ammo. Heavy boots pounded on the ramp above as Guerrero and Naidu came running down in their powered suits, weapons in hand. Jase and Larson opened up on flankers rushing the roof from the north side as a flash of sunlight from the sea wall caught my eye. A squad of rhinos were charging out of the watchtower beside the Cumberland Sea Gate and running along the wall toward an ancient artillery platform opposite our position.

"Heavies on the sea wall," I said, tracking them through my K-8's optical sight, finding they were out of range. "Haines. Can your bunker busters reach the sea wall?"

"Yeah, but those rhinos are small targets."

They spread out along the artillery platform, folded their legs, and converted themselves into fixed artillery. A flurry of explosions thundered around the tower as flankers charged across the roof, triggering camo mines, then the rhinos opened fire. Energy blasts flashed across the water, struck the side of the tower above us and passed through the other side, missing the central pylons, not by accident.

"They're cutting holes in the tower, for the autacs," I said as molten metal dripped onto my girder from above. "Haines, shoot the sea wall below the rhinos."

"Roger that."

Twin hypersonic booms thundered from the observation deck as Haines and Deung fired together, sending a pair of black projectiles hurtling over the shallows. The two bunker busters slammed into the ancient wall halfway between the sea and the artillery platform. Orange flames jetted from the wall as giant cracks fanned out from the impact points and the shockwaves knocked the rhinos off their feet, but the wall held.

"Again!" I ordered, watching the rhinos right themselves through my gunsight.

Two more thunderclaps reverberated through the tower as two more kinetic impactors raced on flat trajectories over the water. When they struck the sea wall, flames and dust erupted from the impact points and the cracks multiplied, reaching up toward the artillery platform, but still the massive structure stood.

"That's it, Kade," Haines declared. "Out of ammo."

"At least you slowed them down."

The explosions on the roof outside petered out, then Larson said, "They're through the mines."

Recon-flankers charged toward the doors while elites fired from the edge of the roof. Their energy blasts smashed through the tower's metal skin, narrowly missing the central columns, while single shots from our rifles rang out in reply. Some flankers were cut down while others reached the doors and began cutting through the locks.

"Grenades. Aim high. Wide dispersal," Dietz ordered

with icy calm.

I sealed my helmet, saw Marie's visor slide shut, then we took cover away from our hatches as the I-F troopers launched N-grenades into the ruins surrounding the comm center. Multiple earthquakes shook the tower as muted booms hammered my helmet and my visor darkened against each flash. The tower rocked crazily, then autacs forced open the tower door, triggering a booby trap that shredded the flankers outside with statically charged shrapnel.

I pumped my second N-grenade into the launcher and fired toward the south. It landed on the road, levelling the ruins beyond and blowing elites off the comms tower roof. The blast struck the tower, tearing skin plates off its side and tilting the tower sharply. A metallic twang rang out as a guy-wire snapped, then the cable whipped away from the tower and lashed the shallows all the way to the sea wall.

Marie clung desperately to her girder as the tower lurched, almost throwing Jase off his cross beam. The metal superstructure creaked ominously, but the novarium blast faded and the tower straightened.

"Too close, Kade," Dietz snapped.

"Just a little," I agreed, relieved I hadn't killed us all.

The already teetering comms building collapsed all around us, burying any autac survivors, leaving only the tower and its mighty foundations standing A dust cloud rose from the ruins and flooded in through open bot hatches, blinding us to the Spawn outside.

"Grenade count?" Dietz called as the breeze carried the dust away. "I'm out."

"Same," Nwibo said.

"Zero," Shen reported. "Down to one mag."

"None," Larson declared.

The I-F troopers had all fired their three N-grenades, turning everything for a thousand meters into boiling lava. When the dust cleared, there were no buildings left standing, no streets, and no autacs this side of the kill zone, only the tower.

"I've got one left," I said, opening my visor again.

"Save it," Dietz said. "If Kade goes down, someone grab his gun."

"Here they come," Nwibo said as flankers began leaping over the lava moat surrounding the comms tower.

They landed on the tower's foundations and charged the base of the tower. Everyone began shooting, thinning autac numbers, then booby traps detonated as flankers forced open the other three doors. Flankers charged in through all four doors at once, spraying energy blasts before them and triggering camo mines. Their shields flashed as static shrapnel shredded their legs and torsos, but the autacs kept coming, flooding through the doors.

"Izin, blow the ramp," I ordered, but nothing happened. "Izin?"

"I'm here, Captain," he replied, ignoring my order.

Flankers poured in through the doorways, leapt over the floor to avoid the mines and crowded together on the ramp. They were shooting up at us, standing shoulder to shoulder, what Izin had been waiting for. The ramp and elevator exploded, hurling them onto the last of our camo mines, triggering more detonations, creating autac carnage.

When the explosions died away, I nodded to Izin, appreciating his calculations, then began picking off the surviving autacs. After several shots, a horizontal energy blast punched through the tower above me, grazed a pylon, and blew out the other side.

"The rhinos are back up," I warned as another blast flashed through the tower close to Marie. She gave me an anxious look. "Stay low. They're avoiding the supports."

She nodded and dropped to one knee, shooting down into the maelstrom below as energy blasts flashed up at us. I destroyed several autacs climbing the walls, then a recon-flanker appeared outside the tower and tried to pull itself in through a hole blasted by a rhino. I put a burst into its torso, knocking it off the tower.

"They're outside the tower!" I yelled excitedly over comms.

"Yeah, we see them," Dietz said calmly.

We were shooting down at flankers on the floor, autacs climbing the interior walls and others scrambling up outside the tower. They were everywhere, and my ammo counter was running low.

A flanker-elite caught Jase's girder and started to pull itself up, but he jammed his gun barrel into its sensor head and blew it away. The flanker tumbled onto the floor below, then a rhino blast smashed through the tower where he'd been standing a moment before. If he hadn't moved, he'd be dead.

Another flanker got halfway up the inside wall, spotted Naidu and an instant later, a rhino blast flashed through the tower and struck the combat engineer in the chest, killing him instantly.

"The rhinos are using the flankers for eyes!" I shouted and blasted the autac that had targeted Naidu.

"Kill the high ones first," Dietz ordered.

I fired several times, then a cracking sound rolled in across the water. Spray was breaking over the rhinos from a big wave pounding the sea wall as cracks spread across it. Another big wave slammed into the sea wall. It shuddered and partially subsided, throwing the rhinos into the sea. A third wave broke over the crumbling wall and it shattered, burying the heavy autacs under a million tons of masonry.

"The wall's down!" Haines declared triumphantly.

It was too little, too late. There were many flankers inside the tower now and many more leaping over the N-grenade dead zone toward us. I ran across the narrow walkway to Marie. She fired several shots down at the flankers, glanced at her ammo counter and gave me a desperate look.

"I'm nearly out."

"Me too," I said, forgetting we were live on comms.

"We can't hold them," Larson declared.

"We've got to pull back to the observation deck," Guerrero said.

"We won't make it," Dietz said as a flanker tried to get above him, then he drilled it before it could fire. "There's too many of them."

"One mag left," Shen declared as she reloaded for the last time.

"Ten rounds," Nwibo said.

"Kade?" Dietz said. "Remember I said no grenades inside the tower?"

"Yeah?"

"Change of plan," he said meaningfully. "Use it."

Marie and I exchanged shocked looks as we realized what he was saying.

She switched off her comms. "I never thought you'd get me killed, before we got married." She reached out, squeezed my hand and nodded.

Jase blasted a flanker as it tried to leap onto his girder, then his K-8 clicked empty. He looked over at me, shook his head, dropped his assault rifle and drew his twin fraggers from his suit's utility pouches. He grinned and started firing with both hands, not caring that his pistols couldn't penetrate contour shields.

Flankers clambered onto a support beam either side of Nwibo. He destroyed one, turned to shoot the other and found his gun was empty. He hammered it with the butt of his rifle, but the flanker's contour shield deflected the blow, then the autac raked his torso with a triple burst. He fell off the crossbeam, dead before he hit the floor below.

"I shouldn't have brought you." I gave her a long look and pumped the last N-grenade into the launcher.

"I chose to be here," she said and emptied her rifle into a flanker that leapt onto our crossbeam.

My finger hovered over the launch initiator, then I

heard a faint buzzing, almost drowned out by the crash of waves and the sputtering fire of our guns as they ran dry.

"You hear that?" I asked, looking through a rhino hole, searching for the source of the buzzing.

"Hear what?"

It wasn't coming from the ground or the sea, but from a dark cloud in the sky. I thought it was the storm, then realized the eye was still passing over us. We had clear sky above us and the wall of cyclonic cloud was still far out to sea. The buzzing cloud dived toward us, separating into long slender strands like demonic fingers, clawing the ground. It had no fixed shape, no clear outline, but grew as the wind carried it toward us.

"What are you waiting for Kade?" Dietz demanded, preferring to die by my hand than theirs.

The black cloud passed over Tamph City. Its claws groped toward the ground as the buzzing grew so loud, it drowned out the roar of the sea and the wail of weapons.

"It's not a ship," Marie said, peering up in confusion.

The flankers stopped climbing and turned toward the black cloud now blotting out the sky. Human and Spawn weapons fell silent as the buzzing became deafening and all eyes and sensors peered up into the darkening sky in disbelief.

"It's the Nisk!" I exclaimed, lifting my finger off the grenade launcher as the great swarm descended like a plague of locusts. "They can fly!"

"My God," Marie whispered.

The winged Nisk opened fire with rapidly pulsing energy weapons, diving out of the sky, raining destruction upon the Spawn below. Strapped to the backs of some, forward of their massive wings, were humans in armored drop suits. They landed on the streets and in the ruined buildings, firing and moving rapidly.

A flying Nisk with a human soldier on its back flew into the comms tower through a rhino hole, followed by hundreds of winged Nisk fighters. The human spoke rapidly into a Nisk translator, issuing instructions, calling tactics, while the winged fighters circled the central pylons, raking the flankers with energy weapons. A few autacs fired back, killing some Nisk before they themselves were destroyed. Other flankers tried to escape by jumping out of rhino holes or retreating through ground floor doors, but the Nisk outside tore them apart the moment they showed themselves.

When the tower was clear, the human Nisk-rider nodded to us as he passed, still issuing instructions to his attack wing. Painted on the shoulder of his armored fighting suit was a mailed fist against a red triangle, the same symbol Dietz and his team wore. He gave us a quick salute and led his coleopteran fighters outside, then Dietz came up beside us to watch the battle.

"They move faster with our people on board," he said with satisfaction.

"Did you know they could fly?"

He smiled for the first time ever. "I knew."

Jase joined us, grinning and shaking his head incredulously. "Humans riding giant flying beetles. Never seen that before."

"Get used to it," Dietz said. "It's the future."

We watched the Spawn fight all across the city, shooting many Nisk out of the air or in the streets, but no matter how many they killed, more came. Spread among the Nisk swarm were thousands of human riders, only a tiny number of whom were Intuitive Fighters. They kept the Nisk moving fast, encircling and slaughtering autacs and spawnwarriors alike, avoiding ambushes and cutting off enemy counterattacks as if they knew what the Spawn would do before they did it–because a few of their number did know.

The others joined us, even Izin ventured out along the girder, overcoming his fear of heights to see the battle for his birthplace. Explosions and energy blasts flashed across Tamph City as human-Nisk attack wings linked up with tamph resistance fighters. Together they drove the Spawn into smaller and smaller pockets while encircling the concentration camps, protecting them from reprisals. The Spawn held out for a long time, but in the end, the human-Nisk attack wings were too fast and too numerous to stop.

A nestship appeared, floating silently above Tamph City. It filled the eye of the storm as millions of winged-Nisk streamed from its sides, fanning out in all directions, along with tens of thousands of troop transports, gunships and escorts. Some descended to the ground, but most fanned out across the sky to liberate distant lands and ruined cities. There was no doubt now, the galaxy's sleeping giant had awoken, he was on our side and he would make the Spawn pay a terrible price for their mistakes, with our help.

"What now?" Marie wondered.

"We rebuild." I gave her a wry look. "And we fight the oldest battle known to man. And woman."

She realized I wasn't talking about the Spawn, and smiled. "Oh really? A battle? Is that what you call it?"

"A minor skirmish. A miniscule feat of arms."

"Better raise the white flag, Skipper," Jase grinned. "You lost that fight a long time ago."

"Everything is a battle with you humans," Izin said. "It is easier for us. The females breathe on us once and all is resolved."

"Our way's more fun," I said, then we watched the flashes of war fade across the archipelago all the way to the horizon and beyond. Sporadic fighting would rage all night and for days to come, but by the time the cyclone had passed, the city–and the world–would be ours again.

Chapter Ten : Free Earth

Human Homeworld
Sol System
1.0 Earth Normal Gravity
498.7 light seconds from Sol
16 Billion Humans
9 Million Terrestrial Amphibians

"You may kiss the bride," Admiral Talis declared. He was in full dress uniform dripping with gold braid, well deserved medals and an extra star.

"I never disobey an order, Admiral," I said.

"Says who?" he asked with a wry grin.

I took Marie in my arms. She was resplendent in white with silver threads sewn through her hair and a beaming smile. When we came up for air, the audience applauded. My best man was grinning and my best tamph was squirming in his dress suit while Lena smiled reluctantly. She might even have been happy for us, although she hadn't forgiven me for showing my face to all of Earth.

Considering Talis couldn't promote me and with every

city on the planet in ruins, he'd decided to provide a makeshift cathedral for the ceremony; the topside hull of the *Solar Constitution*. The Earth Navy battleship floated in New York harbor, flanked by hundreds of other ships, alien and human, many with colored flags and banners flying. With Earth's spaceports unusable, the combined fleet had fallen back on ancient habits, setting down in sheltered anchorages the world over.

Across the harbor, the once glittering towers of Manhattan had been reduced to burned out ruins by Spawn bombardment and constant guerilla warfare. Not one tower remained at full height and the streets were piled high with debris from fallen spires.

It was approaching dusk and the only lights on shore came from camp fires where wretched survivors were celebrating their liberation. At the southern tip of Manhattan, banks of floodlights illuminated navy construction battalions busily bulldozing what had once been the Battery District, making room for a military hospital, shuttle port and food distribution center. They were supported by hundreds of dark brown Nisk workers who were doing much of the heavy lifting. According to Lena, there were ten million more on the way to help with Earth's reconstruction.

The destruction of the Spawn's Am-East base had turned Long Island into a cratered lava plain, although the navy had re-energized the Liberty Island Monument. The original holographic projectors were in pieces at the bottom of the harbor, destroyed on the first day of the invasion. Talis had made restoring the six hundred meter high hologram one of his top morale boosting priorities and had brought along a complete replacement system for the purpose. The original, much smaller neoclassical statue had fallen to pieces millennia ago, but its spirit lived on in the bright hologram now visible from seventeen Am-East conurbations and shining from huge billboard screens hastily erected by the military in every major city on Earth. Millions wearing nothing but filthy rags sat in rubble filled streets and watched her flickering flame in silence for hours, thankful deliverance had come.

"You sure know how to attract a crowd," Marie whispered, glancing at our applauding audience.

"It's not me they're here to see," I said, giving her an appreciative look.

She blushed, then we started down the aisle between rows of applauding well-wishers, mostly Earth Council big shots, high ranking officers and a bunch of diplomats I'd never met. Against our wishes, our wedding had become an event due to my message on the eve of liberation, one that was broadcast to the world.

My brother and Anya sat behind the dignitaries, out of the limelight. He'd refused to be a groomsman, arguing we'd hardly seen each other in years. At least he'd dressed for the occasion, looking almost respectable in formal attire, although the bulges under his jacket indicated he was well armed. Old habits die hard and there were many in the Brotherhood who wanted him dead, so I pretended not to notice.

"You going to be here when we get back?" I asked in a low voice as we shook hands.

"I don't know," he replied.

"You've got a full pardon."

"So they tell me."

Some surviving Brotherhood ships had already slipped away into space without reporting their intentions and others were taking on what supplies they could requisition, almost certainly planning to do the same. They hadn't broken the conditions of their pardons yet, so Talis had ordered none were to be detained.

"Wait for me."

"No promises, little brother," he said, as good as a last goodbye.

Anya hugged Marie, kissed me on the cheek, and like my brother, was discreetly armed. "I hope we see you again…some time," she said.

"Yeah, some time," I replied, convinced they'd soon sneak away.

We moved on to Dietz, Shen and Larson, all wearing uniforms with the Iron Fist insignia on their shoulders, shown in public for the first time now that word of what and who they were was spreading. Many had seen their kind fighting during the occupation, and even though their existence violated human genome laws, they were heroes now and untouchable.

"Two wins in a week." Dietz smiled, equating marrying Marie to the Liberation of Earth.

"It's not a win, just a beginning," I said, shaking his hand.

We moved on to Lena, who smiled politely at us then her voice sounded in my mind. *I hope you know what you're getting into, Sirius. She's going to be trouble.*

"The best kind," I replied aloud.

Marie gave me a puzzled look, glanced at Lena suspiciously, and whispered, "Is she inside your head again?"

"I'm used to it," I assured her, and now that Laleya had done her thing, Lena would never again know what I was thinking.

We continued on down the aisle past a bunch of Fenari, Gienan and Syrman ambassadors from the Orsarlee-M29 meeting. They greeted us in their own ways, then we reached the Nisk, who had their own area behind the seats.

Irukoochati clicked as we reached her. "Praise and acclamation, Human-Kode-Soris. Praise and acclamation, Human-Kode-Mirae."

"Thanks," I replied as Marie's eyes widened in surprise at hearing her name associated with mine for the first time, even if distorted in translation.

"We'll have to talk about the names," she whispered out of the side of her mouth,

I didn't take the bait, then Irukoochati said, "We have

much in common, and much to do together."

I nodded. "Order must be restored."

"And so it will be," she stated.

We'd kicked the Spawn off Earth and had a Tau Cetin designed, Nisk made super weapon that ensured they'd never come back, but the Spawn still held many worlds from here to the Cygnus Rim and they wouldn't give them up without a fight. And as far as the Nisk were concerned, order would not be restored until every one of those worlds were free, which was bad news for the Spawn.

On the opposite side of the aisle from Irukoochati was Siyarn, Gastillion Kalantropis and Laleya. He was dressed in a cerulean jacket with a high neck framing the back of his large head and an array of silver adornments commensurate with his exalted rank.

"Congratulations Captain Kade. I trust your future will be as bright as your past, and as...victorious," Siyarn said, confirming how well Tau Cetins understood humans, after having observed our entire evolution.

"Don't count on it," Marie said lightly.

He gave her an amused Tau Cetin look. Gastillion offered her large hand, being careful not to crush mine, "Congratulations to both of you."

Laleya extended both her hands, taking mine in one and Marie's in the other. She said nothing, gazed thoughtfully into our eyes. "Hmm, your minds are one."

I leaned toward her suspiciously. "I thought you said no one could...you know, look into our minds."

"No one...else," she replied meaningfully.

"Ah," I said with a smile, then she released our hands and I turned back to Siyarn. "So, is the Forum going to approve your recommendation?"

"They will, because they have no choice. Spreading human ships from the Orion Arm to the Cygnus Rim will hurt the Spawn."

"The Empire has already signaled that we support the Ornithian proposal," Gastillion assured me.

With the Tau Cetins, the Empire of D'kol and all the civilizations in their respective factions backing the idea, we had a lot of votes in our favor. And any neutral who feared a Spawn victory would gladly approve allowing tens of thousands of expendable human ships into occupied space.

"In any event," Siyarn added, "we have decided to provide you with the necessary astrographics, whether the Forum agrees or not, as is our right. Article Nine."

"They will agree," Gastillion said, exchanging a knowing look with Siyarn, confirming the two superpowers had already stitched up the deal.

"God help the galaxy," I said with a chuckle.

If our alien neighbors thought humans were a plague of primitives before, they hadn't seen anything yet. We were about to lower their expectations even further. Our ships were painfully slow, fragile as tin foil and would soon be carrying hyper-torpedoes to a quarter of the galaxy, significantly complicating matters for our collective enemy.

The Tau Cetins would keep their fleets united, the D'kol would continue building theirs, and we would scatter our flimsy ships across the galaxy. We'd lose many of them, but a lucky shot from us would allow the Tau Cetins to finish the job and buy time for the D'kol. And in return, untold fortunes awaited the reckless and the brave, so there'd be no shortage of volunteers.

Whether the Galactic Forum liked it or not, whether it meant breaking a tradition reaching back to the dawn of Galactic Civilization itself, the Tau Cetins and the D'kol were letting us out, a million years early. And after what had happened on Earth, and with what the galaxy knew was coming, almost everyone agreed.

The tiny two thousand light year bubble of Human Mapped Space we'd been sealed inside of for twenty centuries would–during the next Tau Cetin update–expand to a quarter of the galaxy, and word was spreading fast. Prospectors, miners, traders, real estate developers, adventurers, colonists, con men, skimmers, scammers, grifters and treasure hunters of every kind were lining up with ships and crews, waiting for the astrographic updates, the hyper-torpedoes, and a place on the next Tau Cetin galactic conveyor heading out. Some would never be heard from again. Others would get a torpedo away in time to ensure the Spawn would die, and a few would return with riches enough to convince others the risks were worth it.

The Tau Cetins, the arch schemers of the galaxy, and their D'kol partners, were banking on human nature to ignore the danger, to take our chances and occasionally give the Spawn a black eye. They weren't doing us any favors, they were opening the door because it suited their purposes, their interests, and we weren't complaining because it suited ours. Earth was in ruins and there was a multitude of volunteers ready to colonize distant worlds that, with Tau Cetin help, were within easy reach.

"Are you ready?" Siyarn asked.

"More than ready," I replied.

Marie furrowed her brow. "Ready for what?"

Siyarn gave me a puzzled Ornithian look. "You did not tell her?"

"It's a surprise."

"Tell me what?" Marie demanded suspiciously.

"About our honeymoon."

"We're going on a honeymoon?" she said, then saw Lena and Admiral Talis were following us.

I grinned. "Just a little trip, to the other side of the galaxy."

She frowned and pointed to Lena and Talis. "With them?"

"They're just hitching a ride."

"I had something more romantic in mind, just the two of us," she protested.

"Sirius has been asked to speak at the Galactic Forum

session discussing the Tau Cetin proposal to expand human interstellar access," Lena explained.

"It's a great honor," Talis added.

"Siyarn's taking us in the Rillesium," I said. "He's even created a honeymoon suite, just for us."

"The Rillesium?" she said with obvious disappointment.

"How many women get to go on a honeymoon to the other side of the galaxy in the flagship of the Tau Cetin Grand Fleet."

"The Forum's meeting on a D'kol palace world," I said, trying to tempt her. It's supposed to be beautiful. Blue seas, perfect weather, and the best food in the galaxy."

"I don't know, Sirius," she said reluctantly, glancing at Lena, Talis, Siyarn, Gastillion and Laleya. "It sounds kind of…crowded."

"Nelosirala is considered the Jewel of the Galaxy," Gastillion assured her.

Marie frowned. "It better be."

A small Tau Cetin ship dropped out of the sky in a streak of light and landed on the *Solar Constitution*.

"Your carriage awaits, Mrs. Kade." I took her hand and followed the others up a short ramp into the Ornithian ship.

The ship's mirrored hull was transparent, giving us a clear view of the wedding guests staring in fascination at the Tau Cetin ship. The entry portal shrank to nothing and we shot vertically into the air under tremendous acceleration. The Am-East mega-urban fell quickly away below us, streaked with smoke plumes from still burning fires, then Sol crested beyond the blue green orb of Free Earth as we raced toward the *Rillesium*.

Marie slipped her arm around my waist and whispered in a sultry tone, "Our cabin better not be this transparent."

I grinned. "It's not. Siyarn promised, no peeking, especially on our wedding night."

For more information on the
Mapped Space Universe
visit the author's webpage at:

www.StephenRenneberg.com

If you enjoyed this book, please post a recommendation and rating on the site where you purchased your copy.

Made in the USA
Las Vegas, NV
05 April 2024